Jo Rees grew up in Essex and went to the University of London's Goldsmiths' College to study English and Drama. She published her first novel, *It Could Be You*, when she was twenty-six, under her maiden name, Josie Lloyd. She went on to write seven internationally successful novels with her husband, Emlyn Rees, including the number one bestseller, *Come Together*.

In 2007, she started writing solo again and *Platinum* was published in 2008 by Transworld. She lives in Brighton with Emlyn and their three daughters.

www.rbooks.co.uk

Also by Jo Rees

PLATINUM

and published by Corgi Books

FORBIDDEN PLEASURES

Jo Rees

CORGI BOOKS

TRANSWORLD PUBLISHERS
61–63 Uxbridge Road, London W5 5SA
A Random House Group Company
www.rbooks.co.uk

FORBIDDEN PLEASURES
A CORGI BOOK: 9780552156240

First publication in Great Britain

Corgi edition published 2010
Copyright © Unomas Productions Ltd 2010

Jo Rees has asserted her right under the Copyright, Designs
and Patents Act 1988 to be identified as the author of this work.

A CIP catalogue record for this book
is available from the British Library.

Addresses for Random House Group Ltd companies outside the UK
can be found at: www.randomhouse.co.uk
The Random House Group Ltd Reg. No. 954009

The Random House Group Limited supports The Forest
Stewardship Council (FSC), the leading international
forest certification organisation. All our titles that are
printed on Greenpeace approved FSC certified paper carry
the FSC logo. Our paper procurement policy can be found at
www.rbooks.co.uk/environment

Typeset in 11/13½pt Palatino by
Kestrel Data, Exeter, Devon.
Printed in the UK by
CPI Cox & Wyman, Reading, RG1 8EX.

2 4 6 8 10 9 7 5 3 1

Mixed Sources
Product group from well-managed
forests and other controlled sources
www.fsc.org Cert no. TT-COC-2139
© 1996 Forest Stewardship Council
FSC

For Araminta

FORBIDDEN PLEASURES

If there was one thing that Savannah Hudson was good at, it was making an entrance. And tonight, at the industry's holy of holies, boy was she going to make damn sure it was a good one.

Her face ached from smiling as she walked into the circus ring arena where the plush dinner tables were laid out below the high trapeze. It was a typically over-the-top venue for the awards ceremony, but a fittingly dramatic one.

Bright spotlights criss-crossed the excited crowd, but fell on her as she walked towards the Hudson Corporation's table in its prime position next to the stage. She felt a gratifying shift in the atmosphere – a hiatus, as everyone realized that the most talked-about guest of the evening was finally here.

Holding her head high, she strode towards her team, her famously bright smile eliciting smiles in return from everyone she passed. The Hudsons had always been the kind of people that others loved to hate, and Savvy was used to causing a stir. Posing, greeting, tripping off those witty sound-bites for the press and being the shining centre of attention was what she did best.

Yet tonight?

Savvy kept her smile tight and wide.

Tonight, this was all one great big façade.

She might be making fairytale copy, but the truth? Christ, she hardly dared *think* about the truth. Because the truth was that she was living a nightmare. And there wasn't a goddam soul in the whole world she could tell about it.

Which meant that she couldn't let her guard down for even a second.

She smoothed the chiffon of her long dress before taking her seat at the head of the table. The white Grecian-style piece was actually a wedding dress – a freebie from one of the designers this morning. After the week she'd had, there'd been no time to find another show-stopping outfit. With her blonde hair piled high and bound with thin golden rope, Savvy hoped she'd pulled off the look.

After all, every move she made, every detail of her appearance, every mannerism, would be scrutinized by her colleagues, admirers and enemies alike. With admiration? Animosity? She hardly cared any longer.

She needed a cigarette *so* badly, she thought, as another photographer flashed his camera in her face, but there'd be no let-up until the awards ceremony was over and the winners were announced. She stared at the glass on the table in front of her, wishing it contained something stronger than water. When she reached out for it, her hand was shaking.

But she would have to see this through. No matter what. Because it was all about reputation and nobody, *nobody*, was going to know that she was anything other than supremely confident.

The future was bright for the Hudson Corporation. That was her message. They were the best. Her presence here tonight proved it. She *would* win the coveted Best Casino award. She'd memorized her acceptance speech already.

But what if . . . ?

She glanced over at the other top table. Roberto Enzo, her father's greatest rival, was in rude good health, even at seventy. He looked like a member of the original Rat Pack, his Italian-American good looks only enhanced by age, with his mane of silver hair swept back from his distinctive tanned face.

And beside him, as always, was Lois Chan. The woman who'd made Savvy's ultimate success so elusive. Her rival.

Lois's long, shiny black hair was piled up into a glossy chignon and she was wearing a dress of heavy red silk. She looked every inch the formidable Asian businesswoman she'd become.

She watched as Roberto Enzo put his hand over Lois's and laughed delightedly at something she said.

Savvy felt her heart swell with jealousy. They looked so united on their table. So together. So much a team. Deliberately so, Savvy guessed. Despite everything that had happened in China in the last few weeks, they'd come out fighting.

But that was why Savvy was here. To fight back. Tonight's awards would prove it. They had to. Because this business was her life.

It was all she had left.

Lois Chan took a long sip of her white wine, grateful that the show was finally starting and the lights had lowered. An expectant hush had fallen over the crowd.

In the sudden darkness, she felt her skin crawl with self-loathing.

How the hell had she got herself into this mess?

But then it wasn't as if she'd had a choice, she told herself. Roberto had insisted that they come here tonight and front it out.

Roberto. Lois swallowed hard, feeling his presence next to her, his hand over hers, but she could hardly bear to look at him.

Dear, kind Roberto. He'd been her rock. The man who had rescued her from the ashes of her marriage break-up and her failed career in the police force and put her back on her feet. He'd nurtured her, trusted her, promoted her. He'd given her the freedom and the tools she needed to make a difference to this industry. And she had. A big one.

Which was why it hurt so much that she was about to betray him.

12

In fact, Lois could safely say that nothing had hurt this much since she'd lost custody of her daughter, Cara.

Lois longed with all her soul to take Roberto away from here and to explain what she'd done. But she knew she couldn't. Too much was at stake.

The irony was that her intentions had been so good. All she'd set out to do was make the world – particularly the gambling world – a fairer and better place. But instead, she'd become embroiled in a level of corruption beyond her wildest dreams.

'I see she's finally here,' Tristan Blake, one of Lois's most trusted employees, whispered, leaning in close and flicking his eyes towards Savannah Hudson. 'I can't wait to see her face when she doesn't win.'

Lois tried to smile back at Tristan. He was wearing an old-school tux with a thin tie, and his bright tanned face and twinkling eyes made Lois realize how much this meant to him. 'You really think we're going to win? After what happened? Come off it, Trist. We don't stand a chance.'

Lois felt Savannah Hudson's gaze on her, even in the dark, like a malevolent force. The cheek of the woman, Lois thought. Flaunting herself here, as if she owned Vegas. And what in God's name was she wearing? Tonight's 'virgin bride' look was surely one reinvention too far.

Lois breathed out, forcing herself to keep calm. But Savannah Hudson's presence riled her.

Well, she hoped Tristan's confidence was justified. Tonight Lois needed to prove to Savannah Hudson that her underhand games hadn't worked. To prove to the entire industry that she, Lois Chan, would not be beaten. Especially by someone as low as Savvy Hudson. The girl would sell her soul for a dime.

How strange, Lois thought, that it had all become so personal, when she had once considered business rivalry to be futile. But then Savvy Hudson had always annoyed her. Even from the very first time they'd met.

It must have been more than five years ago now, Lois thought, but it seemed so much longer. A lifetime ago. Back when they both still had it all to play for. When the stakes were so different to now.

Back when all of this started.

Five long years ago.

That Fight Night in Vegas . . .

CHAPTER ONE

Fight Night in Vegas. You couldn't beat it. On the thirty-third floor of the Enzo Vegas, Savannah Hudson tumbled out of the door of the penthouse suite into the corridor, giggling with anticipation.

'Let's do it, let's do it,' she urged Marcus, pulling him by his sleeve towards the SkyBird – the Enzo Vegas's famous glass-bubble elevator, which provided the occupants of the hotel's most exclusive penthouse suites with a direct and dramatic route down the side of the building to the casino. 'Much as I'm loving your company, darling, we'll miss the fight if we don't get down there soon.'

'O-*kay*, *dah*-ling,' Marcus replied, mimicking her.

Despite his gentle teasing, Savvy knew that, like most American men she met, he adored her accent. Technically she was half-English, even if she hadn't actually lived there since she'd been expelled from boarding school when she was seventeen. But Savvy by nickname, savvy by nature, she knew that impeccable pronunciation, along with impeccable manners, marked her out from the crowd and opened doors for her almost everywhere – especially here in the States.

Savvy punched the button on the wall and the elevator door slid open. She waved her foot, clad in a sparkling sandal, in mid-air before stepping over the threshold.

'Wow,' she gasped, throwing her arms out wide.

The whole of Vegas was spread out before her, the neon blazing so hard it could have been midday, not midnight. Yet in the very distance she could still see the desert, its silky blackness merging into the deepest indigo sky.

Giant billboards glittered, cars streamed along the freeway. She felt immediately humbled, but powerful too – as if she were a god and everything she was seeing was hers.

Down below on the strip, stretch limos queued up bumper to bumper. Two colossal searchlights swept back and forth across the casino's mirrored façade, glittering lake and laser-tinted fountains. News and sports channel helicopters beat the dry air above. This was the kind of publicity money just couldn't buy.

Because tonight would be where millions of people all over the globe would tune in to the Enzo Vegas, where the WBC World Heavyweight champion Cornelius 'The Hammer' Hamilton would defend his title against Russian bad-boy Oleg Olin and settle a rivalry that had escalated from a war of words into a media frenzy.

And Savvy was going to be right there. Right beside the action.

'Come on,' she said, turning and holding out her hand to Marcus. He stared up the corridor, shrugging his leather jacket on to his shoulders and flipping down the brim of his baseball cap, but there was no time for his posing now. Besides, Savvy was immune to it.

Marcus Maitlin, notorious playboy, failed actor and heir to a Hollywood fortune, most of which he'd spent the last ten years frittering away, laughed as Savvy yanked him in next to her. Only now did she realize how high she was – both physically *and* mentally. After the fat line of cocaine she'd just had in their suite, she felt like the top of her head was about to blow off. Marcus had been right that the Peruvian Flake he'd brought along was the best cocaine in the world. This shit was magic.

The elevator started moving and Savvy swayed her arms above her head and bumped hips with Marcus.

'Oh, here we go, baby, here we go,' she chanted.

'That's some dress,' Marcus said, moving behind her. The layers of midnight-blue silk barely skimmed her buttocks and showed off her tanned legs.

'Dress? It's not a dress, Marcus. It's a top,' she said.

Savvy had pointed it out to him in one of the hotel's boutiques shortly after they'd arrived. Marcus had had it delivered just in time for her to change into before they left.

'All the better . . .' Marcus's voice became a husky whisper in her ear as he ran his hand up her thigh and kissed her neck. 'Easy access. I like being able to get at you.'

Savvy pushed her hands up behind his neck, looking at their reflections in the elevator glass. She shuddered as his fingers expertly brushed away her tiny lace thong and dipped inside. She felt the hard bulge in Marcus's leather trousers pressing up against her bottom.

She couldn't exactly pretend to Marcus that she wasn't feeling horny too. He could feel that for himself. But that was more an effect of the cocaine than Marcus's familiar touch.

It amused her that she always managed to get herself into these situations with him. They'd have to stop this mucking about some day soon, but Marcus was an attractive guy. Funny. Generous. The best. A partner in crime.

But the truth was that they could never be real lovers. She wondered whether it was the same for Marcus, but Savvy found the sex rather meaningless. Although as sex went, she had to admit it was pretty good. But to her, it felt like they were diluting their friendship. Because whilst she gave him her fierce and unswerving loyalty as a friend, she gave almost nothing at all as a lover. Nothing *real*.

Then again, after what she'd been through, maybe there wasn't anything left to give.

She laughed now, pulling away from him. Did he really think they had time to do it in the SkyBird elevator? Even by their standards, that was pretty risqué.

'Easy, cowboy,' she said, ducking out of reach. 'You'd better keep that thing holstered, my friend. We've got a long night ahead of us.'

'Aw . . . come on, Sav. Just a quickie. It'll be fun!' Marcus jiggled his thick black eyebrows up and down at her.

'Oh, you'd love that, wouldn't you,' she laughed. 'To do it in front of the whole of Vegas,' she said, pointing to the view.

'I don't care who's looking. It's just that you look so damn horny in that dress . . . top,' Marcus corrected himself.

'Good,' she said, jiggling her famously pert bottom at him, making the layers of her dress shimmy. 'That's the idea. Now . . . let's focus on important business. Drink on the way to the arena? What'll it be?' she asked him, twirling round to lean back against the bar, so that she could face him.

Marcus rubbed the stubble on his chin. 'Hmm,' he ruminated. 'Tequila?'

'Yes!' Savvy said, clapping her hands together, excited at the thought. 'I do so love the simple pleasures in life.' Holding her hand up, she counted off on her fingers. 'Drinking, drugs and gambling. The Holy Trinity of Fun.'

Marcus laughed. 'The Holy Trinity of Fun. I like that. You know, you really are an incorrigible party girl.'

'Oh, like *I'm* the one leading *you* astray.'

She looked down, seeing the ground zooming up to meet them. She could feel the casino's pull just as surely as if she were a silver ball on a spinning roulette wheel, being drawn inexorably towards its centre.

'You know, it's hard to say what would give your father the bigger heart attack. The fact that you're here. Or the fact that you're with me,' Marcus said.

Savvy grinned back at him. He knew as well as she did that being here behind her father's back was giving her a delicious thrill. And it was clearly giving Marcus one too.

Savvy's father, Michael 'Hud' Hudson III, the self-made and notoriously outspoken Vegas casino mogul, had been trying to put Roberto Enzo out of business for years. This, the Enzo Vegas, was his nemesis, the thorn in his side. The reason that his own nearby casino La Paris had never claimed the reputation he craved. As far as Hud was concerned, the Enzo Vegas was strictly out of bounds to his friends and family, or anyone who valued being in Hudson's inner circle.

He'd be *livid* if he knew she was here. Not to mention how much this would get up Elodie's nose, Savvy thought, with a frisson of satisfaction.

Savvy's twin sister had called five times this week to remind Savvy that Hud was flying back from Europe and Savvy mustn't miss the planned family get-together tonight, under any circumstances.

It was so typical of Elodie to suck-butt their father, desperately hunting his approval by jumping every time Hud snapped his fingers. And so typical of Hud to demand everyone come to him exactly when he wanted them to. As if none of them had anything – or any*one* – better to do.

Which was why, when Marcus announced he had tickets for the fight tonight and no date, Savvy had pounced on the chance to join him.

Why not? Her father and her sister clearly thought her life was superficial, so she might as well prove them right and have a good time. She felt it was her duty to enjoy the privileges she'd been given without any guilt. After all, *someone* had to stop and take time out to spend some of the money her father was so busy making. And she sure as hell couldn't see anybody else trying very hard.

Besides, whatever she did, she'd be found lacking. She'd long since got used to being the black sheep of her family – the naughty to Elodie's nice. But secretly it grated. After all, neither Elodie nor Hud had any idea about her private life and all the pain and heartache she'd so recently endured. No fucking idea at all.

But that was a secret that Savvy was keeping to herself. Let them think what they liked. One day, somehow, she'd prove everyone wrong.

In the meantime, she was going to have fun, fun, fun.

CHAPTER TWO

Just metres away, as the SkyBird passed the fourth floor and the Enzo Vegas's high-tech security hub, newly promoted security manager Lois Chan twisted her jet-black hair into a knot at the back of her head and stabbed it in place with her pen. Then she put her hands on the waist of her navy pencil skirt and studied the wall-to-wall bank of high-definition screens.

She cautioned herself to keep her focus. But boy, was it hard. Her toes tingled with adrenalin and she shifted in her high black sling-backs, realizing that she hadn't sat down for nearly eight hours and probably wouldn't for at least the same again.

In her three months here, she'd never seen anything like this. But then again this was her first Fight Night and only now was she finally starting to realize what all the fuss was about.

It was *insane* out there. And she could tell from the

shouted commands of the team around her that she wasn't the only one feeling that it was all about to kick off.

But this is also the opportunity you've been waiting for, she forcibly reminded herself, refusing to allow her fear to overcome her. This was her moment to show the team – *her* team – who was boss.

OK, she might already have one failed career as a cop behind her and she might be a woman in this wholly male-dominated industry, but this was her big chance. She was determined to prove to Roberto Enzo that she was up to managing any task, no matter how big. To show him maybe that one day she would even be up to running the entire Enzo Vegas itself.

Which was why tonight nothing, *nothing*, could go wrong.

She picked up a remote. Screen one ballooned with a view of the Enzo Vegas's grand entrance. Crowds jammed the sidewalk, surging up against the cordon of security guards. Cameras flashed. Fans screamed. Journalists jostled hungrily for position as the slow-moving cortège of limos continued to disgorge its feast of A-list celebrity eye-candy.

Everyone who was anyone was here tonight, the richest and the most famous, the movers and shakers, the stars and star-makers. They were all here to be seen on this, the biggest, most glitzy night of the year.

Right on cue, Lois saw Hollywood legend Todd Lands stepping out of a white limo with his latest svelte blonde girlfriend, to a riot of applause.

Lois smiled to herself, remembering the dreamy crush she'd had on him after all those teen flicks she'd watched as a girl. She had to admit that he'd only got sexier as he'd got older. With the aid of the remote, she zoomed right in and watched him squeezing his date's hand before giving the crowd his famous smile, hardly blinking as the cameras continued to strobe.

But tonight there was no time to linger on the scene. Lois tapped the remote again and screen two switched to the view through the famous golden doors. Inside, the red-carpeted lobby with its dazzling Venetian glass chandeliers was heaving with bodies.

Bobby King, Lois's front-of-house security manager, was standing with his huge black frame squashed against the wall as he ushered people through. He didn't look happy. But then, he wasn't paid a six-figure salary to look happy. He was paid to look unbreakable, uncompromising and totally in charge. But even by Bobby's standards he was looking particularly pissed off tonight.

Bobby hated Fight Night. And he'd assured Lois she would too by the time the night was through.

Another tap and she was inside the VIP baccarat room and she felt her pulse race. A stout Chinese man with a thick mane of glossy black hair and a handsome pock-marked face was joining the game, sitting down at position number eight, with his entourage of Chinese associates – all male, all in black suits – fanning out behind his chair.

So he was here. For real. Dr Jai Shijai was *right here* at Enzo Vegas.

The tycoon of tycoons had finally arrived.

There was a whole department at the Enzo dedicated to luring major players to come and gamble by any means possible – usually by offering them complimentary transport, accommodation, food and drink. These comps guys had been after Jai Shijai for months, trying to make him swap allegiance from La Paris to the Enzo Vegas. Lavish gifts and invitations had been sent to Jai Shijai's home in Shanghai, promises made to his fixers in Beijing.

With Roberto Enzo's blessing, Tristan Blake, the new head of the comps department, had had the number plates of one of the limos changed to the auspicious numbers JS 6688 to shuttle Jai Shijai here from Roberto's private jet, which in turn had been placed on standby for him two days ago in Hong Kong. Lois was sure they'd all be thrilled that their efforts had been worth it. No doubt Tristan himself would be riding high on the triumph of having successfully harpooned such a huge whale.

Which was why it was even more important for Lois to keep a level head. She pressed her radio headpiece to her ear. 'Carl, give me an update,' she said.

'It's not looking good, I'm afraid, Lois,' the chief engineer finally answered.

It wasn't sounding good either. The static on the line was terrible.

'Damn it,' Lois muttered.

The staff intercom system had started bugging out earlier in the evening, and although Carl had worked on it for hours, it still wasn't up and running properly. Without it, Lois felt vulnerable. Being able to communicate clearly and quickly with her staff on the ground was key. Especially with players like Jai Shijai in the house.

Of course, everyone carried a cell phone, but with so many people around, most staff members wouldn't even be listening out to hear the damn things beep.

But before she had a chance to instruct Carl, Mario interrupted her.

'Lois, you'd better get down there,' Mario said. 'Bobby just called. The senator's arriving any minute.'

Lois put her hand on her forehead and blew out a breath. *Focus*, she thought. *Focus*. There was nothing for it. She was going to have to delegate.

Mario, the skinny, bespectacled young man at the station next to her, was a new recruit – Lois's first, and she liked his conscientious manner, even if he did blush every time he looked at her.

She knew that the other guys in the hub had already nicknamed him Clark Kent, on account of the fact he worked so closely with her. But even though Lois got the joke, she didn't particularly care for the analogy. She was nothing *like* Lois Lane. Lois Lane didn't have a goddamned clue what was going on right underneath her own nose. And what kind of supposedly ace reporter could fail to spot that her closest colleague was Superman in a pair of specs?

'Take over for me, Mario,' she said. 'And keep a close eye on Jai Shijai in the baccarat room. You know his reputation.'

They all did.

He wasn't just another punter. He was a potential nightmare to handle. Given the choice, she'd have kept her eyes glued to him like a hawk.

But now an even bigger threat had arrived.

Namely Senator Joshua damn Fernandez.

CHAPTER THREE

Savvy felt a fresh rush of excitement as she and Marcus stepped out into the cavernous main hall of Enzo Vegas's famous casino. The endless rows of throbbing slot machines before them were all full. The noise was deafening: the hubbub of voices, the trill of electronic musical scales, the chime of quarters hitting the pans and the intermittent fanfares announcing the jackpot winners . . .

Savvy loved it. It was the sound of Vegas. The sound of money. Her favourite sound in the world.

She took Marcus's hand as they walked through the hall, following the red carpet past the slots to where the blackjack tables were alive with the tumbling rattle of plastic chips and cheering winners. Perma-grinning waitresses rollerbladed skilfully through the crowds, carrying loaded trays of drinks from the bar, where smartly uniformed waiters tossed colourful bottles into the air with artful abandon.

Savvy had never dared come to the Enzo before, but she should have done. It had a different feel to La Paris, where she always felt watched and on edge. Here she felt like one of the masses, both anonymous and special for it.

Fascinated to check out the layout, she looked in on the plush poker hall, with its French Louis XV-themed décor. Beneath the fancy gilt chandeliers, all twenty-five bespoke tables were fully occupied. An LCD screen covering the far wall listed the pro players' names next to their photographs. The legend at the top revealed that this was the National Poker Forum's annual play-offs.

Shit, she could almost hear her father thinking. Why haven't we already snatched that one from them too?

In contrast to the raucous, frenetic activity in the slots and blackjack halls, the atmosphere in here was intense and reverential. Like a library, Savvy thought. Or a church. Although the last time she was in a church she'd been busy with an altar boy from school behind the pulpit, she remembered with a wry smile.

Yes, this place had class, she thought. It was everything La Paris wasn't. She could see that straight away. It was a stately Rolls-Royce beside La Paris's brash but unlovable Hummer. This wasn't just a machine. It was a thing of beauty. No doubt about it, Enzo Vegas had *soul*.

That was what her father and his cronies just didn't get. People came here for the *experience*, for the *love*.

And that was the irony, Savvy realized, as she took Marcus's hand and ducked back out of the poker hall into the heavy crowd. Despite refusing to take any part in the family business, *she* was the only one really qualified to show her father how to take on Roberto Enzo at his own game, and win. But no one in her family ever took her or her ideas seriously and now she'd given up trying.

'Tristan, my main man!' Marcus suddenly exclaimed, holding his arms out in welcome to a tall, tanned guy with very white teeth. He had a hip sculpted beard and long, immaculately trimmed sideburns.

Savvy rolled her eyes. It was typical of Marcus to bump into someone he knew. Because Marcus Maitlin knew everyone. He made it his business to hang out in the right places, with the right crowd.

'What the hell are you doing here, man? I thought you were in New York?' Marcus said, as the two men embraced.

'I transferred to the big time here. I'm head of comps.'

'No surprise to me. Best organizer in the world, this guy,' Marcus told Savvy, slapping Tristan on the back.

'So are you guys here on vacation?' Tristan asked. Savvy noticed him checking out her legs.

'We're here for the fight. Here,' Marcus said, delving in his pocket and pulling out the tickets. Tristan looked at them and then at his watch. The latest Rolex. Top of the range. Tristan was obviously a very well-rewarded comps guy.

'I hate to tell you guys but you're cutting it fine. Don't sweat it,' Tristan said with a smile. 'I know a short cut. Follow me.'

Tristan led them quickly over to the nearest cocktail bar, where he took a card out of his inside jacket pocket and swiped it on a discreet scanner on the wall. A panel heavily brocaded with green wallpaper slid back to reveal a mahogany-clad elevator.

'It's easier if we go up, then across and down,' he said, as they followed him inside.

He hit a button on the control panel. He stood with one foot crossed over the other, his hands spread out behind him along the brass bar, as the elevator started to rise.

'So who's in tonight?' Marcus asked.

'Well, *you*'re here . . . so everyone who is anyone,' Tristan said, laughing.

Creep, Savvy thought.

'Who else?'

'You ever heard of a guy called Jai Shijai? The billionaire? He's down there playing baccarat right now,' Tristan went on. 'He used to play in the Paris but he's ours now.'

Savvy noted his boastful tone and wasn't surprised by it. She knew all about Jai Shijai. Or rather, she knew all the rumours about him. He was one of the biggest, most enigmatic figures in world gambling.

She felt her hackles rise. How dare this Tristan guy brag about stealing her father's best customer? Jai Shijai being here was costing her father money. And therefore, by association, costing her too – a feeling she didn't like, not one little bit.

'Oh?' she said. 'I thought those Chinese guys were superstitious and always played at the same place?'

Tristan looked at her, momentarily puzzled how someone like her could know something like that.

'Not any more,' he said. 'We made it seriously worth his while to come to us. And trust me, he'll have a much better time at the Enzo than at that jumped-up cruise ship down the road.'

Cruise ship!

God, Savvy would love to see her father's face if he heard La Paris being referred to like that.

The elevator door slid open silently and Savvy saw that they were on a floor that looked nothing like the rest of the Enzo Vegas she'd seen so far.

'We're not supposed to be up here,' Tristan explained, ushering them out of the elevator. 'This is where the security guys hang out.'

Savvy thought about the large wrap of cocaine in her bra as she followed Marcus and Tristan up the corridor, past a glass wall. Through it she could see lots of screens monitoring everything going on in the casino below. Men were stationed in front of the screens, all of them smartly suited and booted like Tristan. What she was witnessing now was obviously the business end of the operation. And every single inch of it was high-tech.

What were all those people doing in there? Even looking through the glass, she could pick up their sense of urgency.

Was there a room like this at her father's casino? She guessed that there must be. Savvy had never given much thought to the inner workings of La Paris before, only the seductive decadence of its public face – the same as every other person who walked through the door.

But she felt funny now seeing all this up close, glimpsing this secret world. A world of intrigue hidden behind closed doors. A world to which she could probably gain access at La Paris if only she chose to knock.

She smiled at her half-reflection in the glass, surprised at how much she suddenly got it. These were the puppeteers behind the glittering show downstairs. She'd just pulled back the curtain and was staring at the Wizard of Oz.

Who knows? she thought. Maybe I will take Daddy up on his offer of a tour around La Paris after all.

'We should go,' Tristan said, clearly uncomfortable that Savvy was lingering.

'Seeing sure is believing,' she said, reluctantly following him and Marcus further down the corridor.

'Excuse me?'

'I'm just very impressed with how, er, industrious it all looks,' she said.

Tristan ushered them quickly to the elevator at the far end of the corridor. But just as they were about to step inside, a pretty, petite Asian-looking woman in a grey business suit rushed towards them and held the door.

'Hi,' she said to Tristan breathlessly, smiling

perfunctorily at Marcus and Savvy. 'You don't mind going over to the baccarat room for me, do you?'

'Actually, I was just taking these guys down to the arena,' Tristan said.

From his shift in demeanour, Savvy guessed that this woman must be his boss and that he didn't like being given orders. But whoever she was, she fixed him with a steely look.

'I'll do that,' she said. 'I'm on my way down. But I need you in the baccarat room. Now.' Her eyes widened with intensity. 'The comms are down, so keep your cell phone switched on. And call me immediately if you think there's a problem . . .'

'Fine,' Tristan said, backing down. 'So Lois here will show you where to go.' He shook Marcus's hand as he ushered him and Savvy into the elevator. 'Have a great night, you guys,' he added, waving them a final good-bye before disappearing from view.

The woman – Lois – joined them in the elevator and pressed a button and the door closed.

'Lois Chan, head of security,' she introduced herself, formally shaking both of them by the hand.

Savvy glanced at Marcus and stifled a giggle. Left alone in the lift with Lois Chan, she felt as if they were naughty schoolchildren.

She slouched against the bar and watched as Lois pursed her lips, tapping her fingers on the skirt of her grey business suit. She had an aura of authority and seriousness about her, despite her small, neat stature.

She noticed that Marcus was scanning her ass

appreciatively. She glared at him, pretending to be shocked, but it only encouraged him. Hidden behind Lois, Marcus increased his ogling, giving Savvy a look that made her realize he had rather salacious thoughts concerning both her and Lois. Marcus obviously had a thing for getting horny in elevators.

Sensing the communication going on behind her, Lois Chan half turned and looked Marcus up and down, clearly flustered. Was she annoyed that mere customers like Savvy and Marcus had somehow blagged their way up into her section to begin with? She had the kind of no-nonsense manner that made Savvy just itch to ruffle her feathers.

Time for some fun, she thought.

'So . . . Tristan was just telling us about Jai Shijai,' she said conversationally, as the elevator began its descent.

'Oh? Was he?' Lois Chan sounded guarded.

'He's the guy in the baccarat room, right?' she pressed, amused to see that this small titbit of information gave her so much power.

Lois Chan tried to laugh it off, furrowing her eyebrows. 'And what else did Tristan tell you?'

'Just that this Jai guy will have a better time here at Enzo Vegas than at La Paris,' Marcus said.

Lois Chan started to look uncomfortable, as if she knew she should know Savvy from somewhere.

'Why's that, do you think?' Savvy asked innocently, staring up at the flashing numbers that showed the floors they were passing.

'Well . . . you know what they say about La Paris?'

'No?' Savvy said. 'What?'

'It's just . . . well,' she said, 'they're uptight over there. A money machine. Nothing but a bank with flashing lights.' Lois smiled wryly. 'As everyone here always says, they've got no Vegas heart.'

As the elevator continued to drop, it became apparent they were nearing the arena. Even through the elevator shaft, you could hear and feel the thump of bass.

'Vegas heart,' Marcus said. 'Sounds like we found it.'

'Just head right and you'll hit the stalls,' Lois advised, raising her voice over the loud rock music as the elevator stopped and the door slid open. Her eyes locked with Savvy's. 'Well, nice to meet you,' she said. 'Have a great time.'

But it wasn't enough. Savvy knew that it was foolish to name-drop, but she'd had enough of Lois Chan dissing her father's business and treating her like a nobody too.

'Thanks for your insight,' she said. 'Very interesting. Especially concerning Jai Shijai. My father's team at La Paris will be very enlightened to know how things run around here.'

Failing to stifle a laugh, Marcus stepped out of the elevator into the corridor leading to the stalls. The crowd in the arena beyond were already going crazy. Lois Chan suddenly put her arm across the elevator doors, blocking them from closing and preventing Savvy from following Marcus out.

'Excuse me? Your father? I don't quite understand . . .' Lois said to Savvy.

'Oh, didn't you know?' Savvy said pointedly. 'I'm Savannah Hudson. I thought *everyone* knew that.'

CHAPTER FOUR

What the . . . ?

Lois Chan gawped after Savannah Hudson as she sashayed away into the crowd, linking arms with her companion.

How dare she! Who the hell did she think she was? The jumped-up little madam . . .

Lois growled with frustration, furious that she'd screwed up. Because she didn't have a leg to stand on. She should have recognized *Miss* Hudson straight away. And she should *never* have discussed a client with a stranger – especially not one as important as Jai Shijai.

But it wasn't just her who'd enabled Savannah Hudson to execute such a whopping snub. What had Tristan been playing at? He really should have known who Savannah Hudson was. Marketing. Publicity. Famous goddamn faces. That was his job.

He'd even walked her up here past the hub.

Lois was going to give Tristan Blake a dressing-down he'd never forget.

'Jesus,' she said out loud, shaking her head as she muscled her way against the flow of the crowd towards the main entrance.

Savannah Hudson . . . Now that Lois had been provided with the name, her brain was busy stacking up further information. Like the fact that Savannah was the bad apple of the Hudson twins. A spoilt little rich girl who was always getting in trouble in the press. Or *shaming her family*, as Lois's own mother would have more unkindly put it.

All of which meant that maybe there was nothing to worry about at all. Maybe Savannah Hudson was just here to have a good time. Just doing her bad-girl act for her bad-boy boyfriend. From the look of her eyes, she'd clearly been wired. With any luck, she might not even remember any of that stuff about Jai Shijai by the time the cold light of dawn swung round.

In fact, Lois was almost tempted to call the PR guys right away and tell them to make a photo op out of Savannah Hudson being here. Frame it as an endorsement of sorts. *'La Paris no longer good enough, even for its owner's daughter'* had a good ring to it. Yeah, Lois would pay to see the look on Savannah's face as her father bawled her out about *that*.

Forget Savvy Hudson, Lois told herself. She didn't have time to worry about her right now. Right now, she had to get out front and deal with Senator Fernandez.

*　　*　　*

Lois finally made it out through the casino entrance to the drop-off bay where the limos pulled up. It was jammed out here too, with press and punters jostling for space, but eventually she reached Bobby's side.

'Just in time,' Bobby told her in his deep gravelly voice, as a large black SUV with tinted windows pulled up. 'Here comes the bride himself.'

Lois followed Bobby's gaze to the car. Two men stepped out of the passenger doors of the vehicle, expressionlessly scanning the cordoned crowd of press opposite. Another, older man stepped out. The same as his two burly colleagues, the tell-tale wire of a comms piece trailed from his ear to his starched white collar. Secret Service. Beyond a doubt.

A fourth man emerged now, towering above the other three. He seemed unfazed as the crowd erupted and the reporters shouted out questions. He smiled and waved, completely in his element. He could have been a movie icon or a pop star, such was the aura around him. But he was neither. He was the junior senator for the state of California, Josh Fernandez himself.

Of course Lois had seen him on TV, but she hadn't expected his presence to be so disarming. He was in his late forties, but he looked much younger. His large, honest brown eyes glowed with vitality and energy. His dark skin was smooth and flawless. Lois was shocked by quite how handsome he was up close.

His clothes belied his star status. He'd dressed down for tonight in jeans, a white shirt and a classic-cut mole-skin jacket. He looked approachable and normal – but then that was what he was selling himself as: a man of the people.

Lois had read all about his humble, disenfranchised upbringing and how he'd fought for every step of his education. A fact that had served only to reinforce his notoriously razor-sharp intellect. And it was that, combined with a prodigious talent for public speaking, which had, many commentators were saying, put him on course to be a potential presidential candidate.

He certainly had the balls to do it if he had the nerve to show up here, Lois thought. On tonight of all nights. Fight Night in Vegas. Where the whole industry would be. The self-same industry that the senator's new legislation was about to pound against the ropes. By taxing the hell out of it and channelling the money raised into federal social projects.

Lois took a deep breath and went forward to introduce herself.

'Mike Hannan,' the older of the security guys said, stepping towards her. He'd obviously done his homework and knew exactly who Lois was. 'We spoke on the phone.'

She'd been expecting a hyped-up know-it-all security type from their brief conversation a week ago, but here in the flesh Mike Hannan was the opposite of how she'd imagined. He was in his fifties, with white hair cropped close to his head, and a slightly stooped way of standing that made him look sweet and bashful. Like someone's dad rather than a Secret Service honcho.

His two colleagues were now standing either side of

the senator, back a little way from him, by the trunk of the limo. There was something ridiculous about the way they tried to seem inconspicuous, whilst their eyes raked over the assembled crowd.

'Agents March and Ransom,' Hannan said. 'They'll accompany the senator into the arena.'

'I've organized seating,' Lois confirmed. She'd been meaning to make an issue of it. Finding three extra ringside seats at short notice had been a nightmare.

But now she felt her gaze drawn to Fernandez, as he turned to face her.

'Hi,' he said, holding out his hand. His voice was warm and smooth. Lois felt a deep flush start inside her, as his hand folded around hers.

'I'm Lois Chan,' she said, her voice catching.

'Lois,' Fernandez said, as if tasting her name and deciding he liked it. 'So you're the eyes-in-the-sky, right?' He held eye contact with her for a moment longer than was necessary.

'Yes, I'm in charge of you – I mean security. Here. Tonight,' she said, thrown by the sudden cloak of intimacy he'd somehow managed to cast over them, in spite of the surrounding crowd. She tried to speak. To say something else. Something intelligent. Welcome him to Enzo Vegas. Give him the Vegas patter. But the familiar words wouldn't come. Instead, she felt powerless to do anything other than stare right back at him, and for a second it seemed as if the whole crowd had melted away and it was just her and him. He had the most amazingly mesmeric eyes.

'I'll take you to your seats,' she said.

'No, that's not the plan,' Hannan said. 'You stay with me. I'm tech-side, not ringside tonight. I'm going to be riding shotgun with you up in your surveillance centre, if that's OK. I always like to see how a spider runs her web . . .'

He said it like Lois had a choice. Which, of course, she didn't. Again, she felt annoyed he'd not notified her about his intentions before. But then again, she considered, maybe this was just how security was at the national level. Ever-changing. On the run. Just like her life had been as a cop. She took a deep breath, concluding that she had no option but to bring herself up to speed.

'No problem at all,' she said. 'My colleague Bobby King will take the senator and his bodyguards through to the arena.'

She waved Bobby over and introduced him to Hannan, who then hurried over to the senator and discreetly beckoned him away.

'Nice to see you all. And I hope you all have a great Fight Night,' Fernandez told the reporters, flashing them a final photogenic smile, before turning away with a polite wave as their relentless barrage of questions continued.

Lois felt a rush of unexpected disappointment pass through her, as Bobby led the senator and his two bodyguards away, scything quickly and professionally through the crowd and into the casino.

She'd been hoping to speak to the senator some more, she now realized. Maybe share with him that she'd grown up in San Francisco too. Now that he'd gone, she couldn't shake her childish wish for him to turn round. Or at least throw her a backward glance, just to show he still knew she was there.

'He's quite something, huh?' Hannan said, as if reading her thoughts.

'He sure is,' Lois answered as the senator disappeared from sight, before turning back to face the Secret Service agent and reminding herself she had a job to do. 'The elevator is just this way. We're on the fourth floor.'

'No, no. Take me by the stairs, I hate those damn things,' Mike said.

As Mike Hannan walked purposefully to the main stairs with Lois, she was suddenly desperate to grill him about the death threats to Fernandez. Now that she'd met the senator in the flesh and been charmed by him, it seemed even more horrendous that someone wanted him dead. She couldn't help turning it over and over in her mind. It seemed impossible to contemplate. Fernandez was so . . . alive. So incredibly vital and forceful.

But Mike wasn't being drawn on whether he had any potential leads. Unsurprisingly, she supposed. Secret Service probably never answered anything specifically. But he did let his feelings be known.

'I tried to persuade him out of coming here tonight. It's not as if he's a boxing fan,' Mike explained. 'On top of which, my wife's upset because I'm missing our anniversary.'

Lois smiled. 'You're married?'

Mike stopped for a moment. 'Yep, twenty-five years. Jeanie is the love of my life,' he said.

Lois didn't know how to react. The words had been said with such honesty, so clearly from the heart.

'So why *did* Fernandez come tonight?' Lois asked, moving the conversation on. 'Just to show who's boss?'

'Pretty much, I guess. Between you and me, he's a stubborn so-and-so,' Mike said, although his tone was affectionate. 'And he's certainly not going to let a little thing like a death threat put him off. But I'll level with you, Lois. Fernandez being here at the fight is just about my worst nightmare.'

Lois remembered ranting to Mario that she didn't want some jumped-up Secret Service guy snooping around her hub telling her how to do her job. But now that Mike was here, she saw that he was only trying to do his job, too.

It was her turn to sound reassuring.

'Don't worry. Safety is our priority. There are twelve CCTV cameras in the arena itself and the exits are covered too.'

She pushed open the swing doors into the corridor leading to the hub.

'To tell the truth, I just want to get this over with and get back home,' Mike confided. 'My son's in the Marines and he's on leave today.' He smiled at Lois. 'You got kids?'

'A daughter.' They reached the door of the hub and she buzzed it open. 'She's eight.'

Mike nodded. 'Then you'll know what I mean.'

Lois wondered why it had been so easy to tell him about Cara, when most people she worked with here didn't even know that she was a mother, let alone any personal details about Cara. But that was just habit. Self protection. If she didn't mention that her daughter lived with her ex-husband Chris and his new wife in Washington, then it might stop hurting so much that her baby had been taken from her and now lived thousands of miles away.

But she felt different telling Mike. Maybe because he was a parent too and his job was every inch as crazy as hers. Or maybe it was just easier telling someone who wouldn't be here to judge her on it tomorrow.

Whichever, Lois soon found herself warming to him even more as she gave him a swift tour of the hub, and brought him up to speed on the various security protocols and surveillance systems they had in place.

She'd been half expecting him to challenge her authority. But he seemed to trust her and believe that she could do her job. And as she showed him the screens and led him to where Mario was sitting at his workstation, she felt a sudden desire to impress him. There was no knowing where a contact like Mike Hannan might lead her in the future.

'Hey, Lois,' Mario said, standing up.

She quickly introduced Mike.

'You following Fernandez, son?' Mike said.

Lois noticed how comfortable Mike was in the hub, how unfazed by the set-up. He'd probably worked in a thousand places like this before.

Mario pressed the remote at the giant bank of

screens. They filled with a picture of the crowded corridor leading towards the stalls of the arena. Lois saw Bobby pushing past the crowds to make a pathway for the senator.

And right then, Lois saw Fernandez look up at the cameras above the doorway. He smiled. 'Hello, Lois,' he mouthed.

Mike Hannan glanced over at Lois, who was busy fighting her smile away. 'Looks like you've got yourself a fan,' he said.

CHAPTER FIVE

In the arena, Savvy Hudson should have been having the time of her life, but all she could think was: How could I have been so dumb? No wonder Tristan Blake had shown them such special treatment. These were the best damned seats in the house. Why hadn't she thought to check with Marcus where they were sitting?

She glanced around. A laser show of lights criss-crossed the auditorium as loud rock music pumped out, cranking up the electrifying atmosphere. Even Todd Lands was on the bank of seats behind her, for Christ's sake. It was like a celebrity who's who in here, and she'd just come out top.

And whilst on one level this was very cool, it also meant disaster on another. Because there were TV cameras everywhere. Anxiously, she looked overhead as a camera above her stretched out on a hydraulic arm above the ring, before swivelling back to face where she was standing.

Quickly, she looked away. And ducked.

Shit, she thought. The last thing she wanted was to be on TV. If anyone saw her . . . Oh God, if Hud saw her . . . *Here. In Enzo Vegas. And with Marcus* . . .

For all her bravado with Marcus earlier, she had to face facts. Another row with Hud would in all likelihood have disastrous consequences. He could cut her off. Deny her income. He'd threatened it before. And she had a hunch that this might just be the straw that broke the camel's back.

She swiped Marcus's baseball cap and pulled it down on her head, only straightening up as the TV camera swung out of the way and pointed in a different direction.

Why had she opened her big mouth and told Lois Chan who she was? For all she knew, Lois could have tipped off the TV people. The press would have a field day with it. Even on a night as packed with celebrity gossip as tonight, there was always room for one more juicy morsel.

'What d'you think?' Marcus shouted at her.

'It's mad!' she shouted back.

Oh yes, she thought, as a Mexican wave rippled round the arena. It was *electric* in here. She could feel the love all around. Enzo Vegas and boxing. Together like fist in glove.

What was it Lois Chan had said? *Vegas heart*. Yes, that was it. *Vegas heart*. She felt right in the middle of its thumping epicentre now.

Savvy reached into her bag for her cell phone and held it up above her head. She often got sent products or clothes to endorse, but this was her latest favourite. A brand new prototype of a phone that could take broadcast quality video.

She held it above her head and took a short burst of film of the boxing ring. She liked the idea of keeping movies on her phone. She'd always hated the thought of keeping a diary, but somehow keeping filmic evidence of her movements appealed. Excerpts from the movie of her life. Featuring her, as always, in the starring role.

A huddle of staff ushered a group of people down the aisle and into the row behind her, but she couldn't see who it was, and she didn't turn round again because the atmosphere had suddenly notched up another level as the MC stepped into the ring.

It was Johnny 'JK' Russell, the Fox Sports anchorman, dressed in a slick DJ and with a mike at his lips. Everyone was on their feet, cheering, the crowd almost drowning out his famous baritone as he announced the arrival of Cornelius 'The Hammer' Hamilton.

The crowd was plunged into darkness. Savvy let out a sigh of relief. The cameras were off her – for the time being at least.

Plumes of fireworks illuminated the pathway from the dugout. Rock music crashed out, louder than ever. This was sensational, Savvy thought, clapping and smiling. She was right here. Right in the thick of the action. Adrenalin pumped through her as the arena glittered with the popping of camera flashes.

Hamilton appeared in a spotlight at the dugout in a black cloak. Cheerleaders in skimpy red satin bikinis flanked him as he made his way down the aisle. Hamilton was huge. Much bigger than Savvy would ever have realized if she hadn't seen him up close.

Once at the ring, the entourage of cheerleaders fanned out, jumping up and down as Hamilton ducked under the ropes, shedding his cloak. The crowd bellowed their approval. His biceps bulged and glistened, the veins standing out on his smooth black skin like ropes.

More fireworks exploded. Thunderous Russian classical music boomed out, as Oleg Olin marched from the dugout to a chorus of hisses and boos. His scarred face was scrunched up into an ugly scowl as he ran down the aisle and clambered up to the ring.

His paleness made him seem smaller, especially with the faded green tattoos that covered his arms. But what Olin might have lost in stature, he made up for in aggression. Immediately, he fronted up to Hamilton, pushing his chest out, his lizard-like eyes boring into his opponent's.

Savvy cheered, awed by the spectacle. In the ring, the referee wriggled in between Hamilton and Olin, pushing them apart. Whatever warning he shouted at them was lost in the roar of the crowd. Johnny JK Russell left the stage and the boxers retired to their corners, to be swabbed down by their trainers.

Seconds later, the bell rang and Olin flew out of his corner. The two men circled menacingly. Hamilton threw a couple of exploratory punches, but Olin was the first to connect.

Savvy gasped as Hamilton's head snapped back from the full force of the vicious uppercut. His huge body lurched against the ropes nearest to where they were sitting, less than two yards away. He struggled up again, only for Olin to land a series of rapid body blows. Marcus was roaring with the crowd, punching the air.

Then Olin caught the American on the jaw. Savvy cried out and recoiled as blood sprayed from Hamilton's mouth towards her.

A fleck of it landed on her shoulder.

She stared at the red bubble on her skin with a mixture of horror and awe.

She turned round to see if anyone else had been hit behind her. Which was when she found herself gazing straight into the mesmeric eyes of a man in his late forties, wearing jeans and a moleskin jacket.

CHAPTER SIX

Up in the hub, Mike Hannan stood next to Lois Chan in front of the bank of screens and sipped the cup of coffee Lois had just handed him.

From the various views of the packed arena, they could just make out Fernandez, but the crowd was so dense, and with everyone on their feet shouting and cheering, it was difficult to keep him permanently in shot. One guy in all those people . . . it was like trying to keep your focus on one bird in a flock.

'That's the best three angles I've got for those seats,' Mario said from where he stood by the screen at his workstation.

Lois was proud of him. He'd done exactly what Mike had asked for so far and Lois could tell that Mike was getting a good impression of Lois and how she was running the hub.

'I'm just trying to patch in the TV feed to our screens.

The overhead view of the ring might be better.'

'Let's use everything we've got,' Lois said.

A nearby movement caught Lois's eye. Turning, she saw Geoff Greenblatch was discreetly beckoning her over to where he was standing a little way off to the right of Mario's workstation.

'Excuse me one moment, Mike,' Lois said.

Greenblatch was losing his fuzzy brown hair and was as dishevelled as usual, with salt and pepper stubble covering his jowly neck and jaw. He was a walking ad for corporate complacency.

But there was no mistaking the panicked look on his face now. Or the fact he wanted her help.

Alarm bells immediately started ringing in Lois's mind. Greenblatch wasn't a panicker. He was a seasoned old pro. So what had got him so rattled he'd had to come to her? Immediately Lois thought of Jai Shijai. He was still in the baccarat room, she knew. But she'd checked her cell phone several times already and there'd been no word from either Anthony, the dealer, or Tristan, so she'd assumed everything must be OK.

'You'd better come see this,' Greenblatch said, as soon as she was within earshot.

'What?'

'Jai Shijai's gone way over the limit.' He kept his voice lowered but Lois picked up the note of fear in it. 'And I mean *way* over.'

A flare of anger burst inside Lois. Why the hell hadn't Tristan called?

The screens showed a single image between them:

table one in the baccarat room. A growing city of stacked-up chips stretched out to Jai Shijai's left and right.

'How much is he up?' Lois asked.

'Nearly three mill,' Greenblatch said.

Lois's eyes widened. Three million dollars? Already? The house limit was one.

'We need to shut the game down,' she said. 'Right now.'

'But we can't. He still might lose.'

It was pathetic. These words. The way he said them. He was as bad as all the other addicts who chanced their lives away in Vegas, always holding out for that one card that would make everything all right.

On screen Jai Shijai was obviously enjoying waging war against the Enzo. In baccarat, the player played against the house one on one. Lois noticed that the other players on the VIP table were all watching Jai Shijai with total awe.

Lois felt torn. Her gut told her to shut down the game. That was her job. But, on the other hand, she couldn't be sure that Roberto would back her if she made the right call. Right and wrong. Black and white. Lois knew how to operate in those parameters, but this situation was an altogether murky shade of grey.

Because Dr Jai was a key figure in the negotiations for Shangri-La. And Roberto Enzo wanted – needed – a piece of Shangri-La more than anything. If Lois could help that happen, then her future was assured. But if she blew it, then Roberto would never forgive her. She'd be out of yet another career before she knew it.

Shangri-La was the hottest news in the whole gambling industry right now. It was a reclaimed ten-kilometre-long spit of land less than thirty miles from Shanghai. The Chinese government were in the process of awarding six concessions to foreign consortiums to develop it into a gambling resort set to rival both Macau and Vegas itself.

Michael Hudson had been the first to successfully politick his way into snapping up a concession and – from the press Lois had read in Vegas – his plans to build a huge casino and conference facility there were already under way.

Roberto's own bid was being considered. If the Enzo Vegas impressed Jai Shijai and he put in a good word, then they had a real chance of seizing a slice of the opportunity of the twenty-first century.

Tristan was standing in the doorway, in full view of the camera and several steps back from Jai Shijai. Lois could see that his cell phone was gripped in his hand.

Everyone watched and held their breath as Anthony dealt another hand. Jai Shijai slugged back his drink, folding his cards slowly one by one, from side to side.

The action sent Lois's mind reeling back to when as a young child she'd watched her father and his friends playing baccarat, behaving just the same way. Baccarat had been his favourite game. He'd explained to Lois once that of all the games, baccarat was the one you could beat . . . the one you could *will* yourself to win. Even back then Lois remembered thinking that having a psychological battle with cards was ridiculous.

How could moving them, bending them over in one particular way, manipulate fate?

She beat the memory away. She didn't want to think about her father. And what gambling had done for him. Or how his lousy addiction had torn her family apart.

On the screens Jai Shijai's associates around him all shouted out, 'Deng.' To stop the bad cards. Just as her father had once attempted to do. Attempted, but not succeeded.

Jai Shijai joined in, calling out *'Sei Bin'* for four patterns. His eyes gave nothing away as he slowly turned over the cards and placed them down in front of Anthony. Jai Shijai's associates cheered as the last card turned. Jai Shijai had won the hand.

Enzo Vegas was down another five hundred Gs.

This had to stop, right here and right now, Lois thought. Jai Shijai wasn't going to lose. And he wasn't going to stop. And if he carried on like this, he would break the house.

She'd have to take full responsibility herself. Either that or duck responsibility and allow Enzo Vegas to keep on haemorrhaging money.

Lois Chan had never been that kind of girl.

And that was why Roberto Enzo had employed her in the first place. To be his white knight. To enforce his law.

She didn't give herself time to reconsider. She hit Tristan's number.

'Lois?' His voice came on the line.

'I told you to call me if there was a problem.'

'But—'

'You're to shut the game down now. I'm telling you this with Roberto's full authority,' she lied.

'We might lose him altogether. He might go back to La Paris.'

'Do it,' Lois barked.

She'd stuck her neck out so far now, she'd just have to wait and see if Roberto decided to chop it off.

But she had no time to worry about it, because as she ended the call and looked up she saw that Mario was standing at the edge of the workstations, waving furiously. Mike was beside him, hunched down over a monitor.

As Mike turned to face her and his eyes locked with hers, she realized that something was terribly, terribly wrong.

CHAPTER SEVEN

As the boxers withdrew to their corners at the end
of the next round, Savvy returned the now bloodied
white handkerchief to the man behind her, who'd lent
it to her to wipe her arm.

'Thanks,' she mouthed.

He pulled a sympathetic face and smiled, as if to
say that getting splattered was just a hazard of being
so close to the ring. His direct gaze was somehow
so reassuring that Savvy smiled back. But her hand
was shaking as she passed the handkerchief back to
him.

And there in his strong brown eyes she saw it, the
same thing she'd seen in so many men's eyes over the
years. A glimmer of desire that had nothing to do with
being a gentleman at all.

Savvy swallowed hard as she turned back to face the
ring. She was so shocked that she'd been blooded that

it took her a few seconds to realize where she'd seen the man before.

It was Josh Fernandez. She was sure of it. Senator Fernandez.

'What was that all about?' Marcus shouted in her ear. 'That guy bothering you?'

But Savvy knew there was no point in telling him that the boxer's blood had hit her. Marcus was too wrapped up in the fight. And there was even less point in attempting to explain to Marcus that the politician intent on wrecking her father's profits and her inheritance was in the seats right behind them.

And he was cute! Despite her shock, she felt a tingle of attraction fizz inside her, like an effervescent tablet dropped in water. She bit her lip as another thought occurred to her.

Hud *hated* Fernandez. But maybe she could finally have hit on a way of ingratiating herself with her father, once and for all. And, even more importantly, help safeguard her inheritance from the IRS.

Here she was, so close to Fernandez. Surely it was fate? Surely this really was an opportunity not to miss? Because Savvy's guts told her that most of the real business that went on in Vegas was up close and personal. Literally.

And what if she could get up close and personal with Fernandez? What if . . . ? No, it was a crazy idea. She was just high, she told herself. She was getting carried away. Reading too much into the moment of connection they'd just had.

But another part of her mind was whirring. What if

fate *had* thrown her into Fernandez's path? What if she *did* introduce herself properly? And then, what if she could engineer a situation where they could talk?

Well, then there'd be no stopping her. Up close and personal: it was what she did best.

She didn't dare to think of the consequences. Sure, she realized it was too late in the day to persuade him to ditch his tax legislation proposals now that he'd already gone public with them. Even someone who knew as little about politics as she did could see that.

But maybe she could persuade him that to make a friend of the influential Hudson family meant doors might open for him where he least expected them to. And in return he might push some tax concessions their way.

Yes, this could be an extremely satisfying situation. Particularly for Savvy if she'd been the one who'd helped grease – or should that be *lubricate*? – the wheels of mutual business. She'd have made a mockery of her father's teams of accountants. How superficial would Hud think her life was then? And how much happier would he be to keep her in the lifestyle to which she'd grown accustomed?

She'd be her daddy's golden girl once more.

The arena swung back into focus. It was the Russian who was taking a punishing now.

The crowd roared for blood as Savvy twisted round in her seat, far more interested in the drama she might be able to instigate with Fernandez. And to her delight she saw that this really might be as easy as she'd hoped. Because rather than watching the drama on the canvas,

Joshua Fernandez was staring right back at her, as if he could read her mind.

But her raised eyebrow let him know that she'd caught him looking too.

She turned back and looked straight ahead. Smiling, she licked her teeth in anticipation.

Game on, she thought.

CHAPTER EIGHT

'There!' Mike Hannan stabbed his finger at the screen.

Lois peered in. At first she couldn't see what he was talking about, but then she saw the blurry grey figure of a man.

'What the hell . . . ? Where *is* that?'

'Get in closer,' Mike told Mario.

Mario clicked his fingers across the keyboard. The screen image enlarged, then transferred to the wall screens.

Even though the view was dark and patchy, compromised by the glare of the arena lights, Lois could see clearly that there was a man scaling the series of ladders which led to the catwalk – the walkway running the perimeter of the arena ceiling above the lighting grid.

The death threats to Fernandez flooded her mind.

Why else would anyone go up to the catwalk? It couldn't be a member of staff. Not at this time. Not during the fight. And with what looked like a backpack strapped to him.

'Is anyone meant to be up there?' Mike asked.

'No. Of course not.'

The man reached the catwalk and quickly cocked his leg over the bar and slid on to the platform. His movements were light and nimble. He removed the backpack and opened it.

'Oh, Jesus,' Mike said.

Lois swallowed hard. The man had begun snapping together what was unmistakably a rifle.

Mike already had his radio pressed to his mouth. 'March? Come in. Come in, damn it. Now,' he shouted. 'Jesus.' He turned to Lois. 'My comms are down. Give me yours.'

'They're not working,' she said, her heart pounding now as she realized – too late – that it might be no coincidence that the staff communication system had gone down tonight. That it couldn't be. Not if Hannan's comms had been disabled as well.

They'd been deliberately taken out.

'What the fuck . . . ? Not working?' Mike's expression was one of anger and disgust. 'Get me down there. *Now.*'

He was already running for the hub door.

'Tell everyone,' she shouted at Mario. 'Tell them it's a code red. Clear the main exits. Now!'

*　　*　　*

Lois caught up with Mike in the corridor.

'We need to come in somewhere he won't see us,' Mike shouted. 'Below him. The base of that ladder he climbed up would be ideal.'

Lois's mind reeled. It was four floors down to ground level from here. Not the elevator, she thought. It would take too long. Worse, she realized, if Mario instigated a casino-wide shutdown right away, then she and Mike might be trapped.

Overtaking Mike, she pushed through the doors at the end of the corridor and out into the open air.

The fire escape ran down the outside of the back of the building. It was dark out here, but this was the fastest way to get to where they needed to be.

'Right to the bottom. Then in,' she shouted to Mike as he ran past.

Lois's shoes clattered on the metal steps as she chased after him.

This was her worst nightmare. Everything that could have gone wrong *had* gone wrong. Every single person in the arena was in terrible, terrible danger. Not just Fernandez. They didn't even know for sure if he was the target. It could be any one of a thousand VIPs in there.

Or all of them. The shooter might not be an assassin at all. Just someone who was here to destroy at random. Or even a fight fan who wanted to fix his hero's chances of a win by blowing the opposition away.

'It might not be him,' she shouted at Mike. 'It might not be the senator they want.'

Mike yelled back, 'He's my priority. I have to protect him.'

She thought again of the senator's eyes. And in her mind's eye, she saw the light dying inside them.

What if the shooter had already . . .

She couldn't even bear to think of what might be about to happen. What could be happening down there. Right now . . . this second.

Mike was way ahead of her. Two floors down.

Her ears were ringing. Her lungs ached. Thank God for all those hours in the gym or she'd be on her knees by now.

Finally they hit base.

Swinging herself down on the handrail, she caught up with Mike in the parking lot.

'This way,' she gasped, overtaking him. She ran diagonally across to the arena's fire doors. She swiped her card. The door buzzed green. No lockdown had been instigated, at least. She hauled the metal doors open.

The noise was deafening as they slipped into the arena behind the stalls. She took a second to look around, orientate herself, her cop instincts kicking in straight away, looking for danger points, exits, angles, the right way to proceed.

She was relieved to see that her hunch had been correct and they'd come in just where Mike wanted them: directly below where they'd seen the man on the catwalk. She pointed her fingers to her eyes, then above them, to signal to Mike where the shooter was.

Mike looked around. The ground rose up ahead

of them, then an aisle led away in between the stalls. In the distance, they could see the boxers in the ring, circling each other, closing in for the kill.

Which meant no shot could yet have been fired, or the fight would be over. And a stampede would have taken its place.

Mike tore off his jacket. He was wearing a pistol in a holster strapped across his chest. Lois recognized the weapon. Mike unclipped the holster and flicked the pistol's safety off. He reached up for the ladder above.

'Get to the senator,' he hissed. 'Get him out. I'm going up.'

Mike climbed. Lois ran.

She'd already worked out in her mind where the senator was sitting. But he still seemed impossibly far away. She raced down the aisle, the stalls stretching away from her to the left and right.

She was terrified. And not just for the senator. For herself as well.

If the shooter saw her running, he might also work out why. Any second now and he might take his shot at the senator. Or whoever the hell else he had come here to kill. Or he might just decide to take her out instead. Figuring that if she'd already realized what was going on, she might also have somehow ID'd him.

Reaching the end of the aisle, she switched left, didn't stop.

There. Up ahead. She saw him. Senator Josh Fernandez. His eyes glued to the ring. Oblivious to her approach.

Nearer now, agents March and Ransom spotted her. Both of them started to rise.

Move him, dammit. GET HIM DOWN.

But then the crowd leaped to its feet. People in the front row stepped forward. Turning. Twisting. Getting in her way.

Ten thousand screams. A shimmer of camera flashes. The fight – it had to be over. One of the boxers had to be down.

Or the shot had already been fired.

Lois fought through the bodies. Didn't care who she hit. Kept going. Then she spotted the senator again. Smiling. Pointing at the ring. He was head and shoulders above everyone else around him.

An easy target.

Lois was screaming now. But her voice was swallowed by the roar of the crowd.

She slammed one man aside, then another. She was nearly there.

A woman in a baseball cap was standing in front of the senator. It couldn't be. It was! Savannah Hudson.

Right in the way . . . her phone held above her head taking pictures.

Lois didn't hesitate. She threw her aside.

Still screaming . . . breathless . . . terrified . . . Lois launched herself at Fernandez.

Lois was in the senator's arms when she heard the shot.

A look of shock on his face. Of fear.

Then they were turning slowly together . . . as if in slow motion . . .

Entwined. Like dancers.

There was a moment of absolute silence. The world shook, shunted sideways. Lois couldn't hear anything. They were crashing to the floor, two lovers pressed together. She stared into his eyes.

An explosion of red.

Blood blossomed across his white shirt.

They've got him, she thought. *I'm too late.*

A wave of white-hot pain ripped across her body. She knew with absolute clarity that she'd been shot as well.

'Too late,' she whispered.

They were both going to die.

CHAPTER NINE

Savvy hadn't run a kilometre since she was fifteen. And never in heels. As she stopped now, folding forward to put her hands on her knees, her chest heaving, she knew that the drugs and cigarettes had taken more of a toll than she'd realized.

'Jesus Christ, come on, come on,' she muttered, as she leaned against the buzzer on the side gate of her father's house.

She looked up at the property's colossal outer perimeter wall, and the palm tree fronds hanging over the top. Once she got inside, she'd be safe. That was all that mattered right now.

Terror still gripped her. Her mind kept jerking back to the arena. She wiped away the tears which streaked her face. She didn't want to think about it. The mayhem. The thunder of feet. The screaming mouths and grabbing hands and the whites of people's eyes.

Fight or flight. It was a reaction that defined everyone. So what did that make her for acting the way she had? A coward, or a survivor? Or both?

The second she'd seen that Chan woman running towards her, flinging herself over the seats, Savvy's senses had screamed out danger.

Gunshots had cracked out. The whole arena had exploded into panic.

Terror, that was what had governed her actions then.

Her instinct had told her to run, so that was what she'd done. Right into the crush, the hysterical stampede.

Her legs were now bruised. Her elbows too. She'd *fought* to get out.

A wave of guilt crept over her. Was Marcus OK? She hoped so. She'd lost him in the crowd. She should go back. To stop herself worrying. To stop him worrying about her too.

But she couldn't bring herself to. All she could think of was the screams, the flailing bodies, the anger and fear. She couldn't return. Not now she'd got away. And besides, Marcus was a big boy. He'd got himself in and out of plenty of scrapes. He'd be OK, wouldn't he?

Sirens wailed in the distance. Only now did she wonder with horror whether everyone else had been as lucky as her.

Deal with what you *can* deal with, she told herself. Worry about everything else later.

But Savvy knew she'd fucked up big time. She should never have gone to the Enzo Vegas. How had she ever thought she'd get away with being at the fight? Even if she'd escaped getting caught on the TV fight footage, the media might still track her down on the CCTV . . .

If she'd been identified as the person right in front of Josh Fernandez, she'd be infamous by dawn.

Stop it, she told herself. Calm down. There's still a chance you might get away with this.

There was the hat for a start. Yes, at least she'd been wearing Marcus's hat.

And secondly, she'd got out fast. Faster than most people. She hadn't been spotted, or cornered for an interview. Like a scalded cat, she'd fled into the night.

She wiped the cold sweat from her brow, as the CCTV camera bolted to the wall swivelled round to scrutinize her. When the gate lock buzzed, she hurriedly pushed through.

An immaculate lawn stretched away from Savvy. A lake rippled in its centre. As the gate clicked closed behind her, it was as if she'd been transported to a different world.

The grand white building with the domed roof had been modelled on the White House in Washington. With his South African background, Hud might not have been able to qualify to stand for President of the United States himself, but he could sure as hell let everyone know that one day he intended to rule this city.

Savvy hated the place, preferring to keep her base in LA. This wasn't a home. It was a fiction. A fairground ride. Again, Tristan Blake's words echoed through her head – a cruise ship. Just like La Paris, the White House had no Vegas heart.

But tonight she'd never been more pleased to see it. Tonight the White House offered safety and protection. Tonight, it really was what her father had always wanted it to be. Tonight it was home.

Savvy took a moment to compose herself, to steady her breathing, to smooth down her clothes.

She gazed up at the White House rising sepulchrally into the night sky. She'd never prayed in her life, but she sent up a prayer now. For everyone who'd been in the Enzo Vegas tonight. For Marcus and the senator. For the cops. She prayed that every single person in there made it out in one piece.

Up ahead, at the end of a well-lit gravel path, the kitchen side door swung open, casting a block of yellow light out on to the walled herb gardens. A shadow stretched out. Martha's big frame filled the doorway. As Savvy hurried towards her, she stretched her arms out wide.

'Baby Girl,' Martha said, in her heavy Cape Town accent, enfolding Savvy in a warm hug.

Baby Girl. That was what Martha had always called her. Martha had been Hud's nanny back in South Africa and remained his housekeeper still, even though she was now nearly eighty years old. Savvy loved the old lady dearly. She'd taken care of her and Elodie after their mother had died. She'd showered them with love when Hud had buried himself deeper and deeper in his work.

A vision of childhood . . . of hot chocolate, lullabies

73

and bedtime stories . . . of their home outside of Vegas in Boulder City, before the White House had been built . . . filled Savvy's mind. She wished she could stay here in Martha's arms for ever, awash with the scent of mint and rosemary and sage. She wished Martha still had the power to make her nightmares go away.

Martha peered hard into her eyes. 'Is everything all right?' she asked.

There was no point in lying to Martha. She always saw straight through Savvy's ruses. But at the same time, Savvy knew there was no way to explain what had happened tonight, not while she was still trying to come to terms with it herself.

'No,' Savvy said, 'but I hope it will be soon . . .'

Martha nodded, deciding not to push her any further. The sprinklers started to hiss across the lawns.

'Ellie's here,' she said, steering Savvy gently inside. 'She was telling me she's not seen you much lately.'

This was true. Elodie had some tedious notion about a joint birthday party and Savvy had been avoiding her and her calls. Because the plain fact of the matter was that Elodie's idea of a party and Savvy's idea of a party were just about as different as you could get.

'You need to be mindful of that, you know,' Martha went on. 'You're twins . . . Which means, like it or not, Baby Girl, she's the closest thing you're ever gonna have.'

Savvy followed Martha through the lofty kitchens, where several members of Hud's staff were clearing away crockery and cutlery.

'You've missed dinner,' Martha said, 'but I can find you a plate of food, if you're hungry.'

'Thanks, Martha, but I'll be OK.'

Martha frowned. 'They're in the drawing room.'

Kicking off her shoes, Savvy held them in her hand and let the coolness of the black-and-white chequered marble tiles soothe her feet like a balm. Ahead of her was a long buttressed hallway and at its far end a strip of soft light glowed beneath a dark oak door. After the frenzy of the Enzo Vegas, she felt as if she'd been through a timewarp.

Savvy walked towards the strip of light, passing beneath the oil painting of the first Michael Hudson, Hud's grandfather, dressed in Victorian hunting clothes, his leather boot pressing down on a dead tiger's head. The portrait was as fake as the White House itself. There weren't even any tigers in Africa. Not that anyone had ever dared challenge Hudson on this point. Or ever would, Savvy guessed.

Savvy stopped at the end of the hallway. She looked at herself in a long antique mirror and brushed the hair from her face, before licking the tip of her finger and wiping a smudge of eyeliner away. Putting her heels back on, she winced at the pain.

She wavered, her hand on the chunky brass doorknob, fighting the urge to run away. She thought about what might be waiting for her on the other side of the door. All the questions and recriminations. Hud's anger.

She could feel her energy levels and confidence dipping, as the vestiges of the coke wore off and the post-adrenalin fatigue kicked in. She'd kill for another line, but there was nowhere she could go. She could feel Martha's brooding presence back there in the entrance hall. If for a second she thought Savvy had ever tried drugs, it would break the old lady's heart.

No, Savvy would have to deal with this straight. By herself. She opened the door a crack, the same way she'd done when she'd come downstairs as a teenager to steal Hud's whisky in the middle of the night.

Holding her breath, she peered inside.

The drawing room exuded power and wealth. A Vermeer oil painting hung in an ornate gold frame. Woven silk rugs patterned the floor around the gilded antique sofas and chairs. Tapestries hung between the floor-to-ceiling sash windows, beside the Steinway grand piano Savvy had never heard anyone play.

The room looked personal, a collector's paradise, but it wasn't. An interior designer had styled it. All Hud had done was pay the bill.

Paige Logan stood with her arms folded over a tailored Ralph Lauren jacket, watching the giant plasma TV screen blaring out from above the marble fireplace. Her face was pinched into a frown beneath her Calvin Klein glasses and thick auburn hair. She might be quite the corporate power dresser these days – she'd matched up her jacket with pinstripe trousers and a white-ruffled shirt – but beneath it all, Savvy still somehow always managed to glimpse her oldest friend, the same geeky kid with broken glasses, buck teeth and braces she'd met when they were both eleven years old.

Savvy had saved Paige's geeky scholarship ass from the bullies in the English boarding school where they'd been incarcerated together in their teens. And two years ago, when Paige had graduated top of her MBA class at Harvard, it had been Savvy she'd turned to for a job.

Paige had always been entranced by the vast business empire Hud had built up from scratch. And now she clearly had ambitions of her own. It had struck Savvy as a business match made in heaven and she'd been only too delighted to set about making her oldest friend's dream come true.

At the time it had been a win-win situation. Hud had already announced his intention to bring on someone young and ambitious with fresh ideas. Savvy had secretly suspected that he'd been fishing for *her* to go and work for him, but she hadn't mentioned that to Paige. Instead, taking her father at his word, she'd recommended Paige and had personally vouched for her. Paige's rock-solid business qualifications, charming manner and sweet looks had done the rest. And from her very first day at the office, of course, Paige had naturally excelled.

Savvy couldn't exactly take back her decision about Paige now, she supposed. Not now that Paige was good news and so integral to the company – a company that Savvy and Elodie would one day own.

But at the same time, Savvy couldn't help feeling sad that her best friend had been gobbled up by her father's all-consuming corporate beast. Paige was so serious these days. So focused on business. So much like Hud himself.

And there he was. Next to Paige. With Elodie – typically – at his side.

They too were staring up at the screen and, as Savvy followed their gaze, she felt like a stone had just dropped into the pit of her stomach. The TV showed the Enzo Vegas surrounded by a buzzing swarm of paramedics, cops and FBI.

Be brazen, she told herself, as she leaned her weight against the heavy door. Front this out. Act like you haven't got a clue what's going on. And don't admit to being anywhere near that place – at least not until you've been accused . . .

Savvy swung the door back fully now and strode into the room, chucking her bag on a high-backed leather reading chair.

'Don't I even get a hello?' she said loudly.

Hud didn't turn round. 'Quiet,' he said. 'We're watching the news.'

'Why? What's going on?'

'Oh, God. Haven't you heard?'

It was Elodie, turning to face her, her baby-blue eyes bright with alarm. She was wearing a pink cashmere dress with a knotted string of pearls. It was a Moschino piece which should have been funky, but she'd somehow managed to make it look square. Her short hair had been cut in an attempt at a jaunty Audrey Hepburn crop, but only succeeded in making her boyish and severe.

If they knew you'd been at the Enzo, they'd already have reacted by now, Savvy thought.

'Heard what?' she said, feeling her confidence growing.

Paige was staring at her in confusion, clearly surprised to see her here in Vegas at all. Savvy hurried over to join them, wanting to know how bad it all was, desperate to discover if there'd been any word on the senator or Marcus.

The news anchorman's voice delivered a breathless commentary: '. . . still no news on Senator Fernandez's condition . . . A second casualty has been reported . . . a staff member . . . But this is not, I stress *not*, a siege situation . . . First indications are that the gunman was acting alone . . .'

So it was nothing like as bad as Savvy had feared . . . Marcus must be safe.

Hud pressed the TV zapper, muting the sound. He was wearing a black polo shirt with a dark tan suit and handmade Italian calfskin shoes. In his mid-sixties, he remained a broad-shouldered bull of a man, tough-looking but ruggedly handsome too. Three years back, he'd been diagnosed with a heart condition, brought on by decades of stress, drinking and smoking, but he'd now given up all his vices and worked out twice a day. His white hair was closely cropped and he was wearing half-glasses, which he carefully removed before fixing Savvy with a piercing stare.

'They shot a senator over at the Enzo,' he said, tapping his glasses on his hand.

'Oh,' Savvy said. 'That's awful . . .'

'Where were you?' he asked. 'Why did you miss dinner?'

'What senator? Who was he?' Savvy asked, avoiding his question. She loaded her voice with concerned sincerity.

'Senator Fernandez,' another man's voice said.

Savvy jolted. She felt her cheeks burning as she turned to see a man rising from a deep leather armchair in the corner of the room.

Luc Devereaux. So he was here. As she'd known he would be.

Because where Paige was Hud's Girl Friday, Luc Devereaux was very much his right-hand man.

Luc was as chic as ever, in an artfully creased cream linen suit, with a white shirt and diamond cufflinks. He was classically handsome, with dark, thick wavy hair and tanned smooth skin. He had a defined roman nose and that unmistakable hint of European nobility about his bone structure that her father so admired. He looked like a man born to rule, but what saved him and made him so undeniably beautiful were the dimples in his cheeks. And now as he walked forward, his hand in his pocket, he oozed charisma.

As usual, Savvy couldn't help but notice the swooning look of adoration in Paige, Elodie and Hud's eyes.

'They haven't yet said if he's alive or dead,' Luc told her, gazing briefly at her before turning away, as if she didn't really matter at all.

Savvy felt her jaw clench as Luc sauntered towards Hud. He knew exactly how much it infuriated her that he was here with her father, at the centre of Hud's empire. After what he'd done. And he knew she couldn't do a damn thing about it.

'No doubt you'd prefer him dead,' Savy said.

She'd meant just to think it, not say it out loud. But now that it was out, she didn't regret it. The flash of anger in his eyes thrilled her. She was delighted she still had it in her to crack his sangfroid.

Elodie glared at Savvy as she walked across to Luc's side. 'Savvy, stop it! What a terrible thing to say. People were hurt.'

'It's all right,' said Luc. 'It's late and I'm sure she meant no offence . . .'

The hell I didn't, Savvy thought.

Because she knew full well that the crinkly-eyed look of concern on his face was nothing but a mask. One of many. He didn't give a damn about any of those people at the Enzo. Oh, sure, on the surface he might be fooling everyone. Particularly sweet, saintly Elodie. *Caring* Luc. *Charming* Luc. *Luc who can do no bloody wrong . . .*

Savvy swallowed hard, sweeping her face of emotion, determined not to let him see that he'd got to her again. She raised an eyebrow at Hud, choosing instead to score a point of her own.

'Well, Daddy, you always said the Enzo was a disaster waiting to happen,' she said. 'It looks like you were right.'

Without actually acknowledging the fact Savvy had spoken, Hud turned to Luc. 'She's got a point,' he said. 'It's going to look bad if we don't do something.

Everyone knows how much we've spoken out against the senator. And Enzo Vegas.'

'You're right, of course,' Luc said, with a bow of his head. 'We have to spin this. Make a statement. Offer our condolences. Even say we'll help. Make sure we end up looking like the good guys out of this.' He turned to Paige. 'Don't you agree?'

'I'll get on it right away.'

Gathering up some papers from a nearby writing desk, Paige shot Savvy a look of warning. It was clearly something to do with Luc. But what?

Elodie brought Hud a drink. Orange juice. He swilled it round his glass and peered at it as if it were medicine. Savvy knew he wished it was whisky instead. But he was under strict doctor's orders . . . and Elodie's scrutiny.

'Thanks, precious,' Hud said, smiling gently as he squeezed Elodie's shoulder.

The dart of jealousy Savvy felt was only sharpened by the look on Luc's face. Ever since he'd been Elodie's guy, the compliments that had gone her way had gone his too.

'I'm sorry I wasn't here earlier,' she said, trying to patch things up, going over to Hud now and squeezing his arm.

He looked down at her hand, making no move to touch her. Her apologies were clearly too little, too late.

'Luc, Paige and I are going to have to deal with this,' he said.

She flinched, feeling the full force of her exclusion.

But you've got away with it, she reminded herself. You've got away without a dressing-down for what you got up to tonight . . .

She should have felt happy. Or at least relieved. But this time the buzz didn't come. She felt deflated. Exhaustion and sadness swamped her. She felt Luc's eyes on her, as if her skin had erupted into a rash.

'No problem,' Elodie said, scooping up a matching pink cardigan from the couch, obviously keen to leave. Savvy saw her flash a look at Luc and then at Hudson. 'We'll leave you guys to it and Savvy and I will go back to mine. To talk.'

Talk about what?

From the way Elodie said it, Savvy suddenly suspected she'd been a topic of conversation for most of this evening, prior to what had happened at the Enzo. She looked across at Paige. Paige was the only one she could trust. Again she caught that flash of warning in her best friend's eyes.

Hud stepped between them. 'We'll go through to my office,' he told Paige.

Elodie already had her car keys in her hand.

You're just being paranoid, Savvy told herself. After everything she'd been expecting – the accusations and drama – she was looking for conspiracies where there was none. The truth of the matter was that what she'd been up to wasn't important. Not to anyone here. They were preoccupied with bigger things. Thank God.

Well, Savvy had no intention of going to Elodie's apartment. She'd only just arrived. Now that the coke had all worn off, she was on a serious comedown.

She didn't feel like the sophisticated young woman she had done earlier. She felt like a little girl. In her father's home. And all she wanted to do was curl up and sleep.

'I'll stay here,' Savvy said. 'Up in my old room.' She moved towards the door. 'It's pretty late, so I'll just—'

'Go with your sister,' Hudson said.

It wasn't a request. It was an order. Luc, she noticed, was smiling at Elodie. Savvy felt like she'd been kicked.

CHAPTER TEN

Savvy hunched down low in the yellow leather passenger seat of Elodie's black Porsche as they joined the line of traffic on the freeway back across Vegas. The hood was down and soft jazz was playing on the CD player. But despite Elodie's best efforts to create a relaxed and intimate environment, it was obvious from the way she kept glancing across at Savvy that she was itching to say something.

But Savvy refused to give her the satisfaction of asking her what it was. If she allowed Elodie to instigate a discussion about her plans for their birthday now, it might never end. Plus, Savvy was way too exhausted to fight her corner. God only knew what she might end up agreeing to, just to get Elodie to shut the hell up.

All she wanted to do was to get inside. To be behind the locked door of Elodie's apartment. She visualized

a claw-foot bath full of fragrant bubbles, air conditioning, pasta and Elodie's soft bed, covered in cushions
and a duck-down quilt. Perhaps she'd sleep in there
with Elodie tonight. Cuddle up, just as they'd always
done as kids.

A burst of sirens. An ambulance slid past them and
weaved on ahead. Even though they were heading the
opposite way from the Enzo Vegas, the freeway was
still jammed.

'Just follow the ambulance,' Savvy said. 'It'll cut right
through. And it's bound to be heading for the hospital.
That's near your exit, right?'

'No,' Elodie gasped.

'Just do it,' Savvy snapped. 'Come on, Elodie, it'll
hurry things up.'

Savvy groaned as Elodie ignored her and stayed at
the same speed in the middle lane, anxiously glancing
in the rear-view mirror. She hated Elodie's over-
cautious driving. It was a travesty that she had this car.
Everything about her was just so *slow*.

They'd resolved long ago that it was better not to
drive in the same car, after all the arguments they'd
had. Savvy remembered now the incident when some
workmen, seeing the twins fighting at a stop sign,
had started clapping in unison and wolf-whistling.
Elodie had been so mortified, she'd told Savvy she'd
never be her passenger again, or vice versa. And until
tonight Savvy had held her to it, but now she felt her
old irritation overwhelming her.

'Goddamnit, Elodie. *Please*,' Savvy urged again,
kicking off her shoes and sticking her feet up on the

smart dashboard. She put her elbows on her knees and clawed her hair.

Elodie glared at her feet, clearly annoyed, but she didn't say anything.

'I'm not an ambulance chaser, Savvy. It's . . . well, it's rude. And anyway – I just thought . . . it might be coming from the Enzo Vegas.' She gasped dramatically, as if she was awed to be potentially so close to dangerous action. She put one hand on her chest. 'I can't imagine how terrifying it must have been in there with someone shooting.'

Savvy let out an ironic, depressed laugh. 'You have no idea.'

Staring out into the neon night, Savvy's eyes welled with tears. She thought again of that drop of blood on her shoulder. She shuddered, thinking of how she'd turned and seen the senator's face, how sympathetic he'd looked and how he'd given her his handkerchief.

Shit. I hope he's OK.

'You know, you shouldn't have said that awful thing to Luc,' Elodie said.

Savvy snapped back to reality. Had she just heard right? Did Elodie want a fucking apology? For Luc? She felt herself flush with fresh anger.

'Don't lecture me. You have absolutely no idea what I've been through tonight,' she snapped.

'Then why don't you tell me? What could be so bad?'

Savvy hugged her arms across her chest, forcing herself to calm down. 'Just drop it. It doesn't matter.'

She glared back at the Vegas skyline. What had

seemed like the Capital of Cool from up there in the SkyBird was now somewhere she just wanted to get away from.

'Savvy?' Elodie asked, quietly this time, finally sensing something was up. 'What *has* been going on?'

Savvy sighed, too tired to keep up the charade any longer. Everything she'd bottled up, she suddenly couldn't hold in any more. 'If you must know, I was there,' she said. 'But if you tell anyone, I'll fucking kill you, OK?'

'Where?'

'*There*. Enzo Vegas.'

'What? Tonight? At the fight?'

Savvy remembered how easy it was to taunt her sister. Particularly with anything shocking. In any other situation, she'd have tantalizingly slow-dripped the details, multiplying the effect of the punchline.

But this wasn't about some crazy party she'd been to. This was different. This was *real*. And as she looked ahead at the traffic and saw the ambulance speed away from them, its siren wailing plaintively into the night, she felt frightened again at how close she'd come to being in one herself.

'Yeah, right. Good one,' Elodie said, snorting.

Savvy wiped her face and shook her head, before hugging her arms tighter across her.

Why had she said anything? She saw Elodie change her grip on the steering wheel and stare at Savvy as she saw her tear-laden eyes.

'Oh, Jesus . . . Savvy? You can't be serious?'

'Deadly. I was right there . . . right in front of the

88

senator when he got shot. You might as well know. Chances are some reporter will turn it up anyway pretty soon.'

Savvy waited for Elodie to clamber down from her moral high horse and say something sympathetic. Because right now it was what she needed to hear. It was too big a deal. Now that she'd come clean, she desperately needed Elodie – anyone – to tell her how sorry they were. That her ordeal must have been dreadful. That she must have been scared out of her wits. Because she had been.

But instead Elodie cleared her throat and said, 'When did you decide to go to the fight?'

'What?'

'You heard me. *When?*'

The question caught Savvy completely off guard. The tears, so close to bursting from her in a torrent stalled, jammed against a dam of incomprehension. She couldn't believe what she was hearing. She could have been killed. Nearly *had* been killed. But all Elodie cared about was that she'd *planned* on going to the fight? That she'd missed Hud's family dinner *on purpose* . . .

'Doesn't it bother you that I was nearly shot?' Savvy asked. Her voice cracked, but Elodie didn't seem to notice.

She didn't even reply.

They still weren't talking as they pulled up at the kerb outside the Chanteuse. It was a boutique hotel – part of a chain which Hudson had acquired last year. He'd given the Vegas site to Elodie to refurbish, and Elodie had been thrilled at the opportunity to try out the interior design skills she'd been busy honing in all her rich acquaintances' homes.

But Savvy knew this was all bullshit. Elodie would never have got the gig if Hud hadn't owned the building. And even then, Paige had employed Giles Winterson, her best project manager, to oversee the work and make sure Elodie got a good result.

Savvy hadn't been to the hotel for over six months and had never set foot in the apartment Hud had effectively given Elodie. The building's scaffolding was down and a mock art deco façade was up. It looked pretty cool too, Savvy grudgingly had to admit. But no doubt that was all down to the architect Hud had employed.

Elodie still wasn't speaking as the elevator took them up to the twelfth floor.

Savvy stared straight ahead. If she'd had any energy, she would have still been picking a fight, demanding an apology from Elodie for being such a sanctimonious bitch. But her own need for comfort was greater. She was too weak to argue any more.

'Can we just deal with this in the morning?' she said. 'You know, when we've both had a chance to catch up on some sleep?'

But Elodie wasn't even prepared to meet her half-way. 'Tonight was meant to be really special. And you deliberately ruined it all.'

Savvy sighed. 'OK, I'm sorry. There. Happy now?'

The elevator stopped. A glass panel slid back. Savvy

stepped into the atrium of Elodie's two-storey apartment.

Last time Savvy had been here, the Chanteuse had been a building site. Now, as Elodie turned on the lights, Savvy caught her breath and swore.

She stepped forward and slowly pirouetted on the intricate spiral pattern of the marble floor, gazing out at the twinkling city through the towering walls of tinted glass. The top two storeys of the building had been combined into one, so that the actual living accommodation was suspended in the space above. A dangling light sculpture stretched down from the high ceiling. A Wurlitzer glowed pink and blue on a giant thick-pile rug at the bottom of a steep flight of stairs.

This is a kick-ass place for a party, Savvy thought, that's for sure.

'You like it?' Elodie asked, smiling and mellowing in spite of herself, clearly having already guessed the answer.

'It's amazing, El,' Savvy said. 'Really. I didn't know you had it in you, but you've done a great job.'

She meant every word. In fact, the effect she felt was even stronger. She felt jealous – of the space itself, of what a great time she could have here. But she felt envious too – of Elodie, and what she'd achieved. Because there was no hiding from the fact. While Savvy had been back in LA getting high, Elodie had been here . . . working . . . putting her stamp on the world. In some way that Savvy couldn't yet fully understand, she suddenly felt terribly left behind.

'Of course it's not finished,' Elodie said, failing to mask the pride in her voice as she walked past Savvy to the steep open staircase, which led up through a cut-away mezzanine floor to the main living area above. 'Mind out for the banisters,' she warned. 'The rest of the glass is being fitted this week before the *Harpers* photoshoot.'

'Oh, OK,' Savvy managed, following her.

She knew Elodie wanted her to ask questions about the photoshoot, but her eyes were stinging. She was desperate for sleep. As she passed the mezzanine, she looked over at Elodie's bed, and saw that it was just as she'd imagined, with an old-fashioned soft eiderdown and fur throw. Maybe she'd have a long, deep soak in a bath and then climb in beneath the duck-down soft-ness.

She joined Elodie at the top of the stairs. Everywhere she looked, there were unmistakable Elodie touches, from the tiger-skin rug on the beige carpet to the circular sofas scattered with stylish cushions. A wall of glass shelves was tastefully stacked with arty books, and on the top shelf were all Elodie's horse-riding trophies.

She kicked off her shoes under the white table. It was crowded with family photos, all beautifully framed in pretty silver fames. Centre-stage was a photo of her and Elodie in matching dresses, when they were four. It made Savvy smile.

'Sav?' Elodie said, gently placing her keys down next to the photos.

'Hmm?' Savvy looked at her sister.

Her eyes were sparkling. The argument they'd had

in the car was forgotten, and Elodie's mind had clearly switched back to the issue she'd been twitching over earlier. 'We need to talk . . .'

Savvy groaned. 'Can't it wait? You know, I'm really, really tired right now, and what I really want to do is—'

'Luc's asked me to marry him,' Elodie said. She was beaming. 'That's why I organized the dinner with Daddy tonight. To break the good news. Isn't it wonderful?'

Savvy felt as if the air had been punched from her lungs.

Elodie was biting her bottom lip, her face lit up in excitement, waiting for her reaction.

'Well?' Still that grin, those happy shining eyes. 'Say something.'

Savvy opened her mouth but nothing came out. There was nothing she could say. Nothing except the truth that would break Elodie's heart.

The truth.

Christ, the truth. Savvy felt the enormity of it rearing up like an iceberg through the fog.

She thought she'd had it under control. That she'd managed to smooth it all over, chain it up, make it disappear. It had taken every ounce of her strength to carry on in front of Elodie as if nothing had happened. But now here it was again.

'Fuck,' she said, out loud.

'I know.' Elodie clapped her hands in delight, completely misreading Savvy's tone. 'It's all so exciting,

I can hardly believe it myself. I've been dying to tell. That's why I got so pissed at you about not showing up tonight.'

If Luc had been here, Savvy would have attacked him with her bare hands. She'd have clawed out his eyeballs. She'd have torn out his tongue.

Poor Elodie had no idea . . .

'You can't marry him,' Savvy said.

'What?' Elodie laughed. 'Why not?'

Savvy had hoped it would never come to this. That Elodie's relationship with Luc would somehow fizzle out. But she could see now that that had just been wishful thinking on her part. That she'd been pulling the wool over her own eyes. Deliberately partying too hard so as not to face facts. And now it was too late.

'I'm serious,' she said.

Elodie's expression flattened. Her smile died and she let out a growl of frustration. 'Luc warned me you'd do this. He said you'd be jealous because you're still single. I didn't believe him. I told him you'd be happy for me.' Tears choked her voice. 'I love him, Savvy. Why can't you just be happy for me?'

'He's not who you think he is,' she said.

'How can you say that?' Elodie's voice rose. 'You don't know him. You don't know anything about him. How dare you judge him when—'

'I slept with him,' Savvy interrupted. Her words were calm. Matter-of-fact. But they couldn't disguise the horrible crawling sense of guilt and self-disgust she felt inside.

Or the betrayal.

'Oh, this is so low,' Elodie hissed. 'So fucking low. You'd tell a lie like that at a time like this?'

'I'm not lying.'

'You are,' Elodie yelled. 'You lie about everything. You're a drug addict. Your head's full of shit.'

She turned away and went quite still. But even though Savvy could no longer see her face, she knew she was listening.

'I had no idea how you felt about him at the time, Elodie, I promise. I thought you were just friends . . .' The words were making Savvy sick. She hated hurting her sister like this. 'That fundraiser we went to . . . at La Paris . . . the one Luc organized. You went home because you weren't feeling well? It was that night. Luc and I . . . we . . . I spent the night with him.'

'No.' Elodie still wouldn't face her. Her voice was a growl. 'You were with Marcus . . . I *know* you were.'

'I was waiting for Luc. To be with him.'

'No . . .'

Savvy's eyes were full of tears. 'It was me he wanted, Elodie. Not you. Right from the start. It was never you.'

Savvy got up and reached out to touch her sister, but the second her hand made contact with the pink cashmere dress, it stretched taut across Elodie's back.

'Take it back!' Elodie screamed, finally twisting round to face her. 'Take it back! Take it back!'

Without warning, she punched Savvy in the face. Savvy staggered backwards, crashing on to the white table, sending the photos smashing to the floor. She put her hand to her nose. Her fingers were wet with blood.

Savvy tried not to panic as she struggled to her feet. She hoped this was it. It was over. But just one look at Elodie told her it wasn't. Her fists were bunched, her jaw set. Retribution blazed in her eyes. They hadn't fought – really fought – since they were kids. Savvy had long ago learned that when she got angry, she turned steely and cold, like ice. But Elodie . . . Elodie was all fire.

'Calm down,' Savvy said, holding out a shaking hand. 'Please.'

She wasn't going to fight Elodie. Didn't want to. And besides, she couldn't. Elodie had been taking kick-boxing lessons for ten years. She'd kick Savvy's ass.

Elodie wasn't listening. She hurled herself at Savvy, screaming. Savvy's ears rang out. The room reeled as she tried twisting away, covering her head to defend herself. Another blow caught the back of her head. Savvy collapsed on all fours.

'Admit you're a liar. Say it,' Elodie screamed, towering over her.

Savvy wished she could. She wished she could say it and mean it. That she could undo the past and make this all go away.

She wished she could lie too. Lying would be the easy way out. All she had to do was tell Elodie what she wanted to hear and all this would end.

But she'd acted like a coward once already this

evening. She wasn't going to do it again. She was going to do what she should have done to begin with. She was going to tell her the truth.

'Luc bought you a watch,' she said. 'He told you he'd bought it in New York, but I chose it from the hotel shop right here in Vegas. You can check the receipt.'

Savvy's nose was bleeding heavily now. She felt dizzy and sick. She squeezed her eyes tight shut and waited for another blow which she knew surely must now come.

It never did.

Savvy opened her eyes. Elodie was backing away from her to the top of the stairs. She sank down, huddled on the floor. She had her arms wrapped around her torso, as if she were freezing.

Savvy was frightened now. She'd seen smack addicts going cold turkey before. She knew what a junkie looked like losing it. But there was something ten times worse about a sane, normal, intelligent girl like Elodie cracking up.

Savvy swept her hair away from her face, smearing the blood across her cheek with her arm. She moved towards Elodie cautiously.

'Please, El. Listen to me. I thought you and Luc would break up and you'd never need to know. Because he was only going out with you to get back at me. And I thought he'd give up the game, not do this . . .' Elodie was still silent. Savvy prayed she was getting through. 'He doesn't love you. Don't you see? Even though he's asked you to marry him. He only loves himself. And no marriage could survive a secret that big. And even if you knowing means that you and Daddy never speak to me again, then that's still better than you marrying Luc . . .'

Savvy would make it up to Elodie. No matter what. She'd find a way. Whatever it took. And Elodie was beautiful and smart. She would find someone who'd respect her and make her happy in a way Luc never could.

'I'm so sorry,' she said, her voice barely a whisper.

But as Savvy reached out to touch her, Elodie kicked out. She smashed her foot into Savvy's jaw.

Instinctively, Savvy kicked back, just as Elodie was getting to her feet. She caught her hard on the shin.

For a moment, Elodie's arms circled in the air, as if she was trying to fly. Then she toppled sideways off the top step, through the space where the glass banister should have been.

There was a split second of absolute silence, then a sickening crack.

Savvy dragged herself across the floor and looked down.

Elodie was lying twenty feet below in the hallway. Her beautiful blue eyes were wide open.

A halo of blood began spreading out around her head, seeping into the grooves of the spiral marble pattern.

Blood they'd once shared in the same womb.

Blood that bound them.

Blood that now told Savvy her twin sister was dead.

CHAPTER ELEVEN

The sky was a cloudless, endless deep blue as far as the eye could see. Lois gripped the plush orange leather seat as the sleek black powerboat sped away from the jetty.

She couldn't help giggling with exhilaration as they skimmed effortlessly across the crystal-clear water. Tenzin, the captain, who'd greeted her this afternoon, had made no secret of the fact that his boss's latest toy, whilst small and compact, was still worth several million dollars. As they reached full throttle, Lois pulled a strand of hair from across her mouth and leaned back, grinning, enjoying the sensation of the wind buffeting her face. It was a pity they had only a few kilometres to travel. This level of style and speed was proving to be quite a blast.

She was heading for the largest and, rumour had it, most exotic of all the private man-made islands in the Arabian Gulf.

In the late afternoon light, Dubai's ultra-modern skyline seemed other-worldly. And with each passing metre between her and the city, Lois felt more and more out of her comfort zone, as if this were happening to someone else.

She felt more than her fair share of guilt. It was one thing not to live with Cara, or to only get to see her one weekend a month, but Lois had always found comfort in the fact that she was in the same country at least.

So this felt as if she'd severed some kind of tie. But she knew it was her own problem. Cara didn't even know Lois was abroad. She hadn't had time to tell her.

It had all been so surreal, flying into Dubai International Airport in Roberto's private jet before being whisked in a gorgeous white Rolls-Royce to the spectacular sail-shaped Burj Al Arab hotel, the seven-star hotel in which she'd just enjoyed two blissful days of luxury.

The pretty yellow floral dress she wore fluttered around her knees and she wondered, not for the first time, whether she looked too casual. She'd been assured that the dress code in the daytime was informal. But the nights . . . the nights were going to be totally different. She thought about the sequinned Christian Lacroix evening dress in her luggage and smiled to herself, remembering how Roberto had bamboozled her into this luxury trip by plying her with a to-die-for wardrobe and a barrage of compliments.

She needed a break, he'd told her gently. A highly paid one. She was to think of this as a working vacation. *A personal favour*, he'd called it. Because he had no one else he could send. She was his most treasured member of staff.

The Tycoons' Tournament was a strictly private annual gambling get-together that Jai Shijai organized for his mega-rich contacts in the Middle East. A poker game for those who couldn't indulge their passion due to the strict anti-gaming laws, particularly in Dubai. Among the players were high-powered businessmen, philanthropists and developers. And Chinese politicians too, albeit in an extremely unofficial capacity, Roberto had explained.

This could be a much-needed foot in the door. After the shooting at the Enzo Vegas and the barrage of bad publicity afterwards, Roberto Enzo had lost the concession in Shangri-La.

It had taken a lot to lure Jai Shijai back to the Enzo Vegas. But he had come back and now considered Anthony, Guido and Rob, three of their most experienced dealers, to be his lucky mascots, and had requested them at his private game.

And who better than Lois to oversee it all and cover the security, Roberto had explained. The cash stakes being carried by the players would be substantial. They'd all obviously have their own bodyguards, but Jai Shijai was keen to bring in his own people to ensure his guests' comfort and safety. Besides, Jai Shijai had mentioned a few times that he wished to meet Lois in person.

So eventually she'd relented, secretly delighted to accept Roberto's generous offer. She did need a break. And could she really live with herself if she passed up the opportunity to meet someone as mysterious and intriguing as Jai?

As the powerboat drummed across the waves, she shifted, trying to get more comfortable, but she still felt a twinge of pain where her scar pulled. She touched the silver St Christopher pendant on her neck.

It had been a gift from Josh Fernandez when he visited her in hospital after the shooting. She'd thought that he'd been injured too, but the blood on his shirt had been her own. She'd completely shielded him from harm and he'd walked away shaken but unscathed.

When she was fit enough, Lois had tried to explain that in saving his life she'd only been doing her job, but Fernandez wouldn't hear of it. She was the bravest person he'd ever met, he told her. He'd taken off his St Christopher and given it to her, telling her to remember that she would always be able to rely on him. No matter what, no matter where, she could call in a favour whenever she needed one.

Lois remembered it like it was yesterday. It might only have been two years, but the shooting at the Enzo Vegas and what had happened afterwards? Well, that craziness Lois would *never* forget.

The Hamilton fight would have hit the world headlines anyway, but the shooting sent the story stratospheric. There'd been a media frenzy, the likes of which Lois hoped she'd never see again. And most of it had focused on her.

She'd been hailed as the woman who'd saved the

senator. And once she was out of danger, people couldn't get enough of the Lois Chan phenomenon.

Even while she was still in hospital, profile pieces had started running in all the national papers. Magazines pestered Roberto's PA to book up fashion shoots. Sponsorship offers and publishing contracts were hustled her way. Even Oprah had been in contact.

At first, Lois had been embarrassed and confused by all the attention, amazed that ordinary people whom she'd never met had sent flowers, gifts, cards and emails from all over the country.

It had been hard not to be dazzled, especially after Fernandez had been so openly generous with his praise on TV. Lois found herself suddenly elevated to a role model, a champion of undervalued, highly trained staff everywhere.

Roberto had even hired her a PR expert to manage it all. To push the attention away. Because that was what Lois had wanted most of all. Time to recover. Time to spend with her daughter. And the privacy that seemed so precious the moment she'd lost it.

She'd turned down everything, apart from Roberto's offer of a promotion. But even Lotty Rosenbaum, the doyenne of reputation management, hadn't been able to keep a lid on everything.

She hadn't figured on Michael Hudson.

Lois was still astounded at the audacity of what Hudson had done. She knew that, deep down, she'd never get over it. In a high-profile smear campaign – one designed to lose Roberto his chance in Shangri-La – he'd launched a savage attack on the Enzo Vegas, calling into question all of its security procedures and the staff who ran them. It was time to stop focusing on the fact that Lois had saved the senator and time to start looking at how on earth a mentally unstable and fanatical lowlife such as weapons expert Vic Benzir, known to have a personal grudge against Fernandez, had been allowed into the arena in the first place.

Hudson had gone on to expound his theory of exactly how it had happened. He portrayed Roberto as a bumbling, emotional old fool who didn't have the first clue about the responsibilities of big business. He'd painted an exaggerated picture of unhappy management and inter-staff rivalries.

But he hadn't stopped there. He'd gone on to question Lois's personal integrity. Who was she to be a national hero? She'd been expelled from the SFPD for a mistake that had cost a fellow cop his life. Was she a fit person to be in charge of thousands of people's safety, on a night like Fight Night?

Not in Hudson's opinion. He'd dug even deeper, revealing a sordid picture of Lois's childhood and how her father's gambling had spiralled into a world of shady debt. Her mother had been hounded by photographers in San Francisco.

Headlines followed about her Miki's murder. None of them had mentioned the sweet, intelligent boy that he'd been. Only that Lois Chan's kid brother had joined the Triad gang in the aftermath of their father's death. Nor did they mention that Miki had joined up solely to find out who had hounded their father into an early grave. Instead, they portrayed him as a violent hoodlum. A gang thug who deserved everything he got. No better than the shooter in the arena, Benzir.

And just when Lois thought it couldn't get any worse, they'd got to Cara. Harassing outside the school gates. Door-knocking her at home.

Lois winced, her mind as always coming back to how much she had to do to mend her relationship with her daughter.

But after lots of negotiation with her ex-husband Chris, Lois had finally persuaded him to extend their allowed time so that she could take Cara to San Francisco to visit her mother. It would be Lois and Cara's first vacation together since the shooting.

And there, in just a few weeks' time away from Chris and Mary-Sue, Lois could start to undo the wrongs that Michael Hudson had done to her daughter. If the shooting had taught Lois anything, it was that life was too short for her to be estranged from the person she loved the most. She had to get Cara back, no matter what it took.

And Hudson? Well, she'd have to bide her time on that one. Not a day went past without Lois feeling the bitter injustice of what he'd done. A situation only made worse because Hudson himself seemed to be going from strength to strength. The building of his monstrosity of a hotel and casino complex in Shangri-La, El Palazzo, well under way.

She told herself that it was just business, that what Hudson did shouldn't concern her. But it did. He'd made it personal.

Sure, she could play him at his own game and point

a finger at Hudson's family. It would be easy to spin his seemingly callous attitude to his daughter's death, or Savvy Hudson's recent and notorious spiral into shame and disgrace, but it would make her no better than Hudson himself.

No, Lois would keep her dignity. She'd find a way to prove that he hadn't cowed her or beaten her down.

'Excuse me, Ms Chan?'

The growl of the boat's engine lowered to a soft purr as they slowed.

The private island was coming into view. It was surrounded by the whitest of beaches and a coral reef. It was larger than Lois had expected, at least half a kilometre across, and dense with green trees and lush palms. Hard to believe that this was all so recently manmade. It looked so solid – as if it had always been here.

But what really blew Lois away, as they got closer, was the sheer perfection of the scene before her. It was like a film set. Although this was in the middle of the Gulf, it really *was* like arriving on the Chinese mainland.

It immediately reminded her of the balsa-wood model of a Chinese palace that her uncle Ed had in a glass case at the front of his restaurant back home in San Francisco. Because nestled in the middle of the island was a palace – a giant wood and glass building, complete with an ornate red and gold roof and a series of fancy balconies. Behind it was a red pagoda, glowing in the sun, stretching up to the sky.

As they pulled up alongside the jetty, Lois saw that the palace was surrounded by exquisitely manicured gardens.

And all of it belonged to just one man. Jai Shijai.

CHAPTER TWELVE

Deep in the heart of the Central American rainforest in a remote corner of Belize, Peace River Lodge was an exclusive rehab clinic whose alumni included Hollywood actors, politicians and infamous rock stars.

Secluded, private and discreet, the complex was set in several hundred acres of unspoilt forest and, for those in the know, its tough love policy had a reputation of working where other programmes failed.

Savvy sat on the veranda of her private bungalow, on the rattan rocking chair, watching the thick, hot tropical rain cascade from the thatched roof. Rivulets of water ran along the shiny slate path, the overhanging fronds of the swaying palm trees nearly touching the ground. Thunder rumbled in the distance and the rain hammered on the roof like a relentless drum.

The oppressive weather suited her mood. She sucked

at the straw in the glass of green detox juice and fought down the urge to retch. What was in that God-awful stuff anyway? It tasted like mould.

This was day four of total sobriety and she still didn't feel any better. In fact, she felt like utter shit. She screwed up the questionnaire and chucked it on to the scuffed floorboards where she kicked it angrily with her bare foot.

What a bloody joke.

The whole philosophy of Peace River Lodge was to rebuild the mind, body and soul. Well, there wasn't a space on the questionnaire to write that her mind was all over the place, her body was fucked and her soul completely crushed.

She stood up. She hated this bloody place. But more than that, she hated everyone who'd tricked her into coming here.

It was so unfair. And it was all Marcus's fault. She'd thought he was her friend. Her true friend. Someone who would defend her, no matter what. But he'd turned on her. Just the same as everyone else.

No doubt Paige had paid him off, Savvy thought bitterly, as she pulled her robe tight across her body and started pacing. With her own money and behind Hud's back. Oh yes, Hud had shown his true colours all right, he'd made it clear how he really felt about her. Because rather than offering any of the support Savvy had needed in her grief, he'd shut her out and treated her like dirt. Well, was it any wonder that she'd gone completely off the rails? *What the fuck had everyone expected?*

At first, after Elodie had died, most people had been sympathetic about the fact Savvy was constantly drinking herself into oblivion. They'd said her behaviour was understandable, given that she'd lost her twin. Her grief had been to blame. The scene that Savvy had caused at Elodie's funeral, when she'd screamed hysterically at Luc that it was all his fault, had been quickly brushed over. Martha had bundled her, kicking and spitting, into one of the black limousines and she had been driven away.

But afterwards, when Luc and Hud had just carried on with their business, waltzing off to China as if everything were back to normal, Savvy hadn't been able to bear it.

Life didn't just go on. It shouldn't. It couldn't. Because everything had changed.

Her life was wrecked. Like a car crash. And anyone who thought otherwise – people like her father and Luc – well, their hearts were made of stone. They weren't even human.

But Savvy *was* human. And every beat of her heart had reminded her of just one thing – that Elodie's kind and loving heart had stopped for ever.

All because of her.

Which was why she'd deliberately embarked on a mission to take as many drugs as she could lay her hands on. She hadn't cared who she'd done them with, or who'd given them to her. Night after night, she'd gone out partying, drinking until dawn, taking so many pills that her vision would blur and reality would disappear. And it was only in those fragmented moments, between the flashing lights of the nightclub, that respite had come.

Eventually someone – usually Marcus – would take her home and slip her some sleeping pills. But no matter how many pills she took, the same nightmare recurred again and again, as soon as she started to wake up. Elodie falling . . . her broken body . . .

The cycle would have continued unabated. Right up to the end. To when that dark sleep she so yearned for embraced her.

But then someone had sent a series of pictures of her to a showbiz website. They'd showed her emerging from a basement club, clearly unable to stand up, her eyes like black spiders and her torn dress hanging around her emaciated thighs.

Within hours, Paige had been on Savvy's doorstep with strict instructions from Hud to control the situation at once.

But Paige hadn't realized how far gone Savvy was. Bringing her back to the White House in Vegas hadn't been the solution that Paige – and Hud – had clearly assumed it would be.

When Hud had finally shown up and accused her of being a spoilt brat and demanded that she pull herself together, Savvy had caused an almighty public spectacle at La Paris, rampaging through the casino and overturning tables whilst ranting, to anyone who cared to listen, that Hud was evil and Luc a total bastard as well.

The press had been on hand to witness it all. Hud, humiliated and furious, was quick to denounce her.

He'd declared both privately and in the papers that as far as he was concerned, both of his daughters were now dead to him.

Given his heart condition – and how recent events had exacerbated it – he'd gone on to announce that Luc Devereaux would be his successor.

Savvy had been holed up in Marcus's Vegas hotel apartment when she'd seen Hud on TV. She'd thrown a whisky bottle right through the screen.

Then the next day Marcus had announced he'd got a surprise. They were getting out of here, he'd told her. They were off on holiday. He'd cashed the last of his emergency funds and splashed out on a private plane. It was too late to change his mind. They were off on an adventure to Central America. All Savvy had to do was meet him at the plane.

But Marcus had tricked her. She'd got to the private airfield but Marcus hadn't yet arrived. A steward named Max had shown her to her seat on the private plane to wait.

She'd been high on coke and booze and when Max had asked her if she'd had all her immunisation shots, Savvy had laughed. It hadn't occurred to her that she'd need them, since she and Marcus were going to a private party in a friend's beach house. But after listening to Max giving her the low-down on all the tropical diseases she might be exposed to, she'd happily let him give her the injections she needed. She *hated* spiders and snakes, she'd told him as she sipped her champagne. She'd giggled as she watched the needle slide into her arm.

When Savvy had woken up, in bed here at Peace River Lodge, the blurry face of the same steward had slowly swum into focus.

He'd explained to her where she was: in rehab. And who he really was. Dr Max Savage. And why she was here: to get clean. No matter how long that took.

Savvy had railed at him, screaming out threats. This was kidnap. It was illegal. It was fucking rendition.

But Dr Savage had stayed calm, producing consent forms bearing Savvy's signature. When had she signed them? She couldn't remember.

Who was paying for all of this? she'd demanded. Who'd chartered the plane to bring her here? Because now that Savvy knew she'd been tricked, she guessed that Marcus's claim of generosity was bullshit as well.

A woman called Paige Logan had made the arrangements, she was informed.

Savvy had sworn out loud that she'd kill Paige the second she got out.

But getting out of here was going to be easier said than done. There'd been two other men in the room. Muscular orderlies in white shorts and shirts. They'd stepped towards her as she moved towards the door.

Dr Savage had explained that she'd be staying here with them until she'd overcome her addictions. Until she was well. And she'd better start getting used to the idea. Peace River Lodge was impossible to escape from, he'd told her. It was surrounded by jungle on one side and the sea on the other – twenty-six miles of uninterrupted coastline.

That first interview had ended when she told him she'd cut his throat. She'd tried to fight her way out of the room. He'd had her restrained, then sedated. He had the power to do that . . . and much more.

It wasn't until last night that they'd finally moved Savvy out of the locked room and here to the bungalow. It was a privilege, the doctor had told her. One that could just as easily be revoked if she failed to behave.

But she'd lost the will to make a break for the coast. Apathy had taken over and the lack of coke and booze had locked her body in a near-permanent cramp. Only cigarettes and mild painkillers – both strictly rationed – were holding her together.

Now she groaned as she heard the swish of the sliding door leading from the bedroom to the veranda.

So this was it, then. This was where the therapy started.

She had no idea who they were sending. Probably one of the over-zealous American quacks she'd seen around the place. But when she turned round, the guy dressed in shorts and a scrappy khaki T-shirt and shaking out his umbrella, was nothing like she'd expected. Where was the white coat? Where were the badges showing his medical qualifications? This guy looked like he was qualified to run a beach bar rather than sort out her head.

He leaned the umbrella against the wall then stood and faced her. The first thing Savvy noticed was his eyes. They were pale blue, with dark rings around their irises, like a wolf's. It was like he was staring right through her. Or, more precisely, *inside* her.

She felt exposed. Ashamed. He probably knew all about her – her temper tantrums. Her refusal to cooperate . . .

His eyelashes and eyebrows were yellowy-blond, but the thick messed-up hair on his head was a dark, gleaming auburn and his skin a mass of joined-up freckles. She saw now that he was much younger than she'd expected. He was probably only five years or so older than her.

'So,' he said, 'you must be Savannah. I've been looking forward to meeting you. I'm Jonny Raddoch.' He spoke with a slight Scottish lilt. 'But everyone calls me Red,' he continued. 'So. How are we doing today?'

We. There wasn't a *we*, or an *us*. Savvy was in this alone.

'Shit. If you must know,' Savvy said, folding her arms.

Red glanced down at the scuffed questionnaire on the floor. With a long-suffering sigh he walked across, bent down and picked it up.

'I know it's difficult,' he said.

'None of it applies,' she said, staring malevolently at the paper in his hand and not hiding her vicious tone. 'Because I'm not a fucking junkie, OK?'

Red pulled up a rattan stool and sat down, clipping the questionnaire on to a wooden board. Savvy noticed some scars on his freckled legs and his flip-flops and feet were splashed with mud.

She looked away. Couldn't they even send a real

doctor? she thought. Who was this idiot? So far, everything about his manner annoyed her.

She couldn't seem to control her temper and as he started speaking, Savvy deliberately tuned out. What had happened to her apartment? she wondered. Her clothes? All the dry cleaning? The twenty grams of coke in the pot on top of the fridge . . . Was nobody looking for her and wondering where she was?

But then she remembered the Vegas hotel, with its pulled-down blinds. Nobody would be looking for her because she'd already shut them all out.

She watched as Red pulled a pen out of the pocket of his T-shirt and clicked the end of it. To Savvy, it sounded like a pistol being cocked.

'Let's get started. Help me out here. Just say yes if these statements apply, OK? Number one. *My job has been affected by my alcohol or drug use,*' he began.

'I don't have a job,' Savvy said. 'I've told them that already.'

'OK. How about, *I drink or use when I'm alone?*'

'Who fucking doesn't?'

Red scribbled something down on the form. *'I have had memory loss after drinking or using? Sometimes I can't remember what happened the night before?'*

Everything was a blur. Savvy couldn't remember whole weeks, let alone days or hours, of the last few months. But that was because she didn't want to. Memory loss was a benefit of drinking and using. Didn't this stupid idiot get that?

'My sex life has been affected?'

'Only in a very positive way,' Savvy shot back.

116

She'd lost count of the number of one-night stands she'd had in the last six months. Lost count . . . or forgotten.

Besides, what business was it of Red's? Why should she tell him anything?

'*My family has suffered due to my drinking or using?*' he continued.

Silence.

'*I have compromised my morals?*'

Silence.

'*I have insomnia or nightmares after drinking or using?*'

'No, my insomnia and nightmares started right here,' Savvy burst out. '*Since* I stopped. Since you fucking people kidnapped me.'

'*Others have suggested that I might have a problem with alcohol or drugs?*' Red continued, unruffled.

'Stop it. Shut up. Leave me alone. I want to go home,' Savvy yelled, standing up and putting her hands over her ears. 'I want to go home.'

But she no longer knew where home was.

And Red wouldn't go away. He stood up to face her.

'Savvy, you're here because your friends and family love you. They want to help.'

'No, they don't,' Savvy shouted at him. 'You don't know anything about my family.'

'Yes I do. I know quite a lot actually. I know who your father is.'

'Oh, I get it,' she railed at him. 'And *you*'re probably loving the fact I'm locked up in here and he's told you to throw away the key.'

'This isn't personal, Savannah.'

'Oh? Isn't it? It seems pretty personal to me. You're the one standing in my space, asking me personal questions.'

Red sighed. She could tell she'd annoyed him and that he was struggling to keep his temper.

'I'm just trying to help you.'

'Well, I don't want your fucking help, OK? I don't need some sanctimonious bastard like you trying to make me apologize for my life. It's my life. My choices.' She thumped her palm on her chest.

'OK,' he said slowly, grimacing. 'So I guess what they told me about you was right.' He rubbed his eyebrow. 'And to think I volunteered for you.' He shook his head, as if he couldn't believe he'd been so stupid. 'I thought we might bond because we're both British. But I hadn't figured out that you're just . . .'

He stopped and shook his head.

'Just what?' Savvy snapped.

'It doesn't matter.'

'Yes it does. Come on. Enlighten me, doctor.'

'I'm not a doctor.'

'*Evidently*. Come on, spit it out. What am I then? Since you think you already know me?'

He stared at her, his face dull with disgust. 'You're just another conceited, spoilt, rich princess who thinks the world owes her.'

'Fuck off!' she shouted, pointing at the door.

'OK, so you want to play it that way, fine. I've got plenty of people in here who need my help, Savannah. People with real problems.'

Without saying any more, he took the questionnaire

118

off his clipboard and dropped it on the floor by her feet, as if it – she – were dirt.

Then he turned and left.

Savvy leaned down, picked up the questionnaire and screwed it into a ball, hurling it as hard as she could after him.

Then she ran into the bedroom and flung herself face down on the bed. Along with the drumming of the rain, she heard the tree frogs and weird sounds of the jungle in the distance and the water falling on to the porch in metronomic drips.

She put her face into the pillow and screamed as loudly as she could.

CHAPTER THIRTEEN

Lois stood at the top of the red and gold ornamental pagoda in Jai Shijai's garden and sighed happily, relishing the chance to reflect on the last, sumptuous twenty-four hours and the even more exciting ones to come.

Last night she'd been invited to dine on the kitchen terrace with Angela Ho, who seemed to be the chief housekeeper and fixer around here, and two other guests who'd come to play poker – an investment maverick, also from the US, called Bill Andies and his friend, an art dealer from Holland, Pieter Von Triers. They'd made a strange foursome, but the conversation had been interesting and, if nothing else, she had secured two future visitors for the Enzo Vegas.

Lois had gone up early to her rooms, unable to stop herself from marvelling at the incredible suite she'd been given, with its enormous bed swathed in pink silk sheets. She hadn't expected to sleep at all but she'd drifted off almost immediately, no doubt due to the fragrant jasmine blossoms outside her window.

Well rested, she was keen to check out the layout of the house and the island. On the way to the pagoda, Kai, an affable young man who seemed to have been assigned to her as some kind of personal servant, had taken her through the enormous kitchens at her request. Teams of chefs had been busily hacking up two giant blue marlin that had just been caught, and perfectly arranging edible exotic flowers and carved pieces of fruit on silver trays.

Lois had been in the kitchens at the Enzo Vegas plenty of times before, but she'd never seen chefs so frenetic or skilled as the ones here. She couldn't help feeling excited about the banquet lunch she was soon to enjoy in such idyllic surroundings. Roberto had been right to urge her to come here. This certainly was a once-in-a-lifetime opportunity.

From up here on the pagoda's balcony, Lois could see that behind the palace was a hill covered in tropical trees, with a shiny stream weaving a lazy path between them. All around, ornate gardens with well-tended flowers and shrubs were divided into different brightly coloured sections. A wooden bridge rose in a high arch over a lake full of ornamental fish. It looked like it had been here for centuries, but it was all new.

Around the island, the water was an enticing deep aquamarine blue. She was about to turn away when something caught her eye. Behind the far trees, almost hidden from view, was the mast of a sleek wooden yacht, mooring up at a jetty. She moved to get a better view. The yacht was beautiful – its smooth lines elegant and neat. Did it belong to one of the guests? she wondered. Or was this yet another of Jai Shijai's expensive toys?

Lois shielded her eyes as a man appeared on deck. He was wearing a pair of blue-and-orange patterned shorts and it was hard to tell how old he was. There was something about him that looked young, like a teenager almost. Especially now as he hopped on top of the cabin and stretched his arms out wide to dive. With incredible agility he somersaulted overboard and landed in the water with barely a splash. A distant exuberant whoop reached her on the breeze.

'Excuse me, Ms Chan.'

Lois started at the sound of a woman's voice. She looked over the edge of the pagoda. Angela Ho was standing on the immaculate grass beneath her. She was wearing a red two-piece suit and high heels, the bow of her lips painted a bright vermilion to match.

Lois couldn't help feeling unnerved by her. There was a steeliness to her eyes that belied the perfect hostess smile. Maybe her ostentatiously charming manner was all a façade and she had the capacity to snap into vicious cruelty in a second. And perhaps Lois wasn't the only one who thought so. Because from the way the staff treated her, with terrified deference, Lois got the impression that Angela Ho was a formidable boss indeed. But maybe Jai Shijai demanded this level of perfection. Maybe, in his mini-fiefdom, he required staff like Ms Ho to make it all run like clockwork.

'Dr Jai will see you now. Kai is waiting for you downstairs. He'll show you where to go,' she said.

Lois felt overdressed in her suit and absurdly Western next to Kai, who was wearing the regulation loose black pyjamas all the staff wore, as she followed him over the ornamental bridge towards the main house.

As they walked in through a grand glass-and-wood hallway into a spacious atrium at the back of the house, the air conditioning hit her like an icy slap.

This was where the poker tournament would take place, Kai explained. An ornate table was set on a raised dais in the middle with ten chairs around it. At the far end of the room was a lavish bar.

Lois followed Kai to the bottom of a sweeping staircase, which elegantly wound up through the atrium. She had to speed-walk to keep up with him, as he started up the shallow marble steps. Lois was no modern art aficionado, but she'd seen enough postcards and New York exhibition posters in her time to hazard a guess that several of the pictures were Picasso sketches. And originals too.

So *this* was what the world of the super-wealthy was like, she thought. She spent her whole time at the Enzo treating all the customers the same, no matter how many chips were stacked up in front of them. It was hard to equate those little discs of plastic to anything real. But here, surrounded by the trappings of extreme wealth, it was impossible not to feel awed and humbled. And as they continued up the stairs, Lois started to feel more and more nervous about meeting the great tycoon in person.

At the top of the staircase there was a wide corridor. At the far end was a floor-to-ceiling window framing another view of the island, showing off its series of interlinked swimming pools connected by waterfalls, cascading towards the sea.

The corridor swung left and terminated abruptly in what looked like a dead end. A man in a dark suit was sitting stiffly on an ornate chair. He stood up quickly and looked Lois up and down. A bodyguard, Lois surmised.

He didn't pat her down or check her for weapons. But then again, he probably felt that he didn't need to. Her luggage had already been searched, she knew, even before it was delivered to her room. They hadn't done a bad job repacking her belongings, they just hadn't done a *perfect* job. And for a girl who'd grown up in a cramped apartment like she had, noticing that someone had meddled with her things was second nature.

The bodyguard moved aside, with a low, watchful bow. Kai stepped forward and knocked on a painted panel. It slid back smoothly to reveal a hidden doorway. Kai gestured Lois through with a smile.

After the tasteful minimalism of the rest of the building, the minute she stepped inside Jai Shijai's personal quarters Lois felt as if she'd arrived in a commercial emporium.

The suite of rooms was crammed with an array of

furniture and artefacts and classical music was bursting from what Lois assumed must be hidden speakers. The walls and ceiling were covered in hand-painted silk wallpaper depicting cranes in paddy fields and ancient Chinese battles. Two antique pillars towered upwards through the middle of the room, with inlaid ivory dragons curling around them. A chandelier carved like a fire-breathing dragon hung suspended from the clear glass dome above.

Kai led her past an intricately carved teak table. On it was a shallow china pot containing a gnarled old bonsai tree. Lois was no expert, but a specimen like that must be hundreds of years old. A pair of scissors and a few minuscule clippings lay next to it.

Western music . . . a Japanese bonsai . . . Jai was clearly a cultured man of the world.

This wasn't a business meeting, she thought, but more like an audience with a king. And now, at the far end of the rooms, where the glass and wooden screen doors opened on to a balcony, was Jai Shijai himself, seated on his throne. Well, on a leather chair, to be precise. He had his back to her, facing the view of the trees and waterfalls, the white beaches and blue sea beyond.

Kai scurried off backwards, without a word.

Lois saw now that a woman was kneeling in front of Jai Shijai, performing reflexology on his manicured feet, a look of intense concentration on her face. Jai Shijai's eyes were closed as he conducted the soaring strings silently in the air.

The woman was wearing a white tunic and trousers

and looked annoyed at the interruption. She squeezed Jai Shijai's bare feet.

'Ah,' Lois heard him sigh.

He dismissed the woman not with a snap of his fingers, as Lois had half expected, but with a gentle whisper and a smile.

Was she his wife? Lois wondered. Or were they lovers? Or maybe Jai Shijai wasn't the sexist ogre his exclusively male entourage in Las Vegas – or the army of neat, meek women here – had led her previously to conclude. In fact, so far all of her assumptions about him had been completely wrong.

Jai Shijai wriggled his toes appreciatively. The woman kept her head bowed as she quickly gathered up the mat she'd been kneeling on. She glanced briefly at Lois and nodded as she passed her.

Jai picked up a remote control from the arm of the chair and pressed a button. The music stopped. Birdsong and the sound of gently trickling water filled the balcony in its place, as he stood up and faced her.

He was wearing utilitarian loose cotton trousers and a blue smock top, its sleeves rolled up as if he were a peasant worker, an affectation Lois had last seen in photos of Chairman Mao. But even so, there was something immaculately groomed about him. In the flesh, he was younger than she'd assumed – even from the live CCTV stream of him playing at the Enzo – probably no more than fifty.

Despite the weight he carried around his face, he

wasn't unattractive. In fact, there was a charisma about him that took Lois by surprise. He was clearly a man in the prime of life.

'Ms Chan,' he said. He had small, neat teeth, which were very white. 'Welcome to my home,' he went on in Cantonese. His accent was sharper, faster than those she'd grown up with.

'Thank you. I am very honoured to be here,' she answered, in Cantonese too.

'Please, talk to me in English,' he said, as they both sat down. It was an order. He placed his hands on his knees and looked at her for a second, then he tutted and wagged his finger. There was a playful twinkle in his eyes. 'Your accent is somewhat *Americanized*, Lois. May I call you Lois?'

'Of course,' she said, embarrassed that the very first time she'd opened her mouth she'd made a fool of herself. But she saw that he was more amused than angry.

'We haven't had the pleasure of meeting in person at the Enzo Vegas when I've been there, have we? But I'm sure you've been watching me on your screens. Am I right?'

Lois blushed. Because, yes, she did spend a lot of time watching him on the screens. After what had happened that first time he played at the Enzo Vegas, *everyone* kept a careful eye on Jai. Roberto had made no secret of the fact that the only good thing to come out of the shooting that night was that Jai Shijai had been interrupted before he broke the house. Since then, *all* players had adhered strictly to the house rules.

'It's always a pleasure to have you at the Enzo Vegas,' she said, trying to sound gracious.

Jai Shijai nodded, clearly aware that she was taking the corporate line when he was trying to get more personal. He looked at her for a moment, then smiled. 'I've been very interested to meet the woman who saved the Yankee senator.'

She bristled. No doubt Jai Shijai had heard all the stories Hudson had spread about her. But even though his public criticism had been downright mean rather than accurate, she'd still spent the last eighteen months back at the Enzo reviewing and changing its security protocols, so that nothing like that night could ever happen again.

'I wish there had been another way to resolve the situation. I regret what happened very much.'

Jai Shijai frowned. 'Regret nothing,' he said, curling his hand into a fist. He thumped it down on his knee, making her jump. 'You are the first woman to save an American senator's life, I think. Be proud.'

There was no point in arguing. He had obviously formed some opinion of her that she wasn't going to shake.

He stared at her and she held his gaze for a moment. Instinctively, she knew that she had to let go of her defensiveness. Blurting out how unfairly the Enzo Vegas had been judged in the aftermath of the shooting, and how devastating it had been for Roberto to lose his chance in Shangri-La, would be the wrong way to play this. Besides, so far Jai Shijai had given her only positive feedback. He wasn't criticizing her. She had to be cool.

'Will you take tea, Lois?' he asked.

As she sat at the table at the far end of the balcony, Lois knew all too well how important the unspoken tea ritual was to the Chinese, and what a big deal it was to be offered it by Jai Shijai. She also knew that one false step in the established etiquette and she'd be judged as lacking in manners and refinement.

What would Grandma have done? she asked herself, searching for memories of the frail old lady who'd tried to teach Miki and her how to take tea like people had done back in Hong Kong. But all Lois remembered was how boring it had been. How *still* her grandmother had required her to be. How watchful. How alert. Every single gesture had a meaning.

Being so close to Jai Shijai like this, breathing in his aftershave, being so alone with him, was making her more flustered by the second. This was a man who, according to the rumours she'd heard, had direct influence over hundreds of thousands of people's lives in the swathes of manufacturing industry and numerous companies he owned in China. Yet here he was, shooting the breeze with her as if it was the most normal thing in the world.

On the table between them was a book Lois had recognized immediately. It was Maxine Hong Kingston's *Woman Warrior*. She couldn't believe that Jai Shijai had read such a famous American – and feminist – book.

'You know this?' he demanded, picking it up and handing it to her.

'Of course.' Lois took it from him. It immediately made her think of her mother and her work at the Chinese Cultural Center in San Francisco. But thinking of her mother, of her mother's world – here, in front of Jai Shijai – only threw her even more. The two of them seemed not just countries but entire worlds apart.

'I read it because I knew you were coming,' he said, confounding her even further. 'You see, I was intrigued to know what it was like to grow up in the United States.'

He'd read a book *because of her*? But why?

'A place of ghosts, but a place of possibilities as well?' Jai Shijai said.

'Yes, very much so,' Lois said, trying to recover her composure. 'I think it's a place where anyone can succeed . . . with enough luck and determination.'

She felt proud telling him this, and relieved too to be asserting her American citizenship. To be asserting *herself*. She believed in the values of the country that she'd been born and brought up in. It suddenly seemed very important to her that Jai Shijai understood that. She was different to him. And she had no reason to feel ashamed.

'Success for everyone,' he said.

She put the book gently down on the table between them.

'Even in the police?' he asked.

He knew. Lois flushed as his eyes bored into hers.

Of course he knew. Why wouldn't Jai Shijai have done his homework on someone he was employing to oversee security in his home on an important occasion?

What happened was in the past, she told herself. She refused to be defined by it. Especially now.

'That didn't work out,' she said.

'So you moved on. Good.'

At least he wasn't here to judge her. In fact, he sounded like he was congratulating her. And how could he sum up her life like this? As if he knew her?

'You know the Chinese are the greatest people on earth.' He said it as a fact rather an opinion. 'The West is finished. Their economies . . . their cultures . . . they have all begun to dwindle into history. Power is shifting to the East. America . . . Europe . . . they will soon become a part of the Third World they have exploited for so long.'

But I am American, she wanted to say.

'Even your friend Roberto Enzo is looking to China now. That, of course, is why he's made you his ambassador,' he added.

His what? Lois's mind was whirring.

'Roberto tells me how much he wishes to profit from the business opportunities in China. Especially since the senator's legislation to tax your casinos at home has been passed. You must approve, yes?' Jai asked. 'Because you will be central to his business interests in Asia.'

Would she be central to Roberto's business interests? What did that mean?

'I know that Michael Hudson is in China right now,

developing his site in Shangri-La,' Jai Shijai continued. 'Even if Roberto were to secure an entry, he would still have a job to catch up with him. He is already . . . how do you say it? On the back foot.'

If? So there *was* an opportunity for Roberto . . . for her.

'They are great rivals.' Jai Shijai sounded gleeful, as if he were savouring the prospect of two gladiators battling it out. He frowned at Lois. 'You don't agree?'

'I think rivalries can be counter-productive,' she said. She didn't want to be drawn on how she felt about Michael Hudson.

'On the contrary, they are often healthy for business.' He smiled and then he paused. 'Of course, at the end of the day, there can only be one winner. So I wonder . . . will it be Michael Hudson? Or maybe your friend Roberto Enzo? Who will wear the crown in Shangri-La? Only time will tell.'

From the way he'd said it, and from the dangerous twinkle in his eyes, it was clear who he thought the kingmaker would be. But Lois could barely hide her sense of elation. So Jai Shijai *could* still make it happen. There *would* be a chance for Roberto after all. Which meant that despite Hudson's best efforts, he hadn't won. Not yet. Not at all.

'But now, tell me, Lois. Do you think women approach business differently?' Jai asked. 'Because I have a feeling, Lois, that women are far more competitive than men. But why is it that in your industry there are so few women at the top?'

Lois could name a hundred reasons. The working hours that were incompatible with family life; the sexism that still persisted across America's boardrooms, despite all the rhetoric to the contrary. The fact that motherhood and gambling were two areas of life which always seemed to repel each other as forcefully as magnet ends. To name but a few.

But none of these reasons applied to her. And this conversation *was* about her. At least, that was what she was beginning to think. Because this felt more and more like an interview. But for what?

'I'm not sure,' she said.

'So how would *you* feel about being at the top?'

'Excuse me?' she said, finally losing her composure, startled by the frankness of the question.

Jai Shijai continued staring at her. 'I'm just interested, that's all,' he said, 'in the kind of person you are. How far you're prepared to go. How high you can fly . . .'

Lois chose her words carefully. If this really was some kind of test, if Jai did have some kind of influence over her future, as he seemed to be implying, then what did she have to lose? She might as well pitch herself straight.

'I think it's important that our industry takes a much greater responsibility for its impact on the environment. And I think it needs tighter regulation. So that it's fair and free from corruption,' she said. 'That's the only way the industry can grow. By attracting all kinds of customers, not just the hard core of gambling addicts. In an industry like that,' she said, finally meeting his eyes, 'I think I could be at the very top.'

He watched her in silence, as if mulling over her words. Then he smiled and stood and bowed. She wasn't sure what had passed between them, but she couldn't shake the feeling that Jai Shijai had somehow changed the course of her life.

CHAPTER FOURTEEN

Savvy rolled over on to her back and stared up at the wooden ceiling fan, as it beat the humid air above her bed in Peace River Lodge. Tears trickled from the corners of her eyes.

She felt hopelessly and completely trapped. If the only prospect of human contact was with that ghastly Red, then what was the point of being here?

Savvy didn't *want* to get better. That was what these people didn't understand. What good would sorting herself out do, when she'd already lost everything she'd ever loved?

She rubbed at her tears with the heel of her hand, her chest shuddering with grief.

She needed a drink so badly . . . A line, anything.

She could feel the walls closing in on her. She needed something – anything – to make the pain go away.

She would give anything to just . . . disappear.

The ceiling fan spun hypnotically above her.

She slowly got to her feet and stood there, watching it turn and turn, as the shadows stretched longer and darker on the walls.

She picked up her dressing gown and its long white cord.

Everything could stop.

Just stop.

The slow beating of her heart was like the ticking of a clock.

CHAPTER FIFTEEN

After the banquet lunch, when all Jai's guests had gathered to eat alfresco on the lawn, the tranquil peace of the siesta hours had descended on the island, but Lois felt too elated to sleep. Adjusting the wide brim of her sunhat and smoothing out the front of her short sundress, she quietly closed her bedroom door and tiptoed carefully along the corridor and down the grand main staircase of the house to the front doors.

She didn't want to bump into anyone. She wanted to be alone. To get her head around all of this. And this was the first moment she'd had to herself to think.

With each passing hour, her audience with the great tycoon seemed to grow in significance rather than shrink. And Jai Shijai's knowing looks across the table at lunch had only confirmed the feeling that something monumental had taken place.

But what? She wished she'd had the chance to discuss

it with Roberto, but he'd be asleep now back in Vegas and anyway Jai Shijai hadn't said anything specific that she could report. And besides, there was something about the way in which Jai Shijai had spoken that had made her suspect that Roberto knew more than he'd told her.

Was Roberto really planning on sending her to China? That was the question on which all other questions hinged. And what would her life be like if he did? She could handle it, couldn't she?

If Cara could spend some time out East – during vacations at the very least – although it might initially be a problem for her ex-husband Chris, it could be the chance of a lifetime for her daughter. A new country, new sights, new friends, new opportunities . . . Cara would love it. And in between Lois could still fly back home and see her as much as she did now. Then later, when Cara was older, maybe she could even join Lois out here. At an international school, perhaps. By then, Lois would have saved up enough money to fund a carefree expat lifestyle.

She let out a long puff of pent-up breath. Then she smiled, rolling her eyes at herself.

One thing at a time, Lois. Don't run away with yourself, girl, she cautioned. Roberto Enzo hadn't mentioned any of this to her. In fact, she had only Jai Shijai's hints to go on. And he was a renowned player of games. Roberto might not be planning half the things Jai Shijai implied he was. She'd have to bide her time, she realized, and wait for Roberto to reveal his hand.

Stopping to look around, she noticed that she'd

already crossed the main lawn leading down from the house to the sea. She'd been so busy thinking, she hadn't been paying attention to where she was going. She was just about to retrace her steps when she saw, through the trees, the far beach and the yacht moored at the jetty that she'd seen from the top of the pagoda.

There was no one around. The sun was beating down as she pressed on through the brushwood. It looked like the perfect place for a swim.

As she reached the shore, Lois saw a man on the deck of the yacht, silhouetted against the bright blue sky.

'Hey there,' he called out. His voice was deep, accented. Australian, she guessed.

She waved her hand vaguely, uncertain whether or not to approach him. Was he inviting conversation, or just passing the time of day?

Was he the man she'd seen earlier? He was wearing the same colourful swimming trunks. His bare legs were tanned and his vest was ripped and covered in oil. He had curly blond hair greying at the temples and a deeply tanned, craggy face. He looked like he'd spent all his life outdoors. But fit as he clearly was, he looked too old to do the boyish somersault she'd witnessed earlier.

She suddenly felt ridiculous being here for no other reason than that she'd been lost in a daydream. She searched for something purposeful to say and remembered the underwater observation tunnel Kai had told her about when she'd first arrived.

'Hi,' she called back, walking along the jetty. 'I

heard there was a tunnel to an aquarium . . . going out towards the reef,' she said, stumbling over her words in an attempt to explain herself.

They were all alone out here. Something about the way in which the man was staring at her made her want to explain herself.

'It's around there.' He pointed half a kilometre along the beach to where a patch of blue glass glinted in the surf.

But Lois could tell he wasn't impressed. 'Isn't it any good?' she asked.

He shrugged. 'Why look at the fish through Perspex? You can do that at a city aquarium. Out here you might as well see them in the wild. The same goes for the dolphins . . .'

'Dolphins?'

'There's a colony here. I'll show you if you like. I was just about to set sail,' he said.

'Oh, I'm not sure . . .' she began, but she had to admit the guy's offer was tempting. She was already fully prepped for the tournament tomorrow night. She couldn't do anything more until Anthony and Guido turned up tomorrow morning and she had to brief them. Until then . . . well, she guessed she was free.

'Why not?' he asked.

'Because . . . because we only just met,' she said, but she was smiling.

He shrugged. 'You look fairly trustworthy to me. You're on this island, so you've obviously been vetted. No seriously criminal past. Anyway, what's the worst thing you can do to me?'

She laughed, trying to think of an excuse, but he was already untying a rope. He lowered a small metal gangway from the yacht on to the wooden jetty by her feet.

Lois didn't even know the guy's name, but she assumed he was a fellow guest of Jai Shijai. Would it really be OK to take off with him on his yacht like this? It felt so indulgent. But it was too late to back out now. He was already reaching out a tanned, muscular arm to help her on board.

Throwing caution to the wind, she stepped on to the passarail and took his hand.

The man's grip was strong, like he'd be able to hold Lois suspended in the air, no sweat, if she slipped.

'Hey, Zak, we've got a passenger,' he called.

Zak?

A teenage boy appeared. He was wearing very similar swimming shorts to the man and there was no mistaking the fact they were related.

'Hey,' Zak said and Lois smiled, everything suddenly making sense.

'I think I saw you earlier from the top of the pagoda. You were doing a dive?' she said, as she stepped on to the yacht's teak deck.

Zak laughed. He was about fifteen, but he already had the confident swagger of a man twice his age. He crossed his arms and stared at her, shaking his floppy fringe out of his face.

'If I'd known I had an audience, I'd have put on more of a show.' He had an Australian accent, too. 'Were you really spying on me?'

'I just happened to see you, that's all,' Lois said.

'And now you're here,' Zak said with a wide grin. 'What did I tell you, Dad? I'm a babe magnet.'

His charm was so over-the-top that Lois laughed. The older guy rolled his eyes. He'd lifted up his Ray-Bans so that they pushed back his hair. He had hazel eyes and he smiled with them, as well as with his mouth. His full lips were pale with sunblock and his face seemed so open and friendly that Lois couldn't help but smile right back.

Zak stepped down into the cockpit. Lois started to follow, but before she'd even taken her first step, both the man and Zak yelled the word 'Shoes!' at the same time, in the same tone.

'Oh.' Lois laughed, slipping off her flip-flops. 'Sorry.'

'I'm Aidan Bailey,' the older guy said, finally introducing himself.

'Lois Ch—' Lois started, but right at that moment a gust of wind tipped her hat off her head. Zak grabbed it, giving it back to her with a flourish, and Lois laughed.

'Take a seat, Lois "Ch",' Aidan said, gesturing to the squashy white leather cushions in the cockpit. 'And let's set sail.'

Soon they were cruising, the wind filling the sails, the boat tipping at a gentle angle. Lois felt like a queen as she sat back, enjoying the sensation of the yacht gliding on the water. She was glad now that she'd come with Aidan and Zak. This was fun. She looked back towards the island with its grand house and landscaped vistas.

It was nice to get away for a while, to let the breeze blow her tangle of worried and excited thoughts away.

Aidan made a final adjustment to a rope before jumping down into the cockpit to join her. Zak stayed at the prow, crouched down, winding a rope around a cleat.

'I take it you're a guest of Dr Jai's too, then?' Aidan said, leaning back in his seat with a contented sigh.

'Kind of. But I'm here for business as well. At least as far as the game's concerned. I'm running security. To make sure it all stays above board.'

She noticed his eyes sparkling with interest. Or was it surprise?

'Not that it wouldn't do otherwise,' she added quickly, not wanting to offend him. 'I mean the other guests I've met seem perfectly honourable to me. And I'm sure you're the same.'

He laughed. 'Honourable,' he said. 'I like that. I've been called quite a few things in my time, but never that.'

Lois shifted in her seat, unsure what he meant. What was he implying? That he was someone to be trusted? Or not?

'I didn't notice you at lunch today . . .'

'Not my thing,' he said. 'I'm here for the poker, not to network.'

Lois was confused. 'I thought all business people networked. Wheeling and dealing. I thought that was the main point of these get-togethers. And the gambling was just an excuse . . .'

'Not for me. I'm in a . . . let's just say . . . *different* line of work to the rest of them.'

'How different exactly?' she asked.

'I run a security company. Military personnel, that kind of thing.'

'You're in the army?' Lois asked.

'Was. For a long time.'

'Dad provides his own armies now,' Zak chipped in, joining them in the cockpit.

'You're a mercenary?' Lois had said it before she realized how rude it sounded.

Aidan winced. 'I don't like that word,' he said. 'It gives off the wrong connotations. Fact is, I'm choosy about who I work for.'

'He fights for the good guys. Isn't that right, Dad?'

'I try my best,' Aidan said, in a tone of voice that suggested, to Lois at least, that sometimes it wasn't as simple as all that.

She'd read lots of press about the private companies contracted to work in places like Afghanistan and Iraq. The way she'd heard it, there were government backhanders involved and plenty of profits too. But who was she to judge? She hardly knew the guy. Maybe he was as principled as his son made out.

'So what's your connection to Jai Shijai?' she asked.

'I've met him once or twice at the tables. There's a private baccarat game I go to in Shanghai sometimes. But then I got an invitation here,' Aidan continued. 'Flights thrown in. Yacht too for me and Zak to stay on. It's our week together, you see, so . . .'

'Dad doesn't think I'm house-trained,' Zak interjected, leaning towards Lois confidentially. 'That's why he won't let me stay in Jai Shijai's palace. He thinks I'm a liability. I might *break* something. What's it like inside there anyway?'

'Very plush,' Lois told him. 'There's more staff than I've ever seen in my life. I have to say, my rooms are astonishing.'

'I'm sure they are,' Aidan said firmly to Zak, patting the cushion on the seat. 'But we're staying here. Us and the stars. Now make yourself useful and fix the lady a proper drink. And bring up some snacks,' he added, playfully kicking Zak's ass as he jumped through the hatch into the galley below.

There was a small pause as they both watched him go. Lois smiled. In spite of all his bravado, Zak was a graceful kid. Lois wondered what his mother looked like. And where she was.

These two seemed so self-sufficient, it was possible she'd passed away, Lois thought. But she doubted it. The phrase Aidan had used – 'our week' – implied he was divorced or separated from Zak's mother. Either that, or still married. But it would have been pretty strange for a married man to invite a woman on to his yacht in front of his son.

Stop playing cop, she reminded herself. It's none of your damn business whether he's married or not.

'So you're a star-gazer then?' she asked Aidan.

'Not in the astrological sense, no. Star signs and all that stuff? Load of old twaddle, if you ask me. But aesthetically, yes. I love the stars. I've spent so much of my life outdoors and on the move in war zones, sharing my space. For me, having this . . .' he gestured out towards the ocean and sky, 'it's my ultimate luxury.

145

What about you? How does a nice San Franciscan girl like you end up policing a tycoon's poker party in the middle of the ocean?'

'Now you put it like that, it does sound pretty weird,' she said. 'But how did you know?'

'Know what?'

'Where I'm from. I never said—'

'Didn't have to. I'm good with accents. And I've worked with plenty of Yanks in my time.'

Lois whistled, impressed. 'You should have been a cop.'

He smiled. 'Funny. You're not the first person to say that.'

'That's how I started,' Lois said. 'As a cop . . .'

She gave him her potted history, skirting around why she'd left the SFPD, sticking instead to the same line she spun most people – saying she'd been offered a job in the private sector that she'd been unable to refuse.

She also skimmed over the whole issue of Fight Night. Aidan seemed like a man of the world, but you could never tell how people would react, or which one of Hudson's stories they might have already bought into instead of the truth.

Jai Shijai's grilling had been enough for one day. Now she just wanted to relax.

So she lied to Aidan instead. She told him an easy fiction: that she'd led an ordinary life, and had worked her way up through an ordinary casino chain. And soon the conversation started bouncing back and forth as if they'd known each other for years.

Lois found out about Zak living in Sydney with his mother and how he was hoping to make the next Olympic team as a free diver. And she heard all about Aidan and Zak's other adventures, including a trip earlier in the year to the base camp of Everest.

Meanwhile, they continued their short journey, travelling on a wide arc around the island and over towards the coral reef, until all too soon it was time to drop the sails.

'Time for a dip,' Aidan announced. 'I don't know about you guys, but I'm boiling. Lois, why don't you use the cabin to change?'

As Aidan and Zak set about dropping the sails and anchoring the boat, Lois went down below. The galley of the yacht was beautifully appointed and looked far more sophisticated than Lois's kitchen at home.

Stepping out of her sundress in the cabin, Lois looked at herself warily in the mirror. She'd got some tone back at last, she thought, even though she'd had to take her training programme extremely gently following the months of physiotherapy she'd had to endure after the shooting. Her scar still ached, even though the last skin graft had been done three months ago. But at least her costume hid its rawness.

She went back through to the galley and was just about to climb the stairs to the cockpit when she heard Aidan and Zak talking above her.

'I get first dibs,' Zak was saying in a hushed whisper. 'She's here because of me.'

'You don't get dibs,' Aidan said. 'You're fifteen. So show her some respect.'

'But she's hot, Dad.'

'You don't have to tell *me* that,' Aidan laughed. 'But just don't go making an imbecile of yourself, OK?'

Lois waited a few seconds before heading back up into the cockpit. Even so, Aidan and Zak both looked like little boys who'd been caught red-handed.

'You heard, didn't you?' Aidan said.

'Every word.'

'Busted, Dad,' Zak called, as he hopped past Lois on to the top of the cabin. Then, like she'd seen earlier, he jumped up into the air and somersaulted into the water.

'Show-off,' Aidan shouted after him. 'Sorry about that,' he added to Lois. It was hard to tell with his tan, but she was sure he was blushing.

'Don't be. I'm flattered. Really.'

It was the truth. She *was* flattered. Aidan was an attractive man. Overhearing him talking about her like that had given her a real boost.

'They grow up quick, huh?' Aidan said, watching as his son cut away from the yacht in a powerful front crawl. 'I sure didn't have the balls Zak does when I was his age.'

'He's a sweet kid. You've done a good job.'

'Nah,' Aidan said. 'It's all his mother's doing. I just stroll in occasionally and take him on holiday. I'm around so little that I still have the novelty factor.'

'I wish I could say the same,' she said. 'My ex-husband looks after my daughter. And . . . well, her father's no

148

fan of mine . . . and she's ended up the same.'

'Oh,' Aidan said. 'I'm sorry to hear that.'

'Yeah, well, it's a long story,' Lois said.

His eyes sparkled as they held hers. 'You could tell me all about it some time . . . if you wanted.' His voice was so soft and his eyes so serious that, for a fleeting moment, Lois felt capable of doing just that. Of trusting him completely with the truth about her life.

But then Zak shouted out from the water. 'Come on, you guys, get in here. It's fantastic.'

Aidan smiled. He held his hand out to the platform at the back of the yacht. 'Shall we?'

The sea was deliciously cool and clear. As she swam, Lois peered down at the blurred view of the coral. She could see so many fish darting in shoals beneath them, she wished they had dive equipment with them. She and Chris had learned to dive on their honeymoon in Mauritius years ago. It had been one of their happiest times.

And it was only now that it hit her how long it had been since she'd had a proper break. A real vacation, when she'd been spontaneous like this and fully opened her eyes to the world around her. She was determined to enjoy every moment.

A little way off, beyond the coral, the surface of the water broke and Aidan pointed. She saw the backs of two dolphins.

'There they are,' Aidan said with a grin. 'Don't be scared. They're really friendly. We met them yesterday.'

They swam to where the water was a much darker, deeper blue. Then suddenly the surface broke again. The dolphins were near this time. Large, shiny and grey.

Lois trod water as she watched them circling Aidan and gently butting him. Then she gasped in amazement as he hooked his arm around the back fin of one of the dolphins and let it pull him through the water.

It was an incredible sight. Something Lois had seen only on TV and at the aquarium in Florida as a kid, but had never imagined seeing up close like this in the wild. Soon Zak had joined Aidan and Lois laughed.

But much as she was enjoying herself, all too soon she became aware of how tired she was. She hadn't been swimming for ages and treading water like this was making her legs ache. But she so desperately didn't want Aidan or Zak to see how weak she felt. They'd been so kind to her, bringing her out here.

She was on the verge of turning to swim back when something hit her. She hadn't seen the third dolphin coming. But suddenly, her eyes and mouth were full of water and she was choking, struggling for air, as pain seared across her back.

Strong arms gripped her, holding her tight. It was Aidan. In a moment, he'd positioned her so that he was taking all her weight. She coughed the water clear from her throat and heaved in fresh air.

Keeping her head above the water, Aidan swam with her back to the yacht. Tears of mortification threatened to swamp her. She was such a goddam idiot. What had she been thinking of? After the last graft, her surgeon had cautioned her against anything strenuous. At the first sign of discomfort, she should have listened to her body and turned back.

Zak overtook them and hoisted himself out of the water. He helped Aidan lift her up into the cockpit.

'Get the first-aid kit,' Aidan said to Zak. 'What happened?' he asked her, grabbing a towel and putting it round her shoulders.

'The other dolphin. It . . .' Her face contorted with pain. Her scar had ruptured, she was sure of it. She touched her fingers against it and winced. When she took her hand away, there was blood.

'Let me see,' he said.

He gently moved aside the fabric of her bathing suit. His eyes widened.

'What's that? A gunshot wound?'

She nodded, grimacing with pain.

'And it looks like you've had graft work on it since?'

'The last one was three months ago,' she said.

She clamped her jaw tight to stop herself from crying out as he examined the wound more closely.

'Well, for what it's worth,' he said, 'the damage you've done just now is pretty superficial. A shot like that . . . you're lucky to be alive.'

His voice was husky and hoarse all of a sudden. His face was so close, she could see the droplets of water on his eyebrows and eyelashes, sparkling like jewels in the sun.

Zak handed over a white padded first-aid box to Aidan. 'What happened?' he asked, noticing her scar for the fist time.

Lois forced a smile. 'I got a short, sharp reminder not to show off to new friends.'

'We'll put a dressing on it,' Aidan said. His hands worked quickly, expertly. It was clearly something he'd done many times before.

'So I guess . . . the bullet . . . it went right through?' he asked.

Lois nodded, grimacing again as he swabbed the scar tissue before pressing the dressing into place. When he held it down, she wished he'd keep his hand there for ever.

'Look away,' Aidan told Zak. 'You're going to have to roll your costume down, so I can bind this properly,' he told Lois. 'I'm going to need to strap it round your waist to hold it in place. Here, use the towel to cover yourself up.'

She did as she was told and a moment later the job was done. She felt the pain dropping off. He was right. She hadn't hurt herself as badly as she'd first thought.

'I can't believe you got shot! I mean, when? Why? Who did it?' Zak asked. He was looking from Lois to Aidan and back.

Lois let out a pent-up breath and turned her attention to Zak. 'There was an assassination attempt on Senator Fernandez two years ago at the Enzo Vegas and—'

'Oh my God,' Zak interrupted. 'You were that chick, the one that took the bullet. I saw it on TV! That is *awesome*.'

Lois felt embarrassed by Zak's reaction. Glancing across at Aidan, she saw that his eyes had darkened. He held her look for a moment, but she couldn't begin to read what he was thinking. He turned away and she felt it as forcefully as if he'd pushed her. Her cheeks were burning with shame, over having lied to him about her career, over having deliberately not mentioned the one act that defined it.

'Zak,' he said. 'Get the anchor up and make ready to leave.'

'No, honestly,' Lois protested. 'Don't turn around because of me. I'm fine, honestly.'

'You shouldn't have gone swimming,' Aidan said. 'You're still healing. We're taking you back now.'

There was such finality in his voice that she shrank back, mortified. All the closeness that had been there earlier had simply vanished. It was as if a shutter had gone up. And now she had absolutely no idea how to get it back down.

CHAPTER SIXTEEN

The following night, as the ten finalists gathered at the raised table area in the softly lit atrium, Lois was still kicking herself about what had happened with Aidan. He'd kept her frozen out on the way back to shore and hadn't given her a chance to explain. Zak's excited chatter had only made matters worse. He'd refused to let the subject drop until she'd told him to, leaving poor Zak as offended as his father.

The simple fact was that she'd been caught lying and now the only thing she could do was to front it out. Tomorrow she'd be heading back home, never to see Aidan or Zak again. She must put the whole sorry and embarrassing episode behind her.

Lois concentrated on checking the packs of cards one last time, shuffling them. She'd been handling cards for as long as she could remember. It didn't even cross her mind, the skill came so naturally, but she noticed a few of the players stop to watch her as she cascaded the packs between her hands. Aidan ignored her, walking past to take his seat, his face a mask.

Dressed as he was, in a smart suit rather than swimming shorts, he looked . . . *handsome.* The word sprang into her head. Aidan wasn't handsome, was he? But when she looked again, she had to admit that he scrubbed up pretty well for a mercenary. Was that why she was finding it so hard to stop looking at him? Because something about Aidan Bailey had got to her. Got inside her. And it was a feeling she hadn't had for a very, very long time.

As the players got ready for the start of play, there was plenty of friendly banter, Jai's being the loudest voice amongst them. Pieter Von Triers, the art dealer Lois had dined with on the first night, had let slip that Jai Shijai had lost nearly two million dollars last year. Over half of it in a single hand. He clearly had old scores to settle and was starting to talk raucously about wagers.

But no matter how fascinating the ensuing duels between Jai Shijai and his rivals were, as the guests now began to play in earnest, Lois's eyes kept being drawn back again and again to Aidan Bailey, until she wondered whether Anthony, the sharpest-eyed dealer she'd ever met both in and out of the Enzo Vegas, had noticed.

But whether Anthony had noticed or not, Aidan certainly hadn't. Yesterday he'd been so open and friendly, but now, at the table, as the players settled and Anthony started to deal, he seemed cold and emotionless. Which was the real Aidan? she wondered.

Was this just an act? Or was this closer to his real personality? She couldn't tell.

In fact, the more Aidan played, the more he fascinated her. At the Enzo Vegas, she'd studied hours of footage of the best players at work. She'd got to watch them 'live' as well, to the point where she now considered herself something of an expert when it came to spotting 'tells' – the minute changes in a player's body language that betrayed their inner psyche.

But Aidan's expression was impossible to read. She'd encountered criminals like this during her years at the SFPD. Men who could commit terrible crimes and appear totally unaffected. Was Aidan really as hard as he seemed, or was he simply using the early rounds to work out the others' styles?

Of course, she'd often seen this strategy work – with gifted amateur players – but as the play continued, Aidan quickly got suckered into upping the ante. It would have been hard not to. No matter how good a poker face Aidan had, the men he was sitting with were some of the richest gamblers in the world. And they were prepared to lose hand after hand to someone like Aidan, knowing that eventually their luck would change. And when it did, and if the ante was sufficiently high, they'd crush someone like him like a fly. And they wouldn't think twice about it.

Such a hand came towards the end of the first session. Aidan got lured into a head-to-head with Pieter Von Triers. And the outcome was cruel. Aidan had a flush, but Pieter had a royal. Aidan lost the lot. A whole lot. Enough to make Lois worry.

But he showed as little emotion when he lost as he had done when he'd won. It was almost like it had never been his money he'd been gambling with.

It was midnight when Lois called the first break. Jai was already down half a million, but she wanted to give Aidan time to reflect away from the heat of the battle. To give him the opportunity to do the sensible thing, take the loss on the chin and walk away.

He might have frozen Lois out, but she still remembered how warm he'd been to begin with. She thought of Zak. No child deserved a father who didn't know when to stop. She knew that from bitter experience.

She hoped Aidan wasn't the kind of man that her father had been – the type who'd go to Jai Shijai and ask to borrow more to gamble with.

Busy as she was, preparing the table for the next session, she almost missed him. When she had a moment, she saw that Aidan was walking out of the far doors on to the terrace. She watched him shaking hands with several of the players, and even from a distance she could tell he was planning on leaving. Thank God. He'd made the right decision.

Telling Anthony she'd be back in a minute, she caught up with Aidan on the lawn at the bottom of the pagoda.

'Aidan, please,' she said, reaching out to grab his arm.

He turned and faced her. Through the door, she saw Jai Shijai glance over towards where they were standing. Aidan noticed too.

'I see our host has taken quite a shine to you. But he's not a man you want to get too close to, Lois,' he warned.

'Why not?'

'Just trust me. With men like that . . . nothing's ever quite as it seems. You cannot afford to cross Jai Shijai. If you cross him, you'll make him an enemy for life.'

'But—'

Before she could ask him what he meant, he cut her off. 'I should be getting back,' he said. 'You know . . . Zak.'

'Aidan, I'm sorry . . . about tonight,' Lois blurted.

He shrugged. 'You win some, you lose some,' he said. 'That's how it goes.' He nodded and, smiling briefly, he half turned to go. 'It was nice meeting you, Lois.'

She took a deep breath. She had to do this. Say this for herself as much as him. Because she wasn't ashamed of herself, no matter how much the press had twisted the truth about her past.

'I'm sorry I lied to you,' she said.

'You don't have to apologize.'

'I do.' She heaved in another breath. 'What happened with the senator . . . the whole media circus that followed . . . I got used to putting up barriers . . . to keeping people at bay.'

He smiled, gently. 'It's OK, Lois. I overreacted. It just blindsided me at the time, that's all.'

'No. I was discourteous to you.'

'Well, thanks for being so honest,' he said. 'Now, I mean.'

He looked awkwardly up from the soft moonlit

grass to the pagoda stretching above them to the starlit sky.

'You know you could check on Zak,' Lois said, 'from up there.' She nodded up at the pagoda. 'It was from there that I first spotted your yacht.'

Aidan looked from the pagoda to Lois.

'Will you show me?' he said.

There was hardly any time. The dealers would be wondering where she was. And what would Jai Shijai do if he noticed that Lois had disappeared with Aidan? But for once, she didn't care. She hoped Anthony would make excuses for her.

Even so, she felt her heart pounding. Was she really here just to show Aidan the view of his yacht? Or was it more that she wanted him alone? Just for a moment.

Either way, she couldn't believe she'd acted so impulsively. She quickly followed Aidan inside and groped for the wooden staircase, struggling up the rough stairs in her tight sequinned dress. She was crazy to be doing this. Crazy. But still she didn't stop.

In a moment they were out through the small wooden door at the top and Lois knew the risk had been worth it. In the distance the moon was full and yellow, surrounded by stars. Aidan stared up into the sky and for the first time all evening she saw him relax, as if he'd shed some great burden. And as he turned to her and smiled, he was suddenly back to being the man she'd first met on the yacht yesterday, laughing with his son, taking her sailing and swimming, before soothing away her pain. This was the face, she suddenly realized, that she'd been longing to see all night.

'Beautiful,' he sighed.

'There's the yacht,' Lois said, leaning towards Aidan as she pointed around the tree to where his yacht was moored. A light glowed in the cabin.

'Zak's still there then,' Aidan said. 'He hasn't gone for a joyride.'

They stood side by side in silence. Lois knew how tight the time was, but it felt wrong to break the sudden peace. She longed for the right words to say, to tell him that she hoped their paths would cross again. To find a way for this not to be the end.

'I suppose this is it, then,' he said.

'I guess so.' She failed to hide the disappointment in her voice.

'I was just thinking,' he said, glancing sideways. 'This is rather romantic, isn't it?'

'I guess . . .'

'Pity it's wasted on us.'

Lois bit her lip. Did he think she'd brought him up here for a romantic moment? He must do. And she hadn't done, had she? This moment certainly hadn't been planned – premeditated – as he seemed to be implying.

This was why she was never impulsive, she thought. Because it always backfired. And she had no way of coping with being put on the spot like this.

Over at the house, she could see the other players were settling back down at the table.

'I've got to go back,' she said, suddenly feeling flushed.

'I know.'

'You're not tempted to come back yourself?'

He shook his head. 'No. I know when I'm beaten.'

She nodded, then stood awkwardly, not knowing what to do. She stepped forward slightly, intending to shake Aidan's hand, although the setting seemed far too intimate for that.

But he stepped towards her at the same time and they bumped into one another. He kissed her softly on the lips. They stayed locked, suspended in a deliciously stretched moment. Then he pulled away.

'I . . . I'm sorry,' he said. He seemed as shocked as she was. As if he hadn't really meant to kiss her at all.

'No, no, it's fine.' Lois covered her mouth with her fingertips. She could feel her lips tingling.

'Lois,' a voice called up. 'Lois? Is that you?'

Looking down, she saw Anthony on the lawn, staring up.

'Go,' Aidan said.

'Call me,' she said.

He stared at her in surprise.

'Next time you're in Vegas,' she continued, blushing. 'On business,' she added, backtracking now as he continued to stare. 'I'll be able to fix you up with good rates – if you wanted to stay.'

He was still staring.

Turning on her heels, she ran down the wooden stairs and back to the game.

What was that? she thought, as she hurried back to the bright lights of Jai Shijai's poker game. But she was smiling, she realized. And she couldn't stop.

CHAPTER SEVENTEEN

Savvy woke with a start from a fitful sleep. She groaned, the familiar thumping headache assaulting her once more.

She felt rancid. Every joint in her body hurt. Her throat was dry and her eyes sore, whilst her stomach churned. It was like the worst hangover in the world, except that this wasn't a hangover. This was detox, pure and simple. And it was hideous.

She lay sprawled out on the large bed, the soft white Egyptian sheet clinging to her skin, soaked in sweat from another night of fevered dreams.

She looked up at the fan, remembering her plan to hang herself with her dressing gown cord two weeks ago. What a joke.

Dr Savage had told her she'd been lucky not to electrocute herself.

She'd got as far as tying the cord round the fan before

she'd slumped to the floor, unable to go through with it. Too useless. Too gutless. Even for that.

She'd torn out clumps of her own hair as Dr Savage arrived, and she'd hysterically begged him to give her something that would make everything go away.

Of course, they'd kept a proper eye on her after that. For the next ten days, a softly spoken nurse, Hannah, had slept in a camp bed right here on the floor beside her.

But they'd relaxed their vigilance three nights ago now. Something she'd said in one of her therapy sessions must have convinced Dr Savage that she was no longer a danger to herself.

And he was right, she supposed. She still felt shit. She still hated this place. But she'd stopped looking up at that fan and seeing herself hanging from it . . . and stopped dreaming of the nearby cliffs and the rush of air beneath her feet.

She had no idea how she was going to handle the future, but she knew that she had to try. Because she was determined to get well and get out of here. Going back to the way she was, slipping back into the cesspool of her old life, would mean that Luc had been right about her. That she was a nobody, a nothing he could trick and push aside. That would mean he'd won. And she wasn't going to let that happen. Not for her sake. And not for Elodie's.

Forcing herself not to crawl back into bed, she got dressed, pulling on the first things that came to hand – baggy white linen trousers and a black tank top. She tied her hair back with a long scarf. When she looked in the mirror, she saw she still had bags under her eyes and that her skin was dry and sallow.

'Past-It-Girl,' she said to her reflection. But her old bitchy comments from her days clubbing with Marcus, when they'd both assumed they were the bee's knees, seemed very, very far away.

She blew out a breath. *Minute by minute*, she reminded herself. That was what Dr Savage had said.

She grabbed the dark shades that were hanging over the wooden mirror, put them on and opened the door to the veranda.

After days of relentless tropical rain, the sun had finally come out and the birds with it. The noise of the rainforest was so loud she instinctively ducked, as if she might be attacked. But after a few moments she realized that the wildlife wasn't coming for her and she straightened up.

She wrapped her arms around her body and walked down the path. It was a familiar view, but somehow today it felt fresh and exciting. As if, for the first time, she was allowing herself to see it not as a prison but as a thing of beauty in its own right.

The trees stretched high up on either side of the pathway, the sparkling sky peeking through the dense canopy. Squawks, whistles and all sorts of strange bird calls came thick and fast from the foliage.

The clear pools of rainwater on the path were almost visibly evaporating and the humid air was filled with scent. All around her, large tropical ferns had sprouted pink fleshy flowers. A wriggling procession of ants crossed the path, carrying pieces of bright orange leaves.

Savvy continued gingerly down the pathway, the mud studded with sections of tree trunks as stepping stones. But instead of following the same route she'd trudged, head down, every day on her way to the communal dining area – where she'd steadfastly ignored any approaches from her fellow inmates – Savvy now chose the path round to the right.

Go wild, she told herself. Let's see what else this island's got to offer. Think positive. It's not every day a girl gets to wake up in a place like this.

Rounding a boulder, she stopped and gasped. Before her was the most stunning view of mangrove swamps and, in the distance, the sea, the waves breaking in white jottings across the coral. But it was the sky that got her. The expanse of baby-blue sky.

She pressed on. A sense of – what? Anticipation? Optimism? – filled her. Just being here. Alone. Somewhere new. But not afraid to walk on. Wanting more.

But now she saw that she wasn't alone at all. Way down the path ahead, halfway between where she was and the sea, was a circular stone seating area with a tiled floor in its centre. A man, wearing only a pair of rolled-up ochre cloth trousers, was practising yoga. She stared at his strong, tanned torso and slim waist as he saluted the sun.

And then she realized it was Red.

*　　*　　*

165

By the time Savvy reached Red, he'd finished his practice. His eyes were closed and his hands were in prayer position in front of his chest. He was standing tall and erect, motionless, like a statue. She noticed that he had some bad scar tissue on his legs. Whatever had caused it must have been painful. Although the scars looked old now.

If he'd heard her approach, he didn't move, or acknowledge her. She watched his face, seeing only serenity in his features.

After a long moment, he opened his eyes slowly, as if he was waking from a dream or a prayer. She got the impression that his inner world was enviably pleasant. She thought of how much she dreaded closing her own eyes and facing the twisted memories her dreams might dredge up.

There was a moment when he stared at her and she felt a deep flush run right through her.

'Oh,' he said. 'Hello. How you doing?'

Savvy swallowed hard and nodded. 'Um,' she began. 'I . . . I should apologize,' she said. 'For before. I was very rude, I think, and—'

'Please don't apologize,' Red interrupted, shocking her by suddenly moving and grabbing her forearms. His touch was firm and strong and she was surprised by how it made her feel. It was . . . nice. Nice to be touched. To be connected to someone else. 'I got it all wrong. I should have handled it differently. I didn't realize you were so . . . fragile. I'm sorry.'

She nodded, surprised. And it suddenly occurred to her that Red had probably got into trouble. He'd been assigned as her counsellor and right after their first meeting she'd hit rock bottom.

It made her very much *not* want to be fragile in front of him again.

Then he surprised her even more by stepping closer and lifting up her glasses. He looked into her eyes. His stare wasn't threatening. It was direct, open and honest. It demanded the same in return.

'Can we start again?' he asked.

'Sure,' she said. 'If you want.'

'Good.'

He grinned at her, as if it was all settled, then stepped away.

Then he picked up a bottle of mineral water and took a long swig, before sloshing some over his face. He wiped his mouth with the back of his freckled forearm. 'Want some?' he asked, handing the bottle to Savvy.

'Thanks.' She never normally shared bottles with people – especially strangers. She felt surprised and flattered that he trusted her to drink from his bottle. But this could be some sort of test. To let her prove she wasn't the princess he'd accused her of being. She took a sip of the water. It was cold, icy.

'Thirst,' Red said. 'Thirst and resentment. Halfway through a detox like you are, I don't know which one is worse.'

He wasn't kidding. Savvy's mouth had been like sandpaper for the last ten days.

She nodded, handing the water back to him.

'It's normal,' he said, sipping the water himself again

and glancing sideways at her. 'Totally normal. You want to drink your own bodyweight in water every half-hour, but can't stomach even the thought of it. And the rest of the time, you fantasize about killing Dr Savage and his entire pain-in-the-ass team, before busting out of here in a stolen seaplane.'

Savvy laughed. 'You've been reading my mind,' she said.

He smiled at her. 'I like that.'

'What?'

'You. Laughing. You should do it more often.'

'Yeah? Well, I haven't had too much to laugh about lately,' she said.

'It'll come,' he said. 'Trust me. It's not so bad here, Savannah,' he said. 'In a week or so, you'll feel better. And then we can take the horses out.'

'Horses?'

'Equine therapy, they call it here. I prefer to call it horse-riding. Because that's what it is.'

Savvy hated horses. It was Elodie who'd been into ponies, when they were kids. Elodie who'd won all the riding trophies. Elodie who'd fallen for Luc because he'd gone riding in the Nevada Desert with her . . .

'I can't ride,' she said flatly, beating the memories away. She wanted to blurt out that getting on a horse was going to do nothing for her state of mind. Even seeing one would only remind her of her sister lying dead and broken at the bottom of the stairs.

'Then I'll teach you,' he said, smiling. 'This place is so big, you've got to learn to ride just to see it all. You mustn't miss out. You know, there's four different kinds of sea turtles,' Red continued, 'that come to lay their eggs on the beach down there. And there's so much more. At the end of your stay you'll get to go diving in the blue hole. It's this amazing atoll. Just incredible. And it's just out there.'

Savvy squinted and followed his gaze to the blue horizon stretched out in front of them. She felt small in the face of Red's unbridled enthusiasm. But sceptical too. What was this guy? Some king of PR for Peace River Lodge? Because if he was, she could do without the hard sell.

Red breathed in and out deeply, filling his lungs with the clear air. He closed his eyes and Savvy looked at the muscles rippling across his stomach and the thick, curly auburn hair of his chest. He really did have an incredible body.

'So,' he said suddenly, opening his eyes again. He clapped his hands together and smiled brightly. 'It's a beautiful day. What about a little exercise? Nothing too strenuous to begin with. Just to get your strength up.'

Exercise? She wished now she'd never opened her big mouth.

But then he smiled again and she realized that he wasn't going to force her. She took a deep breath. *Remember . . . think positive.* She smoothed her hair behind her ear.

'I don't know. I don't do any of this . . .' she flapped her hand dismissively, 'yoga stuff, or chanting. It's really not my thing.'

'OK,' he nodded.

She felt thrown. She'd expected him to try to coerce her into it, but he offered no resistance. He stared at her for a moment, as if trying to get her measure.

'Let's walk,' he said.

He slipped on some battered flip-flops and a tatty straw hat. He had several faded knotted-thread friendship bracelets on his wrist, yet despite his hippy garb, when he moved he looked dignified. Like an old-fashioned city gent.

'Come on,' he said, jumping off the far end of the platform on to the narrow mud path and holding out his hand to her. 'This'll be fun.'

Savvy followed Red along the narrow path, which led down between the giant ferns and into the trees.

'So how long have you been working here?' she asked.

Red pushed aside a fleshy leaf to let her pass.

'I'm a volunteer counsellor. I came here two years ago as a patient, when my addictions got out of hand.'

'*You* were a patient here?' she said, incredulously.

She remembered the serenity in his face when she'd seen him just now, at the end of his practice. Was it possible to be an addict – and then to get to *that*?

'Yep,' he said. 'It took Max months to get me straight.'

'So what happened?'

He didn't slow, setting off now into the dense foliage beneath the tree canopy. He moved quickly and gracefully, his long legs taking effortless strides. His cloth trousers were low on his hips. The scarring on his legs below his knees was even more severe when seen from the back.

'It was the usual cliché, I suppose,' he started. 'My grandfather died and left me and my brother a fortune.'

'What about your parents?' Savvy asked.

'They died in a car crash that my brother and I luckily survived. My legs were pretty messed up when they cut me out of the wreckage. Fortunately, I can't remember it.' He took a big breath. 'Anyway, by the time I was thirty I was living in London, hosting parties, thinking of myself as Mr Big. And when I got Grandpa's estate . . . well, that's when it all went pear-shaped.'

'What happened?' she asked.

Red sighed. 'I blew the whole lot.'

There was shame in his voice and sadness too. It was as if he were talking about a beloved building that he'd burnt down. As if the regret were too much to bear.

'How?'

'Gambling, mainly. I thought I had all the talent in the world. All the luck on my side. The irony was that Grandpa was the wealthiest of the baronets in our line. He left my brother the estate, but he left me his Mayfair house and the casino attached. And it was in that very casino that I gambled away the deeds to them both.'

How sad, Savvy thought. No wonder he was full of regret. She *loved* gambling. Always had and always would. But did that make her an addict? Or did you only get labelled a gambling addict when you lost too much money?

'Then there was the crystal meth on top,' Red said conversationally. 'But it's hardly ever just drink, or drugs, or gambling. One tends to lead to the other, you know?'

She suddenly had a flashback to the SkyBird elevator at the Enzo Vegas, and how she'd felt telling Marcus about the Holy Trinity of Fun.

But thinking of it now, thinking of that whole bubble she'd been in . . . well, suddenly it didn't seem so smart. Not now that it had burst.

They'd reached a steeper part of the path now. Trees were all around them, bathing everything in hazy green light. The noise from the birds and the tree frogs was deafening. Savvy ducked and swatted away a swarm of gnats. Her shoes were wrecked and the bottoms of her white trousers had soaked up an inch or more of muddy water.

A small waterfall trickled down the ruts in the path. Red held out his hands and she took them, so that she could jump over the water on to the path on the other side.

'The thing with drugs is that you come on and off them,' he said, making sure she was steady on her feet before setting off on the path again. 'I went on plenty of benders, but I was smart enough to know that occasionally I had to straighten up my act. I wasn't some junkie sitting in a doorway with a needle hanging out of my arm, even when the drug addiction got really bad. I was quite civilized about it. Being an

172

addict is manageable, as long as you can afford it and have a never-ending supply. I was unfortunate enough to have both.'

'Oh,' she said, unsure how to respond.

'But gambling . . . drugs . . . they weren't my worst addiction.'

'They weren't?' What else *was* there, she wanted to know.

'Sex. That's what really screwed me up and finally made me check myself in here.'

'Excuse me?' She laughed. He was joking, wasn't he? He had to be. But he wasn't laughing. In fact he looked totally serious.

'I was disgusting. I lied all the time to get what I wanted. And what I wanted was thrills. Always involving different girls. I was chasing after a moment of satisfaction that I never found.'

Guiltily, Savvy looked him up and down. He might want to deny it, but now that he'd admitted his penchant for sex, she couldn't say she was at all surprised. Red was designed for sex. He was tactile and direct. And those eyes . . .

She'd bet that plenty of those women he'd lied to had enjoyed the ride too.

'So you're sworn off sex?' she asked, still trying to wrap her head around it.

'Yes I am,' he said firmly.

'*For ever?*'

'Until I find someone I want to have a real relationship with. One where love comes first. And then, maybe down the line, who knows? I'll go back to Scotland.

There's still an island that I'm entitled to – although everyone says it's uninhabitable. Perhaps I'll go there and run a sheep farm. Then maybe I'll fall in love with a local girl, get married, have kids . . .'

He'd just described Savvy's idea of hell.

'Well, I wish you luck,' Savvy said. 'But I should warn you,' she added, almost without thinking, 'true love isn't so easy to come by. And it comes unexpectedly. And believe me, it doesn't always last.'

Red paused and looked at her. 'So what's his name?'

'Whose?'

'The guy you're talking about. The guy that didn't last.'

She was so startled that she thought about telling him to mind his own business. But they were out here all alone in the middle of nowhere. What was the harm in telling Red? After all, who was he going to tell? The birds?

'Luc,' she said. 'The bastard's name was Luc Devereaux.'

'Maybe you can tell me about him some time.'

But at that moment they broke through the trees to where the mangroves spread down to the beach. The sand was a dazzling white, dotted with shells. It was so idyllic, it was as if they were honeymooners stranded on a desert island, especially when they passed a battered, disintegrating row-boat, tied to the low angle of a tree.

Savvy smiled, breathing in deeply. Saying Luc's name

out loud just then, well, she'd felt a weight drop from her shoulders. She took off her shoes and watched her footprints disappearing on the wet sand, washed away by the crystal-clear waves. And with each new step, she began to feel free.

CHAPTER EIGHTEEN

The foghorn sounded across San Francisco Bay, waking Lois. For a moment she didn't know where she was, remembering, for a split second, how she would wake up in her childhood bedroom to the same noise. But she wasn't in her parents' old Chinatown apartment, she was in an exclusive North Beach town house.

She'd rented it for the weekend through a contact of Roberto's, who dealt with all the rich Italians who'd made this area such a des-res locale. Lois had already fallen in love with the pretty blue house with its wrought iron and window boxes full of red geraniums. She loved the exclusivity of the neighbourhood too, with its bohemian vintage shops, cafés stuffed with pastel-coloured cupcakes and spectacular views of the city.

She struggled up in the unfeasibly large bed and saw that her ten-year-old daughter, Cara, was standing by the window, looking out through a small gap in the long blue-and-white flowered curtains.

Cara was already dressed, in sparkly jeans that were way too tight, in Lois's opinion, and a faded jeans jacket covered in badges. The outfit was accompanied by very new black and white sneakers which looked far too big. Her hair that had once been long, like Lois's, had been cut in a short bob and she wore it in an ugly padded headband, straight out of Mary-Sue's dressing table, Lois suspected.

'Hey,' Lois said, smiling. 'What you doing, hon?'

'That noise,' Cara said, not turning round. 'It gives me the creeps.'

Lois could barely believe it. Chris and Mary-Sue had moved Cara to Washington only four years ago, yet she'd already pretty much forgotten all about this place. Or so it seemed. Was she becoming ancient history to Cara too?

Lois threw back the thick cover and, stretching in her pyjamas, walked to where Cara was standing. She loved the sound of the foghorn and even the familiar sight of the early morning fog itself.

She stood behind Cara and put her hands softly on her skinny shoulders, looking out at the view with her. She could see the top of some of the more familiar buildings and the red tips of the Golden Gate towers thrusting up through the blanket of fog into the bright blue sky above.

'Oh, you get used to it,' she said with a smile. But the happy nostalgia was tinged with uneasiness, as Cara slipped out from beneath her grip and turned away.

Lois massaged her brow, remembering her resolve to be calm and gentle. She hoped that today wasn't going to be like yesterday, when she'd clashed with Cara on nearly everything.

She couldn't help feeling annoyed that Cara seemed to be completely ignoring – shunning even – all the effort that Lois had made.

This house, for example, that Lois had hired deliberately so that it would be more cosy and intimate – and might give Cara a taste of what it would feel like for them to live together – had been met with disappointment. Cara had wanted to stay in the Holiday Inn, she'd informed Lois. Because her schoolfriend had told her that there was a buffet breakfast, as well as a pool.

And that had been just the start. In fact, Lois hadn't seen her daughter smile once.

Lois had imagined that it would all be so different. But she didn't know how to explain to Cara that she spent most of her life at the Enzo Vegas, and being away from the workings of a hotel complex felt like bliss to her. As did being away from work itself. As did having the chance to spend time together.

Since she'd returned from Jai Shijai's island nearly a month ago, Roberto had been away and Lois had been working flat out. Cara had no idea how much Lois had had to do in order to take these few days off with her daughter without having to check her messages all the time.

And the fact that Lois's mother had refused to take the day off from the Cultural Center where she worked had made Lois feel even more hopeless and unappreciated. But her mother was unrepentant, seemingly utterly uninterested in the fact that her only daughter and granddaughter were in town for the weekend. She had to prioritize the latest batch of Tibetan refugees, she'd said, making Lois immediately feel small and unworthy.

Stop it, Lois told herself. Getting angry or bitter about her mom wasn't going to help. She wasn't the child here. Cara was. Cara, who needed Lois's love and attention. And Lois was ready to give it. In spades. If only Cara would let her.

And anyway, it wasn't all bad. Her mother *had* agreed to meet Lois and Cara for lunch at Ed's restaurant today. Lois hoped it would be a turning point. That her mother would see what a committed and caring daughter she was. And that she'd be supportive as far as Cara was concerned. Because with her mother on side, surely Cara would remember that she *did* have a proper family – people who would nurture and support her away from Chris and Mary-Sue. Yes, being with her grandma might make Cara see things differently and open her mind to a future with Lois.

Take it one step at a time, Lois told herself, turning to Cara. She had a hell of a lot of bad press to undo, thanks to her darling ex-husband. And the only way she could get through to Cara was by proving what a fun and sensitive mom she could be. How hard can it be? she thought. You're a Vegas casino manager. Surely you can keep a little girl entertained for a few hours all by yourself. Yes, she decided, if Cara was spoiling for a row, she wasn't going to get one. Nothing was going to ruin this precious time together.

'Why don't we go shopping?' Lois suggested, trying to turn on her brightest smile.

Cara shrugged. 'If you want. I don't need anything.'

The fog was clearing by the time Lois and Cara caught the tram to Union Square. Lois tried making conversation with her daughter about her friends at school, but Cara's answers were monosyllabic.

Trying to stay positive, Lois changed tack and started talking about all the sights to see in San Francisco, but again Cara seemed uninterested. Lapsing into sullen silence, Cara turned away and rested her forehead against the glass of the tram window.

Lois gazed at her daughter's reflection. She had so many treasured photos of Cara when she was a baby and she could see that toddler's face still in this older version. She longed to hold Cara's face and kiss the soft apple curve of her cheeks and her upturned nose. But she knew that even looking at Cara made her daughter uncomfortable.

And now guilt slammed into Lois worse than ever before. She was sitting next to the person she loved most in the world and she felt further away than ever. A gulf had grown between them and she had no idea how to bridge it.

At Union Square, Lois stepped out with Cara into the bright sunshine. This was where she'd dreamed of being able to shop as a kid. And now she was here with Cara, with a purse full of credit cards and a morning of free time.

But the happy mother-daughter experience she'd hoped for was not to be. Lois soon discovered she had no idea how to lift her daughter's sullen spirits. It was like dragging around a reluctant dog. Cara didn't seem to be interested in anything, proclaiming everything in the Tiffany store to be ugly, the Disney Store too childish. Lois was amazed and confused too. What *was* her daughter interested in? There had to be something.

They headed on to the shopping mall and took the escalator to the first floor. On the other escalator, coming down beside them, was a man reading a newspaper. On the front was a colour photo of Joshua Fernandez.

He'd kept in touch. Regular emails politely enquiring after her health. Invitations to come visit next time she was in Washington. But Lois had decided to let it lie. She wanted to move away from all that had happened. Not relive it. And as nice a guy as Fernandez was, he remained part of the whole mess that had swallowed her up.

He'd come out of it all smelling of roses. His good looks, charisma, youth and already impressive political résumé, coupled with his survival of the assassination attempt, had given him a JFK-like aura and his nickname of JF Bay.

Josh Fernandez was heading one way. Straight to the top. And in spite of what her Vegas colleagues might think of him, Lois still saw him as one of the good guys. Someone who was trying to make the world a fairer, better place.

And despite all the strife she'd been through because

of it, the fact that she'd come between him and a bullet with his name on still made her proud.

But she felt immediately guilty. As if she were face to face with someone with whom she'd had an affair. Because Cara was glowering at the picture.

'Dad hates him,' she said. 'He says he's a phoney.'

'Yeah? Well, your father's not always right about everything,' Lois snapped back.

Cara was silent, her eyes wide and hurt. Lois saw her comment go inside, stored, she had no doubt, in some horrible squashy, vulnerable place that a therapist would one day spend weeks digging into. She wished she could retract her words. It was wrong to make Cara feel that she was caught in the middle between her and Chris, but that was exactly what Lois was doing.

'Well, I hate Fernandez too,' Cara said defiantly.

'You can't hate someone if you haven't met them.'

But something in the way Cara was staring at her made her see immediately that what she'd said wasn't true. And maybe she was right, Lois thought. After all, Lois hated Michael Hudson and she'd never met him.

And Fernandez – albeit inadvertently – had impacted on her daughter's life.

She tried to put herself in Cara's shoes, to imagine how confusing it must be that Lois had nearly died because of this stranger. And that Cara herself had then been harassed by tabloid journalists outside her school. Who'd interrogated her about her dead uncle Miki who she'd never met. Who'd stuck her photo next to Lois's all over the morning news, with a headline screaming out about Lois being a selfish, career-obsessed absent mother who lived on the other side of the country from her own daughter. With not one mention of why. Or how Lois saw Cara every second that she was allowed to.

Telling Cara that she'd only been doing her job wouldn't cut it. Because the papers had been partially right. While she'd succeeded in protecting the senator, she'd again failed to protect her daughter.

'I'm sorry,' she said, reaching out to put her arm around Cara's shoulder. But Cara shrank back from her touch.

'Don't,' she hissed. 'You're embarrassing me.'

'Then let's hit the shops,' Lois said, trying to put a brave face on it.

Even then, she couldn't shake the feeling that Cara thought she was trying to buy her affection. So much so that Lois began to doubt her own motives as well. Was this really what their relationship had been reduced to? Dollars and cents and arguments? Instead of laughter and memories and love?

CHAPTER NINETEEN

Lois was still trying to break the ice hours later. The morning seemed to have stretched interminably and she was exhausted by the time they headed up into Chinatown for the rendezvous with her mother at Ed's restaurant.

All that time in the gym and these damn hills are still a killer on your thighs, Lois thought. Even so, it was lovely to be back here, with the crowds and the hustle and bustle. Red lanterns hung across the streets and the shops were a riot of colour in the sunshine. And as Lois looked over at Cara, she saw that finally her interest was piqued.

Maybe I should stop trying so hard, Lois thought, smiling at her. Maybe I should just let her be.

But her optimism didn't last long. By the time they reached Ed's, they were both out of breath and sweating. The street was smarter than Lois remembered. Nail bars and internet cafés had sprung up since she'd last been here. Ed's façade looked scruffy by comparison. Cara looked like she'd rather be anywhere else but here, as she stared in at the window.

'Ugh, that's so *gross*!' Cara said, screwing up her nose and making a retching sound. Lois saw that she was looking at the chickens' feet and caramelized pigs' heads on display.

'Some might consider those a delicacy,' Lois said. Now wasn't the time to get into a debate with her daughter about her cultural heritage.

'A *delicacy*? It's like something out of a horror film.'

'Fine,' Lois said. 'But do me a favour, huh? Once we're inside, try and keep your opinions to yourself. The people who work here are proud of what they do.'

This is such a mistake, she thought. Chances were, Ed was going to bring out every one of his specialities, and most of them would make the chickens' feet look positively bland.

But she had no time to dwell on it because Ed came out of his restaurant and laughed delightedly, before wrapping his arms around Lois as if she was a long-lost daughter. Then he kissed Cara on the top of her head and Lois saw her wince. Luckily Ed didn't seem to notice. Lois would hate to see him hurt.

Ed Wan wasn't a real uncle, but a family friend whose parents came from the same part of Hong Kong as Lois's grandparents. Ed's mother – an old-fashioned matriarch of the Chinese-American community – had been a kind of surrogate aunt to Lois.

Lois had known Ed all her life and it was great to

see him again. But now a look of confusion and awe crossed his face as he pulled back and, holding her shoulders, looked her up and down. She'd dressed down in jeans, suede boots and a soft leather jacket, but here on the street, beside Ed, she felt as if her clothes were ostentatious.

'You're rich now, your mom tells me,' he said, ushering her inside his restaurant, the bell on the door jangling in such a way that the sound gave Lois a physical pang of nostalgia. 'The hotshot in Vegas. And you saved our senator. Like a good San Franciscan girl, eh?'

She hated this kind of adulation.

'Here, you can sign my photo,' Ed said, proudly pulling a picture of Fernandez from the shelf by the door and offering a marker pen.

This wasn't the first time she'd been asked to sign a picture of the senator, but she didn't like doing it. Ed smiled at her expectantly. She clearly wasn't going to get away with turning him down.

She took the photo and squiggled on it, catching Cara's scowl of disapproval.

Ed looked at the picture happily. 'There,' he said, with a satisfied grin. 'Now everyone will believe me when I tell them that I know *the* Lois Chan.'

Lois glanced at the glass case by the door and the dusty model of the palace that she'd thought of when she arrived at Jai Shijai's private island. But now, seeing it again, it was nothing like as grand as Jai Shijai's home. And the startling contrast between Ed's world and the great tycoon's hit her full force. Her past and her possible future couldn't have been further apart.

The blue Formica tables were more shabby than she remembered and Ed and his wife looked so much older. Lois wondered how on earth she was going to manage to give them money for the meal. Ed would be adamant it was on the house, but Lois saw all too well the faded glory of the restaurant. This had once been the smartest place in Chinatown, but clearly Ed had been left behind.

'Grab a seat,' Ed said. 'Anywhere's fine.'

He wasn't kidding. They were the only people here.

'And what about you, Cara? You want a soda?' Ed asked with a grin.

'I suppose.' She couldn't have sounded more disinterested.

Lois smiled and ushered Cara to one of the booths on the back wall.

'I don't like anything on the menu,' Cara said, as she slumped into her seat after Ed had gone, humming merrily, to the kitchen doors.

'We're going to eat what we're given. Please don't turn your nose up. These people want to entertain us. It's the custom,' Lois whispered under her breath.

Cara fiddled with the fortune cookie wrapped in foil on her plate. She cracked it open.

'What?' she asked Lois, accusingly.

'They're supposed to be for after the meal,' Lois hissed.

Cara scowled at her. 'I'm going to the bathroom,' she said.

Whilst she was gone, Lois stared at the fortune cookie on her own plate. She shouldn't have snapped at Cara. But the stress of this morning had got to her.

She knew she was doing this all wrong. So what if Cara wanted to open her fortune cookie? Why was Lois being so uptight? She was acting like her own mother, for God's sake. She'd never win her daughter over if she kept on being the fun police like this.

Lois quickly unwrapped her fortune cookie, cracked open the brittle shell and pulled out the flimsy strip of paper. *The man in your thoughts will help you find your destiny*, she read. Who the hell could that be? she wondered. Roberto? Jai Shijai? Aidan? There'd been quite a roll call lately.

A smile played across her lips. She hadn't really thought of Aidan since she'd left Jai Shijai's island. She wondered how he was and if he was still sailing. Or whether Zak had gone back to his mother and school, whilst Aidan had disappeared off to some godforsaken war zone.

It was nice to have come away with such great memories of her time in paradise. And that moment with Aidan at the top of the pagoda. That had been sweet. He'd looked so embarrassed after he'd kissed her. And shocked. As if he couldn't quite believe he'd done it at all. What would have happened if she hadn't had to go back to the game? She supposed she'd never know.

But wherever he was, she hoped he was safe. And that one day he might remember her offer and call her.

She sighed. Being back here in her home town made

all of that seem like a dream. No, more than that, a fantasy. An exotic island . . . a handsome stranger. She couldn't have made it up if she'd tried.

And that was the best part about it. She *hadn't* tried. Hadn't needed to. It had just happened. As if it had been . . .

Ha . . .

She shook her head, staring down at the message in her hands.

As if it had been destined.

Don't be so crazy, she told herself. Just because you're back in one of your childhood haunts doesn't mean you have to start believing again in magic and fate and happy-ever-afters and all of that superstitious baloney your grandmother filled your head with as a kid.

'You look like a ghost has got you,' a familiar voice said.

Lois looked up, startled.

Her mother was standing by the table.

Lois, like her mother and grandmother, had been brought up believing in ghosts. Not the kind from the movies, but real people from the past. People with unfinished business. Loved ones who couldn't settle in the afterlife. Ghosts with sad stories who created a guilty conscience in those who believed in them.

Beverley Chan was a petite woman who'd once been beautiful and immaculately groomed. But since her husband and son had gone from this world – and had haunted her almost continually from the next – she had almost entirely given up on looking feminine.

Her work at the Chinese Cultural Center now took up most of her time and she seemed to have taken on the burdens of all the needy immigrants she saw on a daily basis.

Lois was shocked to see how much she'd aged. She wore no make-up and her hair was greying beneath the black headscarf she now took off. The rest of her was grey too. Her cardigan, blouse and dark grey slacks. Even her sensible lace-up shoes were grey.

Lois smiled at her and rose to kiss her, but her mother's face seemed almost incapable of happiness. Lois couldn't remember the last time she'd seen or heard her mother laugh. It hadn't been for years.

Cara came back from the restroom and Lois held out her arm to her, smiling. She beckoned her forward and reluctantly Cara pecked her grandmother on the cheek, before sitting back down again and standing the menu open in front of her, like a shield.

'She doesn't look like she belongs to you,' Lois's mother commented in Cantonese, as they slid in opposite her in the booth.

'Mom, can we please speak English in front of Cara?' Lois answered in English, determined that her daughter would not feel any more excluded from this environment than she did already. 'Otherwise it's not fair.'

'It would be fair if you'd bothered to teach her your mother tongue.'

Minefield number one, Lois thought, kicking herself for walking straight into it.

'Don't mind me,' Cara said, as if she couldn't care

190

less. 'You want to talk about me behind my back, you go ahead.'

'We don't,' Lois said, putting her hand on the menu to flatten it. But her mother continued glaring at Cara.

Lois winced. She knew that look only too well.

'You should control your daughter, Lois,' her mother said in Cantonese. Then in English, 'I wouldn't stand for such rudeness.'

So now *Lois* was the one being told off? She swallowed hard, counselling herself to keep calm.

'Yes, well, Mom,' Lois began, carefully placing her napkin on her knees. She tried to find the right tone, her eyes pleading with Cara to play ball. 'Cara is her own person and entitled to her own views. I don't want her to feel that anyone is controlling her. She's responsible enough to know how her actions affect others.'

There, Lois thought. Surely that should empower Cara, whilst proving to her mother she was in control of the situation.

But she knew it had backfired almost as soon as she said it.

'Bullshit,' her mother said in Cantonese.

Lois reddened. She saw a smirk on Cara's face. It was a fact of life: you didn't need to speak a language to understand when it was being used to curse. Cara's eyes blazed with triumph. She was clearly thriving on the tension, enjoying the sense of Lois losing her cool in front of her mother.

'Three generations of women. Look at you all together,' Ed said, bearing down on them, his arms outstretched.

Lois saw Cara recoil from the smell coming from his armpits. The apron around his waist was grubby and Lois realized that Ed was doing the cooking as well as the front of house these days. He pinched Cara affectionately under the chin.

'No smile, little one?' he asked. 'I haven't seen you since you were a baby, but we still have a photo of you up in the kitchen.'

Cara turned the corners of her mouth up in a sneer.

'That's better,' Ed said, before turning to Lois's mother.

'Ah, Mrs Chan, you must be pleased to have your daughter home? It's what every mother wants, yes?' he asked in Cantonese.

'What every woman wants is a son. And for their daughters to look after them,' Lois's mother said, deliberately in English.

Lois felt her words like a slap. No matter how well she did in life, she couldn't make up for the fact that her mother had lost her husband and Miki. Precious Miki. The son her mother had prayed for. The son who'd broken the chain of female babies, for her grandmother and mother. The son whose gender shouldn't have mattered in the post-China, campaign-fighting, feminist world of her mother, except that it did. A lot.

And despite everything, Lois felt the weight of all the generations of her family pulling her back down. Pulling her into line, as a woman. It made her want to scream.

What a stupid, idealistic fool she'd been. She'd deliberately instigated this get-together, hoping that it would make all of them bond. But she could see now that both her mother and her daughter were bubbling with resentment towards her. They hadn't come for a reunion, they'd come for a fight.

Despite Cara's obvious hostility, however, Lois still wished she could bundle her up and get her out of here. She couldn't bear the thought of her getting caught up in a painful confrontation. She wanted Cara to be exposed to warmth and kindness and calm. And she could see now that she'd brought her to exactly the wrong place to get it.

But it was too late to leave. As Ed started bringing out plates of food, Lois couldn't help being an observer – watching her mother eating without joy and with wariness and suspicion in her eyes. Cara picked at some snow peas, doing exactly the same – the two of them staring across the table at each other, a generation gap that seemed impossibly wide. She saw a look of revulsion cross Cara's face as Lois's mother sucked up rice noodles from her bowl into her mouth with her chopsticks.

Please not today, Lois thought. Please let me get through this without any arguments.

She staved off any harsh words by babbling a constant stream of cheerful small talk about the food, the weather and the neighbourhood. But there was so much she couldn't mention: her injury, her career, her future. And with no input from either her mother or Cara, inevitably a brooding silence finally descended on the table.

She could see how riled her mother was by Cara,

who'd eaten next to nothing. And when Ed brought out his famous purple rice pudding, giving Cara his usual spiel about how the combination of red bean curd and sticky purple rice was a food so rare that only the ancient emperors could eat it and Cara pushed the plate away as soon as his back was turned, Lois's mother snapped.

'You've been nothing but a little brat since you got here,' she said.

'Mom! You can't—' Lois gasped. 'Please don't. Please—'

'Shut up,' her mother said. She spread her hands out on the table and challenged Cara. 'Since Lois here thinks you're a grown-up, then we'll treat you like one. You can start by explaining yourself. Come on, spit it out.'

Cara's face crumpled. She burst into tears and ran into the restroom.

'Mom!' Lois stood. 'How could you?'

Her mother waved a hand at her dismissively. 'Pah,' she said. 'Histrionics. You know what your problem is, Lois? You've got no backbone. No backbone with your daughter. Your own flesh and blood is a spoilt princess. When you see some of the kids her age I see, who've had nothing . . . *nothing* . . . and she behaves like that? Let me tell you, your grandmother would be turning in her grave if she could see this.'

Her mother had made no bones about the fact she considered Lois's loss of custody of Cara to be entirely her own fault. Lois made ready to defend herself yet again on this point, if necessary. Especially if Cara was

194

still within earshot. She glanced anxiously towards the restroom door.

'But I guess that's to be expected now that you've sold out on all of your principles,' she continued.

The speed with which her mother was getting it all off her chest implied she'd thought out just the right way of sticking the knife in. It didn't surprise her that she continued without letting Lois justify herself.

'When Miki was killed, when those people your father owed money to came, you said you'd find out who was in charge. You'd bring them to justice—'

'I know but—'

'That's why I was so proud of you when you got into that police academy. I thought you would always remember your family. I thought you'd make it right to the top. And make a difference. You said that's where you were going. What you wanted to do with your life. And I believed you.'

Lois felt all her anger deflating in the face of her mother's heartbreak.

'It's not that simple, Mom.' Lois forced herself to remember that her mother was a one-woman fighter against whole ideologies. Her belief that Lois could somehow change the world – could find some sort of justice for Miki – was completely delusional.

'And now what are you doing?' her mother continued. 'You shame your family by working in the same industry that killed your father and brother.'

'It's not like that. It's not,' Lois appealed to her, but she knew she sounded like a petulant teenager. 'Don't you see, I'm trying to make the casinos fair and safe? So that people like Dad don't get hurt.'

'You can justify it to yourself, Lois, but you'll never justify it to me.'

Lois stared at her, then at Ed, whose face was aghast.

Then, growling, she hurried to find Cara. There was no point in arguing any more, or trying to explain the situation to Ed. Her mother shouted something after her, but Lois was no longer listening.

She pushed through the door into the restroom.

Too quiet.

She sensed it straight away. She'd been in this situation a dozen times as a beat cop. Pursuing a perp into a supposed dead end, only to find the bird had already flown.

Lois pushed open the stall door. It wasn't locked. The ghost of a Nike footprint still showed on the toilet seat. The window above it was wide open. Cara had gone.

CHAPTER TWENTY

Panic lanced Lois as she ran out of the restaurant's front door and on to the street. Please don't let her have run far, she thought. How long had she been gone? One minute? Two? Cara might think she was a grown-up and sophisticated, but this was a big city. She'd get eaten alive.

Lois sprinted to the junction at the end of the street. She searched left, then right. Nothing.

But then she saw the bus stop and the stick-thin figure slouched against it. Lois felt relief blossom inside her so violently, it made her knees weak.

She ran to Cara and grabbed her. She was so small she felt like a rag doll in her hands.

'Oh God. Oh Cara,' Lois cried, pulling her towards her, folding her into a tight hug, pressing her precious head against her chest. 'I thought . . . I thought . . . please don't do that again. You scared me.'

Cara stayed limp in her arms. She didn't hug Lois back.

Had she really wanted to run away? Where to? But it was pointless asking her what her plan had been. She'd acted on impulse. Just to get away.

From Lois.

It was time to start building bridges. Fast.

Lois crouched down and looked into her face, holding her shoulders. 'I'm so sorry, darling. I'm sorry that Grandma told you off.'

Cara said nothing. Her eyes were bloodshot, but she wasn't crying.

'Please,' Lois said. 'I'm on your side. I'm your mom.'

'But I've already got a real mom,' Cara shot back.

A real mom. Lois felt as if Cara had punched her. The words hurt so much more than anything her own mother had said in the restaurant. She knew Cara was angry, but she was shocked that she could say something that hurtful.

Lois closed her eyes for a second and took a breath.

'OK,' she said slowly. 'Then, perhaps we could be friends?'

'Friends?' Cara replied, but Lois sensed contrition in her tone. Perhaps she was shocked too by how low she'd just struck. 'I don't even know you.'

'Then let's get to know each other. Please, Cara. That's all I want.'

Cara said nothing. She scuffed her toe on the sidewalk.

'I know we have issues to resolve, but ask me anything,' Lois persisted. 'Anything at all. Let's be open.

Honest. I want you to feel you can say anything to me.'

Lois opened her arms. After Cara's last bullet, she was ready for anything.

There was a pause, then Cara spoke. 'Everyone at school says . . .'

She paused. She stared down at her toe, scuffing it again.

'What? Tell me?'

'They call you a cop-killer.'

Cop-killer.

They'd really said that. Kids? To her daughter?

A spurt of fury shot through her. Chris should have protected Cara from this. But at the same time Lois knew that there was no way he could have. What she'd done . . . her past . . . thanks to Michael Hudson, it had been made public. And distorted.

She should have guessed Cara would have been exposed to some of his lies. She should have anticipated this moment and come prepared.

Lois felt sick. She'd always known she'd have to tell Cara about what had happened one day. She couldn't keep it a secret for ever. But Cara was still a child. And what had happened was complicated. So complicated.

But Lois had asked for this herself. If this was what was on Cara's mind, then Lois had to help her understand. It was time to tell the truth and set the record straight once and for all. And despite all the emotion she felt, she would keep the retelling as factual as she could.

She took Cara's hand and, pulling her, made her sit

199

next to her on a bench. There was a moment when they sat side by side, looking at the view down the hill.

And then Lois began.

Ever since her brother Miki had been killed when they were teenagers, Lois had set her mind on being a cop. A good cop. The kind who would clean up the streets and stop kids like Miki getting killed in the future.

She was driven by a passion, studying so hard she could have aced her exams twice over. When she hit the precinct, she worked twice as hard as all the men. Double the hours and studying on top. She got right in their faces until they couldn't ignore her or refuse her promotion to detective.

Chris was a cop too. A forensics liaison officer. At first, they were a golden couple. They worked and played hard and it seemed like the future was rosy. But as soon as Cara came along, Chris stopped treating Lois as an equal. As far as he was concerned, she was a mom now. She should stay at home.

But Lois had insisted on going straight back to work, determined that she could juggle it all. The arguments got worse and worse, but Lois refused to back down. She had a point to prove to Chris and all the men on her team. She could be a great mom and a cop. Especially when the break she needed to establish herself came with the Lawnton case. She gave it everything she had.

Robert Lawnton was a predatory paedophile who had recently been released from a maximum security penitentiary, following a court appeal that had successfully challenged his arrest on technical grounds.

He'd reoffended – assault – within twenty-four hours of hitting the streets. Then had gone on the run.

Lois and her partner Billy-Ray were assigned the task of tracking him down. And busting him. This time by the book. To ensure that he never got out again.

But then a little girl went missing. Jenna De Souza. Hispanic. Nine years old. Not so different from Cara now. Exactly Lawnton's type.

Only this was where Lois got lucky – if you could ever call dealing with any of these people that. One of her informants harboured a grudge against Lawnton and gave his location away.

Blakeney, Lois's captain, a glory-hunting alcoholic with his lazy eye on a switch to a political career, passed word they were to move in quick and bag Lawnton before the FBI took over and snatched the inevitable slew of headlines such a high-profile grab would bring.

Chris and Lois had a fight an hour before her team assembled to back up the SWAT team on the early morning raid. He told her she was in no fit state to go. She had been up three nights in a row with the baby, he argued. She was running on empty and should hold back.

She told him to back off. She was fine, she insisted. But when he carried on arguing, she snapped. He'd always put his career before hers, and it was clear to her now that the only reason he wanted her to back off was so that he could mobilize the FBI and take charge of the bust himself . . . before her. Well, she was a damn sight better cop than him and now she'd prove it.

The last thing she told him, as she headed off for the raid, was to go to hell.

In the back of the van, Blakeney joined Lois, Billy-Ray and the SWAT team. He looked tired and haggard and despite his drinking coffee and sucking mints, Lois smelt the whisky on his breath.

The SWAT team went in alone to the tip-off address. Lois waited outside with Blakeney and Billy-Ray.

That was when Billy-Ray spotted it: the sudden twitch of a curtain in the building next door. A glimpse of a profile and Lois knew it was Lawnton. Without a doubt. There was no time to call back the SWAT team.

When they broke down the door of the next-door house, it stank of cigarettes and stale beer. The cot in the corner was empty, the mattress stained, a packet of Twinkies spilt on the floor.

Lois motioned to Billy-Ray to go through to the kitchen. He eased open the door with his toe, sweeping the room with his pistol.

Nothing.

Lois was behind, covering his back, Blakeney right beside her.

Then she saw Lawnton through the open kitchen window. He was in the yard, little Jenna with him. Backing into the shadows. Lois took aim.

'I've got a clear shot,' she hissed.

Blakeney gripped her wrist. He took her gun.

He hadn't seen Billy-Ray slip out through the back door into the yard.

A flurry of movement.

Jenna screamed. She was free. Lawnton had decided to run. Billy-Ray stood up straight. Aimed. Shouted to Lawnton to stop.

Blakeney fired.

Billy-Ray fell face down. He had a gaping wound in the back of his head.

Lawnton got himself ensnared in the razor wire on the back fence. The SWAT team poured through and took him down. Blakeney ran to join them. But Lois was frozen.

All eyes fell on Billy-Ray, dead on the ground. Then at Blakeney crouched next to him. He was pointing his finger at Lois.

Then she saw it. The gun. *Her* gun. The one Blakeney had accidentally shot Billy-Ray with.

It was lying by her feet.

Blakeney's eyes were as cold as a shark's. She watched as he swiped his sweating forehead with a red-and-white handkerchief. One she suddenly knew with absolute certainty he'd used to wipe her gun free of his prints.

As Lois recounted those dark days to Cara, she didn't know what was more painful – keeping it in, or letting it out. She'd assumed that finally telling Cara the truth would make her feel better. But now, as she stared at Cara's shocked face, it made her feel worse.

How could she expect her daughter to make sense of it when she could hardly make sense of it herself? Unburdening herself to a child made her feel more guilty, not less. Cara was too young to hear about paedophiles and liars like Blakeney. She didn't need to know how painful the world was. What was the point of protesting her innocence, when in doing so she destroyed her daughter's?

'You let all those people believe you did something wrong, when it was that guy Blakeney?' Cara said incredulously.

'It was my word against his,' Lois explained, her voice much more emotional than she'd intended. 'No one believed me.'

'Why didn't you *make* everyone believe you?'

'The forensic evidence showed it was my gun with my prints on it that had killed Billy-Ray. And nobody had seen Blakeney take my gun or fire the shot.'

'So what did you do?'

'Blakeney stuck with his lie. Billy-Ray was given a hero's funeral. They told me I was lucky I'd not been charged with manslaughter. Your father helped there. I do acknowledge that. I was dishonourably discharged.'

'And after that? With you and Dad?' Cara asked.

'He wanted me to accept I'd killed Billy-Ray. That I was delirious from lack of sleep. That I had imagined Blakeney had taken the shot. He told me that it was OK to make a mistake.' Lois felt tears now, rising in her chest. Unstoppable. Like an old volcano of grief within her that had just been reawakened. 'That was what hurt the most. Chris . . . well, he thought I was going out of my mind. I couldn't live with him not believing me. And it all got . . . nasty. So . . . horribly nasty.'

Lois took a deep breath and swiped at her eyes.

'I thought it could all be settled easily, but then there were lawyers. And before I knew it, we went to court. I wanted to keep you with me, but . . .' She paused, swallowing back the emotion. 'But the judge was the same as your dad. He thought I'd killed Billy-Ray. That I was some crazy gun-wielding idiot who'd made a tragic mistake. Not the kind of person fit to look after her own baby. And that's how Dad ended up keeping you. In the end, I had no choice but to walk away.'

'From me.' Cara's voice was steady, but her eyes were filled with tears.

Lois felt her heart wrenching. How could she possibly make Cara understand?

'Don't you see? I lost everything when I lost you. What was I supposed to do? Follow you to Washington? Sit in a car outside your dad's house? Stalk you at kindergarten? Believe me, I wanted to. But that would only have made things even worse. I had to take the job in New York to keep my sanity.'

Cara's gaze dropped from hers and Lois wiped her face. She longed to hold her. To take her in her arms. To never, ever let her go. But it was too early. She could see that Cara needed time to process everything Lois had said.

Did Cara understand? She doubted it. Just as she doubted now that she'd ever be able to clean up the mess of the past. It would always be there.

And now she didn't know where she stood. She'd told the truth. This should have been her cue to make the promises to Cara she wanted to. To tell her how much she longed for them to live together. But the plan she'd had to do just that seemed pointless and ill-conceived now.

Cara had a home already. A stable one. What right did Lois have to take that from her until she'd built an equally stable home of her own? To claim her right as a proper mom. A *real* mom, as Cara herself had said.

'I think we need to talk some more,' Lois said, as gently as she could. 'So let's go home, eh? But first we'll have to go back to the restaurant and make peace with Grandma. Can you bear it?' she asked.

Perhaps Cara sensed that she did have a choice. She nodded.

Lois was deeply shaken, but she forced herself to stay strong as they set off back up the hill, side by side.

She'd rebuild their relationship, no matter what it took. And she saw now that it would involve being nice to her ex-husband and cooperative, not combative. She'd cut all the conflict she could from her daughter's life.

She remembered Aidan and Zak on the yacht.

Love *could* survive divorce. The two of them proved it.

And looking down at Cara now, the thought of it was a glimmer of hope Lois clung to.

CHAPTER TWENTY-ONE

It was day three of equine therapy. The heat was already rising and the horses snorted in the hazy mist, keen to get going. In the stable yard, Red laughed, pushing his battered Stetson back on his head, as if he had all the time in the world. He crossed his wrists and held the reins as he calmly sat on his horse waiting for Savvy to get on hers.

Savvy was determined not to show Red how difficult she found these early starts. Not just the physical demands of being up at dawn and the technical problems of getting on a horse, but the other stuff – the depression and anxiety that sometimes hit her in waves.

The workshops and sessions with Dr Savage had been both gruelling and humbling. Physically, she'd had to accept that her behaviour had chemically altered her and that in order to regain its balance her body was going to hurt. Emotionally, she'd had to face up to the consequences of her lifestyle and start on the road to permanent change.

At times it felt as if she was unravelling, but more and more frequently when she was with Red she saw for herself that it was possible to come through at least this experience and out the other side, stronger and healthier than ever before. He was living proof of it. Finally she'd realized she wanted to be like that too.

A sweaty mess already, she succeeded in heaving herself into the saddle. She noticed Red was laughing. He gave her a small round of applause and she blushed furiously.

But at least they could get away before anyone else from the group turned up and ruined everything. She'd had enough of Vanessa's success-related drug problems and Dougie's incessant rap-chat, not to mention Kate's laxative dependency following her disastrous plastic surgery.

There were some nice inmates, not people Savvy would want as friends exactly, but decent human beings beneath their addictions. However, a lot of the others seemed hooked on sharing their nastiest secrets, as if the intimacy had become a form of addiction in itself. So much so that for some people this was their third or fourth visit here.

Savvy found the thought of yo-yoing between addiction and this place too frightening to contemplate. Which was why she'd started avoiding those people as much as she could.

But meanwhile, at least she had Red to keep her

company. Strong, kind, wonderful Red.

'That's it. You're getting the hang of it,' he called, as she slipped her bare feet into her stirrups.

Bare feet indeed. Another of Red's ideas, to help her connect with living in the here and now. She'd have avoided him like the plague back in civilization. But here, amongst all the plants and rocks and streams and sky . . . well, out here, OK, she had to admit that Red was kind of cool.

'I still feel like I'm going to fall off any second,' she said.

'Just relax. Let yourself go. You'll be fine,' he said, clicking his tongue and making his chestnut mare turn round in the stable yard and head through the gate to the paddock.

Savvy used her heels gently to prod Mr Ed, the quiet grey gelding she'd grown used to these last couple of weeks, and set off after Red, their gentle clip-clopping on the stable-yard cobbles sending a flurry of birds up into the morning mist.

'My father always says that the early bird catches the worm,' she said.

Red smiled. 'Go on . . .' he coaxed.

'I've been thinking about what you said last time. About how angry he is with me. I wonder how much of that anger is because of my mother?'

'Because she's not around?'

'Because she *chose* not to be around. She overdosed on sleeping pills. When I was six months old.'

'She did it on purpose?' Red said, looking shocked. 'You told me she'd died, but you never told me how.'

'She swallowed eighty of them. I'd say that was pretty conclusive.'

The details . . . Hud had told her once when he was drunk, several years back now, before he'd gone on the wagon. Savvy's mother Clare – a fragile English rose, by all accounts – had left no note. Post-natal depression, the doctors had called it.

Those last few months, she disappeared inside herself, Hud had said. *It was like watching a TV being switched off. Only no one knew how to switch it back on again. She didn't want us, Savvy. She didn't want to be around any of us any more.*

Hud had never spoken about it again. Next morning he'd denied the conversation had ever taken place.

Didn't want us . . .

Switched off . . .

But Hud had switched off too. He'd switched off all the hurt and all the anger.

'So he never talked about her?' Red asked, after Savvy had explained.

'Never.'

'Does he have a partner? Someone he talks to?'

'No. He's married to his business,' Savvy said.

Was he lonely? Savvy wondered now. He'd never remarried, or even had a girlfriend as far as Savvy knew. Perhaps he'd turned off the passionate side of his life and put all his energy into his business.

And now that she thought about the business, about Hud's business, she started to feel curious. How was this new venture in Shangri-La shaping up? Was he excited? Proud? How did he feel about planning the launch of his Eastern empire without either of his daughters by his side? Did it make him sad? Did he ever think about Savvy and wonder how she was? Or had he really closed the door on her for ever?

'So you're all he's got left,' Red said, as if reading her thoughts.

'I guess,' she replied. Except that she didn't know whether Hud would ever take her back. He wanted high flyers, achievers like Paige, around him. What the hell could Savvy offer him that would ever make him proud?

The mist was clearing as Savvy and Red headed into the forest. Perhaps it was talking about her parents or thinking about life outside of Peace River that had done it, but here, her thoughts seemed less like chains that tied her head up in knots and more like butterflies eager to float off into the hazy canopy. All she had to do was voice them. And set them free.

Savvy watched Red as he rode on ahead of her deeper into the forest. He looked so natural, as if he were a cowboy, and with the two of them together, with nobody else around, Savvy felt that she was on an adventure. As if they were frontier people, setting off into the wilderness to build a new way of life. As if it were just her and Red versus the world.

'That's it,' he said. 'Just relax. Feel the rhythm.' He faced forward, walking the horse deeper into the forest.

Fuck, he's attractive, she thought, feeling a familiar tingle in her abdomen.

The thought had just popped into her head. And now, as she continued to watch Red, it wouldn't leave.

But Red was out of bounds, she reminded herself. He wasn't interested in sex. Or wouldn't allow himself to be anyway.

And she wasn't here for sex. She was here to get well.

And he was her friend.

Her very attractive friend.

Christ, what a time for her libido to be waking up. After all the headaches and sickness and thirst.

Out here.

Alone.

With Red. Where no one else could see . . .

Stop it! she told herself. She couldn't wreck things with Red by suddenly trying to seduce him. By getting him to play cowboys and cowgirls with her. Even though the temptation was almost too much to bear. Especially here, where everything seemed so primeval. So Adam and Eve.

Feel the rhythm. That's what he'd told her . . .

And now that he'd said it, she just couldn't stop.

She was so acutely aware of the horse's saddle between her legs that she subtly started rocking with the motion, homing in on the sensation. With each step the horse took, her body moved, making the hard leather saddle feel like a hand cupping her vulva. Tuning in more now, increasing the pressure, she felt herself becoming hopelessly aroused.

Closing her eyes, she began rocking forward on to

her clitoris, arching her back a little more each time, feeling the pressure through the thin fabric of her cotton trousers.

She knew she shouldn't do it, but she couldn't seem to stop. She swallowed hard, unable to rip herself away from imagining what it would be like to lie down naked under the trees on a horse blanket with Red. What it would feel like to have him on top of her. Inside her. How she'd run her hands down over the soft, freckled skin of his back. And how she would cup that gorgeous firm, round butt of his and pull him towards her. Into her. She imagined him deep inside her now, kneeling between her legs, her legs wrapped around his. She pictured what he'd look like as she reached up and kissed his face.

She gasped, feeling the sensation between her thighs mounting higher and higher. Now she imagined herself on her back between these trees. Her legs up. One bare foot on each tree trunk. And Red's kissing down her body . . . his tongue . . . lapping . . . darting inside her, making her so hot that . . .

Oh God, she thought, stifling a groan. *I'm coming*.

Her orgasm rocked right through her. It had been the first for so long, it felt like her whole body was exploding with shimmering sparks.

She gasped, opening her eyes as the heat poured out of her.

Red was several yards ahead, ducking beneath a low branch, blissfully unaware that he'd just been the subject of her unexpected climax.

'You OK?' he asked, as he held back his horse where

the path widened out, so that they could ride side by side.

'Sure,' she said, but she couldn't look at him. She knew her cheeks were burning.

Her body was still awash with endorphins. She knew her fantasy about Red had been just that, a fantasy. But somehow it felt so real, as if something had actually happened between them.

They broke out of the trees into a valley, following the path of a brook. Birds screeched out on either side of them, but they were the only people for miles around.

She noticed Red was studying her face.

'What?' she said, embarrassed by the attention – and guilty as hell.

'Nothing. You've just got that look.'

'What look?'

'The one girls get when they're thinking about a guy . . .'

If only you knew, she thought. 'I never heard of that look,' she said, attempting to switch subject.

'Well, you should go check out a mirror. You're wearing it now . . .'

She couldn't hold his eyes.

'See,' he laughed, enjoying teasing her. 'I knew I was right. So let me guess . . . that Luc guy? Are you finally ready to talk about him?'

'I can't believe you remembered that,' she said, remembering herself now that she'd told Red Luc's name the second time she'd met him, when they'd walked on the beach.

She didn't want to talk about Luc. Not now. Not when she was feeling like this. But Red had clearly sussed that he was on to something.

'I'm guessing that he's behind a lot of stuff that happened when your sister died. Am I right?' he coaxed. 'Don't be scared, Savvy.'

'I'm not,' she said, too quickly. It was obvious to them both that scared was *exactly* what she was. Terrified.

'So who is he?' Red said. 'Start at the beginning. Tell me how you met him?'

CHAPTER TWENTY-TWO

As Savvy started describing the spring day nearly four years earlier when she'd first met Luc Devereaux, it felt as if she were remembering a different person. The future had seemed so easy back then, as if a red carpet would roll out indefinitely ahead of her. She'd been in New York for a film première and when Hud had unexpectedly called her, telling her that he'd flown into town too and asking her to join him for lunch at the newly made-over Scott's, Savvy had jumped at the chance.

She'd got on with Hud a whole lot better then. She'd not yet had her name raked through the gossip columns and he'd still considered her footloose behaviour just a part of growing up rather than a permanent lifestyle choice.

Plus, Hud's borrowed mantra that 'lunch was for wimps' was very familiar to her, but when he did break his rule and dine out, he usually did it in style. Savvy was impressed that he'd booked somewhere as chic as Scott's.

But, as always, he'd chosen to mix business with pleasure. Rather than a cosy lunch *à deux*, as she'd hoped, Hud wanted to introduce Savvy to a potential new member of staff, he'd told her. To get her opinion. He wanted to know if Savvy thought he was all schmooze, or if he really was as smart as people said. The new guy was rumoured to be quite a charmer, Hud had heard.

Savvy was all ears. She'd broken up with a boyfriend a week earlier and was in dire need of some charm.

But there was no point in getting her hopes up. After all, how charming could a potential colleague of Hud's really be? Hud's definition of a charming guy was way off hers. Way off. But still, the lunch should be a distraction, even if this new guy was a tedious business type.

But the moment Savvy walked into the restaurant and saw Luc Devereaux she literally stopped in her tracks. He was sitting at the best table, laughing with her father, and she realized that she was in the presence of quite simply the most beautiful man she'd ever seen. She blinked hard and looked again, astonished by the way in which all her senses seemed to have responded. She was fizzing.

The way the sunlight seemed to bathe him in golden light, the water in his glass shimmering as he lifted it to his lips – it was like Luc had some kind of magical quality – as if he were a heaven-sent gift.

Trying to recover her composure, Savvy walked towards Luc and Hud, her legs suddenly having turned to jelly. She sat down at the table, demurely placing her purse on the white tablecloth. She took off her large Gucci shades and the second her eyes connected with Luc's, she felt a spark. A jolt. Like pure electricity.

She watched his lips as he smiled, immediately wondering what they'd be like to kiss. They had a pronounced bow and were almost girlish. She couldn't take her eyes off him.

But Luc Devereaux wasn't stupid. He knew that Michael Hudson was watching him like a hawk. The perfect gentleman, he asked Savvy her opinion on the movie she'd seen the night before. His sexy French accent was to die for. She tried not to stare too openly at him as he listened politely while she repeated verbatim the opinion of the well-known movie critic she'd got stuck with at the after-show party.

'Well, Michael,' Luc said. 'You didn't tell me that your daughter was so artistic.'

But his eyes said, *sexy. You didn't tell me that your daughter was so sexy.*

'Isn't she,' Hud agreed, winking at Savvy. 'And the best bit is that I have two of them. I invited Elodie to join us, too.'

Even while basking in their flattery, Savvy felt a stab of disappointment. She didn't want to be diluted by Elodie – turned into their usual double act for Hud. She didn't want to be just one of his daughters. She knew with absolute clarity that she wanted to be *the* daughter. The daughter that Luc noticed.

In fact, as Luc continued talking, impressing her father with his tales of the Sorbonne in Paris and his high-flying business career in New York, Savvy hardly heard a word. Luc Devereaux was gorgeous and she wanted him to notice her very much.

She could hardly believe this was happening. All that bullshit about love at first sight . . . well, it was just that, right? Just bullshit. Or at least that's what she would have said before laying eyes on Luc Devereaux.

But now – well, he'd certainly switched on some-thing inside her. She felt lit up, like she was glowing, like she'd been plugged into a socket. And even if it wasn't love at first sight, it sure as hell was close.

When he left the table to go to the restroom, Hud had an even bigger shock in store.

'So what do you think?'

'He's . . . he's great,' she said, unable to lie.

'I think so too. Which is why from now on he's going to be my right-hand man.'

Savvy hadn't even realized such a position existed.

'I can't go on running the show on my own for ever,' he said, taking her hand to break the news gently. 'I need someone to help take the strain – at least until one of you two decides you're going to step up to the mark.'

Savvy resisted the bait. She was having too much of a blast to disappear up a corporate dead end just yet.

'So what will he do? Exactly?' Savvy asked. Hud was a notorious control freak. There was no way he'd delegate important decision-making. Did Luc Devereaux know what he was getting himself into?

'There are potential opportunities on the horizon in China. I'm going to train Luc to spearhead them,' Hud said. 'That's where the future is, Savvy, you mark my words. But in the meantime, he'll shadow me in Vegas until he learns the ropes. He's got great ideas. He's planning a Republican fundraiser at La Paris already.'

Savvy was quick to give her blessing. Having Luc in Hud's orbit would be a dream come true – for her. And he seemed smart, she assured her father.

Amused by Savvy's reaction, Hud was altogether more relaxed when Luc came back. Soon after, he left the table to make a phone call. And finally Savvy and Luc were alone.

Savvy knew in an instant that whatever she was feeling, Luc was feeling it too. She watched him as he tried not to look at her. Then he did and he laughed, blushing.

What the hell? she thought. If she'd read the signs wrong, then she was about to make a total ass of herself. But she was sure she hadn't.

She slipped off her shoe and ran her foot up his trouser leg underneath the table. She knew she shouldn't do it – that it was completely out of order – but she couldn't help herself. There was no point in pretending. This was sexual chemistry like she'd never experienced.

'You know, Savannah,' Luc said, 'I never, ever mix business with pleasure.'

Slowly she withdrew her foot and smiled. 'I'm sure Hud will be delighted to hear that,' she said, raising her eyebrow at him.

But when Luc half stood up and had to use his linen napkin to cover his crotch, Savvy knew she'd got to him. The only bummer was the reason he'd been forced to stand up: Elodie was arriving at their table.

'Look at you two,' Elodie chirped. 'Watching you chatting, it's like you've known each other for ages. You must be Luc Devereaux. Daddy told me all about you.'

And now Hud rejoined the group and gave Elodie a tender kiss, laying his hand on her cheek for a moment.

'It's not like you to be late,' Hud gently chastised her.

'I know. I'm sorry. But there was a Cézanne exhibition down the street and I couldn't stop myself from popping in. And, well . . .' She rolled her eyes. 'You know me . . . I got completely absorbed.'

'The father of Cubism,' Luc said. 'I'll have to visit myself.'

'You're a fan then?' Elodie asked.

'And enthusiast. Certainly.' He turned to Hud. '*Two* artistic daughters,' he said, correcting his own earlier comment. 'You are truly fortunate, Michael.'

Annoyed and feeling, as usual, that she'd somehow been diminished by her sister, Savvy consoled herself that Elodie was looking her usual dowdy self. Her unhighlighted mousy hair was scraped back into a scrawny ponytail and her cheeks were flushed. She was inappropriately dressed, given the unseasonably hot April weather, in a purple turtle neck and boring black trousers. Next to her, Savvy, in her sexy low-cut yellow and white dress, high sandals and tousled hair, positively shone.

She felt herself becoming hopelessly aroused, just watching Luc talk. The way his eyes sparkled as he spoke, his long fingers stroking the stem of his wine glass.

She couldn't stop picturing Luc naked. What would he be like in bed?

Sensational, she decided. French men were all sexy, weren't they? Her mind wandered off into shuttered French bedrooms with four-poster beds, she and Luc nakedly tangled in the softest of linen sheets . . .

For the rest of the meal, Luc hardly looked at her, paying all his attention to Elodie. Savvy was amused at first, thinking it was a tactic to prevent himself from revealing his attraction to Savvy again, especially in front of Hud. But after a while, as their conversation moved on from Cézanne to Matisse and Picasso and then on to Elodie's budding interior design business, it became obvious that Luc had so much more in common with Elodie than he had with her. Luc wasn't interested in live bands, like Savvy was, he liked old school jazz, like Elodie. He wasn't interested in clubbing, he liked to play polo in his spare time, or ski. Elodie was quick to invite him out riding. And of course, he loved that too.

Or was it all an act? Savvy wondered. Was this just part of the famous Devereaux charm? Was he secretly saving up all his real passion for *her*?

*   *   *

After the initial lunch with Hud, Savvy made it her business to find out everything there was to know about the handsome and charming Luc Devereaux. If he thought he could ignore her, he was very much mistaken. She was on a mission to snare him.

His name cropped up often as an A-list bachelor in the glossier magazines, but Savvy's internet research didn't pull up anything unusual. He was straight and hard-working. He wasn't into drugs and he didn't drink to excess. But Savvy could clean up her act easily enough. She'd never had a problem attracting men before.

The more Savvy thought about him, the harder she fell. She'd turned over a new leaf, she told herself happily, and had become a one-man woman.

Soon Luc Devereaux was the talk of Vegas, as well as New York. Hud introduced him to everyone, and from day one he was a big hit.

Luc wasn't the only one to have moved his operation to Vegas. Savvy did the same. She spent more and more weekends at the White House. Hud was delighted. But that was the problem. She never seemed to get Luc on his own.

With Luc so busy, Savvy decided to up the chase. She started taking photographs of herself. Intimate, arty, sexy shots that never showed her face. And she emailed them to Luc from an anonymous account, making sure that she was often in the room with him when he received them. She wanted him to know exactly what he was missing.

Pretty soon, she was sure he hadn't told anyone about

them. The only problem was that the more pictures she sent, the more time he seemed to talk about Elodie at their family get-togethers. She started to wonder whether he suspected that the photos were from Elodie herself. Had Luc confused Savvy's pictures with a secret come-on that he thought was from Elodie?

She was determined to find out.

CHAPTER TWENTY-THREE

Red's hands were on Savvy's hips as he helped her down from Mr Ed. They'd come out of the trees and Savvy squinted in the bright sunlight. In the clearing was a small pool and Red led the horses to the muddy bank to drink.

Savvy sat down in the long grass, breathing in the fresh air. Red came over to her, smiling. He rubbed his thighs, then sat down.

'This is a good place for a rest,' he said. 'Besides, I need to hear more. What happened then?'

Savvy sighed. She knew she'd started, so she shouldn't stop. But she had no idea how she was going to feel telling Red about that night. But it was now or never.

By the night of the Republican fundraiser and Luc's lavish gala in La Paris, Savvy knew that this was the chance she'd been waiting for. Her flirtation with Luc had gone on long enough. It was time to seal the deal.

Yet whilst all the great and good of Vegas turned up, Luc didn't show. Word came through – annoyingly via Elodie – that he was stuck in fog at JFK airport and wasn't going to make it.

But Marcus had. He swooped into the room and gave Savvy a big hug. She could tell he was already drunk.

'Where have you been?' she asked him. 'Seriously?' She hadn't heard from him for weeks. She was more pleased to see him than she'd realized. Marcus always livened up these stuffy events.

'I told you. Disneyland. With disadvantaged children.'

Savvy grinned. 'Still after that nurse?'

'Bagged and tagged,' he told her. 'She wasn't as hot as I'd thought she'd be.'

But then Marcus seemed to remember something and pulled out plastic lighter from his pocket. 'Ta da!' he said. 'I bought you a present.'

She took the lighter from him, laughing. It said *Savannah* on it in loopy writing.

'And that's not all I've got in my party pockets,' he told her. He opened his jacket and pulled out a see-through plastic bag of cocaine, shaking it enticingly.

'Shall we, milady?' he asked, nodding towards the cloakrooms.

Savvy smiled, but she felt torn. She wanted to save herself for Luc. She didn't want to be wired if he did make it tonight. She'd been looking forward to seducing Luc for months. She wanted to savour and remember every second of it. Every touch of his hands . . . and thrust of his hips . . .

But now he wasn't coming, what the hell. She might as well console herself somehow and Marcus was so difficult to resist.

Marcus darted into a cubicle and she followed him in. She watched as he tipped out the cocaine on to the top of the porcelain tank. He chopped several huge lines.

'What's wrong?' he asked.

'Nothing. Why?'

'You seem . . . different. You aren't *sober*, are you?'

Savvy smiled. 'Yes, actually, I am.'

'Good God. Why?'

Marcus snorted the giant line of cocaine he'd laid out.

'I was waiting for someone to show up,' Savvy said.

'Someone?' he asked, amused, making her wish that she hadn't said anything. How she felt about Luc was too precious to be the subject of Marcus's inevitable derision.

Marcus offered her the rolled-up note he'd used with a grin.

'Yes,' she said, snatching the note from him. 'And it's none of your business, so don't ask.'

She turned away from him and leaned down towards the coke.

'Did I tell you that you look sensational in that dress?' he asked, as she bent over.

She felt him slip his hand inside the fabric of the long skirt and reach for the softness of her upper thighs.

'Oh, easy access,' he cooed. 'I likey a lot.'

'Stop it,' she said, slapping his hand away. She snorted the smallest line and turned to face him.

'What?' he said.

But they both knew damn well what. And looking down she saw that he'd dropped his pants and was holding his impressive, throbbing cock in his hand.

'Marcus!' she hissed, both outraged and amused. 'Put it away.'

'Oh, but your old friend is missing you. Come on. Just a quickie. You're mistress of the quickie. I know you want me. I've missed you.'

'Get off me, you idiot,' she said. 'I told you, there's someone else.'

Still not letting go, he buried his face in her neck. 'How can you say that?' he said, lifting her skirt higher and pressing against her.

'Because it's true,' she said, pushing him away.

'So where is he?' he said, shrugging. 'Not here. I don't see him.' He lifted up Savvy's arms, pretending to look.

'Just cut it out, OK?'

'So you're hooked on some new guy? So what? This is us. It's different.'

'I said no,' she told him.

They both froze as they heard footsteps approaching on the other side of the door.

There was a clicking noise, then the squeak of the cubicle door being pushed open.

Their cubicle door.

'What the fuck?' Savvy said, spinning round.

Elodie stood in the doorway. She stared at Savvy. Then her eyes went to the cocaine laid out on the white porcelain. Then back to Marcus, who was still holding his cock in his fist.

Marcus burst into fits of giggles, but Elodie didn't make a sound. She just turned on her heel and marched out of the cloakroom.

'You fucking idiot,' Savvy hissed, shoving Marcus back. 'Now look what you've done.' *How could they have forgotten to lock the door?*

Savvy pulled her skirt down and raced after Elodie. She didn't catch her up until they were on the dance floor.

'El. Please stop,' she implored her, catching hold of her arm.

Elodie's eyes flashed angrily at her. They were wet with tears. 'What you do with your life is your own business. But for fuck's sake, Savvy. *Here?*'

'Elodie, stop it. Calm down. I wasn't doing any-thing—'

'I could see perfectly well what you were doing.'

'It's not what you think—'

'You obviously don't care what I think. Or anyone else for that matter, so just stop pretending.'

Savvy blew out a long, frustrated breath. Elodie was a nightmare when she was like this. She had been this way since they were children. Once she'd made her mind up about something, that was that.

'I'm going home,' Elodie told her. 'I've got a head-ache.'

'Suit yourself,' Savvy said. She wasn't going to justify

her behaviour. Not when Elodie was so clearly in the wrong.

After that, Savvy wasn't in the mood for Marcus's pranks and she told him to leave. And for once, seeing how upset she was, he apologized and did as he was told.

As the coke wore off, she decided to go home herself and cornered her father to say goodbye.

'But you can't go,' Hud told her.

'Why not?'

'Because look who's just arrived.'

Savvy turned and saw what her father meant. Luc Devereaux was standing by the doorway in an immaculate Tom Ford tuxedo.

Even across the crowded dance floor, his eyes picked her out straight away.

And when they did, he smiled.

As usual, however, getting to Luc – and getting him alone – proved extremely difficult. Hud enthusiastically introduced his protégé to the assembled dignitaries and Savvy for once played the part of the dutiful daughter, skirting around the room, always keeping Luc in her peripheral vision.

She switched to spritzers to stay sober, flirting gently with the male politicians whilst charming their wives and girlfriends too. She listened to their boring stories and laughed at their tired jokes. It was all an act, of course, but she knew the part well. She'd had plenty of practice watching her sister playing it for real.

It didn't escape her notice that Luc had been watching

her from across the room as she effortlessly racked up brownie points for La Paris. Oh yes, she thought, I have many strings to my bow, Luc Devereaux. And the perfect corporate hostess is just one . . .

It was the early hours by the time the party finally started to wind down. She spotted Luc heading for the washrooms and made sure she was in the corridor when he came back out.

Even though she'd rehearsed this moment over and over in her mind these last few weeks, Savvy was nervous as hell. This was too important to mess up. *He* was too important. But seducing men was what she did best, she reminded herself. Giving the right signals and pressing the right buttons . . . it was second nature to her. Except that right now all that knowledge suddenly seemed to have deserted her. She stared at him like a tongue-tied teenager, through wide, yearning eyes.

'Ah, Savvy,' he said. 'Are you OK?' he asked, his mouth crinkling into a confused smile.

'Yes, of course.'

'Only you look kind of spaced out.'

When for once I'm not, she thought. Get it together, she told herself. Remember the plan.

'It must be this light,' she said with a shrug, as she linked her arm through his and turned him away from the main function room and towards the service lift.

'Where are we going?' he asked. She could feel his hard muscles through the soft material of his tuxedo. She didn't want to let go.

'Hud wants us to join him for a nightcap,' she said. 'He's upstairs in one of the suites.'

She led him down the corridor, just catching the elevator before it closed. Inside, a maid smiled at her, the button for their floor already lit up.

As the elevator rose, Savvy's nerves multiplied. What if he rejected her? What if he really did want Elodie instead? Or, what if there was someone else, someone she knew nothing about? What if this was a contest she'd already lost?

Infuriatingly, the maid got out on the same floor as them and they still couldn't talk. They followed her in silence down the corridor. With each slow step, Savvy felt her dream fading. This wasn't how it was supposed to have been. It was meant to have been impulsive, fateful, quick. Not awkward and tense like this.

Please let me be right about him, she prayed. Please let him feel the same as me.

It wasn't until Savvy unlocked the suite door and showed Luc inside that he finally spoke.

'There's no one here,' he said, looking round the empty room.

The bed was already turned back. Just as she'd requested, a bottle of iced champagne, two Tiffany flutes and a single red rose were on a silver tray on the bedside table.

Hanging a 'DO NOT DISTURB' sign on the outside handle, Savvy shut the door behind her, sealing them in. 'There's us,' she said.

Now that she'd got him up here, now that there was no turning back, she felt her confidence rise up inside her once more.

'There are people downstairs I still need to speak to,' he continued. But he made no move to leave.

'They can wait.'

Savvy could feel her nipples stiffening, aching to be touched by him.

She let the long green evening gown she was wearing drop to the floor. She stepped out of it and strode towards him in her black suspenders, stockings and strapless bra.

'We can't do this, Savvy,' he said. But he couldn't stop staring at her. She could see the animal lust in his eyes.

'But you want to, don't you, Luc?' she said, reaching him now. Boldly hooking her leg around his, she looked straight into his eyes as she unfastened his bow tie.

'But there's Elodie, your father and . . . we shouldn't.'

He lowered his eyes, as if ashamed, but she put her finger under his chin and made him look at her. She adored his face.

'Tell me you don't want me and I'll back off for ever. And we'll just keep pretending that we're friends.'

Luc said nothing. This time he didn't look away.

'I've wanted you from the first moment I saw you,' she breathed into his ear. 'And you've wanted me, too. I know you have. That's why I sent you all those pictures.'

He pulled back and stared at her then, comprehension dawning.

She saw it then: her gamble had paid off.

Luc grabbed her, picking her up. Then holding the back of her head, his hand clasping her hair, he kissed her, deeply and passionately.

Savvy had fantasized about this moment for so long, but now the reality – the actual sensation of his lips on hers – was more thrilling and exciting than she'd dared to imagine.

He gasped, his tongue finding hers, and he kissed her hungrily again and again . . .

She was so mesmerized, so enveloped by him, she hardly realized that they were on the move, until Luc laid her down on the bed.

'Oh, Savvy, Savvy,' he breathed. He kissed her neck, across her shoulder blades and down to her bra.

She ached for him to pull the material aside, but he didn't. Instead, his lips brushed down over the quivering skin of her belly until he reached her thong. He took in a long, deep breath. Then he grabbed the thin material in his teeth and pulled it down. He lifted up her legs to take her thong off, positioning the backs of her heels on his shoulders.

Then he took her shoes off, flicking them across the room. He bit her toe through the thinnest gauze of her silk stocking. Then sucked her toes, looking at her the whole time. Right into her eyes.

Savvy was lost. She could feel herself trembling. She'd never felt this horny in her life.

Reaching down, he pulled off her stockings one by one. Then starting with her left foot, he kissed all the way up one leg, his tongue making hard circles along the fleshy inside of her thigh. It felt as if he was hardwired into all her erogenous zones. She lay back, her eyes closed, tuning in, gasping as she stretched towards him. She'd never felt exquisite agony like this. As his mouth moved between her legs, she was sure that one flick of his tongue and she'd come.

But he just blew a thin stream of air across her, groaning with desire, as he moved across and down her right leg.

'You are the most beautiful woman I have ever seen,' he breathed.

She felt as if the whole lower half of her body was on fire. She sat up, pulling his waistband towards her, untucking his shirt and ripping at the buttons, pulling it open to reveal his toned, tanned stomach and the line of soft hair between his defined pecs.

She reached up and kissed him, clawing his hair, covering his soft skin with kisses.

Luc undid his belt, letting his trousers fall to the floor. Savvy massaged her hands up him, sliding his shirt from his shoulders, kissing his chest.

Soon he was naked, and she gasped. She was kneeling on the bed now. The taste of him – the way he smelt – Savvy felt as if all of her senses had come alive for the first time.

He slowly, sensuously, stripped her and laid her down. She felt herself trembling uncontrollably as her skin pressed against his.

Then slowly . . . agonizingly, blissfully slowly . . . he was pressing, melting, fusing with her.

They both gasped, suspended, lost in that most delicious of moments, as he slid inside her.

He scooped her into his arms, holding her as close as possible. It was as if every nerve ending was connected to him.

He stroked her hair out of her face and looked into her eyes. He smiled, his eyes soft as he kissed her again, more gently this time, his tongue searching out hers. He let out a long, satisfied groan as if kissing her was the most delicious thing he'd ever done.

'I was hoping it was you,' he whispered. 'Do you have any idea how much those pictures turned me on?'

'Oh Luc, Luc,' she breathed, as they started moving together in perfect rhythm, rolling in the tangled sheets, as if they were both searching for the most contact they could make.

'We can't stop,' he breathed, kissing her ear, sucking her earlobe. 'We can't ever stop.'

And she realized that he was as lost in her as she was in him.

CHAPTER TWENTY-FOUR

Savvy blushed, covering her eyes.

'Don't be embarrassed,' Red said gently. 'It's better that you tell it like it was.'

Savvy swallowed hard. She'd been so caught up remembering that amazing night with Luc, she'd forgotten how this must all be sounding to Red. Was it weird for him, talking about sex, when he was a recovering sex addict? She thought about asking him, but then she changed her mind. Red was so easy to talk to and she felt good unburdening herself. And it was easy. In this wonderful place with just them and the open sky, it felt like the most natural thing in the world to talk like this.

'So . . . passion on a grand scale, by the sound of it,' he prompted.

'I guess it was. Have you ever had sex that's so

powerful, it makes you feel as if your whole life has changed?' she asked him.

Red pulled at a long blade of grass. 'No, not really. Oh, don't get me wrong – I've had plenty of sex. But I guess that was always my problem; quantity, not quality. And I've had great sex sometimes when I've been high, but that doesn't really count.'

He shrugged bashfully and Savvy couldn't help wondering what he must have been like in his wild days. In another life, would their paths have crossed? she wondered. Yet he was different now. Serene and at peace. She watched him stretch out his long, lean legs. Then leaning up on one elbow, he chewed on the piece of grass.

'So, come on. What happened with this grand love affair?'

Savvy remembered now how she'd woken up in Luc's arms, their limbs wrapped around each other, as if their bodies fitted perfectly. She snuggled her head on to his chest, hearing his heartbeat and his soft breathing. She smiled, loving the way her body felt against his.

Of course, Savvy knew that Elodie would freak when she found out. But in the thin dawn light, she also knew that she'd never felt this content. This wasn't a conquest, or a one-night stand. This was the start of something. Something amazing.

Savvy didn't want to be a bad person, or to upset her sister, but as of this morning everything was different. The future she'd dreamed of for so long had just arrived. She and Luc were together. And they really were in love. Elodie would just have to understand.

'I'll tell her,' Savvy offered, watching Luc as he got dressed.

'Who?'

'Elodie, of course,' Savvy said, confused he'd even had to ask. Surely he'd already sussed that Elodie had a thing for him too?

'No, it's better if I do,' he said, with a sigh.

Savvy stood up on the bed behind him, wrapping her naked body around his. She looked at them in the mirror opposite. A perfect knot, she thought. Was this what they'd look like, their heads side by side like this, in their wedding photos? Yes, Savannah Devereaux had quite a ring to it.

'Oh, Savvy, what am I going to do?' Luc said, suddenly looking upset. 'I feel so guilty. I feel like I've given Elodie false hope. Like I've led her on.'

'Why?' Savvy asked. 'Nothing's happened between you two, has it? Nothing physical, I mean?' *Nothing emotional*, she wanted to ask. But she didn't dare.

'No,' Luc said. 'No,' he repeated, shaking his head. 'Nothing like that, but we have, you know, become friends.'

Savvy grinned, oozing with relief. So he really was hers then. Just hers.

'And you can stay friends,' she said, kissing his neck. 'She's my sister. I'm delighted you two get on.'

Luc would be the only boyfriend Elodie would ever have deemed suitable, she almost told him, but she didn't. Instead, she pressed her tongue against his salty skin. God, he tasted great.

239

Yes, she thought, she could afford to be magnanimous where Elodie was concerned. And it touched her too, that Luc was such a gentleman. The fact that he cared about Elodie's feelings made him even more special.

'Don't worry about El. She'll get over it,' she said.

'You really think everything will work out?'

'I know it will,' she said. And she meant it. She'd do everything in her power to make it so.

Savvy waited all that day for Luc to call and all day she couldn't stop smiling. When the phone rang and it was Elodie, she sat down, prepared to be contrite. She'd planned out what she was going to say. That she and Luc *had* to be together. They were born to be together. Elodie wouldn't be able to argue with that. She hoped she'd be happy for them too. That would make it even more perfect.

But rather than sounding cross or left out, as Savvy had been expecting, Elodie sounded ecstatic.

This was the best day of her life, she told Savvy breathlessly. Luc had been to see her this morning. Obviously, he'd been exhausted, having flown in from New York and straight to work at the party. But he hadn't been able to wait to see her.

'What did he say?' Savvy asked, thrilled that Elodie had responded so positively to her news.

'That . . . well . . . that he's been doing a lot of thinking. And . . .'

'And . . . ?' Savvy prompted, biting her smile back, waiting for Elodie's gushing congratulations.

'And he says he wants to take our relationship further.'

Savvy gripped the phone. 'What?' she managed, but she could barely speak. 'What did you say?'

'Luc asked me out.'

'*You?*'

'Yes, Sav. He wants us to be together properly. Him and me. Boyfriend and girlfriend.'

'But—'

'*And*, I've got to tell you – oh my God! He is just the most amazing kisser. Like . . . ever,' Elodie went on. 'I just can't believe it, Sav. I'm over the moon. Like on a cloud. I mean, isn't he just such a total dream? And such a gentleman. He even held my hand when I rang Daddy to tell him the good news.'

Red stared at Savvy. She could tell that he was trying to work it out. How Luc could have gone straight from the night Savvy had just described to asking Elodie out.

He whistled, stunned by Savvy's story. 'Let me guess,' he said. 'Elodie had told Luc about what she thought she'd seen you and your friend – what was his name? Malcolm? doing . . .'

'Marcus, yeah.'

'That was a bit harsh of her, wasn't it?'

Savvy sighed, staring at the butterflies skimming over the grass. She picked a lazy blade and watched the drops of warm dew fall from it like tears.

'At the time, sure, I was livid,' she said. 'But looking back, I doubt she did it maliciously at all. El just isn't, *wasn't* like that . . .' she corrected herself. 'To her it was

241

just a bit of naughty gossip . . . at worst, something she'd mention to make her own halo shine that bit brighter by comparison. And you've got to remember, she was completely in the dark about me and Luc.'

'But Luc believed her. That you and this Marcus guy had been . . .'

Savvy nodded sadly. She could still feel all the bitterness, as real as if it had happened yesterday. 'The one time I did get to speak to Luc on my own, he told me I was a slut and a liar who'd been playing some messed-up power game with him.'

'How did you respond to that?'

'With the truth, of course. I told him he'd got it all wrong. That I loved him. That he didn't love Elodie and never would. He was making a mistake. That he was dragging Elodie into it, just to get back at me.'

'How did he react?'

'He told me to go to hell. He told me I was the mistake. And that if I tried to mess things up between him and Elodie, he'd show her the photos of me. The ones I'd sent him. And he'd show Hud as well . . . if that was what it took. He'd let everyone know what a conniving sicko I was.'

Red's eyes were bright blue in the morning light. 'What did you do?'

'I backed off, of course. What else *could* I do? I'd lost him. And that should have been it, I suppose. But it wasn't. Because I really was in love with him. No matter how vile he'd been to me . . . no matter what he thought of me . . . I still wanted him back. And hearing about him . . . about him and Elodie. And worse . . . *seeing* them together. It broke my heart. *He* broke my heart.'

'You didn't tell anyone? What about your friends?'

Savvy thought about Paige and how she'd longed to confide in her. But by then, Paige had bought into Luc's golden boy image. And she was too involved in her job at La Paris to notice that anything was wrong with Savvy. And Hud? Well, Hud was over the moon that Elodie had found her handsome prince. A prince who'd one day become family. Someone he could control for now, but who might one day take over the reins.

'No,' she said. 'You're the first person I've told.'

Red shook his head. He sat cross-legged in front of her, eager to know more. 'So you were hurt. I get that. But what about all the anger? The sense of injustice? How did you cope?'

Savvy hugged her knees. 'I reinvented myself as the fun party girl,' she said with a bitter smile. 'I drowned all my feelings with drink. I drugged the anger with pills and powders. Until . . .'

'Until what?'

Savvy fought back the tears welling in her eyes. 'Until Elodie told me that they were getting married,' Savvy said. 'And everything I'd tried to bury . . . all that anger . . . all that pain came bubbling up.'

Her tears were flowing freely now. Looking down, she saw that Red had taken her hand.

'That's when I told her about me and Luc . . . because I wanted her to know the truth. And I wanted him to pay . . .' Savvy scrunched her eyes tight, willing it never to have happened. 'And that's when she fell.'

'That was a brave thing to do. To tell her.'

243

'No,' Savvy said, sniffing loudly. 'It was stupid. I should have kept my mouth shut. If I'd kept my mouth shut, she'd still be alive.'

She'd told Red everything now, apart from the fact that she and Elodie had actually fought. It was the closest she'd got to telling anyone the truth about what had really happened that night. She'd admitted more than she'd done to her father, or Paige, or the cops.

'And how do you feel about Luc now?' Red asked.

Savvy thought for a moment. 'As if everything I tried to block out is all still there. And just as raw as ever. It feels as if he's robbed me. Of everything. My self-respect . . . my sister . . . for a long time, even myself.'

'Oh, no,' Red said. 'Trust me, Savannah Hudson is still very much here.'

'So what do you think I should do now?' she asked.

'Only you can make that decision.'

'That's what a counsellor would say . . .'

He blushed, caught out. 'I am a counsellor.'

'What about a friend?'

A seagull soared overhead, mewing. Red stared up at it for a moment. Were they friends? Savvy wondered. Or was this all part of her therapy? It suddenly felt terribly important it was the first.

'You talk about love,' he eventually said, still not looking at her. 'But is that what love is? Wanting someone? The way you wanted Luc?' He did look at her now. 'Some people might say that was just obsession.'

Anger swelled inside Savvy. The old indignation. The same fire that had burned whenever she'd seen Luc and Elodie together.

'No,' she said, 'what I felt was love.'

Because if it hadn't been love, if it hadn't been real, then Elodie . . . Elodie would have died for nothing. Luc might never have actually said the words to her, told her that he loved her. But Savvy knew that he had.

'So my advice to you as a *friend*,' Red said, 'would be to let it go. Put it all behind you. And move on.'

'And if I can't?'

'Then one day you're going to look back at your life and realize that you never really lived at all.'

CHAPTER TWENTY-FIVE

Under the glare of the bright neon signs, the night market in Temple Street in Hong Kong was buzzing. Lois wandered through the crowd, taking in the noise of the traders and the jostling hubbub of locals and tourists. The market stalls were endless, crammed with an astonishing array of goods as far as the eye could see: tacky Mao memorabilia, statues, costume jewellery and DVDs, knock-off designer T-shirts and perfumes.

It was so strange to feel foreign and yet look local. She was amazed by the way in which the fortune tellers and palm readers called out to her in Cantonese. It made her feel weirdly displaced, yet thrilled too. Because in a crazy way, this did feel like part of her heritage. As if she were coming home.

The pace was so frenetic and everything seemed to be hurtling forward to the future so rapidly that there was no choice but to get on board and enjoy the ride.

And yet there were moments of sheer peace, too. She'd walked through the park this morning and seen a group of old men and women doing t'ai chi in the early sunlight. She'd been mesmerized by the silent harmony of the scene, stopping to catch a feather that floated past in the haze.

Who'd have thought it? she considered, an amused smile on her face. Who'd have thought that Lois Chan, the little girl who'd grown up in San Francisco watching *Sesame Street*, would be walking along the very streets her grandmother used to talk about?

And not just as a tourist either. She had a purpose. In the midst of all this noise and colour, her mind whirled. In just two days' time she'd be meeting Roberto Enzo to discuss her future. Lois had a weekend stretching out before her to wonder exactly what his intention was. He'd hinted at a special task. But what? That's what she wanted to know. And *where*? Because Jai Shijai's talk of Shangri-La still weighed heavy on her mind. She was itching to know if that was where her future really lay.

Since the poker game at Jai Shijai's island, Roberto had been preoccupied with a whole series of clandestine business meetings both in the States and here in Hong Kong. Lois had only spoken to him on the phone and he'd dodged her conversation-openers about the future of the business.

But here she was now. Why else would he have insisted on meeting her out here in Hong Kong, the commercial gateway between East and West? He must have decided to take her into his confidence at last. Excitement and apprehension tingled over what the weekend might bring, as she continued to weave her way through the stalls.

She found herself distracted once more by the trinkets on show. She stopped at a jewellery stand, where a pretty pair of silver earrings had caught her eye. Under the watchful gaze of the stall owner, she picked them up and studied them. They'd be perfect for Cara. They were pretty and sparkling, just like her.

Lois bought them. She didn't even bother to haggle, even though she knew it would have horrified her mother and grandmother.

But Lois didn't care. She wanted them quickly, because she'd had an idea. Impulsively, she pulled out her phone and asked the store owner to hold them up, which the woman did with a shy smile.

Lois took a photo with her phone and attached a message: *I wish you were here. Keep an eye on the post. I'm sending these back for you. Love Mom.*

Since their trip to San Francisco, Lois felt that the ice had finally been broken between them. Cara had started talking to her. Hesitantly at first, but each week she'd shared a little more, until Lois realized that she'd fallen into an unfamiliar role as Cara's confidante. It was as delightful as it was hard. Because her instinct was to immediately muscle in on the classroom politics Cara told her about, or to give stern warnings about the flaky best friend, or to rail against Mary-Sue's strict rules. But instead Lois had learned to listen. And at this rate the two of them might become – God, Lois could barely contain her excitement, even at the thought of it – something close to friends.

And it had been Cara herself who'd put Lois's mind at rest about this trip to Hong Kong. She'd spent so long tying herself up in knots about how Cara would feel about her being abroad, but her daughter was surprisingly pragmatic, telling Lois how many of her friends' parents had to travel for work. It was no big deal. Not so long as they got to text and phone. It was her job, Cara pointed out to Lois. She had no choice. There was no point in feeling guilty, certainly not on Cara's behalf. Lois had felt humbled and amazed at how wise her child had become.

Now, with the earrings safely tucked away in her pocket, she felt satisfied that Cara would know she was thinking of her.

Realizing that she was hungry, Lois made a beeline for one of the busiest stalls, ducking under the awning, into a hiss of wok steam and chattering diners and loud pop music blaring from the strung-up radio. She ordered shrimp noodles and squeezed on to the stool at the last remaining plastic table. The man sitting next to her had two live cockerels in a cage by his feet and they fluttered noisily. He nodded and smiled at her with a toothless grin.

Soon, she had a plate of steaming noodles in front of her, which smelt delicious. She took the paper napkin and spread it out over her lap as she snapped apart her chopsticks. But just as she was about to taste her first mouthful, she felt the buzz of her cell phone in her pocket. She checked the screen but didn't recognize the number. She smiled. It must be Cara. Her own phone must have run out of credit, so she'd borrowed a friend's.

But it was a man's voice which came on the line and said, 'Hello, Lois.'

'Hello?'

'It's Aidan. Aidan Bailey.'

Unexpectedly, Lois felt blood rushing to her cheeks as she remembered the kiss at the top of the pagoda. 'Aidan,' she said, smiling. 'My God. How are *you*?'

'Fine. Well, hungry, actually. And I was just wondering whether you wanted to join me for something more exciting than those shrimp noodles?'

How the hell?

Lois lowered her phone and swivelled round. Aidan was standing in the alley next to the food stall. He shrugged as she looked at him and smiled.

And that's when it happened. She felt as if she'd just tipped over the top of a roller-coaster. Like a love-struck teenager, she felt her palms sweating and her heart thumping.

It was impossible. But he was here. Aidan Bailey was here.

And he was . . . Christ, she'd forgotten . . . he was *gorgeous*.

His smile. She'd forgotten how infectious it was. How his eyes seemed to beckon her to forget everything.

Don't be crazy, she told herself. You're just surprised, that's all.

And yet she was grinning like a cat. And she couldn't take her eyes away from his.

He was wearing khaki trousers and a T-shirt and trendy short-sleeved shirt. He folded up his phone and dropped it into his top pocket, before shooting her a grin with a theatrical bow.

Pull yourself together, she told herself, placing her chopsticks on her plate. She dabbed her mouth with her napkin, unable to hide how happy she felt to see his face.

Unfinished business. That was the phrase that sprang to mind. Or should that be unfinished *pleasure*? Because they had crossed a line, hadn't they? When they'd kissed?

Feeling her knees shaking, she walked towards him. They met, squeezed in together by people. He kissed her quickly on the cheek and put his arm around her shoulder, to stop her getting knocked by a man with two buckets hanging from a yoke across his shoulders. His touch felt warm and reassuring. She stared at his chest, thinking how nice it would be to be enfolded in a hug. She'd forgotten how good he smelt.

She smiled back at him, thinking how tanned and healthy he looked. And altogether too clean for the marketplace. Amongst all the Asian faces he looked extraordinary, with his golden skin and blond hair.

'Hey,' she said. 'Well, this is a nice surprise.'

She put her head on one side, confused. Even though she knew Aidan spent a lot of time here in the Far East, this was way too much of a coincidence. Even supposing Aidan was in Hong Kong anyway and had fancied a stroll around the night market, this was still one of the most crowded places she'd ever been.

Did he really expect her to think he'd simply wandered past and had somehow managed to pluck her face out of the crowd?

Again she tried not to laugh. Because, crazily, the word *destiny* had just popped up in her mind again.

But this was nothing to do with destiny, she told herself straight away. More like *technology*. The Dark Arts. Black Ops. Call it what you want, the fact remained: Aidan Bailey must have used some gizmo to track her phone over the GPS network.

Impressive, Lois thought. Illegal. Cool . . . but flattering, too. Or maybe stalker-ish? The jury was still out on that one.

'So how are they?' he asked.

'What?'

'The noodles,' he said, nodding behind her to her plate. She'd been so wrapped up in the shock of seeing him, she'd entirely forgotten her food.

She smiled. 'Oh, those? They're good. In fact, I've been craving them all day. Why don't you join me?'

Aidan walked with her over to the small plastic table, grabbed a spare stool and chopsticks from a table nearby and sat opposite.

'Help yourself,' she said. 'There's far too much here for me anyway.'

Lois continued digging into the noodles.

'Go ahead,' she said, amused that she was suddenly sharing her dinner with him. But she was interested to see how he'd react. The guy was a multi-millionaire.

Would he really enjoy slumming it with the locals, like she did? But somehow she knew he would. Somehow Aidan seemed to fit in anywhere.

'I take it back. These are great,' he said, as he savoured his first mouthful. 'But I'm putting extra chilli sauce on my side.'

Lois laughed, amused that they'd slipped into such easy familiarity. As if they ate together every day. 'You can't beat street food in my opinion. I'd rather eat here than some stuffy restaurant.'

Aidan looked at his watch. 'Maybe I should cancel my booking at Lung King Heen, then.'

Lois had been in Hong Kong for barely twenty-four hours, but she'd picked up enough to know that Lung King Heen at the Four Seasons Hotel was the only Michelin three-star restaurant in Hong Kong, as well as the first and only Michelin three-star Chinese restaurant in the world.

She blushed. Was Aidan joking? He might as well be, because she'd already claimed that she preferred noodles like this to a stuffy restaurant, so she'd just have to front it out.

To her relief, Aidan swiftly moved the conversation on. She soon found out that he'd just returned from a stint in the Middle East. She didn't push for details, but she could tell from the way he spoke that the last few weeks had been hard and he didn't want to talk about them.

'And what about you, Lois?' he asked, gazing intently at her. His eyes sparkled. 'What are you doing here in Hong Kong?'

Lois shrugged. That was a question she longed to find out the answer to herself. She told him how she was going to meet Roberto, but she didn't yet know why.

'I'm sure it will all become clear,' Aidan said, as if he knew something that she didn't. But that was impossible, she told herself, beating the thought away.

'Do you fancy going for a drink? I know a great bar near here,' he said, as they finished up the last of the noodles.

His offer was so genuine and Lois was enjoying his company so much and was still itching to know how he'd engineered their meeting that – forgetting her pledge to go directly back to the hotel to sleep – she agreed.

CHAPTER TWENTY-SIX

In his office at Peace River Lodge, Dr Max Savage – or Max, as Savvy now knew him – scribbled on the form in front of him. Then he laid his glasses on top of it and swivelled his chair to face her.

After the two months they'd spent getting to know one another, Savvy could read his expressions pretty well and she saw now a bittersweet mixture of sorrow and affection. How high must she have been to fall for his ruse of being an air steward? Savvy thought incredulously.

The thought of Max as a flight attendant was ludicrous. He was far too old and far too unconventional. He had a deep tan and thinning blond hair. Today, he wore one of his customarily loud jungle-print shirts and jeans with his sandals.

'So, that's it,' he said.

Surrounding him on the walls were lots of

photographs and letters from ex-inmates – or patients, as Savvy had finally come to acknowledge them to be – of Peace River and they flapped in the breeze thrown down from the overhead fan, like a distant round of applause.

'You really mean it? I'm good to go?' Savvy asked, squeezing her hands between her knees. She couldn't believe he was telling her this. With such certainty. How did he know she was well enough to leave?

Sure, she'd made a start on coming to terms with why she'd got so messed up to begin with. Survivor guilt over her mother and sister – along with a whole load of therapy-speak labels, which basically added up to a bad case of low self-esteem and responsibility avoidance, she'd been told. But, as far as she was concerned, she was way too wobbly to go back to the real world.

She still sometimes woke up screaming or weeping after yet another nightmare about Elodie falling. Or woke up, her heart pounding, having dreamed she'd started doing coke all over again.

Control. Sure, she had it now. But it could just as easily slip through her hands like sand. All she knew for certain was that she sure as hell didn't want her old life back. She dreaded it. Feared it.

And now that she was being told she could go home, she realized how much she desperately wanted to stay.

Was it money? Was Dr Savage making her leave because of that?

'You know, if it's a question of finance, I can always find a way to pay for myself and—'

Max held up his hand to stop her. 'Savvy, you wouldn't be the first and you certainly won't be the last person who wants to stay on here. But this isn't a holiday camp. The best thing for you is to get back to your life. Sooner rather than later. From what I've seen and what we've talked through, you've got all the tools you need to cope.'

'But—'

'Listen.' His normally jovial face had turned serious. 'Talking about one's emotions in a safe, nurturing environment like this is very comforting. Deliberately so. But it's not real. And if you become too dependent on the kind of connections you have with certain people here, then, in my opinion, you are in danger of transferring your addictive behaviour.'

Savvy blushed. Did he mean Red? Was he implying that she'd somehow crossed a patient–carer boundary? Just because they got on so well together?

Because Red had been amazing. It had been Red more than anyone – more even than Dr Savage with his qualifications and years of experience – who'd helped her through. She felt a debt of gratitude to him that she could hardly describe.

But was she confusing this emotion – this gratitude – for something more? Was that what Max was saying?

Of course it was possible. But what if she wasn't confusing anything? What if her feelings for Red were nothing to do with her therapy, or this place? What if they were real?

This connection . . . this bond . . . this feeling that they fitted together . . . and yes, incredible physical

attraction – well, that all certainly felt real to Savvy.
Real enough that she hadn't dared admit it to Red.

She'd pictured them together, as if they were in
a movie. In the desert somewhere. In a beaten-up
combi van covered in stickers. Taking it slow. Living
the dream. Yes, she'd fantasized about all those places
she'd never seen – all those places Red had told her she
must see – well, he could take her to them. India, South
America . . . and his beloved Scotland.

'I've been in contact with your friend . . .' Dr Savage
continued, interrupting her thoughts. He picked up his
glasses again and looked at some notes. 'Paige Logan.
She's arranged a flight to Miami. It leaves in three
hours and you're to be on it. Paige says she'll meet you
in the usual place as soon as you arrive.'

Today?

Savvy was reeling at the terrifying solidity and sud-
denness of the arrangement.

Wasn't there some kind of leaving process to go
through? It felt like a horrible ejection. One she'd had
no time to prepare for.

And Paige? Even the thought of Paige made things
feel even more precarious. First there'd be Paige. Then
Vegas . . . her father . . . Luc Devereaux . . .

Paige was from her old life. Things were different
now. She was different now.

But it wasn't her old life.

This second realization hit her just as hard as the
first. It was her *actual* life. The life she had to face. The
life in which she had so many apologies to make and
bridges to build.

And a score to settle.

'You'll be fine,' Max said, with a reassuring smile. 'You're a survivor, Savvy. You might have had a few knocks, but you're much stronger than you know. I saw that in you from the beginning. You're different to most people I see. People who are actually broken. You were never broken, just wounded. It's time to start marching again.'

Savvy nodded, looking at her hands. She felt tears pricking her eyes.

'It's time to pack up and say your goodbyes.'

That was Peace River Lodge, she thought, as she stood up and hugged Max. Tough love. She should never have expected anything more.

CHAPTER TWENTY-SEVEN

Lois had envisaged an upmarket cocktail bar, but the place Aidan took her to was like an old pub, with scruffy wooden tables and a scuffed floor, and cigarette cards for decorations. There were pool tables at the back and an old jukebox lit up and playing fifties rock 'n' roll. The place had a cheerful happy-go-lucky atmosphere and Lois immediately liked it.

The barman greeted Aidan like a long-lost friend. It wasn't long before their drinks were followed by whisky chasers. Soon all Lois's resolve to leave and go back to the hotel to sleep was forgotten.

But the best part was that Aidan was so easy to talk to and the more whisky she drank, the easier it became. Before long, she found herself telling him about her trip to San Francisco with Cara and her family situation. And as the evening wore on, she found herself telling him other stuff too. About her life at the Enzo Vegas.

'I still don't understand how a nice cop like you ended up in such a nasty industry.'

Lois laughed. 'It's not all nasty. But it does need people like me to balance it out.'

Aidan still didn't look convinced. 'You've never been tempted to gamble yourself?'

Lois took a sip of her drink and sighed. 'No. Never. My father was a gambling addict. It wrecked his life. My mother's . . . our family's life . . .' She trailed off, amazed that she'd told him something so personal.

'I'm sorry,' Aidan said. 'But I still don't understand. I'd have thought that going through an experience like that would've put you off casinos for life?'

'You and my mother both. But I don't see it like that. I think this industry needs policing properly. It makes me feel good to know that on my watch there's no intimidation, humiliation, or the kind of hounding from loan sharks that finished my dad. I keep it safe and fair for the little guy. I show the punters the door when their credit runs out, even comp them a car to the airport. I have the power to stop their adrenalin ride long before they sell their homes and the shirts from their own backs.'

Aidan raised his glass to her, impressed.

'Put it like that . . . and I can see why Roberto Enzo is so proud of you.'

Lois smiled and looked at him curiously. 'Proud?' How would Aidan know that Roberto was proud of her?

'I mean he must be, right? Otherwise he wouldn't have sent you to oversee Jai's game.'

Lois shrugged and took a sip of her whisky. 'I guess. Roberto calls me his white knight. Keeping his casino clean in a dirty city.'

'That's good.'

'And that's why I hated all the media attention after the attempt on Senator Fernandez's life. I was only doing my job.'

Aidan scratched the side of his face. He looked embarrassed.

'Seriously. I was mortified that Zak had heard of me,' she continued. 'I didn't want either of you to have a preconceived idea of me. And . . . well, I'm sorry. I'm sorry again that I lied about it.'

'No . . . no, it wasn't just that you'd lied to me. That's not why I reacted like I did.'

'It wasn't?'

Aidan sighed. 'It's just that someone I loved very much once died of a gunshot wound. Just like yours. And seeing you like that . . . well, it brought it all crashing back. All the hatred I felt . . . at myself . . . for it having been her, not me . . .'

He trailed off.

'I'm sorry,' Lois said.

'No, let me explain,' he said. 'I'm not very good at talking about this stuff, but I want to tell you how it is. You see, I married my wife young. We were infatuated. But once that burnt out, we had very little in common. I thought that was it. That I wouldn't ever fall. But then I did.'

'For the girl who got shot?'

He nodded. 'Her name was Becky. She worked

with me in the Middle East. She died in my arms.'

'I'm so sorry.'

'It was a long time ago. Seven years.'

Lois thought of Miki. 'Things like that never go away,' she said.

'I got drunk. I told my wife everything.'

'And she didn't take it well?'

'No. She took me to the cleaners.' He sighed. 'And she took Zak, of course.'

'I know the feeling.'

'The worst,' they both said. The fact they'd said it in perfect unison made them both smile.

'Enough of the past,' he said. 'We should think about the future.'

He reached into his pocket and pulled out a coin.

'Heads or tails?' he asked.

'Heads,' she said, automatically.

Aidan raised his eyebrows. His eyes were amused, as if he'd caught her out. 'You're sure now?'

'Yes,' she laughed. 'I don't understand?'

He flipped the coin, but as soon as it landed he covered it with his hand.

'Fun, huh?' he said, taking a look, shielding it from her. 'I know you're not a gambling girl, but I bet you're itching to know what it is?'

She was. 'So tell me. Did I win?'

He shook his head. 'Ah-ah. Not so easy. Best of three.'

Again, he flipped the coin. Once again it landed. He covered it with a flourish, then peered again and pulled a face.

Lois suddenly realized that she'd forgotten about the coin and was staring at his craggy tanned face and greying blond curls. She blushed as she watched him flip the coin the last time.

'Ah,' Aidan said, satisfied. He was looking at her and his eyes had a soft smile in them.

'What?' she asked. 'What is it?'

He turned the coin over. It was tails. 'You lose. Which means I get to choose,' he said.

'But that's not fair. I didn't see the other two times. It might have been heads. Anyway, choose what?'

He smiled. 'Choose where we're going next, of course,' he said. 'I thought that was obvious.'

She stared at him with frustration and amusement. 'And where exactly are we going next?'

'Ah, that'd be telling.' Returning the coin to his pocket, he signalled to the waiter for the bill.

'So tell,' she said.

'Not a chance,' Aidan said. 'It would ruin the surprise.'

CHAPTER TWENTY-EIGHT

Red was waiting for Savvy on the veranda of her cottage. She felt so relieved to finally find him. She'd been searching for him everywhere in all their usual haunts. He stood up quickly and from his expression she saw that he knew that Dr Savage had told her it was time to leave. He was dressed differently, in long trousers and a shirt. As if he were about to lead a safari expedition. He looked nervous.

'Hey,' she said.

'How did it go?'

'Max is throwing me out.'

Red nodded. 'I know. You OK with that?'

'Not really.'

They stared at each other. She felt like she had done when she'd first seen him – as if she could drown in his amazing wolf-like eyes. Only it was worse than that. Because now she knew the man behind them.

She loved them right as they were now: so soft and knowing and forgiving that it brought tears to her eyes.

'What's the matter?' he asked, stepping towards her.

'It's just . . . you've done so much for me,' she said. 'I really don't know how to say thank you.'

'You can repay me by staying clean when you get out of here. And by having a fabulous future. By putting the past to rest.'

She didn't like his tone. He was making this all sound so final. Her fantasy of travelling with him seemed to be disappearing like a mirage.

She felt as if he was letting her go. Just like Max had done. She felt like screaming for him to hold on to her. How did he know she'd land on solid ground? How did he know that she wouldn't just go on falling, back and back?

'Why don't you come with me?' she said quickly, before she lost her nerve. She no longer cared about what Max thought of her feelings for Red. Here, close to him, she knew they were genuine. She reached out to him.

Red took a deep breath. But his arms stayed by his side.

'What? It's against the rules?' she said, her tone making it perfectly clear how stupid that particular argument was now. 'There can't be any rules. Not now. Now that they say I'm better—'

'It's not that,' Red said.

'Then what?'

His eyes bored into hers and she knew in an instant that what she'd suspected all along was true. *He did feel something for her too.* It wasn't her imagination. This was something powerful and real. So why wouldn't he give in to it? Why wouldn't he admit that he cared?

He lowered his eyes from hers. He was putting up the counsellor barrier once more.

'Tell me,' she implored.

'You want the truth?'

She nodded. 'We're friends, aren't we?' But even as she said it, she knew how desperately she wanted them to be so much more.

'The truth is that I can't tell whether this is old behaviour,' he said. He looked down, almost as if he were ashamed for saying it.

She recoiled, shocked. 'It's not, I—'

'Let me finish, Savvy,' he said, gently stopping her. 'I don't mean just you,' he said. 'I mean me. When I look at you . . . when I think about you . . . I get scared it's the bad old me clawing its way back out again . . . trying to reduce me to nothing but a mass of compulsions.'

'But what you're feeling might be real,' Savvy said. 'Isn't it just possible that it's *not* that complicated? That we're not different to a thousand people who meet every minute of every day . . . people who like each other . . . who want to be together? Normal people, Red. Like you and me.'

'But that's it. Don't you see? I'm not sure I *am* normal yet. On a conscious level, yes, of course I think I am. But deep down? I don't know.'

'Red, I don't care if you're normal or not,' Savvy said. 'I like *all* of you. Even the bad bits.'

'I can't risk it, Savvy. I'm sorry, but I can't. Not with you. And until I know for sure that I'm well, then I can't possibly know that what I'm feeling for you is real.'

He looked so sad when he said this, but his eyes blazed with determination.

She was aching so hard with longing that it hurt. But she knew it was impossible – and wrong – to try to persuade him. Her time here had taught her that. *He* had taught her that.

Savvy felt her eyes welling with tears. She'd opened up to him like no one else. She'd never had this kind of connection with anybody. Ever.

But now he was saying goodbye.

'Oh, Savannah.' This time he did reach out to her. He cupped her face in his hand and stared deeply, unflinchingly, into her eyes. 'My lovely, beautiful Sav. We mustn't undo everything we've worked for.'

Lovely. Beautiful. The words echoed like church bells through her mind.

'But—'

'You're going back to your life,' he said. 'And I'm leaving too. Today. Now. On the boat.'

'What?'

He stepped back from her then. She felt the memory of his hands on her face, like a burn.

He nodded to the wall and she saw that leaning up against the veranda table was his rucksack, his yoga mat strapped to the bottom of it.

'But where?'

'I don't know yet. I'm not sure that it matters where exactly. Just that I go. And keep going until I'm sure I'm really ready to settle down in one place.'

'So this is it?' she said. She let out an aghast laugh. It – they – couldn't just end here . . . could they?

'You need to find some answers,' Red said, regaining his composure and taking on his counsellor tone of voice again. 'You need to follow your heart. Learn who you are. And so do I. And we've both got to go it alone. Here. I want you to wear this,' he said, pulling a friendship bracelet from his shorts pocket. He put it around her wrist and knotted it. For all the amazing jewels Savvy had ever worn, this seemed more precious than everything put together. 'So you remember our time here. And that I'm always with you in spirit.'

'What am I going to do?' she asked. An emptiness she hadn't felt in weeks, she now felt in her bones.

'Do what you have to do,' he said. 'You're so much stronger than you think you are.'

'Am I?'

He smiled gently at her. 'Of course you are. Now do something for me.'

'What?' she said.

'Make a wish.'

Savvy closed her eyes. She wished that Red would take back everything and hold her in his arms and promise to look after her for ever. But when she opened her eyes, he was walking away from her.

He didn't look back and she didn't call him back.

As Red disappeared out of sight, she wrapped her

arms around herself, listening to the noise of the wildlife and the distant hiss of the sea. She'd been cut adrift.
But in another sense, she knew that he'd set her free. To
perish or survive. To wilt or grow. The choice was hers.
He'd given her that.

And now the future beckoned. And home . . .
wherever that might turn out to be.

She thought of the rough and tumble of city life
and all the things she loved about it. The airports and
shops and restaurants. The constant noises, smells and
colours and the messy edges that made it real. And the
people waiting for her there.

Max was right. And so was Red. She could do this.
On her own. Her way.

She could stay strong. She *would* stay strong.

This was the start of the rest of her life.

It was time to live again.

CHAPTER TWENTY-NINE

Aidan's mystery destination turned out to be right across the city. The journey took nearly an hour, partly due to the bicycle rickshaw that Aidan insisted every first-time tourist should try, but also because he kept getting the poor guy on the pedals to stop so that he could point out the sights.

Next came a water taxi, all diesel stink and growl, that carried them across the harbour to the peninsula.

It was gone midnight by the time they were back on dry land and Aidan was leading her through the brightly lit maze of harbour streets. Lois knew she should really turn round and take her tired bones back to her hotel, but she was having too much fun.

They hadn't stopped talking since they'd left the pub. And not about anything serious this time. Just fun stuff. Movies, books they'd both read, places they'd been.

Lois felt like pinching herself. How had she let Aidan sweep her off like this? She hardly knew the guy and yet here she was on another adventure with him.

At the landing jetty, Aidan took her hand as they crossed the road, although there wasn't much traffic. She hurried along beside him, amused that he hadn't let her hand go.

He took her through a green iron gate into a small, well-kept park. She tried to keep her footing as they stumbled in the dark past a temple.

'What is this place?' she asked. Despite being so near the city, she could hear the wind rustling through the trees and the wind chimes tinkling in the temple eaves.

'Come on, this way.'

Aidan led her through a gate in the railings and Lois saw that they were at the water's edge. Hong Kong's brilliantly lit skyline stretched up into the black sky across the bay, a never-sleeping cathedral of commerce. No wonder people called it the New York of the East.

'Incredible,' Lois sighed.

'Isn't she? I bought her from a naval architect.'

She? Lois turned to Aidan, only to see him gazing proudly at a nineteenth-century wooden barge, moored to their right, lit up by a string of brightly coloured paper lanterns swaying in the breeze.

He smiled. 'Like to take a look?

What did *that* mean? Did that mean he thought she was staying the night? With him? Here on the boat?

Don't jump to conclusions, she told herself. She didn't

have to do anything she didn't want to. She could call a taxi and get back to her hotel whenever she wanted.

'Sure,' she said.

He stepped down on to the stern of the boat and reached out to her. She took his hand and allowed him to lift her down. He opened a small gate in the boat's gunwales, which had been built up for privacy and security, and she walked through it on to the wooden deck, which was festooned with potted plants and flowers. The scent of jasmine filled the air.

Aidan opened a painted wooden hatch and ushered her inside, down a short flight of steps into the darkness below. At the click of a switch a brass ceiling light flickered into life, illuminating everything in a soft yellow glow.

Inside, the whole craft had been hollowed out into one living space. In the stern, a tinted window showed the water level outside and the lights of the city opposite.

In front of it was an enormous bed, covered in cushions and a fur throw. In the centre of the space was a large sitting area with two low bamboo and cushion sofas facing each other. An old-fashioned wood-burner sat in between, a chimney jutting up into the sandalwood ceiling.

The galley under the stairs was cluttered with copper-bottomed pans hanging from hooks, spice racks and coloured tins on the open-plan shelves. There was a wooden island with a butler's sink and an old-fashioned tap. Next to it stood an enamel jug filled with pale mauve roses and a champagne bottle unopened in a bucket of half-melted ice.

Aidan crossed to it and popped the cork. He handed her a glass.

'You set me up,' Lois said.

'Guilty.'

'So what happens now?'

'You take another gamble. To stay or to go . . .'

Like she really had a choice. Because who was she kidding? Right now, there was nowhere else she'd rather be.

Aidan took her glass from her and put it down next to the flowers with his own, then he slipped his arm around her waist. As he pulled her towards him, she gasped. Gently he brushed his lips against hers.

She closed her eyes, giving in to the sensation, letting her inhibitions go as the delicious feeling of indecent intimacy overtook her.

She loved the way his lips felt – shifting from soft to yielding – as his tongue parted her lips and started searching out her own. She felt a dart of pleasure between her legs. She shifted to put her arms around him, desperate to hold him close. Wanting . . . needing more.

This is mad, she thought. I shouldn't be doing this. But God, she wanted him.

Still kissing, Aidan gently steered her towards the bed. It was like they were engaged in an exquisitely slow dance. She trailed her fingertips down his arms, feeling the muscles there flex and swell.

She clawed her fingers through his hair, kissing his neck, breathing him in. *Christ, this feels good . . .*

She began quivering with excitement as he

unbuttoned her shirt. She felt his hand softly run over her chest. He leaned down and kissed from her white lacy bra to her stomach. Then he softly laid her back on the bed, unhooking the buttons of her jeans. She tensed as she felt him kiss across to her scar. Then relaxed. His touch, his tender kisses, bought tears to her eyes.

Tugging at the waist of her jeans, he slowly slipped them down over her hips. She sat up, desperate to feel the touch of his skin against hers. She pulled at his T-shirt and watched him lift it over his head. His chest was muscular and defined, with an old faded scar down one side of his ribs. She traced it with her fingertip, then leaned down and flicked her tongue over his nipple, feeling the skin pucker in her mouth. Running her fingers into the hair on his chest, she began exploring him, feeding her senses with the taste of him, the smell of his skin, the feel of his soft grey-blond curls beneath her palm.

Rolling across the bed, Aidan pulled aside the fabric of her bra, kissing her breasts, his soft lips pinching her nipples hard enough to hurt exquisitely.

Holding her tight, he kissed her again, his hand sliding inside her knickers. She gasped as he found her clitoris and began rubbing it. She was shaking, breathing so heavily. Her eyes closed as she surrendered to the pleasure, letting it sweep her along like a deep ocean current. The waves of pleasure began to shimmer through her loins.

But she didn't want this to be over yet and was determined to make him part of it too. Resisting the urge to climax, she rolled over on top of him and pushed him back.

Grabbing the sides of his shorts, she pulled them roughly down.

She moved down on him. Her nostrils flared as she breathed deeply in, savouring his glorious aroma. As she took him in her mouth, she heard Aidan moan with pleasure.

Soon, he sat up and reached for her hips, pulling her round. He swivelled her so that she was positioned above him, then tugged the fabric of her knickers aside. Lois felt herself shuddering, pressing down on Aidan's mouth.

She didn't know how long they stayed there, exploring each other's bodies, twisting, turning, entwining themselves around each other like vines. But finally he moved away from her and took a condom from a box in the bedside table. She noticed the box was already open. But what did it matter who'd gone before? She was here with him now. And it felt so fresh to her. This place. This man.

This might not lead to love or anything like it. It might all lead nowhere at all. But what mattered was how she felt right now.

She pulled out her hair clip and let her long black hair cascade down over her breasts.

She could see herself reflected in the tinted glass of the window. Her pulse was racing, her breath shuddering. His skin shone like burnished gold in the soft light as he held his arms out to her.

She straddled him, gasping as he entered her. She

began grinding herself back and forth on top of him, slowly and sensually, her eyes locked with his as she massaged her hands up his chest.

He sat up, his face pressed against hers, kissing her again as they moved together, locked in the unison of pleasure. He sucked her nipple and she strained towards him.

When he finally came, he gripped her tightly, quivering and shaking as she bore down on him. Then she felt them again, the waves of hot pleasure, building up inside her. But this time there was no hesitation. She abandoned herself to them, surrendering to the rush and release of her orgasm, rocking with Aidan, with the boat, feeling the water swell beneath them, as she gasped for air.

CHAPTER THIRTY

The moment Savvy stepped out of the cab from the airport and found herself in front of the sleek silver façade of the Montrose Bar and Club in Miami Beach, she wanted a drink. Forget that. She wanted *two* drinks. *Ten*. She wanted a bottle of tequila and a wrap of pharmaceutical-grade cocaine. She wanted some buffed-up stud of a barman to take her back to his place and throw her down on the bed and . . .

Stop it, she told herself. Take control. Take control right now.

Dr Savage and Red hadn't been kidding. Getting herself clean out there in Belize had been just the start. Being back here in her own world, and keeping clean . . . well, this was where the battle really began.

It wasn't just the culture shock of being in the US that was killing her, after having been in the rainforest only hours before, it was much more that she felt as if she'd been spat into an entirely different reality. One as scary as hell. It felt as if a connection with the strong person she'd been had already snapped.

But she *was* strong, she reminded herself. She could do this. Red had told her that and she had to believe he was telling the truth.

She glanced across at the beach. The sails of luxury yachts littered the horizon. Powerboats churned up the water nearer to the shore. Young guys cruised the streets in their sparkling Ferraris and Porsches. Perfect girls in bikinis sashayed up from the beach, looking tanned, toned and provocative.

Everything *looked* the same and yet everything had changed. Because she'd changed. Instead of looking enticing, it looked artificial. Its glitz had been permanently tarnished in her eyes. Because she now knew the sordid reality that lurked beneath this fun. Addiction. Self-destruction. It was all still here. Waiting to claim her back.

The Montrose was where she and Paige had spent their first summer together, partying, when they were eighteen, before Paige headed off to college. Savvy had commandeered a free yacht for the season and had flown Paige out from England to join her for a summer of hedonism. It was here that Paige had lost her virginity. Here that Paige had learned to let her hair down. Here that the two of them had laughed until dawn and slept until dusk. This was the only place that Paige could have meant in her message.

But the comfort Savvy expected to feel at this familiar location didn't come. Instead, she felt jittery with nerves as she stood on the sidewalk with her heavy holdall and watched the cab drive away.

With no access to money other than the stipend Max had given her to cover her journey here, she'd had to travel in the best of her old clothes from Peace River Lodge. She'd always taken such pride in her appearance, knowing what a powerful tool it was, but now she was fully aware of what a mess she looked.

Hanging around with Red in flip-flops and going horse-riding had given her a deep, uneven tan and her nose was still peeling from the last few days she'd spent on the dive boat. And since her make-up had mostly melted or curdled in the tropical heat, she'd had no chance to patch herself up.

She wished she'd had time for a makeover before meeting Paige. Because she wanted to be taken seriously. For Paige to understand the efforts she'd made. To see that she really had changed. And looking like a refugee from Woodstock wasn't exactly going to help.

Still, Savvy had done her best. She'd put her hair up in a ponytail, but it didn't hide the fact that it was out of condition and ratty, the ends bleach-blonde and split. And her ripped jeans didn't look retro, she realized, they looked what they were – dirty last season's. Even her 'cool' T-shirt was unfashionable now, with its faded logo and stained armpits.

As if to rub in her lack of confidence, two girls arrived at the Montrose's famous red-carpeted entrance. They were both wearing tight, short dresses and high heels and they looked immaculate. *Young* and immaculate. They were giggling as the doormen un-roped the entrance and let them through, with compliments and smiles. Savvy felt like she looked old enough to be their mum.

But she had bigger worries than just her appearance, she remembered with a sinking sense of dread. She had to find out how things stood with Paige. She had no idea whether their friendship had survived. For all she knew, Paige could easily have come here to tell Savvy that getting her to rehab was her last gesture of friendship and from now on she was on her own – financially and emotionally.

And that would be a disaster.

Because Paige was her only way back in with her father. She needed Paige to smooth the water, to make things OK. To convince Hud that his little girl had come home chastened. Then he might give her back her allowance. Or – hell – let her move into the White House. *Anything* so long as she didn't end up walking out of here with nothing but loose change in her pocket.

Savvy took a deep breath and crossed the road towards the familiar entrance to the nightclub, realizing that her old power strut wasn't possible in Converse sneakers.

The Montrose Bar and Nightclub had had many revamps over the years, but somehow it still managed to be *the* place to be seen – at least Savvy guessed it was, judging from the number of young studs and babes on display in here.

As she walked through the terrace with its sleek

white tables and low lounge beds and the DJ pumping out cool summer beats, she felt more and more out of her comfort zone.

Nobody recognized her. It was as if she were invisible. But then, her face hadn't been in a magazine or paper in a positive way for over a year and a half and she'd been in rehab for the last two months. Enough time to become a nobody.

She almost lost her nerve and was about to turn round when she saw Paige sitting on one of the high stools over by the long bar at the back of the terrace. Her back was to Savvy, but there was no mistaking that auburn hair, or the tilt of her head, as she listened to the barman, who was polishing a glass and talking intently to her.

How long had it been since she'd last seen Paige? Socially, that was? Soberly? Over two years, certainly. Before Elodie's death. Her memory served up vague flashes of conversations they'd had since then. But all of them were out of focus, obscured by the fug of drink and drugs.

Savvy shuddered, half remembering now the way she'd railed at Paige the last time she'd seen her. Could Paige ever forgive her for the things she'd said? For the appalling way she'd behaved?

She'd spent the first part of her time at Peace River *hating* Paige, but now she felt so overwhelmed with gratitude for what her friend had done.

Had Paige spoken to Dr Savage? Had he reported back favourably? Was Paige expecting the old Savvy with added fury and resentment? Or something new?

Paige still didn't turn round or notice Savvy approaching. Savvy couldn't help smiling at the familiar trill of Paige's laugh, as she talked to the barman. It was no wonder that Paige was getting chatted up. She looked good. She was wearing funky white trousers, high wedge heels and a halter-neck top which showed off her tanned, freckled shoulders and her glossy hair, which curled sexily in long tresses. In fact, the more Savvy looked, the more amazed she was. When had Paige grown to look so womanly and cool?

She was used to Paige being her sidekick, her frumpy friend, but she could see now that the tables had well and truly turned.

'Hello, stranger,' she said, startling Paige.

Paige lowered her glass.

There was a moment as they faced each other when Savvy thought it was over between them. Then Paige slipped off the barstool and stepped forward, pulling Savvy into a tight embrace.

'Come here,' Paige said.

Savvy felt tears springing to her eyes.

This was Paige. Her old buddy. The person she'd known for almost all her life. Her rock.

When Paige finally pulled away, Savvy could see that she was emotional too. 'Let me look at you,' she said, her green eyes raking over her face for a moment. 'You look different,' she concluded. 'Healthy.' She lowered her gaze. 'You've put on weight.'

Savvy bit her lip.

'In a good way,' Paige hurried on. 'It's just that

before . . . before you went away . . . you looked . . . well, too thin. Like you were . . .'

'Halfway to the grave,' Savvy finished her sentence for her.

'Can I get you a drink?' the barman asked. He was polite enough, but Savvy could tell he was annoyed that his time alone with Paige was over. And she saw, too, in his eyes, that he didn't think enough of Savvy to want to flirt with them both.

'Mineral water, please,' she said, without missing a beat.

He looked at Paige. 'Same again?' he asked, with a smile.

'I'm fine,' Paige said, putting her manicured hand over the top of her mojito glass and glancing at Savvy.

'You've really done it then, you clever girl,' she said, once the waiter had left them alone. Her smile was genuine but her voice was still nervous. 'And the other stuff?'

Other stuff. Savvy smiled. So some things, at least, hadn't changed. Paige was still too prim, too good, to even say the word cocaine out loud.

'That too,' Savvy said.

They fell into small talk for a minute or so, about their journeys here. But Savvy wasn't really concentrating.

Seeing Paige, hearing her voice, smelling her familiar Chanel No. 19 perfume, brought memories flooding back. Giggling in the dorm at school, ducking out to the cinema on a winter's evening, sobbing into their popcorn. Learning to dive in the pool and having underwater swimming races. Hanging out in cafés, working out strategies for snaring boys. Trying out new hairstyles on one another and taking mountains of clothes into the changing rooms at the most expensive stores they could find. Having their first manicures and pedicures side by side . . .

But the bad memories came straight after. Standing Paige up. Taunting her with Marcus. Mocking her. Excluding her. Making her feel small. Savvy felt a blast of remorse for the horrible person she'd been the last time they'd been together.

'I'm sorry, Paige,' she said, cutting her off mid-sentence as Paige started talking about how much the Montrose's new refurb had cost. 'You have to know,' she went on quickly, needing to unburden herself, 'that I'm sorry I took you for granted. I'm sorry that I said all those things. I didn't mean them.'

Didn't mean them? God, that's only half the truth, Savvy thought. Because the whole truth was that she couldn't remember half of the things she'd said.

Paige flapped her hand, embarrassed by Savvy's honesty. 'I'm just so glad you're OK.' Then she laughed, as if thinking of something ironic. She put her hand on her chest, covering the small silver crucifix she always wore.

'What is it?' Savvy asked.

'It's just that I thought you'd be angry with me.'

'For tricking me into going to Peace River Lodge?'

Paige pulled a face, waiting for Savvy's onslaught.

'I was mad as hell at first,' Savvy said. 'But actually, I've got to tell you that you did me the biggest favour.'

'You really mean it?'

Savvy grasped her hand and squeezed it. She didn't let go. 'Oh Paige, I found out so much in there. So much about myself. And I honestly feel completely different. About *everything*. Making me go there . . . Well, you saved my life.'

It was on the tip of her tongue to tell her about Red, but something stopped her. Quite what, she didn't know. Because nothing physical had happened? Because she still couldn't find the words to express the deep connection between them? Or simply because Paige was so inexperienced with men – so uninterested – that she wouldn't understand anyway.

Instead she told Paige all about how difficult the withdrawal had been in the early days. She told her about the other people there and all the therapy sessions she'd had, which had helped her understand her addictive behaviour. She told her about the place itself too – about the beaches and the rainforest and the horses. Everything she missed.

'Wow,' Paige said. 'It sounds pretty intense. But you know, Sav, it's still early days. You'll have to go easy on yourself. You'll still be getting over . . . you know . . .'

'Elodie,' Savvy said decisively. She didn't want Paige to treat her with kid gloves. She didn't want Paige to think she was still fragile and vulnerable. She wanted her to know that she was strong. 'It's OK. We can say her name. And yes, I am still getting over it. I always will be. But I have to carry on. That's what she would have wanted.'

Paige nodded and was silent for a moment. She twisted the straw in her glass. 'So have you thought about what you might do now?' she finally asked.

Savvy shrugged. 'Concentrate on staying clean is the first thing. But Paige, before all that, I want you to tell me what's been going on: in Vegas, I mean. With the business. And with Hud?'

She pictured his face when he'd heard that Elodie was dead. Slumped in an armchair, like an inflatable version of himself which was slowly having the air sucked out of it. Like he was heartbroken. Finished.

Even though he'd turned his back on her, she still loved him. And pitied him. Because she'd suffered the same loss and knew just how deep it had cut.

'Hud's on his way back from China. With Luc, of course.'

Luc . . .

Savvy had been determined to take Red's advice, to try to put Luc behind her, to move on. But just hearing his name in the same sentence as her father's, so cosy and close, working side by side, made her realize how hard that was going to be.

'China?' she asked.

'El Palazzo in Shangri-La. We've all been working on it around the clock. We're going to make a killing, Savvy, and—'

Paige suddenly stopped and put her hands over her mouth. 'Sorry,' she said.

Savvy was desperate to hear more of what was going on. But Paige seemed to have remembered something.

'What?' she asked.

Paige shook her head. 'No, I'm doing what I always do, aren't I? Talking about the business again.'

'No, please. Go on . . .'

'Oh, come on.' Paige laughed, embarrassed. 'You don't want to know about all of that. It must be so boring for you.'

Boring? What on earth did she mean? Paige couldn't stop now. Savvy had dozens of questions already stacked up in her head. When would they open? How big was El Palazzo going to be? What was Shangri-La like, anyway? And what would it mean for the other parts of the business? What was happening in Vegas? La Paris?

This was her world. The world she'd grown up with. The weird and wonderful world of Michael Hudson. The world Savvy now desperately wanted to belong to again.

But Paige was adamant. 'No, really. I always do this to you.' She smiled decisively. 'Let's talk about something fun instead. Let's talk about you.'

She couldn't believe that Paige was ripping the carpet out from under her, slamming the door to the business in her face, telling her to go hang out in the playground instead.

She should have expected nothing less. More flashes of memory from her wasted past hit Savvy right between the eyes. Enzo Vegas. On Fight Night. Before her whole world had been torn apart. Staring through the glass of the ops room. Peeping behind the curtain of the Wizard of Oz. Making a fool out of that woman – what was her name? Lois Chan. When only twenty minutes later she'd saved the senator's life. And Senator Fernandez himself. Her crazy plan to seduce him. To win back Hud's favour, even then.

All that money. All that power. Had she really been cut off from that world for ever?

Savvy had had plenty of time at Peace River to think it through. To prepare herself for the fact that Hud still might not want to see her. To harden herself to the possibility of being cut off financially.

But it was only when she'd finally psyched herself up enough to ask Paige where she and Hud now stood that she realized it wasn't the financial severance that was frightening her. It was the horrible concept of being permanently emotionally rejected that now sent a tremor down her spine.

'So how is Hud?' she asked. 'With regard to me?'

Paige grimaced. She'd clearly been dreading the question. 'Hud? I guess he's pretty much the same,' Paige said, but there was something in her tone of voice that made Savvy remember the night at La Paris, when she had been on her drunken rampage.

'Does he know you sorted all this out? Does he know you're here?'

Paige nodded. 'Yes,' she said, but Savvy noticed a hesitation.

'But . . . ?' *What's he told you to say? Doesn't he even care how I am?*

'Sav, he's still very bitter,' Paige said.

'You mean he doesn't want to see me?'

'No. Not yet . . .'

'Not even now that I've sorted myself out?'

'He knows rehab might have helped . . .'

'Only *helped*?' Savvy couldn't believe she'd been to all that effort and none of it meant anything to him.

'Listen,' Paige said. 'And this isn't easy for me to say. But your behaviour – particularly around Elodie's death . . . your behaviour compared to hers . . . the comparison between what he's lost and what he still has . . . It makes it all ten times worse, don't you see?'

Hud still hated her. She'd been measured against her saintly sister and found wanting *again*.

'I've been giving it a lot of thought,' Paige said. 'And I hope you don't think I'm interfering, but I was thinking that maybe you could . . . I don't know . . . go to college?'

'College?'

'Well, Sav, you've got to do something,' she said. 'And it'd be fun. And you know, that way you could prove to everyone that you've really changed.'

She didn't have to say it for Savvy to realize what she meant. It was clear that Hud required some serious grovelling. Penance, no less. Even to be in with a chance of forgiveness.

But college? Savvy was still reeling. Was that really how Paige, Luc and her father viewed her? As a messed-up kid who might just about be ready for a college education? Was that what they said behind her back? *Better late than never.*

'Just think about it. You don't need any pressure in your life right now. But some structure would be good. There are so many fabulous courses out there. If I had my time again, there's so much I'd like to do . . .'

'I'll think about it,' Savvy said.

'There is some good news, though,' Paige said. 'An attorney is going to contact you anyway, but I thought I'd tell you to your face myself.' Paige smiled. 'Elodie left a will. Your father challenged its authenticity, which is why it's only just been settled. Elodie's attorney said she tried contacting you several times last year . . .'

Savvy pictured the mountain of mail that had piled up in her apartment.

'I wasn't exactly corresponding back then.'

'Elodie named you as her next of kin. The apartment, her car, her money and shares – everything she owned separate to your father – are all yours. And she was quite a smart cookie. She'd made some great investments of her own in the last few years. If only half the banks and businesses had had the foresight she did.'

It was as if Elodie had reached out from beyond the grave and come to Savvy's rescue in her hour of need.

'I'd like you to come back to Vegas with me, Savvy,' Paige said. 'I've got keys to the apartment.'

Savvy felt momentarily giddy. She remembered suddenly how she'd lied to Paige about how Elodie had accidentally tripped down the stairs. How she'd come out of the bathroom to find Elodie on the floor. How she'd had to repeat the same story to Hud. And the look in his eyes as she'd told him . . .

'No. Not after what happened.'

'I understand. But remember that she loved that place. It was her pride and joy.'

'I can't go back there. Ever,' Savvy said.

'Then maybe we can find you somewhere else in Vegas,' Paige said. 'I've got a flight back booked for us both.'

'No.'

Paige seemed startled by the forcefulness of Savvy's reply.

'I mean . . . not yet,' Savvy clarified. 'I want to go back to my own apartment first. It's part of the rehab programme. I need to clean up what I messed up. I need to take control, not run away.'

'Yes, I see,' Paige said. 'But I just thought it would be a good idea if you were closer to me, so I can . . .'

Keep an eye on you. She didn't need to say it, but they both knew that was what she meant.

'No,' Savvy told her. 'This is something I need to do by myself.'

And when I'm ready for Vegas, I'll arrive on my own terms, she was already thinking. Feeling good and looking good. And with a plan in mind. A future. Goals. Something more ambitious than college. Something that would make all of them – Paige, Hud and Luc – sit up and pay attention.

'Suit yourself,' Paige said, with a disappointed smile. 'But it's a shame. I was looking forward to hanging out.'

She reached into her Anya Hindmarch bag and pushed a wedge of fifty-dollar notes across the bar's polished surface.

'Living expenses,' she said. 'You can pay me back when you've settled things with your attorney.'

'Thanks, Paige,' Savvy said. She smiled, genuinely grateful for Paige's friendship and trust. And also for the fact that she no longer felt an automatic urge to peel off the top of these crisp bills and roll it up into a tight cylinder, ready to stick up her nose.

Paige excused herself to go to the bathroom, leaving Savvy alone at the busy bar. The place was louder now than when she'd arrived, the faces redder, the beautiful people getting stuck into happy hour.

They all looked like they were having a great time, but Savvy just wanted to leave. She'd resisted temptation. She'd had no drink. No drugs. Her sheet was still clean. Just as she'd promised Red.

She closed her eyes for a moment, remembering the rainforest, the cry of the birds and the musky smell of the earth. And she remembered Red too, picturing him once more walking away from her. She wondered where he was. What he was doing. Would she ever see him again?

And then, before she could stop herself, she was thinking of Elodie, about when they'd been little kids, chasing across a burning hot beach in the sunshine, laughing, crashing hand in hand into the surf.

Oh Elodie. I was never much of a sister or a friend to you once we grew up, was I?

She remembered how she'd tried to exclude Elodie from her friendship with Paige. 'Three's a crowd,' she always used to tell her sister, making up excuses for seeing Paige alone. How they'd partied here in the Montrose that summer whilst Elodie had gone to Europe with Hud, tagging along on business trips and visiting museums and galleries alone. Had Elodie been lonely? Jealous? she wondered now.

Several times these past few weeks she'd felt like her sister was somehow still here. Maybe it was a twin thing. Maybe it was just the way Savvy's grief process was playing out, but the more sober she'd become, the more in tune with herself, the more the feeling had grown. Was she imagining it? Was she pretending she had some kind of sixth sense? Or was she just holding on to something Red had once said about letting Elodie live on inside her? Because she felt more protective now of Elodie than she ever had before. And the feeling gave her an odd kind of strength. Like goodness had been poured into her, where before there'd only been bad.

When Paige came back, they both gathered up their belongings ready to go.

'Are you sure you won't come with me, Sav?' Paige asked.

Savvy shook her head. 'Quite sure. But Paige, in the meantime, there's something I want you to do for me.'

'Sure.'

'Tell Hud . . .'

'Yes?'

'Tell Hud that I love him.'

Paige smiled and raised her eyebrows. 'Really? You're sure?'

'Yes, I'm sure. He's always said that blood is thicker than water. We're family, Paige. He can't ignore me for ever. Tell him I'll be home soon. As soon as I can.'

CHAPTER THIRTY-ONE

Lois woke to the buzz of powerboats. A wave of nausea swept over her as she opened her eyes. Squinting into the gloom, she realized the room was moving. *The boat. Of course.* She was on Aidan's boat.

She couldn't tell whether it was Aidan's boat rocking on the water or her hangover that was making her feel worse. She put the sheet up over her face and groaned.

Oh my God! She'd had a one-night stand.

But the wave of remorse or shame she'd been expecting didn't come. Instead, she found herself smiling like the twenty-year-old she suddenly felt.

Lois bit her lip as flashes of last night came back to her. The sex had been great. Better than great. Fantastic.

Somehow, with Aidan, she hadn't felt shy, but able to do anything. The dawn had broken by the time they'd finished and had drifted off, utterly spent, in one another's arms.

But that was last night. And this was this morning. And Lois was old enough and wise enough to know that sex *always* complicated things. Especially sex as great as that. She couldn't help wondering what the hell Aidan must think of her now. The opinions men formed after sex were always so unpredictable. Would he have categorized her already? Slut . . . conquest . . . partner . . . lover . . . or still just friends?

Friends with Aidan was one thing, but there was no way she could get involved in a relationship. Not now. She had her career to think about. Cara. She didn't have time to get emotionally involved with anyone.

Plus, he was far from perfect, she reminded herself. The guy was a ferocious drinker and a gambler. Could she really contemplate a relationship with someone who had such a different attitude towards money from her? Not to mention the risks he took with his own life. After all, those trips he'd described – could she really handle the stress of being involved with someone who regularly went to the world's worst war zones?

But her thoughts were running away with themselves. Aidan hadn't at any point suggested that this might be leading anywhere.

But where the hell was he anyway?

She twisted and looked out on to the water. But even with the tinted glass, the glare of the sun on the horizon was too much for her. She groaned and got out of bed.

In the bathroom, she found a cotton kaftan – purple

296

and yellow, not her colours. She put it on, thinking how typical it was of Aidan not to have a mirror in here. She picked up a bottle of aftershave and pressed the nozzle to her nose. God, he smelt good, she thought to herself, her face breaking into a smile.

She opened the hatch door heading out on to the deck and blinked in the bright morning light. She hadn't been able to see too clearly in the dark last night and, judging from the way her head felt, had probably been more drunk than she'd realized, but she saw that Aidan's barge was at the end of a row of equally beautiful and idiosyncratic houseboats.

But what was truly astonishing was that the whole of the city was right there, just across the water, towering over them. It looked impossibly close, like a child's drawing where the perspective was all wrong.

The choppy harbour in between was buzzing with activity. She could hear the distant honk of tuk-tuk horns, the low murmur of road traffic and the chugging of diesel engines nearby. The smell of brine and fuel mingled in the air with the sweet perfume of the potted jasmine plants on Aidan's deck.

'Mr Aidan, Mr Aidan . . .' she heard. She saw now that Aidan was crouched near a hatch in the bow of the boat. A couple in a dilapidated water taxi with a torn yellow canvas awning were passing him a wooden crate of exotic fruit, which he lifted aboard. He also took in two suit carriers and what looked like a hat box, before paying the man, who waved and zoomed away.

'So you're awake,' he called, as he turned and saw Lois.

Was he as embarrassed as she was? She couldn't tell. He was wearing three-quarter-length cotton trousers and an undone short-sleeved shirt. He looked calm and collected and, compared to her, surprisingly fresh. She sensed a sudden stirring within her as she looked at his body, remembering how great it had felt pressed hard against hers last night.

She put her hand to her hair. She had crazy bed hair and she knew it. She could feel herself blushing.

'Yes you do,' he said with a grin, walking along the gunwale towards her now, the wooden crate in his hands.

'Do what?'

'Look like you've been dragged through a hedge backwards.'

She laughed. 'Thanks.'

'But don't worry.' He patted the roof of the cabin. 'Despite appearances, this old tub's got an excellent power shower, complete with a fine array of lotions, potions and perfumes from some of the world's finest hotels.'

Lois laughed. But his filibuster wasn't over yet.

'All of which is a very long-winded way of saying that you look just as beautiful this morning as you did last night.'

Beautiful? She grinned back at him. It was comforting to know that he was charming *after* as well as *before*. Not that it mattered. Because she wasn't planning on getting involved with him, she reminded herself.

'I've got breakfast,' Aidan said, putting down the box full of ripe pineapples, mangoes and papayas.

'What are those?' she asked, nodding behind him to the suit carriers.

'Oh, those?' he said. He seemed caught out and bashful. 'They're clothes. Stuff for the races.'

Lois nodded. But then she saw that one of the suit carriers was slightly open. She spotted a flash of orange. Which could mean only one thing . . .

Aidan had someone else on the scene. He wasn't as single as he'd made out . . .

For all she knew, he could be married for a second time. Or have a serious girlfriend. Now it all made sense. The open condom box. This kaftan – *oh, gross*. Did this belong to . . . ?

'I should leave,' she said.

'What?' Aidan looked crestfallen. 'No, no. Don't. Stay,' he said, hurrying over to her, 'I've got the whole day planned. Tickets for the Hong Kong races. I know gambling's not your thing but it's more of a cultural event out here. And look,' he went on, racing off to collect the suit carrier and holding it out to her. 'I even got a friend at the Four Seasons to get you some clothes delivered in time. I had to guess your size, but . . .'

He was so flustered, so schoolboyish, that Lois felt her suspicions melting away.

'I don't usually do this,' he said. 'I mean, I would have taken you out before . . . you know . . . but things got a bit out of hand last night. I only meant to bring you back here for a drink, I swear. But will you? Will you come with me today?'

299

Lois felt a laugh of relief escape her. And shock too. Aidan was nervous about asking her to go with him. How ironic that they'd slept together but he was fumbling around now.

And of course the answer was yes.

'OK,' she said, her hand on her hip. 'On one condition.'

He flushed. 'Anything . . . what?'

'Tell me how you tracked me down last night.'

He hadn't stopped smiling, but there was an added alertness to his eyes. 'You mean you don't believe it was just fate?'

Lois rolled her eyes. 'Tell me.'

'OK,' he admitted. 'I'm here in Hong Kong to meet Jai Shijai's people. For business.'

Jai Shijai. That name again. Wherever she seemed to go these days, it just kept on popping up.

She was tempted to ask Aidan exactly what that business was, but she doubted that he'd tell her. And anyway, she didn't have the chance.

'And, well, Angela Ho let slip your boss Roberto was coming to town to meet you. So . . . I called in a favour and got an ex-military contact to track your cell with GPS . . .'

'You must have some powerful friends,' Lois said, impressed and outraged in equal measures.

'Comes with the turf, I guess,' he said, a twinkle in his eye. 'Now we're going to have to hurry. I don't want to miss the first race. I promise you, it'll be worth it.'

'But I'm just going for the experience,' she said.

'Because you know I'm only here for two days. And then I'll be gone.'

She felt she had to say it. To lay down her cards. To make sure there was no confusion later.'

'Sure. Just for the experience,' he assured her. 'I mean, what else is there, right?'

CHAPTER THIRTY-TWO

Happy Valley Racecourse was a green oasis in the centre of Hong Kong Island. It was surrounded on all sides by tower blocks, as if the very buildings themselves were leaning in, ready to place a bet, watching in anticipation beneath the bright blue sky.

As soon as Lois stepped out of the cab with Aidan, she was glad she'd come, just to experience the sheer craziness of the atmosphere. The street outside the stadium was a logjam of screaming cabbies, blaring their horns. It seemed that everyone in Hong Kong was here – locals from all walks of life, crowding around the makeshift noodle stands and beer stalls and swarming around the ticket touts. Tic-tac men teetered on packing crates, shouting out in a rapid, high-pitched code to one another, adjusting odds and offsetting their risks.

'Come on,' Aidan shouted, gripping Lois's hand. 'This way.' Hauling her through the crowd – it was like wading through mud – he finally got them past the turnstiles and into the stadium. Everyone was jostling against each other, gripping their betting slips as they vied for a position with a good view of the track. It made Fight Night in Vegas seem sedate by comparison.

They reached an elevator and waited their turn in the chattering masses, until they managed to squeeze a ride up to the seventh floor. Even in the elevator, the talking didn't stop, nor the sense of good-natured anticipation.

As soon as they came out of the elevator, Lois had her first glance at the racetrack spread out below. With its lush green infield stretching into the distance beyond the crowd, it was an impossible, awe-inspiring luxury in a city where real-estate values were some of the highest in the world and overpopulation and pollution were threatening to choke it to death.

'So what do you think?' Aidan shouted, above the constant roar of the crowd.

From his broad grin, it was obvious that he'd already read the excitement on her face.

'Miraculous.' She could think of no other way to put it. She laughed and said, 'It's like Central Park . . . with hooves.'

Aidan knew the stadium well. He led her on an efficient dance through a maze of corridors and automatic doors, flashing the gold-braided enclosure passes at the various flunkies they encountered, until they finally reached Hong Kong racecourse's inner sanctum, the private members' enclosure.

Gold-framed photos of previous winning owners, horses and jockeys crowded the walls. Champagne corks popped. The brightly lit room was loud with excited, drunken chatter.

Lois was glad she'd dressed for the occasion. She was part of the scene in the gorgeous burnt-orange dress that Aidan had magically provided. The designer chiffon and silk fitted her perfectly, but then, as he'd said himself, he'd had time to study her body in detail last night.

Last night. Flashes of it kept coming back. Neither of them had mentioned it yet. But now, having kissed nearly every inch of Aidan's body and abandoned herself completely to him, it was proving more difficult than she'd anticipated to stick to her resolution that they were just friends.

Just as well then – before she made a complete fool of herself or complicated things even further – that Aidan had brought her to the one place where contemplation was almost impossible.

It was electric up here. Through the UV-protected window, the racetrack below was a perfect green oval. The windows were soundproofed, but speakers in the ceiling conveyed the cacophony of the swelling crowd of race-goers below.

The horses paced in loops in the owners' enclosure with their jockeys in their bright vests. Amidst all the noise, most of them seemed calm and focused; only a few horses broke rank and they were quickly controlled.

She'd never have dreamed of coming here on

her own, even though she knew that Hong Kong's obsession with horses was the biggest part of the city's obsession with gambling. But gambling like this, away from the sleek lights of the casino, made it all the more understandable and attractive. Seeing all the guys huddled excitedly over the race forms, talking animatedly, reminded her of sitting at a bar as a small child in a smoke-filled room late at night with her father and his friends. But it was the camaraderie, the bonding experience of participating in something together, that she remembered most clearly. The sense of belonging. And she felt it here too.

And yes, now that she was here, she knew that whatever this was, it *was* in her blood. She'd spent so long controlling the gambling in the Enzo, skirting around the peripheries like a non-smoker who liked being around smoke, that dipping a toe in the water like this felt deliciously dangerous.

Being here with Aidan doubled the kick.

'There's nothing like it,' Aidan said, sighing happily and rubbing his hands together. He clearly couldn't wait to get stuck in.

She saw his eyes scanning the track, concentrating. Aidan wasn't here as a tourist. He was here because this was his thing. The thing that gave him the biggest buzz.

And that's when it hit Lois. She was wrong to fall for this place, wrong to allow herself to be seduced. Just because something was in her blood didn't mean she had to give into it at all.

She had a sense of déjà-vu she couldn't escape. It

was a feeling of exclusion. The same feeling she'd had as a kid, when she'd tried to distract her father from gambling and he'd taken no notice of her.

Yes, the smell of this place. The atmosphere. The babble of voices. It was making it all come back.

She tried desperately not to think of her father. The unpaid bills. The broken whisky bottles. The bruises on her mother's face.

But the ghosts wouldn't leave her alone. Wasn't Aidan doomed to end up like her father? Weren't all gamblers destined to end up that way? And whoever was with them, wouldn't they be dragged down and destroyed too?

She shifted uncomfortably in her dress. She didn't fit in here with this crowd, no matter how much she looked the part. She was police, not a gambler. She couldn't get her kicks from this like Aidan and all the other people here. She felt like a fraud. A killjoy. And entirely out of her comfort zone.

'What's the matter?' Aidan asked.

'Nothing.' Lois forced a smile. You're his guest, she thought. You shouldn't have come here, but you did. And he's made such an effort. The very least you can do is pretend you're having fun.

'So, what do we do now?' she asked.

'Now? Oh, that's easy. Now we pick a horse.'

Aidan bought a race programme and together they studied the runners for the next race.

'Hey, look at this one,' she said. 'Orchid Sunrise. It says the owner is Angela Ho. Do you think it could be the same Angela Ho that we met at Jai Shijai's place? If she pushes her jockeys as hard as her staff . . .'

'Good point.' Aidan laughed. 'But you'd better keep your thoughts to yourself because over there is the lady herself.'

Lois turned to see Angela Ho gazing steadily back at them. She was several metres away, at the centre of a group of businessmen. She raised a champagne glass to them and Lois followed Aidan's lead in returning the gesture.

'It's her we've got to thank for our enclosure passes,' Aidan said.

So *she* was the favour he'd called in to get them here. Wherever she turned, Jai Shijai's influence twisted through her life like a creeper.

Aidan ducked away and placed a bet by phone and then they edged through the champagne-swilling throng towards the window.

A pistol cracked. The crowd roared. The horses shot out of the gates and the race began.

Lois tried not to pay attention, tried to distance herself and not get involved. But something – the will of the crowd, Aidan's excited shouts – kept her eyes glued on the track. Within seconds, she'd picked out the distinctive yellow and blue polka dot of Orchid Sunrise's jockey. It was halfway back in the field as the horses rounded the first bend.

The sporadic shouting around them evolved into a roar, a wall of noise. Aidan began pumping his fist. The horses were coming back into view now, rounding the final bend before hitting the home straight.

And there . . . Lois couldn't believe it. Aidan's horse was still in the running, up there lying in third, no, moving into second . . . now closing on the lead . . .

Lois was amazed at how much adrenalin she felt. No wonder so many people got off on this, she thought.

'Go on, boy,' Aidan bellowed.

His arm was around her, squeezing her tight. But Lois didn't care. She was fixated on the track.

Orchid Sunrise had drawn neck and neck with the leader. There was less than ten yards to go.

'Come on,' she shouted as well, finally losing control.

It was impossible, of course. But it was like the horse had heard her. Because the exact moment she cried out, the sleek bay beast's stride seemed to lengthen . . . its slender neck stretched out . . .

One stride, two strides, three . . .

The jockey was up in the stirrups, slapping the bay's neck, saluting the crowd. Orchid Sunrise had done it. He'd won by a length.

Aidan picked up Lois and spun her round and kissed her full on the lips. Then he put her down and they both backed away, startled. Here in the crowd, in front of all these people . . . it had taken them both by surprise. But worse than that, it had somehow felt wrong. Like it was to do with the race, and nothing to do with them.

'You won!' he said, with an awkward grin.

'I won?'

'Sure. The bet I placed. It was for you. All you had to do was pick the horse.'

'How much was it?'

'Enough for another one of those dresses.'

'Give it to charity instead,' Lois said.

'Are you serious?'

'Yes. Of course I am.'

Aidan didn't seem to believe her. He pulled an amused face and rubbed his hands together. 'How about another bet?'

'No.'

'Come on, you might be on a roll.'

'I said no.' It came out more harshly than she'd intended.

But she'd had enough. She was annoyed with him. For putting her in this situation. And annoyed with herself. For having got pulled into the race. For having got fired up, when she'd been determined not to lose her cool.

But before the conversation could go any further, she saw a familiar face. A man, just over Aidan's shoulder, was staring at her with a look of complete surprise.

CHAPTER THIRTY-THREE

'Mike!' Lois said, breaking away from Aidan. It had been nearly two years since she'd seen Mike Hannan, but he'd hardly changed at all.

'Lois,' he said, still looking shocked, then more warmly, 'Lois.' There was an awkward moment when they didn't know how to greet each other, then Mike stepped towards Lois and hugged her and they both laughed.

'How you doing?' he asked. 'You look terrific.'

A woman was standing next to him. She had a fragile, elegant air about her. Her eyes were a beautiful grey that sparkled like wet slate.

'This is my wife, Jeanie,' Mike said.

Lois put her hand out to shake Jeanie's hand and saw her flinch. She wondered what she'd done, but as she looked down she saw that Jeanie was missing two fingers on her right hand.

'I had an accident in an elevator a couple of years ago,' Jeanie explained.

Lois stared at her mutilated hand.

'I'm so sorry,' she said.

'Don't be. It's amazing how you adapt. And besides . . . I'm getting prosthetic fingers soon. It'll stop me feeling so self-conscious about it, I hope.'

'Yeah, well, there's no need to feel like that in front of Lois, honey,' Mike said. 'It's Lois here who took a bullet that night in Vegas with me. So she's been through the wars herself.'

'It's an honour to meet you at last, Lois,' Jeanie said. Without warning, she stepped forward and kissed Lois on the cheek. 'Mike told me how wonderful you were. I'm so sorry you had to go through what you did.' She looked like she was going to cry.

Lois smiled, embarrassed by the attention and unexpected intimacy.

'I was just doing my job. No different to Mike.'

She became aware of Aidan standing by her side. 'This is my . . . um . . . friend.'

Aidan's expression surprised her. He was smiling pleasantly enough as he politely introduced himself, but Lois noticed a hardness to his eyes.

She quickly explained her connection to Mike, saying he'd been the true hero at the Enzo Vegas.

Aidan remained polite but seemed completely uninterested in the man who'd saved her life. Was he jealous? Was that it? It made no sense.

'So, how have you been? You know . . . since?' Lois asked.

Since . . . Since you shot that man dead . . . Since you saved the senator's life . . . Since we last spoke when you visited me in hospital . . . when my face was plastered across the nation's newspapers and websites . . . while yours had been kept secret . . . shielded from the public eye.

Since . . . The word conveyed so much of their silent history together. History that they'd probably never discuss. History that would never be recorded.

'Oh fine. Fine,' he said. 'I still look after your pal, Fernandez.' He laughed. 'He's just as difficult to keep up with.'

'So what brings you to Hong Kong?' Lois asked Jeanie.

'We're on vacation. You know, soaking up the atmosphere. The guidebook said this place was a must.'

'You must have a good travel agent,' Lois said. 'Aidan was telling me that tickets for this place were like gold dust.'

'Yeah, we sure lucked out there,' Jeanie said.

'We sure did,' Mike agreed. 'But listen, Lois. We're just leaving.'

'Leaving? But there's loads more races to go,' Lois said.

'I know, but there's a lot to do on this island and we've only got twenty-four hours left.' He leaned in and lowered his voice. 'Gambling's not really my thing.'

'Nor mine,' Lois told him, suddenly wishing they would take her with them.

But almost as if sensing her desire to flee, Aidan put his arm around her.

'Trust me,' he told Mike. 'You're not going to find anything as exciting as this.'

Mike shrugged. He tapped his watch. A gold Rolex, Lois noted. He'd probably been promoted after the Vegas affair, she thought. Deserved it too.

'We're out of here,' Mike said. He smiled warmly at Lois as he kissed her on the cheek. 'But I'm glad we bumped into each other.'

'Me too,' Lois said with a smile.

She meant it. Even if they hadn't had much of a chance to talk, it was good to meet Mike in a non-work situation. It made Fight Night seem even more like something they'd all left behind.

Mike and Aidan nodded at each other and stiffly shook hands.

Then Jeanie stepped towards Lois and took both her hands. Again, Lois saw the tears in her eyes. Maybe this meeting hadn't been so good for her. Maybe it had been an altogether too real reminder of what her husband did in the line of duty.

'I'm so glad you're all right,' she said. 'I hope you have a wonderful life.'

Mike smiled awkwardly, clearly embarrassed.

'Come on, honey,' he said, gently placing a hand on Jeanie's shoulder. 'We really do have to go.'

Lois watched Mike and Jeanie fade into the crowd.

'Lunch?' Aidan said brightly, as if nothing had happened. 'We've got half an hour before the next race starts.'

* * *

Lois sat at the crowded seafood bar beside Aidan, picking at her lobster salad. It looked and tasted great, but she'd lost her appetite. Her glass of champagne stood untouched at the side of her plate. She felt more churned up than she could account for.

Aidan was doing his best to be charming, but for her, the day had lost its magic. It was the TV screens showing the betting, the drunken laughter, the platinum cards and endless cash being flashed around. This wasn't fun for her any more. It felt too much like Vegas. Too much like work.

Seeing Mike had brought her reality and responsibilities crashing back. She remembered all at once why she was here in Hong Kong. She shouldn't be here gambling with Aidan Bailey. She should be back at the hotel, checking her messages and preparing for her meeting with Roberto.

'What are you thinking about?' Aidan asked. 'You seem distracted.'

'Work,' she said.

'Ah, and the mystery project with Roberto Enzo,' Aidan said.

Lois remembered now that she'd told him about it last night. But for the second time, something in his tone unnerved her.

'Where's *your* work taking you next, Aidan?' she asked him. She hadn't meant to sound so direct. There was no denying that it was a challenge.

'I'm not sure yet,' he said distractedly. More like he couldn't, or wouldn't, say.

Lois held her breath for a moment, beating down an

314

unfamiliar emotion. It had been so good pretending that they were a normal couple having fun. But they *weren't* normal. They hardly knew one another. And she was way out of her depth.

Her cell beeped. She got it out of her bag and saw that there was a message from Cara.

Like the earrings. When r u coming home?

'So,' Aidan said. 'Time for the next race.'

'I'm sorry,' Lois lied. 'One of my meetings . . . it's been brought forward. I'm going to have to bail, I'm afraid.'

'But . . . we're having so much fun,' he said.

'I know, but this is business. I've got no choice.'

She put her phone away quickly and stood up. Now she'd made the decision, she wanted to get out of there before Aidan realized that she was a liar. Or that she was deliberately running away.

But how could she explain to him that her emotions towards him were too complicated, especially after last night? She needed time to work it all out.

Still, she had no idea how to say goodbye. To shake his hand would be ridiculous, so awkwardly she reached up to kiss him on the cheek.

'Thanks for . . . you know . . . well, everything. It was great bumping into you,' she said. The words immediately embarrassed her. Too graphic. Too callous.

It was too late to take them back.

'You too,' he said and nodded. There was a small beat as they stared at one another. 'Can I see you again?' he asked.

She'd known that the question was coming, but it still shocked her to hear him say it. She wanted so much to say yes, because she liked him. She'd liked him *so much* last night, just the two of them, away from all this.

But she had to protect herself. Aidan was too big a risk. So instead she sighed and said as gently as she could, 'I don't think that's a good idea.'

His face clouded with disappointment, but before he could say anything Lois saw Angela Ho extricating herself from her companions and beginning to weave through the crowd towards them. Jai Shijai's eyes and ears was the last person Lois wanted to talk to right now. Especially before she'd found out from Roberto why she was here. And it would be far too embarrassing to try to explain how she and Aidan came to be together.

'Don't think I haven't had a good time. I have. It's just that your life is complicated,' she said, feeling more emotional than she'd expected. 'And mine is too.'

'I'm sorry you feel that way,' he said.

Oh God, she thought. Now it's gone too far the other way. It's like we're not even friends any more. Like last night never happened.

But it was too late to fix it.

'Goodbye,' she said, turning round and quickly walking away.

She didn't look back. She didn't want to see him staring after her. In case she changed her mind. And in case she'd just made one of the biggest mistakes of her life.

CHAPTER THIRTY-FOUR

In the exclusive salon on Rodeo Drive, Savvy stared in the mirror as Sebastian, the world-renowned hair technician, revealed Savvy's new crop.

'It's pretty radical, Savvy. You look totally different,' Sebastian said, looking at her in the mirror and gently patting the short blonde hair, before pulling an individual strand at the front.

Savvy smiled. 'Good,' she said.

'It's a real statement. It's certainly saying something...'

'What? Like "Don't underestimate me, sweetie, or I might just cut off your balls"?'

Sebastian laughed. 'Yeah, exactly.'

'Then your work here is done,' Savvy said, smiling. She stood up, shaking off the gown.

'You can open up shop again,' she told her old friend, placing the gown on the back of the chair.

She'd been flattered that Sebastian had not only granted Savvy a last minute appointment when she'd touched down in LAX less than two hours ago, but had offered to close the salon for the morning, so that she could have a complete overhaul with the beauticians as well as a consultation with Mimi, the stylist and another old friend from Savvy's It-girl days, in peace and privacy.

Mimi was still the best stylist in the biz and arguably the biggest gossip in LA, and had responded straight away to Savvy's call, eager for the lowdown on her time in rehab.

Who did she meet? Who did she have an affair with? Was she really going to give up her old partying ways?

Savvy had been happy to set the record straight. It wasn't the story they were expecting, but dramatic nevertheless. Savvy wanted the word out there and this was the best way to do it. Savvy Hudson was back. And she'd changed for good.

As she'd riffled through all the clothes Mimi had brought, she'd thrown out every outfit. She didn't want low-cut tops or sky-high sandals. She wanted clothes that were elegant . . . classy . . . *serious*. The only way she'd be taken seriously was if she looked serious, she told Mimi, who set to work, sending out her assistants along Rodeo Drive to find the outfits that would complete Savvy's new look.

And now, as Savvy stepped confidently out of the salon, the bags containing kick-ass trouser suits and power-woman skirts swinging by her newly waxed legs, her brand new heels clipping the sidewalk, she pointed the beeper at the hired silver Lotus parked up against the kerb and finally felt as if she really *was* different.

She saw her reflection in the tinted glass and put her hand up to her new haircut, delighting in the way it felt.

If only Red were here to see her. He'd hardly recognize her.

But there was no time to get distracted with thoughts of Red. There was too much to do. She got into the car and, turning up the radio, did a fast U-turn in the road, the car's brand new tyres screeching on the tarmac.

Today was a day for taking the bull by the horns.

Savvy pressed Marcus's door buzzer for the fifteenth time, but still there was no answer. She squinted back down the drive, through the heat haze to where the date palms cast long shadows over the wide private road.

It was one of those humid, hot LA afternoons where the air doesn't seem to move. She saw that the lawn was going brown at the edges, as if the sprinklers hadn't been turned on for a while. An empty whisky bottle protruded from the hedge.

Marcus hadn't returned any of her calls. Giving up on the front door, she walked over to the carport that stood alongside his once stylish but now dilapidated home.

Peering through the tinted glass doors, she saw that

the carport was as empty as a squash court. His canary-yellow Lamborghini was gone.

So that must mean that Marcus had gone, too, right? But where? On holiday, perhaps? Because without Savvy, who knew who Marcus had been up to. Who he'd replaced her with.

But just as she was about to give up and turn away, she heard the bolts being moved and the heavy oak front door swung open.

Marcus was naked except for a dark-blue hand towel wrapped around his waist. His hair was greasy and mussed up and from the expression on his unshaven face, Savvy could tell that she'd woken him from a deep sleep, even though it was four in the afternoon.

'Fuck,' he said, when he saw her. He shook his head and rubbed at his eyes like he must be hallucinating.

'Nice to see you, too,' she said, taking off her shades.

'You look . . .' he said. He didn't finish the sentence, but waved his arm for her to follow him inside.

'Where's your car?' Savvy asked, walking behind him into his house, scrunching her nose up at the hideous smell of stale smoke and alcohol.

'The repo men came,' Marcus said.

The grand piano was gone from the hall, she saw. As was the Hockney that had once dominated the wall at the bottom of the stairs. All that remained was two wires sticking out of the wall, and a slightly grubby outline of where the picture had been.

The painting had been left to him by his grandmother. 'My "Get Out of Jail Free" card', Marcus had always called it. Which meant that he'd only sell it when the shit had truly hit the fan.

And now it was gone. No doubt he'd flogged it, or put it up as collateral. Or worse – Savvy noticed the playing cards strewn across the baize card table in the other room – lost it in a bet.

'I had a party,' Marcus said, picking up a bottle of vodka from a table crowded with empty bottles and squinting down its neck. He shook it and, realizing that it still had a dribble of liquid in it, took a swig. 'You should have come. I didn't realize you were in town.'

Marcus had had this place built for parties five years ago. After his mother had died of toxic shock on a now discredited Beverly Hills plastic surgeon's table, he'd flown in his favourite Tribeca designer to do the job.

The louche interior with its bar and low sofas was perfect for looking out at the wide terrace, pool and the view of the Hollywood hills beyond.

Marcus's notorious circular bed had been wheeled through to the sitting room some time during the long night and Savvy noticed that a pair of feet were sticking out of the end of it. From what she could ascertain from the feet, and the contours of the body beneath the red satin sheet, Marcus's latest conquest was a slim and very tall black girl.

'I didn't realize you had company,' she said. 'Sorry.'

'Come on,' Marcus said, grabbing the unknown woman's ankle and shaking it. There was an annoyed groan from beneath the pillow. 'Come on, get up. Time to get going.'

'New girlfriend?' Savvy whispered.

'Trixie,' Marcus said, as the woman sat up in bed, blinking into the light, her fingers on her forehead, the diamanté studs on her long acrylic nails glittering. 'Meet my . . . um . . . friend, Savvy.'

'Tracy,' the girl said, correcting him.

Tracy slowly unfolded her extraordinary body out of bed. She was wearing a black lace teddy – the crotch poppers still undone. If it weren't for the folded dollar bills wedged in her ample cleavage, Savvy would have pinned her for a fashion model. She eyeballed Savvy as she strolled casually towards the bathroom as if she owned the place.

'Charming,' Savvy said, as the door clicked shut. 'And quite a conversationalist. Known her long, have you?'

'She's from an agency,' Marcus confessed.

'You're getting prostitutes now?'

'She's a call girl.'

'There's a difference?'

'In price. Yes.'

'You'd be better off spending your money on a cleaner. It stinks in here,' she said, her tone making it perfectly clear that she wasn't only referring to the physical smell. 'I'll be on the terrace.'

The evidence of Marcus's continued downward spiral during Savvy's absence was even more marked outside. His vintage Harley Davidson motorbike was at the bottom of the murky pool. Someone had graffitied the back wall. Profanities and crude sexual drawings. Nothing smart.

Savvy had wondered what she'd feel like seeing

Marcus. She'd feared that she'd see him and crave her old lifestyle back. But standing here, feeling so shiny and new in the midst of all the stale party debris, brought her nothing but a sense of relief.

Her own reflection stared back up at her as she leaned over the pool. She looked so different. Older and more confident. And, she had to admit, hot as hell with her new haircut. But not anything like she used to be. Sure, she'd been hot sexually before, but now she was a different kind of hot. As in the kind of hot where you might just get burned if you didn't treat it with respect.

She guessed that Marcus probably thought so too, considering the speed with which he'd kicked Tracy out of his bed just now.

It was hard to believe that she'd once been part of all this. Almost as hard as it was to believe that she and Marcus had once been intimate.

She turned to see him emerge wincing into the daylight. He looked painfully thin. Much more of his lifestyle and she was certain he'd end up as broken and forgotten as the bike at the bottom of the pool.

Which was why she was here. She wasn't just going to reach closure with Marcus on their old life together, she was determined to kick him into shape to join her in her new one too.

He was wearing large aviator shades, with an unlit cigarette between his teeth.

'So out of ten,' he said, 'how pissed were you that I tricked you on to that plane?'

'Eleven,' she said, sitting down in one of the pool

chairs. 'I can't believe you managed to keep the act up long enough to pull it off.'

'Valium helped with the sincerity,' he said. He lit his cigarette and sat down, crossing his legs and sucking on his cigarette, his knee shaking up and down. Savvy wondered whether he'd done a line before or after she'd arrived. She recognized his familiar, weasely smile and the way he squinted through the smoke.

'So how much did she pay you?' Savvy asked.

'Who?'

'Paige, of course. To get me on that plane. Come on, you can tell me.'

Marcus looked bemused. 'Paige? She never paid me a cent. Just arranged it. The whole thing was your father's idea.'

'Hud?' Savvy thought she'd misheard.

'Sure.'

Marcus scrunched up his nose as if astonished that she didn't know this already. 'He was pretty upset when he came here. He said I'd been leading you astray. I did point out that it was the other way around, but—'

'Hud . . . was here?' Savvy said.

Marcus picked a bit of tobacco from the end of his tongue. 'Sat more or less where you are. Had a man-to-man. He and I have never seen eye to eye. But it was quite gratifying seeing him ask me for help.'

'I bet it was,' Savvy said, trying to imagine it all. She shook her head, struggling to digest the information. 'I had no idea. I thought . . .' She trailed off.

'You may have had your rows with him, but you're

still his little princess – no matter what he calls you to your face.'

'He doesn't call me anything. He won't even speak to me. Didn't you read the papers? I'm dead to him.'

'Bullshit. You're all he's got left, Savvy.'

Savvy suddenly thought of Red. He'd told her the same thing. And now, coming from Marcus, it felt obvious. True.

But why hadn't Paige mentioned any of this in Miami? She'd given Savvy the impression that it was she and she alone who'd organized and paid for the Peace River retreat. And that Hud was still furious with her.

But perhaps she was just managing her expectations, Savvy guessed. Diplomatically smoothing the waters. Knowing that just because Hud had paid for her treatment, it didn't necessarily mean he wanted her back. Typical of Paige to want to give Savvy as soft a landing as possible.

'You know, given all that, I don't think Hud would be that delighted to see you back here . . . with me,' Marcus said. 'But it's great to see that they didn't brainwash you after all. I always knew you were way too wicked for that.' He grinned at her broadly. 'So once Sleeping Beauty's finished showering off in there, what say you we go out and score? Just like the old times.'

Savvy winced and shook her head. 'One of the pledges I made when I left Peace River was to deal with my past . . . to face up to the destructive relationships I've been in.'

Marcus's eyes darkened. 'Oh. I see. And there I was thinking we were friends.'

'We were,' she said quickly. 'Are.' Oh God, this was coming out all wrong. 'Which is why I came to see you. Because I don't want you to carry on with all this . . .'

He was going to hate her, she knew. But someone had to tell him. Just like she'd been told by Red at Peace River. Someone had to tell him before it was too late.

Marcus laughed. 'So you've come here to preach? Are you some kind of evangelical convert now? Jesus, Savvy.'

'A stint in rehab would do you good. And as far as I'm aware, you don't have anybody else who'd have the nerve to tell you that. Certainly not someone who can pay for you to get straight.'

He half stood to leave and Savvy thought she'd lost him. But he didn't go. He sat back down and stared at the ground, cradling his head in his hands as Savvy began to speak.

She started telling him about her experience at Peace River Lodge and tried to describe what she'd learned. How much happier – better – she felt. But she didn't bullshit him either. As well as the pros – his new future – she told him the cons. The pain. The sickness. The fury. But she told him she believed he could do it.

By the time Savvy had finished, Marcus's eyes were red-rimmed and full of tears. He tried to make a joke. 'Are there hot chicks in rehab?' he asked.

Savvy smiled. 'I went, didn't I?'

She stayed with him for another hour. He fixed coffee and they drank it by the pool. He told her he'd think about her offer. And when she stood up to go, she believed he meant it too.

It had been a gamble coming to see Marcus. He was from the past, from her old life. But just because she'd thrown away all her old habits, it didn't mean that she had to throw out everything. And she was going to drag Marcus into her new life whether he liked it or not. Because Marcus had stuck by her side, through thick and thin. And she had the feeling that she might just need an ally now.

CHAPTER THIRTY-FIVE

Roberto Enzo had always described himself as 'the doorman who took over the Ritz' and Lois had to admit that, for all his wealth, the description was pretty accurate. Especially now, as he drew out Lois's chair in the café of the Mandarin Oriental hotel in Hong Kong and walked round to sit opposite her.

'I don't like those chairs,' he muttered, shaking his head and jutting out his jaw from his collar. 'Backs are too low. All wrong.'

Lois laughed, delighted as always to be in Enzo's company. He was a stickler for detail and competitive to his core. He might be paying several hundred dollars a day to be here in these beautiful surroundings, but all it represented to him was an alternative business model. To be scrutinized and analysed, before being criticized or admired.

'Ah, I *love* this stuff,' he said, rubbing his hands

together, as the waitress placed bamboo steamers of dim sum on their table.

Lois smiled, unsurprised that Roberto had ordered already. He wasn't one to waste a moment. He'd already told her on the phone this morning that today was going to be a big day, and in Roberto's book that meant having a full stomach to deal with it.

'I'm their best return customer and they know it,' he told her. 'Hong Kong's one of my favourite places in the world. And "the old Mandy" is still one of the best pieces of real-estate ass the island's got to offer.' He smiled at the waitress, the comment for her benefit as much as for Lois's.

Lois looked around her. The room, unlike many places she'd seen in Hong Kong, was flooded with natural light and had amazing views over Statue Square below and the green double-decker trams and the new-age glass skyscrapers beyond. She thought immediately of Aidan's barge and the incredible view of the buildings from there.

Aidan . . . knowing that she wasn't going to see him again was affecting her more than she'd like. Was he still here in the city? she wondered. Somewhere in all those buildings? Or had he already left Hong Kong?

It's over. We're wrong for each other, period. Get over it.

Roberto took the lid off the top steamer and breathed in the aroma of chicken and water chestnuts. 'Come on, Lois, tuck in,' he said, picking up his chopsticks.

Lois helped herself, but unlike Roberto she felt too nervous to eat.

'You know when I first came here?' he said. 'In

329

'sixty-one. I was eighteen years old. A radio operator on the USS *Constellation*. We were based here in the Pan Shan Shock Anchorage for two years. I grew up round these streets. Became a man.'

Lois tried picturing Roberto as a fresh-faced kid in crisp navy whites, but the image wouldn't stick. The man before her was too removed from that boy. He was her boss and she couldn't see him any other way. 'I bet you've got some stories to tell,' she said.

'You got to have the place to have the stories in,' he said, waving his chopsticks around. 'That's why it's so important to take notes. You know, up here.' He tapped his temple.

'It's all in the detail,' she said, his familiar mantra clearer to her now than ever before. Even here in the café with its dark timber panelling, its pewter-grey table mats and the pale-yellow silk wall coverings, there were gorgeous silver bowls of fuchsia and green dragon fruit.

'So come on then, Lois. Tell me. Who's the guy?' Roberto asked, raising his eyebrows at her.

'What?' Lois felt her cheeks burn.

'There. I knew it. Look at you now . . . looking like you swallowed all the glow worms in China.'

'It's nothing. No one.'

He stared at her. In silence. That old negotiator's weapon. Waiting for her to fill the void with words. But she said nothing, until he eventually smiled. He seemed to relax as he picked up his chopsticks again.

'Good,' he said. 'It's not that I don't wish you happiness. I do. Some day. And not that you're not entitled to a private life. Of course you are. But I'm glad that whatever it is between you and this "nothing, no one" person isn't too serious. Because right now, I need you, Lois. All your attention. All your dedication.'

'Roberto?' she asked. 'Let's be straight with each other. I need to know what this – me being here – is all about.'

Roberto let out a laugh. 'Ah, Lois, my Lois. This is way too big to simply *tell* you. I've brought you here to *show* you. Show you everything I've been dreaming about for the last two years.'

Roberto's private plane was waiting for them at the airport. He was keen for Lois to sit by the window.

As she strapped herself into the soft cream leather seat, she felt her apprehension increase along with her annoyance that Roberto was clearly as excited as a little boy, but still hadn't put her out of her misery.

'Just tell me, Roberto. Please. Where are we going?'

'Shangri-La,' he announced, with a clap of his hands.

So she'd been right. Roberto did have a plan after all.

'You see, Beijing is determined for Shangri-La to be a shining advert for the new China. They're keeping a very watchful eye on the Western investors. They know that the first sign of this turning into bad propaganda would allow the hardliners at home to shut the whole project down.'

'And . . .' Lois prompted.

'And that's what nearly happened. The French

331

consortium behind one of the concessions went into financial meltdown. Which meant the French were kicked off the project and their concession was up for sale again.'

But Lois was still confused. 'I still don't get why this is good news for us,' she said.

Roberto laughed. 'Because our friend Jai Shijai put in a good word for *us*.' He grinned in triumph. 'Lois baby, I gotta tell you . . . this is the opportunity of a lifetime.'

'You mean you've bought the French concession? You're going to build one of the casinos out there?'

'Me and several of Jai Shijai's other friends. Private investors mostly. In fact, you met some of them at the game on his island.'

'You mean that was a set-up? You already knew we'd be involved?' Lois was outraged. 'Why didn't you tell me?'

'Because I'd signed a confidentiality agreement. None of it was official then. Not like it is now. But the new investors wanted to meet you. Wanted to know what – *who* – they were buying into. So Jai Shijai set up that little tournament on the island. To showcase your talents and to prove what a classy act the Enzo Vegas is.'

So it had been a job interview all along. She'd been paraded that whole weekend without knowing it. The information left her reeling. She remembered how shocked she'd been that Jai Shijai had described her as Enzo's ambassador. But that was exactly what she had unwittingly been.

She didn't know whether to be furious at being manipulated like that, or relieved that she'd passed their test.

And what about Aidan? Oh God! She felt sick. Was Aidan one of the investors too?

'I didn't tell you because you would have got nervous if you'd realized how much was at stake,' Roberto said. 'And anyway, I trust you. I knew you wouldn't screw up.'

Lois forced herself to concentrate. She'd figure out Aidan later. For now she had to deal with Roberto.

'But if Jai Shijai's got all these other investors, why does he need us?'

'Know-how,' Roberto said simply. 'No point in putting in a bid unless you know what to do with the concession once you get it. You need someone to run it. To make it work. Us.'

There it was. That us word. Not me. Not just Roberto. But Lois too.

'And what about Jai Shijai? Has he invested too?'

'No. I'm sure he'd love to. But his government is very clear on that. His position has to remain strictly advistory. His role is to help broker the deal. Shangri-La is about bringing money into China, not sending it out.'

He took a bottle of champagne out of the ice bucket by his feet. 'Shangri-La will be even better than Macau. This is where the market is. There are millions to be made. Millions. And we'll be the first to open,' he added, with a twinkle in his eye. 'The French were way ahead of Hudson. Way ahead.'

Lois stared at him, trying to take it all in. So this was about him and Hudson after all.

'And what about me?' she asked. 'You still haven't told me why I'm here.'

'Because you're in charge,' Roberto said, as if this were a given, his eyes boring into hers.

'*What?*'

He took her hand and squeezed it. 'I'm not getting any younger, Lois. And I gotta be back home in Vegas. So I'm relying on you. You've got to make this thing happen. You're going to make Shangri-La happen.'

'Oh Roberto,' she said, 'I don't know what to say.'

'Yes, if you've got any sense.'

CHAPTER THIRTY-SIX

Savvy was still in a good mood and feeling positive as she drove to her apartment. But the moment she walked in and breathed in the stale, fetid air, the reality of her old life came crashing back.

She had to physically force herself to step over the threshold. Dust motes swirled as she pulled back the blinds and opened the windows.

The place was an utter mess. Like a snapshot in time, evidence of her former existence lay all around. A torn VIP wristband for the Slits' backstage party. Cigarette butts floating like dead fish in a half-drunk bottle of Coca-Cola. A make-up mirror speckled with white powder and a dirty rolled-up twenty-dollar bill.

She felt like a burglar walking in here. As if it wasn't really her apartment at all. It certainly wasn't a home. It was nothing more than a glorified changing room. She looked in at the bedroom with its unmade bed, the wardrobe doors hanging open. Piles of designer clothes, shoes and bags spilled out over the floor.

She'd make herself a pot of coffee, she decided. Then tidy up. She walked through to the kitchen.

That was when she saw it. Perched precariously on top of the refrigerator. The sparkly silver box winking at her in the late afternoon sun.

Of course, she'd known it was here – waiting for her. The stack of wraps. Her emergency rations of coke. Seeing it . . . right there in reach . . . made her feel momentarily light-headed. She had to clutch the back of the kitchen chair to keep on her feet.

She hauled the noisy chair across the tiled floor and shoved it up against the refrigerator door. She climbed up and grabbed the box, then shakily removed the lid.

Do it, she told herself. *Do it right now.*

She couldn't give herself time to think. She ran into the bathroom and lifted the toilet seat, tipping the box upside-down so that the wraps cascaded into the water. Then she flushed. She watched them swirl. Round and round. Down and down. Until they were finally gone.

She drank black coffee, sitting hunched by the open window in the sitting room listening to the sirens and car horns and watching the jets etch vapour trails like chalk marks across the board of the sky.

She smoked the last two cigarettes in the packet. She

336

knew that she ought to give up, but somehow this last remaining vice offered some kind of comfort and the one or two a day she smoked was hardly the end of the world.

She'd been so excited about coming back to city life when she'd left Peace River, but now she felt small and hemmed in. Sucked into a city that she no longer wanted to be a part of. The trouble was, she didn't know where she belonged. Peace River was gone and this place was wrong.

She needed change. New horizons, new challenges to keep her mind occupied. The college prospectuses that Paige had given her were scattered across the cushions of the sofa, but she couldn't seem to find an answer in them either.

There was no point in tying herself up in knots, she thought, hearing Red's voice in her head, as if he was speaking to her. She was here to deal with her life. Right now. Just concentrate on the here and now, she told herself again, getting up and walking through to her bedroom. The message light on the phone by her bed was a continuous red, signalling that the tape was full.

She pressed the button, knowing what awaited her. The first message she'd heard a thousand times before. For over two years now, she'd never found the will to delete it.

'Sav, it's me.' Elodie's voice was clear and bright. 'Hud needs you—'

The beep sounded and other messages followed. Recent ones. But Savvy went back and played the first message again. Each time, the message ended in static as Elodie's cell phone cut out.

The full message could have been about almost anything that had happened over two years ago. Hud needs you to talk to him about money. Hud needs you to discuss plans for the party. Hud needs you—

But did he still need her now?

She picked up the phone. It was now or never.

Regardless of what Paige had said, about it being too early to contact him, Savvy felt spurred on by what Marcus had told her. Hud did care, didn't he? And if he did, then he would want to hear from her, right?

She dialled Hud's cell. He was probably in the White House, she thought, biting her lip as she heard it ring, imagining him in the Oval Office, the sun streaming through the window.

Would Paige have told him about their meeting in Miami – how healthy Savvy was, and determined? Had Paige passed on her message? Her heartfelt sentimental message. But it was the truth. Surely if Hud had heard that his only daughter still loved him, his heart would have softened?

She bit her lip, trembling with anticipation, waiting to hear his familiar voice.

But it was Paige who answered Hud's phone.

'Savvy? Is that you?'

Savvy realized that her caller ID must have come up on Hud's cell.

'Is he there?' Savvy asked, wrong-footed. 'Paige, what's going on?'

'Oh Savvy, we've been trying to get hold of you,' Paige said. 'It's Hud . . .'

Savvy gripped the phone. 'What? What's happened?'

There was a sob. 'He had a heart attack last night. He's . . . he's dead.'

CHAPTER THIRTY-SEVEN

Even though she was wearing her darkest shades, as Savvy walked out to the arrivals hall of McCarran International Airport in Las Vegas, the camera flashes of the waiting photographers were blinding. She held up her hand as a reporter ran forward, thrusting out his microphone, barging into her so forcefully that she was almost knocked to the ground.

'Get off me,' Savvy yelled.

She realized now that she should have listened to Paige and waited for the private plane to pick her up, but she hadn't wanted to wait. Her gut instinct had told her to leave LA and get to Vegas as soon as she could. Only some bastard on the flight must have tipped off these vultures.

Savvy clutched her purse to her chest and strode forward, as a TV camera crew snaked along beside her, filming. A buffed-up celeb reporter strafed her with rapid-fire questions: Was she aware of her father's drug habit? Was he a sex addict? When did she get out of rehab herself? Was it true he hadn't spoken to her in months?

Her father was dead, she wanted to scream at them. Did they have no shame?

She looked past the baying pack of reporters to the glass doors. A mirage of heat beat down on the tarmac. Where the hell was Paige? She said she'd be here.

'Savannah, did you give your dad the drugs that killed him?' one of the reporters shouted.

Savvy pushed past him, desperate to get away. Desperate to get away from these lies.

'Miss Hudson, did you ever meet the call girl in question? The girl who had been with him on the night he died?'

Girl? What girl? Hud had been with a call girl before he died?

A numbness spread through her. She stopped for a moment. She felt herself crumbling, like she was being dissolved, like she was about to disappear.

But then a figure burst out of the crowd. Paige. She put her arm around Savvy's shoulder, shouting at the reporters to leave them alone.

'Quick,' she hissed in Savvy's ear, covering her head with her coat. 'Don't say anything. The car's just outside.'

Savvy felt herself being led, as if in a dream. Through the doors into a wall of heat outside. More shouted questions. An open limo door.

Paige bundled Savvy into the back. They sat behind the tinted windows watching silently as the reporters lurched in close. It was like being attacked by a plague of locusts. But these scavengers wanted more than her flesh. They wanted her soul.

Savvy could hear herself pant. Don't cry, she told herself. Keep it together. Give in to the tears now and they're not going to stop.

She took a deep breath and turned away from the window, taking off her shades. She realized that she and Paige were not alone.

A grey-haired man in a dark suit was sitting quietly opposite Paige. He looked vaguely familiar.

'Savvy, I don't know if you've met Len Johnson before. He was a good friend of your father's and has agreed to work the case for us.'

'I'm sorry for your loss,' Len said, leaning forward to shake her hand.

'Who are you? A cop?' Savvy asked.

'He's better than a cop,' Paige said.

A detective then. Ex-FBI. He had the look about him. There'd been plenty of Lens on Hud's payroll over the years.

'This woman they were talking about in there?' Savvy's eyes flashed at Paige. 'It can't be true. Tell me it's not true.'

Paige couldn't meet Savvy's eyes.

'You didn't *tell* me?'

'I didn't know what to tell you,' Paige said. 'We're all shocked. Devastated.'

Paige handed Savvy a newspaper. As she saw the

342

picture of her father, fresh tears threatened to choke her. The article's headline was unbearable.

Vegas Tycoon Dies in Drug-Fueled Sex Romp.

Len cleared his throat. 'They're saying it was a severe heart attack. Whoever the girl was, she panicked. She left him there to die.'

Savvy's eyes blurred as she tried to read the words that she could hardly comprehend. How her father had been found dead in the White House having had a heart attack, apparently after a rampant sex session. How Hud had a notorious predilection for up-market call girls. How 'several sources close to Hudson' had suggested that his secret habit was the reason for Savvy's mother's suicide.

'Who are these sources?' she snapped. 'Who has been talking? Peddling this rubbish?'

'That's what we're trying to find out,' Paige said.

'The police are all over the White House,' Len said. 'We've got to wait our turn. But we will get to the bottom of this mess.'

'You're not trying to tell me there's any truth in this bullshit?' Savvy shook the paper at Paige.

Paige didn't answer.

'Tell me it isn't true,' Savvy shouted.

'I only heard the rumours,' she said. 'I never saw anything – anyone – myself.'

Savvy felt sick. She watched her best friend, Hud's greatest fan, rub away a tear on her cheek.

'What rumours?'

Paige sniffed. 'That he used ... well, had used agency girls.'

Savvy thought of Tracy, the girl at Marcus's apartment. But Marcus and Hud . . . they weren't the same. She couldn't bear to hear any more. Hud had been snatched away from her and already her memories of him were being sullied as well.

'And the drugs? That can't be true, can it? It doesn't make any sense. Daddy was a fitness freak. He was so careful. He'd never have done drugs. He hated drugs. You know that.'

Paige glanced at Len. 'The preliminary blood tests show that there were several milligrams of cocaine in his system,' Len said.

This was all wrong. Savvy refused to believe it. Wouldn't believe it.

'You're going to get to the truth,' she told Len Johnson. 'You're going to find out whoever's responsible for what happened to Hud. No matter how long it takes. Or how much it costs.'

There were more photographers waiting at the White House. A helicopter thwacked overhead.

As the limo slid through the gates, as sleek and sedate as a hearse, Savvy saw the yellow police tape across the side entrance to the house and unfamiliar cars parked at random angles on the drive.

She closed her eyes for a second and took a deep breath, bracing herself.

Paige held out her hand to Savvy and together they hurried up the front steps, knowing full well that telephoto lenses would be trained on them from above.

In the domed hallway, a uniformed officer stood guard at the bottom of the staircase.

'I need to see him,' Savvy said, walking towards the stairs.

Paige grabbed her wrist. 'He's not here. They've taken his body. And the police are still upstairs.'

'Where's Martha?' Savvy asked, looking towards the kitchen. She knew that she'd be devastated by what had happened.

'She's resting. You can see her later. There'll be plenty of time.'

Savvy looked longingly again at the kitchen door, needing the comfort of Martha's familiar embrace now more than ever, but Paige was already on the move. Savvy followed her into the Oval Office and Paige shut the doors behind her.

Three men in grey suits – people Savvy instantly recognized as her father's lawyers – stood crowded around Hud's polished desk. They all stopped talking immediately and turned to face her. Their looks were searching, ashen.

Peter Murasaki, the head of her father's legal team, came to her side. He'd been one of her father's favourite employees. Hud had poached him from a career at a Japanese bank after they'd hit it off one night at La Paris.

'I'm so sorry, Savannah,' he said. 'We're all going to miss him terribly.'

The other two attorneys were quick to follow suit, offering up their condolences. But Savvy wasn't listening.

345

The oil portrait of Michael Hudson stared steadily down at her from the wall behind them, as if he'd caught them snooping.

'Well, now that everyone's here, let's get on, shall we,' Paige said. She seemed to have taken strength from being in the Oval Office. The tears from the limo had vanished. Her voice had changed too. She seemed confident and businesslike.

Savvy stared at her and she knew all at once that Paige hadn't told her something. Something important.

In the corner of her eye, Savvy caught a movement over by the bay window. She turned to see Luc standing there. He looked weary, his eyes bloodshot. His suit was crumpled and his tie was crooked. Hud's death had clearly hit him hard.

All this time, Savvy had wondered what it would be like to see him again, how she'd feel. But now that he was here, what she felt wasn't a surge of hatred or love. Just embers. Sadness. The need for warmth. The need to be held by someone who'd cared about Hud. And who'd once cared about her too.

Luc walked forward. For the first time in so long, he looked at her directly without hostility in his eyes. She thought immediately of all the terrible things she'd said about him to Red. And to his face in the wake of Elodie's death.

Luc was saying something. Savvy stared at his soft lips. His voice was a gentle half-whisper. He was telling her he'd take care of everything, that everything would be all right. It was all she could do not to step forward and lay her head against his chest.

But Paige butted in. 'Peter wanted to explain to you as quickly as possible what we've got in mind. What Hud would have wanted to happen in the event of his death.'

Savvy felt her whole body tense. The warmth faded. Coldness came in its place. Because once more she remembered the last words she'd heard Hud say.

She felt fear rip through her. Was the whole empire – everything Hud had worked for – now Luc's? Was that the news the lawyers were here to break to her?

'I'm afraid there's rather a lot of urgent paperwork,' Peter Murasaki said, 'relating to your father's estate. None of us were expecting this to happen.'

He led her over to the big desk by the window and she sat down in Hud's chair. Peter started talking then, leafing through the triplicate sheaves of papers laid out.

He was speaking in lawyers' language, using words Savvy had never heard before.

There would have to be a funeral, she thought. She'd have to lead the mourners. Would she bury Hud's ashes next to Elodie's? Would they lie together and look up through the great oak trees of the cemetery? Memories of Hud flashed up at her from her childhood. She thought of all the things she'd never got a chance to tell him, or thank him for, once she'd grown up.

She was aware that Peter had fallen into an expectant silence. He smiled gently at Savvy as he pressed an ink fountain pen into her hand and pointed to the first of the many documents he wanted her to sign.

'I know this is difficult, Savvy,' Paige said gently.

'But the fact is you don't know anything about the business. And there's so much you want to do. College ... travelling ... All you have to do is sign and then we can take the business forward. You won't have to do anything. You'll be a wealthy woman and free to do whatever you want. You'll never want for anything.'

'You mean ...?' she said, looking at Paige. 'He left it all to me?'

Paige and Peter glanced at each other. Savvy sensed that Paige had wanted to break this news to Savvy alone, but had been overridden. And now she'd proved Peter wrong, as Savvy hadn't taken in anything he'd just told her.

'Technically, yes, you are Michael's heir,' Peter said.

'Technically?'

'Michael had talked of structuring his eventual legacy in a different way, but unfortunately his wishes hadn't been put in writing,' Peter said. She noticed the look between him and Luc.

Unfortunately? Unfortunate for who?

'As you might already know,' Peter continued, 'he'd already assigned both Paige and Luc a five per cent equity share, based on performance, of course, but—'

'But the rest is mine,' Savvy said. 'The company is mine. To do with as I choose?'

'Michael worked very closely with Paige and Luc. There were many facets of the business he was expecting them to take forward. When you sign these papers, it'll mean that everything your father wanted to do can happen.'

Savvy still held the pen in her hand. It was shaking.

All at once she saw the friendship bracelet Red had given her slip down her wrist.

Do what you have to do . . .

You're so much stronger than you think you are . . .

Was this her final chance not to let her father down? To step up to the mark and prove to him how worthy she could be? Or was she being crazy even thinking like that? Would her getting involved be the last thing he'd want?

Savvy stared at the framed photograph on the desk. It was of Hud with Elodie and Savvy at their twenty-first birthday party. In it, he looked so happy – as if he were glowing with pride. He had his arms around both his daughters. They seemed so solid. So united. As if they could never be torn apart.

This was a Hudson business. Hud's hard graft had built it and now she, the next Hudson – the only surviving Hudson – would make sure it went to the next level. No matter what happened. No matter how hard. No matter how much she had to learn along the way. Her father's legacy would live on. She'd make damn sure of it.

Savvy put the pen down on the desk and, taking up the papers, tore them in two.

CHAPTER THIRTY-EIGHT

Lois Chan felt as if her heart was about to burst with excitement.

It was finally here: launch night at the Good Fortune. Two incredible and long years since Roberto had first shown her the site.

In her office, she pressed her lips carefully together and smoothed down the front of her long Christian Dior evening gown. Her stylist, Sue-Lin, nodded at her in the mirror, satisfied that Lois was ready and the final slick of lip gloss was perfect.

Lois stared at her reflection for one more second. After spending the last three days in the same clothes, working round the clock to get ready for the launch tonight, she couldn't believe how glamorous Sue-Lin had made her look now. Her eyes were sparkling, her hair glossy and her skin was glowing.

She let out an excited, pent-up breath. *It was really happening.*

'Go, go, go,' Sue-Lin told Lois. 'They'll be waiting for you.'

Thank God for her girls, Lois thought. She'd made sure that the workforce was split fifty-fifty men to women and she couldn't have been ready to host the biggest night of her life without all the women who'd made it possible.

She kissed Sue-Lin on the cheek, then, picking up her long skirt, she rushed out on to the raised walkway of the hub.

The walkway ensured that Lois could see everyone and everything she needed to, at a glance. Unlike at the Enzo Vegas, Lois had had this space designed so that all of the security staff could move freely and communicate easily. The curved back wall was filled with floor-to-ceiling screens. In front of them, Mario's team were going about their business in an atmosphere of control and calm, which made Lois feel nervous. Would they really cope when the casino went live in just a few hours?

But Mario was the boss of the hub. It was his job to ensure that they did, she reminded herself. He'd worked tirelessly with the computer technicians to make sure that every system was the best it could be.

'You all set, Lois?' Mario called, as she walked towards him, fiddling with her diamond pendant earring. He looked surprisingly relaxed, considering what a big deal tonight was, and how much rested on his shoulders.

But then, Mario was hardly the young foot soldier he'd been back at the Enzo Vegas. He looked older and more self-assured tonight than Lois had ever seen him – probably to do with the smart dark-blue suit he was wearing, as opposed to his usual scruffy jeans and T-shirt. She suddenly saw that, without his glasses, Mario was a very handsome man.

'As ready as I'll ever be,' she replied.

'It's going to be awesome,' he said, a grin on his face. 'You look sensational, by the way.'

She smiled. 'Thanks. Everything's up and running?'

She knew he'd been overseeing a final round of the performance tests she'd insisted on, governing every-thing from the cashing-up procedures to the emergency protocols. They were leaving nothing to chance.

'All A-OK,' he said in a soothing tone. 'The floor staff are all set as well. They can't wait.'

'Good.' Lois checked her watch. It was half an hour until the dignitaries and celebs were due to start arriving.

Lois looked over to the screen which showed the outside of the Good Fortune, where the crowd had been gathering all day, soaking up the atmosphere and the rising sense of occasion. Lois knew from experience that Chinese people were a lot more good-natured about waiting than Americans. Even so, she was pleased to see that they were taking advantage of the free drinks and free Good Fortune paper umbrellas she'd sent out to thank them for their patience in the unexpected heatwave.

She sure hoped it was going to be worth the wait.

She'd done everything in her power to ensure that it was. Tonight was about putting the Good Fortune on the world map as the first of the mega casinos in Shangri-La to open its doors. The first and the best. And what a party it was going to be.

She now saw that Roberto was waiting for her by the main swing doors out into the casino with LJ, the events manager Lois had hired. She'd enticed her from one of the best hotels in Shanghai and the small, feisty Chinese girl had been worth her weight in gold. She was a stickler for detail, worked incredibly hard and had brought some of her finest staff with her, as well as enticing Leighton Wan, the celebrated Hong Kong chef, to head up the Good Fortune's catering and fine dining. Roberto was thrilled.

Lois knew that this must be the busiest time of the whole night for LJ. The champagne reception was being set up in the atrium downstairs and the band in the ballroom, and the final nerve-racking adjustments were being made to the net containing close to twenty thousand balloons, all embossed with the Good Fortune's dragon logo. But LJ was full of smiles as Lois hurried towards them, knowing that Roberto was waiting to escort them both down to the waiting press in the courtyard.

'Knock-out dress, Lois,' LJ said, feeling the silky skirt. 'Couture. Lovely.'

'Thanks,' Lois said. 'You look great yourself.'

It was true. LJ was wearing a traditional Chinese silk dress embroidered with green and red flowers. Roberto didn't look half bad either. He was immaculate in a vintage tux, his hair swept back from his tanned forehead.

Roberto had his hand behind his back and now Lois saw why. He was holding a bunch of red peonies which he now handed to her.

'Oh Roberto, you didn't have to.' She kissed him on the cheek.

'You know what they're calling you out there?' he said.

'Something good, I hope?'

'Lady Luck. The Queen of Shangri-La.'

Lois flushed at his praise. She looked down at the beautiful blooms, smelling them.

'You know they call these the king of flowers here,' LJ said to Lois, her English perfect but heavily accented.

As usual, she wasn't missing an opportunity to translate customs and idioms for Lois and Roberto's benefit. Goodness knows how many *faux pas* Lois would have made if it hadn't been for LJ. She'd brought her up to speed culturally and linguistically, teaching her all the nuances and customs to help her get by. If Lois's grandmother could see her now, even she would nod with approval.

LJ carefully pinned one of the blooms into Lois's chignon.

'It's the perfect touch,' she said with a smile.

Lois gave the bunch of flowers to LJ and plucked a bloom to put in Roberto's buttonhole. She pressed her palm against the lapel of his jacket, suddenly overcome with gratitude. He'd given her a free rein out here on

354

everything from the interior design to the hiring and firing of staff. He'd been as good as his word, and as a result the Good Fortune truly was hers. All hers. She felt overwhelmed by his faith in her.

'Thank you,' she said.

'You've done a sensational job,' Roberto said proudly, squeezing Lois's hand. 'I couldn't have done it better myself. Now go knock 'em, dead, Lois. This is your moment.'

On the podium in the Good Fortune's central courtyard Roberto applauded Lois, stepping away so that she could make her address to the press. They were banked up ahead of her, with the giant Good Fortune dragon fountain behind them, glinting in the late afternoon light.

To one side were the huge golden gates, closed for now, and to the other the casino doors, draped with the red ribbon that Lois and Roberto would cut.

Bring it on, she thought, seeing the TV cameras pointing her way. She hoped that her mother would be watching this on the entertainment channel in San Francisco, and Cara too would be viewing the live webcast.

She'd made it. Nothing had gone wrong and they were all ready. She smiled at the press, the flashes blinding her.

This was her baby – everything she'd worked flat out for. Now was her big opportunity to show the world a different Lois Chan. Not someone whose claim to fame was that she had once been shot, or had had a brother who'd been killed in a gang fight, but one who had created something innovative and amazing.

'In being the first casino to open its magnificent gateway, we are sending out a statement that the Good Fortune is *the* face of Shangri-La,' she began. She knew these words by heart. She'd practised for this moment over and over, but now that she was in it, it was even more nerve-racking than she'd anticipated. 'Tonight we are here to present to you the world's first ever eco super-casino.'

She heard applause and smiled as she continued. 'Our philosophy is *consumerism with a conscience*. We are sending a message to the world that China has the capacity to lead the way in vital green technology.'

The idea had been Lois's own. Roberto had been sceptical at first, but he was won over as soon as he realized that Lois had universal approval from the architects and authorities, and green tax breaks into the bargain.

'How?' someone asked.

'We have harnessed the power of the waves, the wind and the sun to provide all the energy for the casino. We've also completed an ambitious water recycling project – one of the first of its kind in the world, which allows us to irrigate our beautiful gardens and supply the waterways and water park.'

'Is it true that you built schools for the workers' children?' someone else asked, in Mandarin.

'Yes. And safe housing,' she answered in the same dialect. 'We have made sure that, in every aspect, the Good Fortune has had – and will continue to have – a positive impact on its environment and the surrounding community.'

'Critics have said that this is the most expensive casino built in recent history. Isn't your strategy risky?' another reporter asked.

'We believe that the investment has been worth it. Looking at the bigger picture, Shangri-La is an important geographical site for world entertainment. It's here to stay. The blueprint of the Good Fortune's environmental and ethical strategy will mean that we're here to stay as well,' she said.

'How do you think you'll compare to the other casinos being built here, once they're up and running? El Palazzo, for example?' An American CNN journalist had a mischievous glint in her eye.

Lois smiled. 'I think the very fact we've opened first speaks for itself,' she answered.

'To the victor, the spoils?' the journalist said.

'Quite so,' Lois agreed, knowing full well the journalist's quote would be attributed to her in tomorrow's press.

'Savannah Hudson might have something to say about that,' another American journalist – Fox News this time – said.

Lois held up her hand and smiled joylessly. 'I am not interested in what Savannah Hudson has to say,' she said.

She had to admit – she hadn't wept when she'd heard of Hudson's death, but she had been taken aback to learn that his wild-child party-girl daughter had come out of rehab to run the Hudson Corporation.

For one fleeting moment, she'd thought that a woman in charge might change the way things stood between the business empires, but the Hudson Corp's PR machine had carried on exactly as before, since its founder's death, pushing its own agenda at the expense of its rivals' reputations.

Savannah Hudson was complicit in this, Lois was sure. But she also suspected that Savannah was in charge of the corporation in name alone. A pretty puppet with a big mouth in a business suit. It was Paige Logan and Luc Devereaux who pulled the strings.

'Have you invited Savannah Hudson to your launch tonight?'

Of course Lois had invited her. It was a neighbourly courtesy. One she'd discussed long and hard with Tristan Blake, who'd been her right-hand man in Shangri-La from the start. They were both intrigued to see whether she'd have the nerve to turn up. She glanced across at Tristan and caught his private smile. He was standing along from Roberto and Susie, Lois's PA and Tristan's girlfriend.

'Everyone's welcome here. That's our philosophy,' Lois said. 'Even Savannah Hudson.' She tried, but she couldn't resist the jibe. 'Particularly since, as I understand it, it's going to be several more months before El Palazzo is even vaguely habitable.'

There was a ripple of laughter. She'd judged her ad-lib jibe well. The press were on her side.

Suddenly, there was a sound of drums beating.

'Please, turn round,' she instructed the crowd, all thoughts of Savvy Hudson forgotten. The drums got louder as the giant golden gates slowly opened. In a few moments, the world-famous Ko-Xin Acrobatic Dance Troupe she'd flown in from their sell-out show in Beijing for tonight would be flipping and tumbling up the red carpet, followed by the Good Fortune's sixty-metre dragon ushering in the guests.

It was show time.

CHAPTER THIRTY-NINE

Savvy stared up at the ceiling of the Sistine Chapel and swore. The plaster section showing the finger of God giving life to Adam had come away and now lay cracked on the floor, pointing at her like a terrible omen.

The giant reproduction of Michelangelo's masterpiece in Vatican City had been painted in Europe and shipped in sixty sections to the casino hall of El Palazzo in Shangri-La, where it had been resurrected. But the exterior roof tiles had been fitted with the wrong type of cement and the whole thing had leaked overnight.

The resulting flood had caused tens of thousands of dollars' worth of damage. And now there were workmen everywhere trying to rescue the situation.

Drills screeched in the cavernous, gloomy space, scaffolding poles clanked. Above it all a Chinese radio station blared and echoed, making the decibel level ear-splittingly high. A huge crane was lifting ten engineers in a cage to survey the damage up close. A team of artists and artisans were already on their way over from Italy.

Savvy held on to her yellow hard hat and quickly stepped in to a gritty puddle on the concrete floor, as another shower of dust swirled down from the ceiling. Shit, she thought. Her new Louboutins were trashed.

She'd flown into Shangri-La an hour ago, but so far her visit to the El Palazzo complex had been an unmitigated disaster. Luc had lost his temper with the builders twice and he seemed as if he might snap at her at any minute. At this rate, if the guy bit his tongue any harder, he'd draw blood.

After hearing about this latest disaster to throw El Palazzo even further off-schedule, she'd decided to fly over herself and see how bad the situation really was. Luc was clearly in the middle of a full-blown crisis and was making it plain that Savvy was the last person he wanted to see.

She hadn't been alone with Luc like this for a long time. After Hud had died two years ago and Savvy had torn up the documents that would have put Luc in charge, he'd been furious. But she'd stood her ground. In the arguments that followed, she'd been sorely tempted to fire Luc and ditch the whole Shangri-La project altogether. But she'd quickly seen – mostly thanks to Paige spelling it out – that there was no way she could extricate herself from the complex financial deals that Luc and Hud had struck to get the Shangri-La concession.

So she'd dispatched Luc almost immediately and told him to run the entire project on the ground over here. It had been an arrangement that suited everyone, except perhaps poor Paige, who seemed to spend her life on a plane, flying back and forth between Shangri-La and Vegas to report on progress.

But the reports – even with Paige's rosy twist on them – hadn't been good. Delay had followed delay, until the head start El Palazzo had secured over its rivals had been lost. First there'd been the fact that the foundations weren't dug deep enough, leading to subsidence so that the main concourse needed to be demolished and rebuilt. Then there'd been a series of disasters over local labour relations.

All of which threw Luc's management ability into doubt. But Savvy had already got Paige to secretly employ an independent analyst to check up on him, and they'd concluded that Luc had done as good a job as anyone could have done in the circumstances.

Savvy watched now as he slumped down on to the boards of a scaffolding tower and rubbed his eyes. He was wearing jeans, brogues, a designer stripy pink and white shirt and, like her, a yellow hard hat. And he was still just as handsome as ever.

'So there it is,' he shouted above the cacophony, gesturing to the ceiling. 'Totally and utterly fucked. So,' he said, lifting his eyes wearily to hers, 'I guess you're going to fire me.'

His accent . . . In spite of all the cruel words he'd said in the past, she still loved the sound of his voice.

'No, Luc. I'm here to discuss how you're going to put it right,' she said.

As Paige frequently told her, the Hudson Corporation's best asset was its staff. And now her gut told her that balling out Luc when he was clearly exhausted and demoralized was not going to help.

'It's not your fault. I know that,' she continued, glancing up one final time at the ceiling. Savvy already knew that it was the Chinese sub-contractors and the confused surveyors who'd caused the problem this time. And the ever-present language barrier. Luc had fired six translators in the last two months alone. She knew he was trying his best to keep on top of the situation.

Besides, Luc might not think it but by Savvy's reckoning there was lots to be positive about. Hud might have had a romantic vision of a noble European palace, but the truth was that, behind this big centrepiece, El Palazzo was crammed with small, cheap hotel rooms with the bare minimum of facilities to pack in the customers. Most of them were almost ready.

'Excuse me, Luc?' a short, squat man interrupted them.

'Ah,' Luc said, smiling for the first time. 'Chester. I'd like you to meet Savannah Hudson.'

The man, who had a gingery goatee beard over his roll of chins, was sweating profusely. 'Miss Hudson,' he said, extending a fat hand. 'I was a great admirer of your father's,' he said. 'Chester Malone. Very pleased to be at your service.'

'So, Chester,' she said, 'how is security coming along?'

He glanced at Luc. 'Well, slowly. It's a problem training these . . .' He paused and Savvy was convinced he was about to say something horribly racist. He realized in time that it would not be wise in front of Savvy. 'Training these newcomers to the control room of a casino,' he said judiciously. 'But I think I've got it covered.'

'I'm glad to hear it,' she said. 'Now then, you've set up the meeting tomorrow, right?' she asked Luc.

Savvy had insisted on calling together the heads of all the contractors working on El Palazzo. It was time to show them who was boss and give them the face of the chairwoman and owner of the Hudson Corporation.

'Yes. Tomorrow morning,' Luc said. He sounded as if he didn't think it was a good idea, but Savvy ignored his tone.

'I'd like Chester to be there, too,' she told them both.

She didn't tell either of them that she'd be announcing that they were going to open in six weeks. Three weeks ahead of the planned schedule. Savvy had heard that Lois Chan had invited Jai Shijai to a baccarat championship and she knew she had to get El Palazzo open if the high rollers were in town. Whatever it took. She had to lay out her stall. El Palazzo was the competition and everyone was going to know it.

Savvy thanked Chester and politely dismissed him, before walking on through the casino with Luc.

'I don't know if Paige emailed you, but I worked out a bonus structure for the new contractors,' she said.

'That was *your* idea?' Luc was obviously surprised – and impressed.

364

His praise shouldn't be important, or his approval, but somehow it was. More than she'd care to admit. Because no matter how much she told herself otherwise, the last two years had been dominated by just one secret desire. To make Luc Devereaux respect her again. To prove to him that she'd filled Hud's shoes.

'Of course,' she told him. 'We're going to get this place back on track. And fast. Now show me the roof.'

Up on the damaged roof of El Palazzo, Savvy leaned back against the scaffolding. It was such a relief to be away from the noise and stress inside and up here in the fresh air.

She wondered what Hud would have said, if he'd been here today. Would he have handled Luc the same way?

She was full of remorse that she hadn't taken her father – or his business – more seriously when he was alive. It had all been there for her, right under her nose, if only she'd just looked. And now she'd missed out altogether on having Hud as her mentor.

On one level, his death was still very raw, but on another, she felt more connected now to Hud than she'd ever felt in the past, now that she was running his business. She was determined to see his vision through. She had to. She was the only one left.

A fact made more apparent when she'd attended Martha's quiet funeral a month ago.

Poor Martha had died peacefully in her sleep after heart problems had left her unable to work for the past year. Savvy knew that she'd never really got over Hud's death. Savvy had solemnly promised Martha that she'd get to the bottom of what had happened to Hud in his final hours.

And now it was on the tip of Savvy's tongue to tell Luc what she'd heard about the latest call girl kiss-and-tell that would hit the headlines in Vegas this week. They kept on coming. Women who wanted to make a quick buck by spreading sleaze about Michael Hudson.

Each one cut a little deeper. But the mystery woman Hud had allegedly been with on his last night seemed to have vanished into thin air. The police investigation had turned up nothing and Len Johnson, the PI Paige had hired, had got no further. Nobody had been held to account for Hud's death, and it rankled more than ever.

Which was why Savvy had taken matters into her own hands. Since all official lines of inquiry had failed, she'd decided to employ someone she trusted, someone well accustomed to operating in a city's seedy underbelly. Before she'd flown out to Shangri-La, she'd enlisted Marcus's help to track down the agency who'd supplied girls to Hud.

Marcus, at Savvy's expense, had come through a short stint in rehab and was a changed man. Much to Paige's disapproval, Savvy had thrown him in at the deep end and given him a job as head of comps at La Paris. Just as she'd expected, Marcus was thriving. He'd just clinched next year's MTV awards.

None of which she intended to discuss with Luc. She

had the sense to know that Marcus would probably always be a sore subject between them.

Reaching into her bag, Savvy pulled out her packet of Lucky Strike and lit one.

'You haven't given up then?' Luc said.

'No,' she said, inhaling and putting the lighter back in her bag. 'I will. One day soon. A girl needs *one* vice.'

Luc nodded. 'You've done very well, Savvy,' he said quietly.

He didn't look at her. Did he still think of her in terms of her vices? she wondered. Did he still assume she was the slut and liar he'd declared her to be all that time ago?

But now she could never raise the issue with him. Because life had moved on. And because Elodie was dead. And that, more than everything – Marcus, Hud, her decisions in Vegas – was something that they could never broach. Ever.

She sighed. 'Look at it,' she said.

A vision of Shangri-La was rising up from the mud right before their eyes. Giant cranes stood sentry on the skyline, huge diggers chomped at the ground like modern dinosaurs. She breathed in the hot stink of the tarmac pouring from the burners. And that humid, exotic smell that told her she was in the East.

A large red sun was sinking beyond the horizon across the sea, and in the moment of silence, the distant sound of music, which must be from the Good Fortune's opening party, drifted over to them on the breeze. She could hear drums and cymbals clashing. But Savvy ignored it, turning the other way to survey

El Palazzo's leisure complex in the grounds below. She had to focus on the positive.

'The pool and the golf course are all nearly there,' she said. 'It's like Vegas must have been. Nothing there, and then . . . Bam!'

She knew he was looking at her as she continued to stare out.

'I'm glad you're here, Savvy. Thank you for keeping faith in me. I can turn this around and I will.'

Savvy smiled. 'Good. That's what I want to hear.'

'Maybe you should have come before.'

Savvy crushed the cigarette beneath the toe of her shoe.

'Actually, I think our arrangement has worked rather well. Don't you think so?' she said. Any other arrangement and you'd have quit, was what she was actually thinking. Leaving me with no one to run the project at all.

He nodded down at the workers still toiling on the site, even at this late hour. 'Those people down there,' he said, 'they work for money, sure. But sometimes to get the best out of them . . . they need to hear something more. Like what you just said about Vegas . . . that they really are making history here.' He turned to face her and looked her in the eye. 'I think it'll mean a great deal to them that they're finally going to meet the boss.'

The boss. He'd actually said it. Like he meant it.

As if he'd finally accepted that she was the real deal.

Her triumph should be complete. She'd worked so hard for this moment. From day one, she'd taken on

Hud's mantle. She'd worked 24/7, eating, breathing and (barely) sleeping the business. She'd learned hard and fast, pumping Paige for information, shadowing Hud's team, learning his business models, mastering the finances. And in the back of her mind, all along, she'd wanted just one person to take notice and be impressed. Luc.

And now he had.

So why didn't she feel triumphant? Why did she feel sorry for him?

She forced herself to turn in the opposite direction.

'Well, I'll do my best. You know, I like it here,' she said. 'I didn't think I would. But I think Shangri-La is going to be very special.'

Luc sighed. 'Do you? It has no soul yet for me,' he said. 'It's not like Macau with all the Portuguese buildings and the old town.' He sounded so wistful and exhausted.

Savvy turned to Luc. His face was softly lit in the setting sun.

'You sound like you could do with a break,' she said. 'You know, Luc, I'm going back to Vegas the day after tomorrow. But I'm flying via France. I'm stopping in to meet some people in Monte Carlo.'

'Oh? Who?'

'Some disgruntled investors from the failed French consortium. They still want to get in on Shangri-La. They've been hunting us down for a share in El Palazzo.'

'You're not going to give them one, are you?' He sounded suddenly alert.

'Why don't you come with me? I could do with your opinion.'

'I can't. I mean – I can't *possibly*. There's far too much to do here.'

'Luc, you need some perspective. It'll also give us time to plan who to bring from Vegas. We're going to have to throw people, power and money at this thing to get it done.'

'I appreciate that, Savvy, but—'

'You're exhausted and you need to get out of here. Fix it with whoever you need to. That's an order,' she said.

Luc bowed his head deferentially. There was a small silence. Again the music from the party at the Good Fortune drifted towards them.

'Come on then,' Savvy said, standing and putting her hands on her waist. 'Let's do it.'

'Really? Are you sure you want to? They're not expecting us to actually turn up, you know.'

'Which is precisely why we're going. It's all about face. If you lose face, you lose the war,' she said. 'And I'm not losing.'

CHAPTER FORTY

As Savvy got changed in one of El Palazzo's minuscule bedrooms, she knew that this was *exactly* why she'd avoided Luc all this time. Because she couldn't trust herself around him. And now she'd gone and invited him to Monte Carlo with her.

And she shouldn't have, she now realized. Not if she still had feelings for him.

What good would getting any closer to him do? They had a professional relationship which just about worked. But all the other personal stuff – all their past, Elodie, everything – was still there. Buried. Where it should stay.

Savvy threw open her suitcase on the bed. She pulled out the mint-green and silver dress, then stood in front of the mirror on the wardrobe.

She held the figure-hugging evening dress up against herself. She'd worn it to a party at La Paris and Marcus had told her it was a knock-out. But how would Luc think she looked in it?

Stop it! she scolded herself. Who cared what Luc thought of her? Anyway, for all she knew, he had a local girlfriend out here. Someone like these grinning Asian girls on the dreadful tourist posters on the walls.

But even as she thought it, Savvy knew it wasn't true. Luc Devereaux looked like a man who'd not had any female attention for a long time.

She saw the glint in her eye as she mussed up her hair in the mirror. Because now a deliciously naughty thought occurred to her as she remembered how she'd seduced him at La Paris all that time ago. The moment when he'd not been able to help giving in to her.

OK, so the past was the past, but . . . but what if . . . ?

What if she could make Luc desire her again?

Well, surely she'd win, really win, if that were to happen? How delicious would that be? To hear Luc overcome with passion again? To see him lose all his principles and the moral high ground and admit that he was a slave to the lust he felt for her . . .

She smiled at herself. Being his boss was one thing, but she knew she wouldn't feel satisfied until he was grovelling at her feet.

Because only then would she get her real victory. Because the moment he admitted that he wanted her – truly wanted her – she'd tell him that he couldn't have her.

Not ever.

And then she'd be even. Once and for all.

Her reflection stared back at her. She knew she was contemplating a dangerous game. One that she'd never dare to play if Paige was around. But wasn't it only by doing this that she could truly put the past to rest and quell the what-ifs that still haunted her, whenever she spent time with Luc? Wouldn't she be taking charge of her life in exactly the way Max Savage had counselled her to do from the start?

She bit her lip and smiled at herself. Was that why she'd packed a green dress? To remind Luc of the green dress she'd worn the night they'd made love? Had this plan been in her subconscious all along?

Savvy deliberately didn't look at Luc as they walked out of El Palazzo and across the road with its orange and white cones, to where the crowd had gathered outside the Good Fortune. He'd changed too and was wearing a tuxedo with a black shirt, which showed off his tan and made him look – Savvy had to admit it – damn sexy.

If he thought she looked great in her dress, she didn't give him the chance to tell her. Instead, she remained calm and professional. They were to go to the Good Fortune and find out as much as they could about their rival casino, she told him. This was a spying mission pure and simple. They had to find any evidence, any chink, any fault they possibly could and twist it to their own advantage. It was no good waiting for someone else to do it. Luc and Savvy were here tonight. They had to be proactive. *Nowhere* and *no one* was perfect. If Lois Chan was going to open first and hold herself up to scrutiny, then scrutinize they would. Savvy was sure there had to be some way to gain the upper hand tonight. They just had to find out how.

Up ahead, the limos and the camera crews with their bright lights trained on the red carpet made the place feel like Oscars night and, with the crowd glittering in the camera flashes, Savvy felt her confidence surge. Walking and talking, meeting and greeting, posing and smiling. It had always been her bread and butter. It was what she did best.

She took Luc's arm firmly, falling into step demurely beside him.

'Smile,' she said, through gritted teeth. 'We're a united front. Nobody is to take a photo of us looking anything other than relaxed, OK?'

Savvy steered him on to the red carpet and turned on her brightest smile. She heard her name and turned and posed for the cameras, stopping by a gaggle of journalists. A woman from the *South China Morning Post* was clearly delighted they'd shown up.

'Are you upset that the Good Fortune has opened ahead of schedule?' she asked Savvy. 'Your father made it very clear that El Palazzo was going to spearhead Shangri-La.'

'And it still will. There will be nowhere on earth like El Palazzo,' Savvy replied, with a charming smile. 'We will be the biggest and undeniably the best venue in the whole of China. Perhaps the world. You wait, you'll see,' she said as she moved on, exuding confidence.

'Go easy, Savvy,' Luc said. 'Don't promise them the earth.'

'Why not? They're going to get it.'

'But—'

She squeezed his arm and he looked down as she rubbed her fingers together. 'Shangri-La is about gambling,' she said, 'not some crusade for the environment. We'll give them good old Vegas razzmatazz right here in their backyard. Not all this eco bullshit.'

She'd seen the glossy brochure for the Good Fortune already. She knew just what to expect. This place was more of a hippy holiday resort than a gambling haven. And people wouldn't travel halfway around the world and pay these prices for that.

Oh yes, Roberto Enzo might have won Savvy's approval for the way he ran the Enzo Vegas. But he'd betrayed his own old-school principles here. This place was a hybrid. A nothing. It would never win anyone's heart.

They stopped and posed for the cameras again.

'Can you put your arm around Miss Hudson, Mr Devereaux?' one of the photographers asked.

'Sure,' Luc said, grinning and putting his arm around Savvy's shoulder. 'United front, right,' he hissed, so that only Savvy could hear.

She smiled, grateful that she and Luc were not alone. Because it would be too easy, she now realized. Too easy to be seduced by his touch . . . too easy to let it smooth away everything that had gone before.

When the cameras finished flashing, she firmly stepped away from Luc. She was here for business. Nothing more.

'So what do you think of the Good Fortune, Miss Hudson?' another reporter asked.

'The façade looks fine,' she said. She had to say it really. Because it would look like sour grapes if she said nothing. She gazed at the Good Fortune's glass structure rising into the pink sky like an elaborately cut jewel. It was quite magnificent, she had to admit. The clever melding of the twenty-first century with the traditional Chinese elements shouldn't work, but it did. Rather stunningly.

'But looks can be deceiving,' she carried on. 'And usually are. So give me a chance to have a look around inside and I'll tell you if I'm right,' she said, walking on.

'You're pretty good at dealing with the press, you know,' Luc said.

'I used to do it all the time,' she reminded him.

But God, she thought, it feels so much better to be doing it like this. Talking about something real. Something I'm involved with. Not just someone else's perfume or DJ night. How silly and inconsequential and far away that seemed now. And the very best thing of all, she thought with a smile, is doing this clean. And with Luc by her side.

But the second she walked through the golden gates into the glorious courtyard of the Good Fortune beyond, she felt her spirits sink.

Because the brochure she'd flicked through had in no way done this place justice.

And how could it?

This was un-photographable. This atmosphere.

It was immediately recognizable as a casino, but it had an ambience to it that was different to anything Savvy had ever experienced, as if the building site of the rest of Shangri-La was a million miles away, not just out there.

The sound of water was everywhere. Tinkling, splashing chimes. The courtyard's stone arches looked like they'd been here for ever. Savvy caught a glimpse of the lofty glass-sided casino and saw how the Chinese theme had been taken inside from the courtyard.

Any hope she'd had that Roberto Enzo had gone off-message on his Vegas principles was dashed. This place oozed just as much class as the Enzo Vegas ever had. Roberto hadn't just reinvented his business ideals, he'd adapted them. To this new city growing out of the dirt. To bring in new people itching to gamble their money away.

And that was the hardest part for Savvy to swallow. The people. They already loved it here. She could see it all around her. They felt like they belonged. No matter where Savvy looked, she could see a sense of wonder and joy on every face.

She could now see what a fool Hud had been to insist on European designs for El Palazzo. She knew that he'd deliberately planned the Italian-themed casino as a snub to Roberto Enzo.

But it was no wonder that El Palazzo's building contractors had floundered over the complicated replicas of Italian masterpieces. There was no cultural context for them here. The workmen didn't know what they were, so had no clue how to install them. So how the hell were the clientele supposed to be impressed?

Savvy saw now that Michael Hudson's unshakeable pride had backfired. Instead of being an innovator, he'd achieved the opposite. He'd created an old-fashioned monstrosity compared to this, leaving El Palazzo looking like yesterday's news before it had even opened.

But Savvy couldn't go backwards. She was stuck with Hud's vision. They'd invested way too much money and time to start rethinking their plans now.

Which meant that Savvy would just have to get over the fact that her casino would never be the most beautiful – or even somewhere she'd choose to go herself. But it could still be the biggest and most profitable. Which meant she would have done Hud proud. Because in his eyes, those were the only things that mattered.

OK, so they might have lost the design battle but they could still win the business war, she told herself. She needed to become her father's daughter in more than just words; in belief as well.

She meant what she'd said to Luc. Gambling was where El Palazzo would get its edge. Whatever Lois Chan did, Savvy would undercut her. She'd make sure that the masses would come flocking to her casino. She'd hook them in and get them to spend, spend, spend.

'Look, it's only a case of one final push and we'll be opening ourselves soon,' she told Luc. 'Only bigger and better. We'll show these Chinese how to really throw a party, right?'

They followed the crowd past a magnificent fountain

– the centrepiece, a dragon with its golden claws resting on a golden tree trunk. Already, the bottom of the pool around it was shimmering with coins from people who had made a wish.

Savvy stared into the water. Then she quickly slipped her bag off her shoulder, opened it and pulled out a dime. She threw it into the water and made a silent, secret wish.

Hud might have been a fool in his choice of design, but Savvy was the bigger fool. Because she'd underestimated Lois Chan. And it was a mistake she'd never make again.

CHAPTER FORTY-ONE

Lois couldn't keep the smile from her face as she walked through the casino, past the slot machines. She'd grown to love the sound of them. Roberto had told her years ago that they were always tuned to the key of C and now, hearing them all live, all trilling their musical scales, she realized how harmonious they sounded with the happy burble of voices above them and the tinkle of coins.

Unlike the energy-guzzling, brightly lit emporiums of Vegas, the Good Fortune's cathedral-like casino hall had one side made entirely from glass and now, in the last rays of the sunset, the whole place was filled with a shimmering orange-gold light.

She waved to various friends and acquaintances, thrilled that everyone had turned up. There were so many familiar faces from Shangri-La and from Vegas too. She knew that amongst the crowd now swarming through the casino were a whole contingent of seasoned Macau and Hong Kong regulars who'd made the special journey to see what the fuss was about. But there was also a swathe of newcomers from the provinces who'd never seen a casino before, and she heard their sighs and exclamations of awe as they filled the tables.

But one thing had been clear in Lois's mind from the start – especially after seeing for herself the race-goers in Hong Kong: the Chinese would always gamble. Which was why she was so proud to have created the safest, most entertaining place they'd ever had to do it in.

Lois had insisted on a responsible public relations programme, employing locals to take the Good Fortune's message deep into the heart of the mainland. She wanted people to be clear about the hazards of gambling, as well as aware of the exact expenses they'd encounter in Shangri-La.

She'd heard horror stories of whole villages pinning their hopes and life savings on one of their men making a fortune in the casinos of Macau, with devastating consequences.

But she knew as she moved through to the blackjack tables that she was looking for one face in particular.

Aidan Bailey had been invited tonight, along with all the other investors, and Lois hoped she'd have a chance to talk to him. She hadn't seen him since she'd run out on him at the races in Hong Kong. As time passed, she'd started to feel increasingly foolish for acting the way she had.

She'd been so quick to dismiss him from her life,

thinking his only connection to gambling might be through his own compulsions and addiction. It hadn't occurred to her that it might be through business or that he might be connected to the Good Fortune.

She'd checked the books, and although he wasn't a large investor by any stretch, she still wanted to know whether he thought that his investment had been worth it. It was a point of professional pride.

But there was another reason she wanted to see him too. To make him a reality again and not just a fantasy. Because that night . . . that magical night in Hong Kong . . . well, Lois hadn't been able to forget it.

She needed to see Aidan to remind herself of all the reasons why they couldn't be together. To remind herself that he was still a gambler – just like her father – even if he'd made a business out of it too. To remind herself that he was still in the business of war, making money from exploiting other people's misery and conflicts. To remind herself that he'd deceived her whilst he was sleeping with her. That he hadn't had the courtesy to tell her that he was involved as an investor in the business she was about to run single-handedly.

But still she scanned the faces, looking for his familiar grey-blond hair and disarming smile.

'Ah, there you are.'

Lois heard a familiar voice and turned to see Jai Shijai standing behind her. He'd lost weight since the last time she'd seen him. It made him look younger. More attractive too. But then, she had yet to see a man tonight who didn't benefit from being in black tie.

'Hello,' she said.

He smiled, his eyes glittering. 'Look at you. Lois Chan. Right at the top . . .'

Lois was flattered by his words and the reference he was making to their conversation on his private island.

'It's easy to be at the top when only one casino is open,' she replied, with a modest smile.

'But you won,' Jai said. 'You got there first. The Good Fortune will always have that now. The first and the best. I wonder how Savannah Hudson will retaliate.'

As usual, she heard the tone of glee in his voice, as if this were all a game and he was revelling in the spectacle. But it wasn't a game to her. It was her life.

She had no desire to discuss her rival with Jai Shijai.

'We are very honoured that you're here tonight. And also that you are coming to the inaugural International Baccarat Championship,' she said, keeping things formal. Jai Shijai had been the main reason she'd arranged the event in six weeks' time, when she'd learned from his fixers that his schedule would be free and that he was planning on coming to Shangri-La. Six weeks would give her just enough time to iron out all the glitches and make sure they were fully operational as a world-class hotel.

Jai Shijai's presence here would almost guarantee the Good Fortune sufficient status for the championship to become an annual and internationally recognized event. It would also mean that the other billionaire gamblers who followed Jai Shijai's lead would follow him here to the Good Fortune.

Jai Shijai smiled, but he didn't verbally commit himself either way.

'Show me the baccarat room,' he said.

'Of course. It would be my pleasure.'

He glanced at his minder, putting out one finger to tell him to stay. Realizing that she'd be accompanying Jai Shijai alone, Lois began weaving through the crowd with him towards the far corner of the casino.

The suite of baccarat rooms had been designed with Jai Shijai specifically in mind. She was thrilled to be able to show them off, but she felt a flutter of nerves as she pushed open the heavy door and showed him inside.

Unlike the rest of the casino, here Lois had used Jai Shijai's personal quarters in his home on the island as her inspiration. The walls of the large room were covered in antique tapestries and the ceiling was painted with an image of Good Fortune's dragon. At the far end of the glossy tables, there was a curved bar adorned with gold carvings. The smoke from the incense burner swirled, a waft of sandalwood coming towards them. The squashy black carpet and soft lighting gave the room a chic, intimate feeling. The door swished back quietly, sealing them inside.

Lois stood behind one of the fringed black velvet chairs at the table, smiling at Jai Shijai, seeing that he was impressed. This was a room fit for a king, let alone a tycoon. Yet, infuriatingly, he made no comment.

'So tell me, Lois. You have enjoyed being in China, yes? Getting back to your roots?' he asked.

Lois chose her words carefully. 'It has been

384

illuminating,' she said, not wanting to offend him. Because the last two years *had* been illuminating. Illuminating, exhausting, amazing, as well as down-right frustrating at times. Her American standards had been hard to impose here and culturally she'd had to accept that she was a million miles away. But she'd made it work, through sheer determination. The quiet respect she'd earned in Shangri-La from the developers and the locals was precious to her. And so yes, in that sense, she did feel as if she'd put down roots here. She'd grown in stature and experience because of this place. It was a fact the benign look on Jai Shijai's face served only to confirm.

He walked the length of the table, trailing his finger-tips over the soft baize.

'When was the last time you took a vacation, Lois?' he asked. He smiled, his eyes scanning her face.

'I can't remember,' she said, thinking of the last break she was supposed to have had with Cara, which Chris had cancelled at the last minute. She hadn't had a moment to think about doing anything for herself, for as long as she could remember.

'Which is why I thought a gift might be in order.'

'A gift?' she asked.

He walked back to her. *Too close*, she thought. He gazed into her eyes.

'After your party tonight, you will accompany me to Beijing. I have some interesting contacts for you to meet. And then I thought you might like to come back to the island in the Gulf. You found it restful there . . .'

It was an invitation, she realized. But he'd said it like a command. One that she couldn't refuse.

And any lingering doubt that he might be making a business proposal was lost as he now leaned in close, putting his hand over hers.

Immediately, she found herself thinking of the last man who'd touched her like this. Aidan Bailey. And she remembered how she'd felt when he'd first taken her hand in his. Safe. Excited. Not intimidated or confused. Nothing like this.

'That's a very kind offer, but I couldn't possibly. There's still so much to do here and—'

'But I don't think you understand, Lois, what I'm offering you . . .'

Lois glanced up at the camera in the ceiling above them, wondering whether Mario was seeing all of this, whether Jai Shijai knew it was a possibility, or whether he even cared. But she doubted the audio would pick up Jai Shijai's voice as he whispered, 'I can offer you riches . . . a lifestyle, Lois, of a kind you've never dreamed of.' His eyes were deadly serious. 'You'd be a fool to turn me down.'

This can't be happening, Lois thought, beginning to panic. Why is he compromising me like this? Jai Shijai was central to the success of the Good Fortune. Without his patronage . . . without him on side, the whole enterprise could so easily fail. If she turned him down now, she could be risking her future success. But if she agreed, then she would have given him all the power.

Lois slipped her hand out from under his. The

gesture gave her strength. 'But I've got what I want already. Success. And I worked hard for it.'

'Ah yes,' Jai Shijai said. 'But I think you will agree that your building project has gone exceptionally smoothly. As well as the extra funds you needed for your . . . ideas.'

What was he saying? That he'd had a hand in making sure the Good Fortune had opened ahead of schedule?

But how?

Even if he'd put pressure on the investors to release extra finance for Roberto, did that really make her beholden to Jai Shijai in some way? Was that what he was implying? That she *owed* him? That he'd somehow done it all for her and now he was here to claim his prize?

'You and I are alike, Lois,' he said, his dark eyes glinting. 'We like to get what we want. And you see, I have admired you for a very long time . . .'

Admired her as what, exactly? Lois wondered. Not as an equal, if he assumed he could snap his fingers and she'd go to him like an obedient dog. And not as a businesswoman either, if he had the presumption to think that her success was somehow his.

'Jai, I'm very flattered, but I'm afraid my answer is no. And now I'm sorry but I have to go,' she said.

'I see. Then so long, Lois,' Jai Shijai said. His tone was icy. Final.

He turned and marched out of the room. The door swung shut, leaving her alone.

'Fuck,' Lois said out loud.

She knew that she'd just caused Jai Shijai to lose face. And if the last hard months had taught her anything, it was to handle Chinese men with delicacy and diplomacy. But it was too late now. She'd rejected him on instinct. Completely. She'd acted as a woman, not as a businesswoman. Because everything inside her had told her that what he was suggesting was wrong.

You cannot afford to cross Jai Shijai. If you cross him, you'll make him an enemy for life. Suddenly, Aidan's warning rang clearly in her head.

What would the consequences be now? she wondered. Would he withdraw his patronage of the Good Fortune? Or even the Enzo Vegas? Or would his revenge take a more personal form – against her?

She would just have to wait and see. She would have to see how Jai Shijai played his next hand and keep her wits about her. She wasn't going to be cowed or intimidated. Not tonight. Not on *her* night, she thought, walking swiftly to the door to take control of the party once more.

CHAPTER FORTY-TWO

Savvy Hudson was still holding court at the champagne reception in the glass atrium of the Good Fortune. In a sea of black tuxedos, Savvy, with her short blond hair and shimmering green dress, was causing quite a stir.

Now, late on in the evening, many of the guests had ventured into the ballroom where Ko-Lee Rai was performing her much-anticipated set on stage, to rapturous applause. But the scantily clad Asian sensation wasn't the only woman getting attention tonight.

Luc had introduced Savvy to a whole host of people he knew at the party. She had no doubt from their reaction that her It-girl reputation had preceded her – particularly with some of the government officials from Shanghai. Several of the men, on introduction, had looked her up and down as if she was a Shanghai hooker. As if they'd been about to ask her how much. But one by one she'd shot them down and stripped away their preconceptions. Until she'd left them looking at her more like they might have done her father: in awe.

They weren't the only ones whose opinion she was actively battling to revise. She'd also relished the opportunity to shine in front of Luc. He clearly hadn't been expecting her to be so informed about the Good Fortune and its shortcomings, tripping off wittily damning sound-bites for the press. She didn't waste a single opportunity to plug El Palazzo either. And, as a steady procession of journalists continued to be drawn to her like moths to a flame, they could be forgiven for forgetting that Lois Chan was supposed to be the centre of attention tonight.

Soon Luc excused himself, winking at her and mouthing that he'd be back in fifteen minutes. Savvy nodded, but stayed where she was. She was busy negotiating the sale of exclusive documentary rights to a film producer interested in profiling Savvy and filming the launch of El Palazzo.

By the time there was an announcement from the stage and the crowd were invited to move outside to the gardens for the fireworks, Savvy had managed to raise the expectations for El Palazzo ten-fold and create the impression that this launch at the Good Fortune was just a warm-up to the real thing.

Luc caught up with her in the crowd, walking through the casino towards the doors in the glass wall leading to the gardens. 'Where have you been?' she asked.

'Everywhere.'

'So come on then, my fellow spy,' Savvy said, pleased to hear it. 'What have you found out?'

He leaned in close. 'Lots. This place is not at all as finished as it looks.'

'Really?'

'One of the waiters I spoke to said that over half the hotel rooms aren't habitable yet . . . and that the spa they've been making such a fuss about in their brochure is a total dump.'

'So it's all a smokescreen,' Savvy said, gratified to discover that El Palazzo wasn't as far behind as she'd previously assumed. 'Just like this firework display we've been promised. Nothing but pretty lights to stop people focusing on the truth.'

'Exactly,' Luc said. A wicked glint crept into his eyes. 'And you know what I think?'

'What?'

He held up his camera. 'All we have to do is mail some damning evidence to Paige and she'll do the rest.'

Savvy smiled, getting a real buzz now out of the conspiratorial atmosphere that had risen between them.

They broke away from the crowd and snuck off down a maze of corridors which led to the spa. Savvy ducked under the yellow tape and 'KEEP OUT' signs and pushed open the opaque glass double doors with their etched Good Fortune dragon motif.

She thought immediately that Lois Chan must have been infuriated that the spa wasn't ready in time for tonight. It was certainly going to be worth showing off. A series of rooms connected to a central pool. The pool lights were on beneath the still blue water. Three channels branched off the main indoor swimming area, running like rivers beneath brick arches, clearly leading outside.

The pool lights and the emergency lights above shed a soft radiance over everything, as if they were in a moonlit grotto. After being on show in front of all those people upstairs, it was heaven to be somewhere so relaxing and quiet for a moment.

She walked further into the spa and saw a whole series of treatment rooms, and at the far end a wall which had been made to look like luminescent rock. Savvy could see how much detail had gone into the design. It looked as if a steam room at the end was still being constructed. There was evidence of workmen's materials and large barrels of paints and sealants. Neat ropes and toxic hazard and flammable liquid signs separated off the unfinished area.

But despite all that, Savvy could see that this was another clever use of space. Big enough and yet intimate, functional and yet classy, and although Savvy wanted to hate it, her first thought was how lovely it would be to have a treatment and then stretch out on one of the squashy poolside beds.

'Savvy, what are you doing?' Luc said suddenly. He put his hand out and grabbed her wrist.

'What?' she asked, looking up at him.

She was only about to light a cigarette. What was the big deal?

'The sealant,' he said, pointing back at the barrels, then the walls. 'Can't you smell it?'

'No.' She shrugged.

But now that he'd mentioned it, yeah, she supposed she could smell it. All around, in fact.

'Thanks,' she told him, slipping her Lucky Strikes and her lighter back in her bag and getting out her phone. 'I wouldn't make much of a spy if I set fire to the joint, now would I?'

As Luc got to work with his camera, Savvy got out her phone and started to take snapshots. Of the signs and the barrels of chemicals left lying around. Then of the half-finished mosaics on the pillars leading up to the roof. She felt guilty, but justified too. If the Good Fortune had been her casino she would have opened tonight too, but that wasn't relevant. Lois Chan was a fool to claim she was ready to open when half her complex was in this state. She'd left herself vulnerable to criticism. And it wasn't as if she and Luc were going to get caught spying. Savvy could see the surveillance cameras on their perches up above, still waiting to be wired in.

'We can make this look terrible,' Luc said.

She smiled. 'Too right. There's nothing like a photo to get someone's attention.'

She'd said it without thinking and now Luc stared at her, frozen. Did he remember that she'd once taken photos of herself and mailed them to him? She felt her cheeks reddening and looked away quickly.

But she could still feel him watching her, as she mailed the photos off to Paige. She waited for a moment longer, trying to compose herself. Then she dropped her phone back into her bag before meeting his gaze. Uncertainty filled his beautiful eyes, mixed with something she'd never seen before. Timidity? Doubt?

Was this it? So soon? Was Luc about to make the declaration she hoped he would? It would have been fun to spin the game out longer.

She sensed danger too. Because once she rebuffed him, who knew how he'd react? With an ego like his, for all she knew he might freak, flip out, quit and leave her high and dry without a project manager. Or he might be more gentlemanly and take it on the chin for what it was: payback. The settling of a balance once upset, a place they could move forward from, freed from the ghosts of the past.

But she never found out. There was a thunderous boom, followed by loud crackling, like fire-crackers, as the fireworks exploded outside, breaking the moment.

'Come on,' Savvy laughed. The noise had made her jump. But she'd seen Luc do the same, only now he was trying to look so cool. 'Let's get out of here. I want to see the hotel rooms.'

'OK, but nature calls first,' he said, smiling bashfully. 'Wait there, OK?'

He hurried off down a corridor signposted wash-rooms. He turned around and pointed at her. 'Don't leave me here. I hate fireworks. They make me nervous.'

She laughed. Not so cool, after all, then. 'Just get on with it,' she called after him.

She forced the smile from her face as he disappeared out of sight.

This is just a game, she reminded herself. So don't go falling. Not even a little bit. Because you're going to come out on top.

Luc might think they were having a good time, but she was still planning on tricking him, she reminded herself. Getting close to him was just a means of luring him into her trap.

Wasn't it?

CHAPTER FORTY-THREE

Outside in the gardens leading down to the water park, the crowd collectively gasped and cheered as the fireworks exploded against the black canvas of sky.

Lois picked up a glass of champagne from one of the waiters. She smiled and raised her glass towards Roberto, as a flurry of pink and yellow sparkles briefly illuminated his face. Xan, the pyrotechnic expert she'd hired, had assured her that these fireworks tonight were going to be literally visible from space. She could see that Roberto was already impressed.

'Unfortunately, Jai Shijai has left already,' he told her, as she made it to his side. 'I was hoping he'd stay.'

She flushed, guiltily, as she took a sip of champagne. Should she tell him what had happened earlier? She decided against it. She still didn't know what the fallout would be. So why bother Roberto with it? Especially on a night like this that was otherwise a runaway success.

Besides, she knew that Roberto would back the call she'd made. Not only as a friend, but as a businessman too. She needed to see the opening of the Good Fortune through. She needed to be there for her team. Jai Shijai's suggestion that she should walk out of here with him was unthinkable.

'Hello,' a loud voice said above the crackling of the fireworks above.

She turned to see Aidan Bailey standing right beside her. Their eyes locked for a moment and she felt herself grinning at him.

So he was here after all.

But he didn't smile back. His eyes were cold as a shark's.

Lois felt disappointment slam into her. She hadn't exactly expected him to be overjoyed to see her, not after the way they'd said goodbye in Hong Kong . . . the way *she*'d said goodbye . . . the way she'd left him. But she hadn't expected this look of almost naked hostility either. Aidan was a man of the world and it wasn't like she'd led him on. She'd explained how temporary an affair their brief dalliance in Hong Kong was likely to be.

He could at least have had the courtesy to congratulate her on tonight's launch, like everyone else had. Or be grateful for the money he'd make as an investor. Or at least tell her that he was having a good time?

There was a thunderous boom of rockets launching

and exploding in the sky. Lois watched Aidan's lips as they moved.

'What?' she shouted, cupping her hand around her ear.

'Can we talk?' he asked, still with no trace of a smile.

'What, now?'

'Right now.'

'Fine,' she said. 'Inside.'

She led him back towards the casino.

'Aidan,' she asked, when they'd broken through the crowd, 'what's the matter?'

'Not here.'

As he took her by the arm, she tried to break free, but he just gripped her more firmly. He steered her through the nearest doorway into the poker hall.

A few players were still at the tables, but now they were inside, the noise of the fireworks and music was muted.

'Let go of me,' she hissed. 'How dare you just—'

'Quiet,' he told her, his expression suddenly altering.

All the anger, hostility towards her . . . whatever it was . . . now dissolved. Only for something even more worrying to take its place.

It was a look she'd seen before. On Billy-Ray's face at the raid on Lawnton's lair, on Mike Hannan's face too at Fight Night in Vegas. It was a look of fear. A look that said some major shit was about to go down.

'Burning,' he said. 'Something's burning. Can you smell it too?'

But she never got to answer. The boom of the fire-works above was suddenly swamped by the noise of a massive explosion somewhere much closer to the ground.

Lois stumbled and fell into Aidan's arms.

What the hell was happening? An earthquake? She stared into his eyes and saw the terror she felt reflected there.

Steadying herself, she clamped her hands to her ears, screaming as the ear-splitting noise of the fire alarm filled the air and the sprinkler system kicked in and a cloudburst of cold water rained down.

CHAPTER FORTY-FOUR

Savvy opened her eyes, choking and gasping for air. She'd been thrown across the room by the force of the blast.

Black smoke filled the area.

Deafening alarms wailed.

She struggled on to her hands and knees.

Groping now in the dark for the wall . . . trying to remember the way out.

Shielding her eyes with her forearm, she looked behind her. Flames leaped into the darkness. The barrels of sealant . . .

'Luc!' she screamed, then coughed. 'Luc.'

Please God . . . Which was the corridor he went down? *Please God, let him be safe.*

She got to her feet, lurching towards the double doors she'd come through earlier. The emergency lights were still there – barely visible beyond the smoke. But now a wave of flames leaped up before her, blocking her escape route. She threw her hands up to protect her face.

She screamed, but her voice was lost in the roar of the fire.

CHAPTER FORTY-FIVE

Lois Chan threw the newspapers one by one on to the table. Her team – Mario, Tristan, Susie, LJ, Sven the architect – all flinched in silence as each one landed, as if they'd just received a physical blow.

The headlines had been universally damning. It was the same on the net.

Bad Fortune

Casino Turns to Water Park

Washout

'That's not the worst of it,' Tristan said.

'So what is?' she asked, because right now she couldn't imagine feeling any bleaker. She put her palm on her forehead and paced away from him and Mario, then back again. Her long dress, ash-smeared and ripped, flapped against her leg but she didn't care. How could this have happened? How could her launch night have turned into this?

'Savvy Hudson and Luc Devereaux were here last night,' Mario said.

In all the mayhem, she'd forgotten that they'd even been invited.

'So what?' Lois said. 'Don't tell me that bitch has tried to make capital out of this. Even she wouldn't stoop that low, surely?'

'The thing is . . . she was nearly killed.'

Lois stopped still. 'What? But you told me everyone got out safely from the casino. That no one had been injured.'

'She wasn't in the casino.'

'Then where the hell was she?'

'The spa,' Tristan said.

Lois stared at him, stunned. A chill ran through her.

'But it wasn't even open to the public.'

'I know. But that didn't stop her going down to check it out. When I realized everyone else on the guest roster was accounted for, I finally tracked down Luc Devereaux. He was stumbling around in a daze – smoke inhalation or shock, I guess – and he told me he couldn't find Savannah Hudson. He got kind of hysterical in fact. That's when he admitted where they'd been. He started crying . . . he was terrified she'd been lost in the fire.'

Lois shook her head. *Luc Devereaux and Savannah Hudson had been in the spa area . . .*

The news put everything – all the headlines – to the back of her mind. Because the Chinese authorities had already returned their unofficial preliminary findings.

That an electrical fault was to blame for the explosion and resulting fire in the spa area.

But Lois trusted the foreman working down there. They'd had a long conversation about how the spa would be out of bounds to the public until it was finished. She knew that the workmen would have left it safe, knowing how many people would be in the casino.

'It was a miracle she made it out alive,' Tristan said.

'So how did she get out?' Lois asked.

'She swam.'

'What?'

'She jumped into the pool. Swam down the channel leading under the archway and into the outdoor pool. Devereaux and I spotted her at the same time. She was slipping under. Devereaux dived in and got her out. The two of them are in hospital in Shanghai, being checked over. Taken there in a medevac chopper. At our expense.'

'Jesus,' Lois said. Savannah Hudson had been bloody lucky to survive that. Of all the people in the Good Fortune, why, oh why, did the drama have to happen to *her*?

Because everyone else had been fine. The fire had been limited to the spa and put out quickly; turning off the fire alarm and sprinkler system had proved more difficult. There'd simply been no choice but to evacuate the guests.

But Savannah Hudson had been down in the spa. Right where the fire had started.

'What are you thinking, Lois?' Mario asked, stepping towards her.

She looked at him. Because all of a sudden, Jai Shijai's comment earlier rang in her head.

I wonder how Savannah Hudson will retaliate . . .

No, Lois thought. You're exhausted. Being paranoid. No one would be crazy enough to do that.

Lois's head was still buzzing with doubts and suspicions as she walked into the spa area with Tristan and Mario. Sven, the architect, carried the large torch and pushed past them at the broken double door to see inside.

Chinese officials – several of them, working silently – were measuring various objects near the blast centre and taking notes.

'Holy fuck,' Tristan said, standing in the puddles of water on the floor. It was the first time any of them had been allowed in here since the fire.

Lois stared around the once serene and beautiful spa, blackened now from the smoke and flames. The glass dome above the pool was charred and cracked. The half-completed mosaics were ruined. The pool itself was as dark and dank as a swamp.

'Look around,' she told Tristan, Mario and Sven.

'For what?' Tristan asked.

'Anything,' she said. 'Anything that's wrong.'

They split up and began searching the room. Mario was the first to call out.

'What's this?' he asked, as Lois rushed over to him. He crouched down and pulled out something from under one of the poolside beds. 'It looks like an evening bag . . .'

Lois undid the zip. She reached inside and extracted a packet of cigarettes and a lighter.

She weighed the lighter in her hand. It was a tacky plastic one – the same as a million lighters all over the world – except that this had one word written on it in gaudy lettering: *Savannah*.

'Are you thinking what I'm thinking?' Tristan asked.

She didn't have to answer him. Because here it was. In her hand. *Proof.*

Proof that Savannah Hudson had caused the fire. She had wrecked the Good Fortune. Deliberately. Out of jealousy and spite.

She was almost breathless as she pulled out the phone from the bag. She handed it to Mario.

Oh yes, she had enough proof for herself that Savannah Hudson was guilty as hell. But for the authorities? For a court of law? She'd been a cop for too long not to know that she was going to need more than this.

'What do you want me to do with that?' he asked.

'I want you to find anything, and I mean *anything*, that's evidence. Anything that will prove that she did what I think she did.' Her voice trembled with anger.

Mario whistled. He turned the phone over in his hands. 'I guess I can try. This is an old phone. There might be something stored on it.'

'Lois, you've got a visitor.'

It was Susie. She was standing in the broken entrance to the spa, staring at the carnage in disbelief. 'It's a man called Aidan something. Aidan Bailey. Shall I tell him to go away?'

CHAPTER FORTY-SIX

Aidan was waiting for Lois outside in the courtyard, sitting on the wall of the Good Fortune dragon. He stood up when he saw her approaching and pushed his sunglasses to the top of his head.

The terracotta tiles were littered with thousands of strips of gold paper from last night's party, which sparkled in the morning sun. A Good Fortune balloon floated across the courtyard in the breeze.

'You must be devastated,' Aidan said.

She nodded, swallowing back an unexpected surge of emotion. She'd lost him almost straight away last night, in the stampede of guests trying to escape the sprinklers and the noise of the fire alarm.

'We're all here to fight another day,' she said, as she shivered and hugged her arms.

'Here.' Aidan slipped off his jacket and put it around her shoulders.

She smiled, grateful for the small kindness. Whatever was wrong with him last night seemed to have passed, but she was still wary.

'It doesn't look so bad,' Aidan said, trying to sound reassuring. 'Out here at least.'

'You should see inside,' Lois replied. But even so, she reached out and touched the gold scales on the dragon's back. It was still intact. Aidan was right . . . it could have been so much worse.

'Looks like whoever put your fire and evacuation systems into place did a good job. You did a good job,' he said.

'It doesn't feel like it right now,' she said, although it was good to know that one investor, at least, wouldn't be calling for her head on a plate. Roberto, panic-stricken, had left a few hours ago, to fly back to Vegas to talk to the insurers.

'Seriously, if you'd got it wrong . . . if that fire hadn't been shut down as quickly as it was . . . they'd be wheeling dead bodies out of here right now.'

'I know,' she said. 'But it's the damage to our reputation that hurts the most, not the damage to the building. All of which can be repaired. But I guess that was the whole point.'

'What do you mean?'

She told him about finding Savannah Hudson's bag by the pool, with the lighter inside. And about how Luc Devereaux had already confirmed that the two of them had been snooping around down there before the fire began.

Aidan whistled.

It was a big allegation, Lois knew. And it sounded even bigger as she told Aidan.

'You're going to have to be pretty sure of your evidence before you accuse her,' he said. 'It's just as possible that she was the victim of an unfortunate accident.'

But Lois knew she wouldn't be defeated on this. Whatever it took, she would find out the truth.

'I don't think this is a good time, but I do need to talk to you,' he said.

She remembered now, before the explosion, the way he'd been acting. As if he'd been looking for a row. He didn't look like it now. He looked like the same kind and charming man who'd surprised her in the Temple Street night market in Hong Kong. But at the same time, if it was a fight he was looking for, she couldn't afford for it to happen here in public, for her authority to be challenged any more than it already had been.

'OK,' she said, 'but do you mind if we go back to my place? I need to change.'

Lois led Aidan through the short cut to the back of the casino and on through the gardens beyond. They looked spectacular in the early morning sunlight, as if the fire had never happened. She'd sourced experts to make sure that all the planting was indigenous to the area and would flourish in the climate. After the recent rains, everything was greener than ever and the dove trees were flowering, their petals like white handkerchiefs fluttering in the breeze.

The grounds were intercut with waterways, designed

so that the guests could travel on traditional boats to the cottages and residential complexes that stretched down to the beach and the water park.

She could tell, as Aidan nodded to himself, that he was impressed, but she was in no mood for showing off the Good Fortune now.

She felt too bitter. This morning, the grounds should have been full of guests exploring the paradise she'd created for them. And she should be walking tall, proud to have carried off an amazing opening night. She looked at the main canal with the row of gondola-like dragon boats lined up and empty, the waterways and hotel rooms deserted.

Empty firework shells littered the ground and she kicked at one of them. What a bloody waste of money. The drama of last night had been made all the worse because they'd had to carry out the evacuation under the pomp and ceremony of the firework display. The two events would be forever intertwined in her mind. It was a sour thought.

'Here, it'll be quicker if we use one of these,' she said, pointing to the Good Fortune's customized golf buggies. 'I'll navigate, you drive,' she said, hitching up the grubby skirt of her dress and getting in.

Apart from the sporadic directions she gave, they drove in silence over the bridge of the main canal and along the new pathways of the golf course itself. It felt weird having Aidan here when the hotel was so deserted. It felt like they were in a computer game – eerily silent except for the whine of the golf buggy and the chirrup of starlings.

'It's beautiful,' he said, looking around him at the hotel's eco-buildings. 'You know, when I heard you were going to build this, I couldn't picture what it would be like – but this place is pretty amazing. Usually once the daylight comes, you want to get the hell out of a casino, but this isn't tacky. This feels like a luxury resort. And being here with just you,' he said, 'the person who created it, well, it's a real privilege, Lois.'

She had spent weeks wondering whether he'd turn up at the launch, and whether he'd be impressed if he did. But now, after last night's PR disaster, it no longer mattered.

'Follow the path over there,' she said, pointing to the bridge across another waterway.

The landscaping team Lois had employed had created the village of recycled antique teak and tiled cottages beside the furthest saltwater lake, as luxury accommodation for guests who preferred to spend their nights far away from the madding crowd. In the meantime, the Good Fortune's senior staff had moved in. And Lois herself had been living here for nearly a year.

The lakeside water, thick with lush green water lilies, rippled against the whitewashed walls. Palm trees, all of which she'd imported from a remote village in the north, bent in at an angle towards the group of cottages.

Once she'd pressed the combination on the gate and they were through to the enclosure, she saw her own cottage. Her sarong still hung over the carved wooden rail of the veranda, her flip-flops by the door as if nothing had changed. And yet everything had.

She led Aidan up the steps and in through the thick teak door. In the tranquil silence of the early morning, she felt as if she were sneaking home with a lover.

Lover. There. The word had crept into her mind. Because that's what he was. Had been. Once.

But not today, she reminded herself. Today they were here because he wanted to say something to her, something she was too exhausted to listen to yet. She needed to freshen up before she could face anything emotional.

In the centre of the cottage was a large teak bed and an antique chest beside it, with polished brass hinges. A soft throw lay on the bed and two big red embroidered cushions.

Lois walked straight past.

Further back was a small living area, with two armchairs, a desk and Lois's laptop in the corner. There was a fridge in the other corner by a sink and a drinks tray. Small, rush-shaded windows let in the soft morning light.

She should have taken him to her office, she now realized. This was too intimate. Too personal.

'What a great place,' Aidan said, admiring the cottage. 'I love these walls. They must be a foot thick.'

She grimaced, catching her reflection in the mirror, seeing how bedraggled and dirty she looked.

'Listen, make yourself at home. I'm going to take a shower, if you don't mind.'

'Sure,' Aidan said. 'I'll fix us a drink. What do you fancy?'

'After last night – I need a whisky,' she said.

He smiled at her and she looked into his eyes, remembering all too well the last time she'd drunk whisky with him and what had happened afterwards.

But that was a long time ago. Had Aidan moved on? He was probably in another relationship by now. A man as attractive as he was must receive so much female attention. Especially in the casinos and clubs he frequented.

She felt her legs shaking as she took off her shoes. She opened another small teak door with a high wooden doorstep at the back of the cottage. Behind it was her favourite part of the bungalow – the open-air shower room.

'You want water with it?' Aidan called after her.

'Sure. Use the tap water,' she said.

'Tap?'

'I put in a reverse osmosis system so it gets ultra-filtered,' she explained, as she unclipped her earrings and put them on the side.

He smiled. 'Neat,' he said, stepping into the open doorway. He was holding two tumblers of whisky in his hands. The way the sun caught his hair . . . the wrinkles around his hazel eyes suddenly made something in her burn.

It was crazy. She had no idea why he was here, or what he'd been doing for the last eighteen months. She'd had the most exhausting night of her life, and yet every nerve ending was on fire as Aidan's eyes bored into hers.

Then, suddenly, he seemed to remember himself. 'I'll, um . . . wait,' he stuttered, pointing behind him.

Lois quietly closed the door of the shower room. Now that Aidan was gone, she wanted him back. She wanted to feel the touch of his strong hands on her skin. She wanted . . . needed . . . to press against him, to forget all about last night.

Stop it, she thought. She was just tired. She didn't know what she wanted any more.

She let the dress fall to the floor and pulled out the clips in her hair, the withered peony bloom dropping on to the white tiles. A smile played on her lips, which she couldn't control, like a schoolkid with the giggles in class, like it was only a matter of time before she got caught.

Aidan was on the other side of the door. And she was naked.

She shook her head, shivering as she stepped into the shower and turned on the water.

The shower head was designed to drench the person underneath and as soon as the water came on, she gasped, letting it cascade down over her. She closed her eyes, feeling her skin tingle and goosebump under the flow. She turned up the heat and soon the small bathroom was thick with steam.

She filled her hand with fragrant shower gel and started massaging it over her breasts. She closed her eyes, pushing her face up into the falling water, wondering what he would think if he could see her now. Would he still want her? Would she still want him?

She slipped her hand between her legs and softly moaned.

Why fight it? a voice inside her said. *Why fight the desire?*

Impulsively, quickly, she reached out to the door and lifted the latch. As it slowly swung open, she turned her back. She felt her whole body tense, as she waited to see what Aidan would do.

And then, a second later, she heard a sound . . .

She didn't open her eyes as Aidan stepped into the shower behind her. She felt his hot naked skin against her, his hard cock pressing into her, as he put both arms around her, sliding his hands over her shoulders and down her arms. She gasped as he buried his face against her neck, kissing her skin. He uttered a long, sensual groan that made her insides sing.

Then he turned her round in his arms. He ran his hands over her wet hair, pulling her head back so that he could kiss her. Slowly. Deeply.

Neither of them spoke. It was as if they'd been taken over by pure, animal lust, and neither of them could explain it, or justify it. Still kissing him, their tongues dancing together, she felt him hoisting her up, lifting her legs so that they were wrapped around his waist.

She loved the way she felt in his strong arms. As if she were light as a feather. She was shaking, she realized. Wet with desire. She needed him inside her. Needed him more than ever before.

He felt deliciously familiar and yet so new and exciting. She pushed down on him, crying out as he slid into her.

He gasped as she squeezed her muscles and leaned back, closing her eyes, the warm water running over her hair and face as she rocked, tuning in to the sensation of the water over them.

She dug her heels into his firm buttocks as he hoisted her up again, leaning in to suck her nipples. They felt so engorged – as if they could explode – and each flick of his tongue brought exquisite torture.

Cradling his head, she planted kisses over his wet cheeks. She tensed her thighs, so that she slid up him, then bore down again and again. They stayed locked, fused, kissing beneath the water.

She was shaking uncontrollably as she slipped away from him. She leaned down and flicked her tongue over him, tasting herself on him and groaning, then she took him deep in her mouth.

As he began shuddering, he pulled her up and turned her round, rubbing soap over her shoulders, massaging her back again and reaching around to soap her breasts.

She pressed back against him, desperate to have him inside her again. Water cascaded over her, washing away the soap from her breasts. He reached around to the small triangle of her pubic hair and began to massage her clitoris as he continued to thrust deep inside her.

She cried out as she came in a violent, shuddering orgasm.

He held her, turning her round in his arms in the water as she continued to gasp. Gently, he took her hand and guided it down on to him. She squeezed his cock just once and his knees buckled slightly as he came.

Then he was smiling. And she was smiling too. She turned off the shower and they held each other in silent joy, as the sun shone down overhead, bathing them in a rainbow of steam.

CHAPTER FORTY-SEVEN

Lois was still dazed as she sat in her robe on the bed. Should she feel bad? She couldn't tell. All she knew was that out of the ashes of last night, Aidan had come to her and made her feel ecstatic.

She knew she would have to leave soon, to talk to her team and deal with the millions of problems stacking up. But Aidan had done the most wonderful thing and made her forget them, just for a moment. It had been more rejuvenating than any sleep could ever have been.

He had a towel wrapped around him as he sat down on the bed beside her now and handed her another whisky. He smiled softly at her as they clinked glasses. But she was aware that this easy intimacy was just an illusion. They hardly knew one another and now she didn't have a clue where she stood.

'So you were about to tell me . . .' she said pointedly.

Whatever it was he'd wanted to talk to her about, there was no sense in putting it off now.

'Ah, yes.' Aidan frowned heavily, as if contemplating a tricky problem. 'Well, you see the thing is . . .' He put the whisky glass down on the chest next to the bed. Then he looked at his hands and clasped his fingers together. 'You're not going to like this.'

Again she saw it, that look in his eyes she'd seen last night. But he couldn't still be harbouring a grudge against her, could he? Surely not now?

'That doesn't sound good.'

'No.' Aidan winced. 'You see, I haven't been entirely honest with you.'

'I see,' Lois said. But she didn't see at all.

'I'm not really who you think I am.'

She already knew he was some kind of mercenary, some kind of gambler. How much worse could it get?

'Then *who are you*?'

'I'll need your word that what I'm about to tell you will stay strictly between us.'

'What?' She laughed in disbelief. He couldn't be serious. 'You want me to sign a confidentiality agreement when I don't have a clue what you're about to tell me?'

'I said, I need your word. Nothing more. That's good enough for me.'

'Fine,' she said. 'Fine. You've got it.'

Aidan took a deep breath and let it out again. 'The thing is . . . three years ago, I was seconded to an undercover international task force to investigate the trafficking of heroin into the US from China,' he said.

'You mean you're not a—'

'A mercenary? I think that's how you once so charmingly put it,' Aidan said. 'No. That was just a cover. Ex-army, yes, but actually this special task force is government. DEA.'

'The DEA?' Lois asked. 'As in Drug Enforcement Administration?'

Every time she'd thought about him, she'd forced the image into her head of Aidan in a war zone, making money out of other people's misery.

But no wonder it had been such a struggle to conjure up the images that put him in shady situations. Because Aidan was a good guy. *DEA*.

That night. The races . . .

If she'd known this about him, everything would have been so different.

'Why didn't you tell me before?'

'I wanted to. Believe me, I was dying to. But I was undercover. I hinted at it far too much as it was.'

'And what about the gambling? Is that all bullshit too? Part of your cover?'

Aidan raised his eyebrows at her. 'What do *you* think?'

She laughed incredulously, remembering how out of his depth he'd been that night at the poker game. 'Well, that sure explains a few things,' she said.

'I got into so much crap for losing all that government cash at Jai Shijai's table, I can't tell you. When we went to the pagoda that time, I was in shock.'

'So why are you telling me this now?' she asked.

'Because I trust you, Lois,' he said, his voice soft and

low. 'And because I care about you too much not to tell you, even though this has serious implications for you.'

She didn't like the sound of where this was going, but equally she knew she couldn't back out now.

'Go on.'

'You see the thing is, my investigation has all been focused on Jai Shijai. And his business interests, of course. The US government . . . through me . . . invested in the Good Fortune in order to see where the funds went. To see how Jai Shijai's finances flow . . .'

'But why? What's he done wrong?'

'We suspect that Jai is using this casino, as well as his other businesses around the world, to launder funds from his narcotics operation. The heroin he exports to the West.'

Lois stared at him. 'And you've got evidence of this?'

'That's what we're still trying to get.'

Lois remembered Roberto sporting a new suit and how he'd admitted that Jai Shijai had given it to him. One of the finest from his factories in China, he'd told her proudly. She remembered how Roberto had claimed to be a convert, saying that Jai's people had Italian design and cheap production all sewn up. A miracle of modern efficiency.

'But Jai Shijai's a businessman. Legitimate. He's got textile factories all over China. His government trusts him so much they even let him organize the whole Shangri-La deal.'

'Ghost factories,' Aidan said. 'At least the ones we can

directly trace to him. Condemned low-output operations. Worth next to nothing, unless you're looking for a front.'

Lois got up from the bed and started pacing. Her mind was rushing ahead. Roberto trusted Jai Shijai completely. It was thanks to Jai Shijai that Enzo had won the concession in Shangri-La in the first place. The Good Fortune's success and Jai Shijai's patronage were inextricably linked.

'But what about all his assets? His private islands?' she asked.

'Just because Jai isn't legit, it doesn't mean to say he's not wealthy. In fact, quite the reverse. He's extraordinarily cash-rich. That's why he gambles at the level he does. Either way – win or lose – he gets to launder some of his money.' Aidan stood up too and stared at her across the bed. 'It's taken me so long to track down his actual assets. He has an elaborate spider's web of aliases. And he diverts money through his contacts.'

'So that's why you were at Jai Shijai's island for the game?' she asked him.

'Yes, I wasn't sure then. But I had a hunch. I went to find out who his business associates were. The best cover was to pose as an investor in the Good Fortune myself. Through being part of the set-up, we were hoping to get access to his accounts, but so far we haven't been able to turn up a damn thing.'

'But the bankers . . . all the people Jai brought to the table? All the money behind the Good Fortune? Surely you're not telling me that it's *all* corrupt? It can't be.'

'Our thinking is that this is the biggest money-laundering operation ever to come out of the East.'

'What about Roberto? Does he know?'

'To be honest, I doubt it. We checked out the Vegas operation and it's all clean. He's acted in good faith.'

Lois could barely begin to comprehend the implications of what he was telling her.

'So what's going to happen?' she asked.

'I have to find proof. To take to the Chinese authorities. And soon. But so far all the evidence I have is circumstantial. I have nothing to link it together. Every time I think I'm on to something, the trail vanishes.'

Lois rubbed her forehead, Jai Shijai's proposal the previous night haunting her. Not just the words, but the way in which he'd said them. The way she'd felt threatened. He was a man who was used to getting what he wanted. She'd sensed that then, but Aidan's revelation and suspicions put him in an entirely new light.

'What are you thinking?' he asked her.

She told him about Jai Shijai's proposal.

'But you told him no?' Aidan said. He looked worried and, Lois saw now with a glimmer of satisfaction, jealous.

'Of course I did.'

Aidan rubbed his chin and Lois realized that he was mulling over the repercussions of her decision. He wasn't going to ask her to go back on it, was he? He couldn't. He *wouldn't* . . .

She'd thought Aidan was her friend, but a horrible sense of dread filled her now. Because he wasn't a friend. He was a man who was about to detonate her entire life. Because finding the means and the evidence to bust Jai Shijai was going to be bad enough. But if he succeeded . . . then the Good Fortune, Roberto, her team and the future was just a house of cards that Aidan Bailey was going to bring crashing down.

CHAPTER FORTY-EIGHT

Savvy was sure that delayed shock must be about to kick in, but for the time being she felt euphoric. At the top of her game. Thrilled to be alone with Luc here in France. Or maybe it was just that she felt lucky to be alive.

And *this* was what life was all about, she thought. Tonight she felt like herself for the first time since Elodie had died. Tonight she was having fun.

So much so that the problems at El Palazzo, her responsibilities in Vegas and all the craziness of the last few days, starting with the fire at the Good Fortune, seemed to have faded into the background.

'Let's go again,' Luc said, his eyes shining. 'We're on a roll.'

Savvy laughed and agreed. In all the time she'd seen him at La Paris, Savvy had never known Luc to be around any of the tables in the casino, but now, hours into their night at the Casino Royale in Monte Carlo, Savvy realized that she'd found her gambling soulmate at last.

He was just like her. Not only did he share her passion for roulette, but he stacked his bets just like she did, with the same amount of determination and crazy faith in lucky numbers.

In the busy hall, below the chandeliers of the famous casino, Savvy felt very much the part at the VIP tables. It was so much fun being with Luc. He had charmed the people around their table and a cosy sense of camaraderie had descended on them all.

The sleek French croupier wrapped up the other bets, quickly and professionally stacking the chips on the green baize, his hands moving rapidly and nimbly in the white gloves, like a magician.

He picked up the ball and held it briefly aloft, as if he was showing it to the players before he made it disappear. Just before he dropped it, Savvy flashed him a flirtatious smile and mouthed the word 'red'.

The ball clattered into the outer groove, the wheel spinning fast and smoothly, like the spoked tyre of a vintage car. The colours flashed as Savvy tracked the silver ball, her heart whirring in tandem. She loved the thrill of waiting for fate to take its course. It was this moment of hiatus – of life in freefall – that excited her the most. For this split second, the future was wide open and anything was possible.

'Red! Red! Red!' she chanted, under her breath, as the ball started losing momentum.

She saw Luc's brow furrow with concentration. He

glanced to where she was standing next to him and grinned, holding up his crossed fingers and pulling a face, as the ball whooshed around the wheel once more.

Savvy watched it, acutely aware that Luc's shoulder was touching hers. Neither of them broke the contact, both leaning into it instead.

She clasped her hands together, willing the ball to land on red. She'd read somewhere that an experienced croupier could probably make it do so nine times out of ten if he wanted to. She wondered now whether this guy had already rigged it for her. She glanced up at him and, sure enough, saw straight away that she'd captured his attention. He was staring directly at her cleavage.

Embarrassed, he looked quickly away, concentrating on the wheel, but she noticed a smile playing at the corner of his lips.

The wheel slowed and the ball whooshed slower and slower around the outer ring, in ever-decreasing circles, before teasing and rattling over each groove.

The tension was unbearable. Luc was pressed right up against her.

Bang on cue, the ball landed on red.

Luc won and punched the air, grinning at her. The French croupier congratulated him, whipping the chips across the green baize in a businesslike way, calling bets for the next round. Luc stacked his chips, running his fingers sensually along their smooth sides.

Savvy smiled at him, but just then a waiter interrupted them, muscling in between them to place a glass of champagne in front of Luc and one in front of Savvy. She pushed it away politely. He talked to Luc, who then turned round and waved, raising his glass to two players at an adjoining table.

'Who are they?' Savvy asked, impressed. She liked seeing Luc in France, seeing his mannerisms come alive in his own language.

'Old friends. Gérard Paul used to be a manager here. He knew my father,' Luc explained.

'Oh?' she asked. She didn't break eye contact with him.

'Papa used to bring me here to the casino when I was young.'

'Really?' Savvy was intrigued. She'd never heard him talk about his family before.

In fact she'd only really seen him before in terms of Vegas and how he'd been around Hud and Elodie. He'd taken up so much of her head space for so long, but she realized now that there was a whole lot she didn't know about him.

Sure, she'd looked into his love life once, to see what kind of girls he'd gone out with, but that was only to discover how attractive he might find *her*. How immature and childish that seemed now. All the important stuff – his past, his family, even his tastes – she knew almost nothing about. She felt ashamed now that she'd been so selfish. And shallow. That she'd made so little effort to find out the truth about him.

'Your father liked gambling?' she asked.

'He owned a casino.'

'I had no idea,' she said. 'So it's all in the blood?'

'I guess. Although my father would never have approved of El Palazzo, or La Paris for that matter. He loved this casino.'

'So when you were talking to me at El Palazzo,' she said, thinking that it seemed like months ago already, although it was only a couple of days earlier, 'and you said you thought Shangri-La had no soul yet, was this what you meant?'

'You look surprised,' he said.

'You and Hud, you always seemed to want to build big, brash places. I never thought this was your thing.' Savvy shook her head, amazed. 'And I thought . . . well, I thought you agreed with his vision.'

Luc smiled gently. 'He made it impossible to do anything else. You know, he would have been proud of you for seeing it through. Keeping his business philosophy alive,' he added.

He said it so matter-of-factly, as if it were a *fait accompli*. But Savvy saw a new possibility opening up. If neither she nor Luc agreed totally with Hud's vision of the future, why should they slavishly keep attempting to make it come true? Sure, it might be too late to make any great changes at El Palazzo. But as for the rest of Hud's empire, for any new venture they might undertake . . . well, what was to stop her and Luc steering the business down a different and altogether more exciting path?

Perhaps that was what she should do. Get all the senior members of her team together and be democratic about it. Perhaps now more than ever was the right time to pin down their business strategy in the long term. She made a mental note to call Paige about it so that she didn't forget.

It was so frustrating not having her phone, but her bag had been lost at the Good Fortune. And Paige had gone into full panic mode. She was all fighting talk about suing the Good Fortune for negligence. She hadn't stopped saying how Luc and Savvy might have been killed.

But they hadn't been harmed, Savvy had pointed out several times. Neither she nor Luc had suffered from smoke inhalation and after a once-over by the medics they had left the hospital in Shanghai straight away.

And looking on the positive side, the fire at the Good Fortune had only played into their hands. The Good Fortune had flopped on its very first night. Now El Palazzo could capitalize on all the bad press and come out on top. The only really annoying thing was that the photos Savvy had sent Paige from her phone hadn't reached her. In the aftermath of the fire, it infuriated Savvy that she didn't have pictures of the barrels of sealant to show the world. Luc's camera had been totally trashed when he'd dived in to save her.

'If you don't mind, I must go and give them my regards,' Luc told her.

Savvy smiled. 'Sure. I'll be at the bar. I need some water after all this excitement.'

Excusing herself from the table, Savvy walked over to the bar to get a drink. She smiled, watching Luc laughing with his two old acquaintances. God, he was handsome, she thought.

'Filly, two o'clock,' she heard the fatter of two guys at the bar say to his companion. Lost in thought as she was, her ears pricked up at his Scottish accent.

He had freckles and ginger hair and there was something familiar about him as he turned round to make room for her. He stared at her, grinning.

'Do I know you?' she asked.

'It shames me to say you don't.' Now he actually swaggered as he smiled at her. 'Sir Angus Raddoch,' he said, holding out his fat hand.

Raddoch. She stared at him.

'Are you related to Jonny Raddoch, by any chance?' she asked.

'You know Red?' He looked momentarily shocked. 'Yes, well, that figures. Little Bro always has had exquisite taste.'

This bloated, older, red-faced version of the Raddoch genes only served to remind Savvy how handsome Red had been in comparison. She pictured him now at Peace River Lodge standing so tall and calmly in the meditation area, and how he'd opened his eyes slowly and smiled.

Her life was so different now, but she remembered Red's measured strength and his empathy. She felt sad that her life had hurtled away so fast from the peace she'd felt back then. And she was sad too that he'd never been in touch. She'd tried to send him an email through Peace River but had heard nothing back. She assumed he'd moved on and, in the chaos after Hud's death, she'd moved on too.

But in the rare quiet moments she had alone, she

still often thought about him, as she'd last seen him when he admitted that their relationship had messed with his head, too. She'd felt so close to him, she remembered. As if they were on the verge of something amazing. A closeness she'd never had with anyone else.

But then he'd left her on her own.

'How is he?' she now asked.

'You haven't heard?' Angus asked. He swilled his wine around in his glass and took a swig. There was something both angry and frustrated in the gesture.

'Heard what?'

'He's buggered off to the back end of beyond. To become a bloody sheep farmer of all things.'

Savvy smiled, remembering how Red had told her that living on his family's Scottish island was his ultimate dream. She wondered whether he'd fallen in love with a local girl, as he'd planned.

'God knows how long he'll survive, though. He's got no money. After the last time he cleaned me out, I'm not stumping up a bean.'

Savvy made small talk and excused herself as soon as she could. Hearing that Red was living his dream only confirmed his rejection of her in her mind. She felt as if a small part of her had been cut loose. Knowing that he was living his life somewhere that she couldn't imagine, made her feel as if a link between them had been severed for ever.

She looked down at her wrist. She still wore the friendship bracelet that he'd given her. She'd got used to it, hidden as it was in the rack of silver bangles. But now, for the first time since leaving Peace River, she thought about taking it off. It was silly to still wear it. Especially now. Red had told her that it was to remind her that he was always with her in spirit. But he wasn't. Not any more.

CHAPTER FORTY-NINE

It was three days after Aidan had left Shangri-La that Mario summoned Lois to a meeting out of hours in their favourite bar in Shanghai.

They were both exhausted. The clean-up operation at the Good Fortune was in full swing and, after the stress of the past few days, she was glad of the opportunity to slip away from work into the bustling streets of Shanghai, where no one knew her name. And no one was going to ask her to make a decision.

Everything Aidan had told her had been relentlessly whirring round and round in her mind, until Lois thought she was going crazy. She wished he'd never voiced his suspicions about Jai Shijai. Because every decision, every enthusiastic comment from a member of her team, now had a cloud hanging over it. Because the Good Fortune's future had a cloud hanging over it too. If it turned out it had been built on drug money, it would not only put her and Roberto out of business for good, it would also bankrupt Roberto and ruin both his and Lois's reputations for ever.

She knew that Aidan had warned her so that she could be prepared. But she had no idea what she should be preparing for. Should she jump ship now? Tell Roberto? But tell him what? Because Aidan hadn't got any proof.

All she could do was wait.

She pushed open the door of the diner-bar and saw Mario sitting on a high chrome seat at the counter. She smiled and waved, but she saw immediately from the look on Mario's face that he had news.

She slid on to the stool next to him. He had a beer waiting for her on the counter top. He slid it across.

'It's about Savannah Hudson's phone.'

She felt her breath catch. Was this what she'd been waiting for? Proof, at last?

'You know I told you I copied the memory card?' Mario said.

'Yes?'

'Well, there was no doubt she was planning a stitch-up of the Good Fortune. She'd taken damning pictures of the spa area. From what I can tell, she had tried to mail them to Paige Logan back in Vegas.'

Lois slumped. Another shit storm coming her way, then. Did Savannah Hudson have no shame?

'Well, that wasn't all. There were . . . let's say . . . fairly explicit pictures on there,' Mario said. He looked away sheepishly. 'And some film footage too.'

'Go on . . .'

'It was just, I was looking through it all late last night.' He put his hand in front of his mouth and coughed and Lois realized all at once why he was so embarrassed. She felt oddly riled that he'd been looking at pictures of Savvy Hudson.

Mario moved quickly on. 'She must have thought she'd deleted them, but I found some old files. Amongst them were some of the Enzo Vegas on Fight Night.'

Lois felt anger rise up inside her. 'Let me guess,' she said, remembering now how she'd first met Savannah Hudson waiting for an elevator outside the Enzo's hub. 'More snooping, right? What did you find? Footage of the hub?'

Mario shook his head. 'No. It was of the arena. And at first I didn't think anything of it. It was footage of the Hamilton fight.'

Lois frowned. This wasn't what she wanted to hear. She wanted to know that Mario had found hard evidence that Savannah Hudson had set fire to the Good Fortune deliberately. Lois wasn't interested in the past – only in nailing her rival once and for all, in the here and now.

But Mario clearly thought he was on to something. He took a deep breath. 'I couldn't work out what was bothering me until I looked again. Savannah Hudson was standing just in front of Fernandez. She'd taken a video file probably seconds before the shooting, when Hamilton was down in the ring . . .'

'And your point is?'

'Well, it occurred to me that the angle at which she

was holding her phone gave her direct line of sight between where she was standing and the person in the gallery who fired the shot at Fernandez. And hit you.'

'Benzir fired the shot. We know who the shooter was,' Lois said, startled. She took a deep slug of beer. She wanted to move the conversation on. Even talking about that night was making her scar ache.

'That's what I thought too,' Mario said. 'But when I slowed down the footage to individual frames, they were so blurry I couldn't make out Benzir's face in any detail at all. And something about the whole scene didn't seem right. So I sent the file over to a contact in M.I.T. He used the latest photo enhancer software he's developing to generate some much clearer stills.'

Mario lifted a large brown envelope from the counter next to him. He pulled out some photographs.

'He mailed them to me yesterday. I think you'd better take a look,' Mario said, handing them to her.

Lois frowned, intrigued now in spite of herself. Benzir. She'd only ever seen his face in the press. Mug shots. Even the few bits of footage the Enzo's own surveillance cameras had picked up of him had been compromised by the hat he'd worn to cover his face.

But here was an opportunity to see him up close. To see the look on the face of the man who shot her, seconds before he fired.

She took the envelope and slipped the sheaf of photos out.

The first showed a man pointing a rifle into the arena. A body was clearly slumped by his feet.

'It's a fact that this footage was taken before the shot

was fired . . .' Mario said, 'and there are clearly two people up there.'

But Lois put her hand up to stop him, her brain working overtime, as she stared at the face of the man holding the gun, pointing out into the arena, to where Senator Fernandez was sitting.

The face of the man who had shot her.

'Oh, Jesus,' she whispered.

CHAPTER FIFTY

Savvy watched the ball rolling round and round the wheel. Luc was on a lucky streak and he was sure that this latest ball was going to be the luckiest ever.

If it lands on red, I'm going to bed. If it lands on black, I'll stay . . .

No! Staying is too dangerous.

She could already feel herself slipping out of control. Winning like this was making her want to risk more and more. All her old behaviour was being triggered. It made her want to order bottles of champagne at the bar. It made her want to do lines and lines of cocaine. To take this high to another, new high. To prolong this amazing night for as long as she possibly could.

The ball landed on red.

'Well, that's me done,' she said, stepping away from the table. 'Goodnight, everyone. It's been fun.' There were gasps from her companions. Nobody wanted the night to end, least of all Savvy. But she had to remember where she was. And who she was with. Luc Devereaux – her gorgeous companion . . . her colleague . . . and the man who must not see her lose control.

Only days ago, she'd wanted nothing more than for Luc to admit that he cared for her, so that she could reject him. But now, especially *right now*, she realized what a stupid and dangerous game she'd been playing. Who was she kidding? *She* was the one with feelings. Call it chemistry, call it hormones, there was an undeniable attraction that she couldn't control.

But she had to control it. To resist. No matter what.

There was no future for them, apart from a professional one.

'Goodnight, Luc,' she said. She didn't look at him. Couldn't look at him. Because if he looked into her eyes, he'd know in an instant what she was feeling.

'I'll walk you to the hotel,' he said.

'There's no need, honestly. You stay,' she urged, but he was already collecting up his piles of chips.

They walked back through the casino to the connecting doors that led to the hotel. Savvy tried making polite chit-chat about the people they'd met, but she'd fallen silent by the time they stepped into the old-fashioned hotel elevator.

They stood together, side by side, looking up at the numbers on the floors ticking past on the elevator panel.

Was he, like her, remembering the time she'd taken him up in the lift to the hotel suite at La Paris? Was that why he was so quiet? Was that what he was thinking about?

How self-assured she'd been back then. How confident that she'd seduce him. But now she felt terrified. All she had to do was get to the room. Put a solid wall between them. Lock the door and then she'd be safe.

But she could feel Luc next to her. Feel the warmth of his body. She couldn't deny how aroused she felt.

They strolled down the thick carpet of the corridor to her suite.

'Our flight leaves at eleven,' she said, as they reached the door.

'I know.' He paused. 'I'm glad we had this time, Savvy. To, you know, reconnect. I thought we might always avoid one another.'

She said nothing, but felt the weight of his words. He'd been avoiding her, too? It hadn't just been one-sided? She forced herself to smile and shrug, as if it didn't matter.

'Time changes things,' she said. 'We've both moved on, haven't we?'

He nodded. 'I guess we have.'

'Well, goodnight,' she said.

He sighed. It was his cue to say goodnight and move away. He didn't.

'There's still so much we never got to talk about,' he said.

All that time after he'd rejected her and gone out with Elodie, she'd done nothing but want to talk to him. But he hadn't let her. He hadn't believed her.

'We could talk now . . . ?' he said.

No, she thought. Too much had happened. Too much time had gone by. They had to leave the past alone.

But as her eyes met his, she realized that they couldn't spend any longer running away from it.

They'd once been an 'us'. To move forward to the future, they both needed closure on the past. She owed him that conversation at least.

Savvy didn't turn the light on in the room. Instead, she walked out to the private balcony and looked down at the bay, lighting a cigarette. She shivered, despite the warm breeze. She stared out at the dark water.

She gripped the balcony rail, bracing herself, as Luc stopped behind her.

What the hell are you doing? she asked herself. She was his boss. She had control . . . was in control. Raking up emotions . . . it was too dangerous.

'I'm sorry, Savvy. Maybe I shouldn't have said anything . . .' Luc began. 'Maybe it's too painful.'

There was a beat as she turned and stared at his handsome face. She knew that this was probably the only chance she'd ever have to get to the bottom of where they'd gone so wrong.

But it took all her strength to start speaking. 'If you want to talk now, then you have to tell me the truth,' she said.

He nodded. 'OK.'

'Did you honestly think that you could marry Elodie?

Did you think you'd be able to keep such a big secret? That we'd been together?'

She could tell that he hadn't expected her to dive in at the deep end and mention their brief affair and Elodie in the same sentence. But she had to speak her mind. She had to tell the truth. It was all or nothing now. Or what was the point?

'No, I didn't,' he said quietly.

This wasn't the answer she'd expected. She'd been expecting Luc to defend his relationship with Elodie, but instead he shook his head. His dimples pitted his cheeks as he bit his lip. He looked so sad . . . and so beautiful in the moonlight. 'Poor Elodie,' he said. 'You know, I didn't really ask her to marry me at all.'

'*What?*'

Luc sighed. 'You know what she was like, Savvy. I know this sounds callous . . . but Elodie was very manipulative. In the nicest way, of course. In the way she wanted everything to be right, to be perfect. There was a conversation we had about the future. She twisted my words. And then she was so overjoyed that I got swept up in the whole thing.'

He looked so earnest . . . so confused himself.

She knew exactly how Elodie had been, and how hard it would have been for him to stand up to her sister. She'd found it hard enough herself at times. But even so, that didn't stop the fact that he'd been weak. So weak. He couldn't blame Elodie.

'You could have told her no,' Savvy said, hating the way her voice trembled. She'd thought that she'd processed all of this, but now that they were talking, she realized that the emotions she was feeling were still uncontrollably strong.

He stared directly at her. 'I could have told her no. But I didn't.'

'You loved her, then?' Savvy asked.

Luc paused. He looked down at his feet, then into her eyes. 'I guess what I loved were the parts of her that reminded me of you.'

'But . . . but *I was there*. I hadn't gone anywhere,' she said.

'Hadn't you, Savvy? It didn't seem that way to me.'

He was talking about Marcus, about what Elodie thought she'd seen. She stared at him defiantly.

'I don't care what Elodie told you,' she said. 'What she saw that night never happened. Could never have happened. I hadn't been near another man in months. I was saving myself for you.'

She turned her head and looked up at the cliffs, willing herself not to cry. What did it really matter now? she told herself. What they were talking about happened so long ago.

'But I thought—'

She glanced at him. 'Yes, I know what you thought. But you were wrong.'

He seemed to slump. 'I didn't listen. I know that. I judged you.'

All or nothing. The whole truth.

'I told her, you know. Elodie. About us,' Savvy said.

'You told her?'

She looked at him and nodded slowly.

'What did she say?' Luc asked.

444

Savvy remembered that night at Elodie's apartment. 'She didn't believe me. But when I made her believe me, she was furious.'

What was she doing? This was a secret she was supposed to be taking to the grave. Not telling Luc. Luc, who'd believed all this time, along with Paige and Hud, that Elodie's death had been a tragic accident. One in which Savvy had played no part.

But she couldn't help herself. She had to release it. He had to know. He had to know what she'd had to carry around, because of him.

'We had . . . we had a fight. A physical fight.'

'A fight?'

'She punched me in the face. My nose was pouring blood. She wouldn't stop hitting me. It was like she was possessed. In the end I was on the floor and she was above me. She was about to slam down on me and I . . . I kicked her. And that's how she fell backwards . . . backwards down . . .' She struggled to say the words, picturing the halo of blood. '. . . and broke her neck.'

Luc said nothing. He stared at her, unblinkingly.

'She died because of me,' Savvy said. 'I killed her.'

In one step Luc was right up close. He gripped her arms tight. 'Don't say that. It was an accident, Savvy.'

But Savvy shook her head and pulled herself free. 'She's gone, Luc. She's gone. Because of what we did.'

She turned away. She'd thought that talking about the past would settle it and put it to rest, but she realized now what a mistake she'd made. She didn't feel relieved, or vindicated. She felt guilty and broken all over again. As if all the strength she'd garnered since leaving Peace River had now been torn away.

She swiped angrily at the tears which had sprung to her eyes. She didn't turn round. 'You should go now. Please. Just go.'

Savvy waited for Luc to leave, but instead he spoke.

'I wanted you to tell her,' he said. 'About us. I hoped you'd have the guts to say what I couldn't bring myself to.'

Savvy turned to face him. Hadn't he heard what she'd just told him? About Elodie. About what she'd done? But she could see in his face that he had. He'd heard every word of it, but he still hadn't gone away.

'I hoped you'd tell her and that Elodie would break our engagement. And that somehow, crazily, you might take me back.'

'But why? After what you thought had happened between me and Marcus?'

'Because I still loved you. I loved you desperately. I always did.' He looked at her then. Right at her. 'I still do.'

She was shaking uncontrollably as she felt Luc's arms go round her. She felt him lean in close, holding her tight.

'I never wanted Elodie, Savvy. Not like I wanted you. You have to know that,' he whispered. 'I always wanted you. It was you I wanted to marry.'

Her heart was racing so hard, she could barely breathe. She couldn't seem to pull herself away, as if she was melting against Luc, fusing with him. As if the force were just too great for her to resist any longer.

'That night we spent together. It changed my life,' he said. 'I've never felt like that. That connection we had. I have been living in the shadow of it ever since. Until right now.'

'But we can't. I'm . . . there's the business . . . every-thing . . . everything's changed.'

But his lips were moving towards hers.

'Will anyone really care, Savvy? When we have to be together. Does anything really matter, apart from this? Apart from us?'

And then his lips were on hers in the moonlight.

CHAPTER FIFTY-ONE

Banyan's Boatyard in Shanghai's oldest quarter was a stunningly preserved piece of colonial heritage. More recently it had been a private members' club and hotel, and its splendid bookcases, solid billiard table, giant ostrich-feather lampshades and brass and wooden fans harked back to a bygone era. The décor seemed to stir up faint echoes of the nineteen-thirties gin-slinging set that had once made this destination infamous and desirable in equal measure, throughout the Far East.

The carved wooden bar was stacked with antique gin bottles and a waiter in white gloves stood polishing the crystal glasses, watching the blurred scene of the harbour beyond through the rippled glass of the old French doors. Motes of dust twirled peacefully in the shafts of late afternoon light that patterned the black and white chequered tiles with blues and greens from the overhead stained-glass dome.

In the corner, a man in polished brogues sat on a studded leather reading chair beside the newspaper stand. He selected a broadsheet which had been ironed and folded into a wooden baton and pulled it open.

In the centre of the room, near the bottom of the wide marble staircase which swept up to the first-floor terrace, Lois Chan sat by the fireplace in a pretty lavender and white tea-dress, sipping tea from the bone china cup set out on the low ottoman in front of her. The scene looked tranquil enough, but Lois's senses were on red alert. And now here it was. The moment she'd been waiting for.

In the gleaming brass trumpet of the old gramophone Lois saw the reflection of Mike Hannan entering through the main doors with his wife, Jeanie.

He was wearing a straw trilby and a light brushed-cotton fawn suit. Lois stood up as he approached.

'Mike!' she exclaimed.

'Lois,' he said. 'What a surprise.'

She went forward and kissed his cheek. 'Well, actually I've been waiting for you,' she said, smiling brightly at Jeanie. 'I'm here on business, and I happened to see your name on the register. I'm so glad we got to bump into each other.'

'You remember Jeanie, don't you?' Mike said.

'Of course.' Lois stretched out her hand to shake Jeanie's, remembering the last time they'd met. She noticed that her hand was different. Two prosthetic fingers had been fitted. 'How lovely to see you,' Lois said, remembering how emotional Jeanie had seemed the last time they met. And how much more sense that made now.

'You know, Mike, I was wondering, do you have a moment?' Lois asked, gesturing to her table. 'I hope it isn't inconvenient, but I could really do with asking your advice on something.'

'I'll be up in the room,' Jeanie said. 'I hope we'll get to have a drink together later.'

'Me too,' Lois said with a bright smile, as Jeanie departed for the stairs.

Mike joined Lois on the sofa by the fireplace.

'So, this is an unexpected pleasure. How can I help you, Lois?' Mike asked.

'Something has come to light,' she said. The smile had gone from her face.

'Oh?' he asked.

She reached into the bag by her feet and pulled out the picture that Mario had given her.

Mike Hannan stared at the photo for a very long time. Finally he looked at Lois.

'Who else knows about this?' he whispered.

'What if I told you no one?' she asked. 'Would you shoot me again?'

He was silent for a long moment. They both stared at the photograph. Even further enhanced now than when Lois had first seen it, the image showed Mike Hannan aiming the gun into the arena, with the supposed gunman, Benzir, dead – murdered – at his feet.

450

She saw that Mike was using his peripheral vision to scan the room for ways out.

'There's no point in running. All the exits are covered. The guy behind the bar is DEA. The building is completely surrounded.'

He glanced up the stairs.

'Someone will be with Jeanie by now,' she said.

The disappointment and bewilderment that had swamped her since Mario had shown her that photo didn't diminish. She'd been hoping it would, but the photograph said it all. Mike Hannan wasn't even denying it. He *had* tried to shoot Fernandez in the arena. And instead he'd shot her.

All of the pain, all of the heartache she'd suffered, was because of this man right here beside her.

'Why have they sent *you* to get me?' he asked.

'Because they were worried that you'd try and do something rash. Like run. Or fight your way out. And because we're friends. Because I thought you might listen to me. Because you owe me that.'

He sighed and half smiled. 'In all of this, Lois, I never factored in how good you'd be at your job. I never expected you to make it to Fernandez before I did. I . . . well, I thought I'd killed you.'

'That's why you visited the hospital so many times? Guilt?'

He nodded.

'But you killed a man. Murdered Benzir.'

'He was a murderer himself, Lois. A professional hitman. Someone the CIA already had a death warrant

451

out on. I just hired him unofficially and did their job for them.'

Death. Murder. The way he spoke about it was like it was just business. The thought made Lois sick.

Mike seemed to deflate right there in front of her. He looked away from the door and back at the photograph in his hands.

'So what do you want to know?' he said.

'Why did you try and kill the senator?'

'Oh Lois. I didn't really want to kill him. I just had to make it look like I'd tried.'

'Had to?'

'Three days before the fight, LA Triads affiliated to Jai Shijai kidnapped Jeanie.'

So Aidan's hunch had been right. When Lois had first shown him the photograph, he'd immediately thought that Jai Shijai was behind the hit. Partly because it explained Mike Hannan's presence at the Hong Kong races that day, where Aidan had later seen him talking to Angela Ho. But mainly because Jai Shijai had always been the one who stood to gain most from Senator Fernandez's death.

'They told me that unless I killed the senator, they'd kill her. They tortured her to make me play ball. They FedExed her fingers to my home. There never was an elevator accident.'

'Oh God. Oh Mike . . . no,' Lois said. She recoiled, horrified. No wonder Jeanie had reacted like she had at the races. Her experience must have been horrendous. Lois felt bile rise in her throat, imagining her own fingers being severed. And horror at the thought that someone had done that to Jeanie. It only went to prove how ruthless Jai Shijai was. And what a dangerous world both she and Mike had unwittingly become involved in.

'But why would Jai Shijai want Fernandez dead?'

'Because he'd heard through one of his sources that Fernandez would be setting up a DEA task force to break the chain on heroin imports from China. It was only a matter of time before they linked the main supply back to Jai Shijai. He needed to buy time to cover his tracks. Having Fernandez out of the way would give him a window to move his operation. He wanted to invest in the new casinos out in Shangri-La. He planned to use the Good Fortune initially to launder his money and make it legitimate. Then to get out of the drugs game altogether. He liked to think he was following an old Vegas plan. All those guys used drugs money to build the casinos. Jai Shijai thinks he can do the same again, only here in China.'

'So why didn't you walk away, Mike? Or blow the whistle? Or tell Fernandez?'

'Because once I'd fired the gun, I was on Jai Shijai's payroll. He had someone film the shooting too. He could have handed me over to the cops whenever he liked. He summons me to report to him every two months. That's what we were doing in Hong Kong when you saw us there. And here. I met him two days ago.'

No wonder Aidan's task force had been having such trouble. Mike knew what Fernandez knew. And in turn gave the details to Jai Shijai, so he could always stay one step ahead.

'So what are they going to do? Lock me up and throw away the key? Or take me outside and shoot me?' he asked. 'That's what I deserve. Let me tell you, being Jai's kept man is a living hell.'

'No, they need your help to nail Jai Shijai. You remember my friend Aidan Bailey?' she said.

Mike nodded. His eyes were raw as they looked up at her.

'Well, that DEA task force the senator set up? Aidan's bossing it. Take his offer, Mike. If they can prove you were coerced . . . and if you help them now . . . then this might not be so bad for you after all.'

'Jai is a dangerous man,' he said. 'If he suspects that you know . . .'

'I know,' she said. 'That's why you're going to help me. Because otherwise he'll get to me, too. I'm giving you a last chance to do the right thing, Mike. Take it.'

CHAPTER FIFTY-TWO

It was eleven thirty at night and Luc and Savannah's surprise engagement party at the White House was winding down. Most of the guests – mostly La Paris employees – had returned to work. The rest were in the kitchen. But for Savvy, the place that had once been the heart of the house wasn't the same without Martha.

Savvy watched Belinda, Martha's replacement, topping up some glasses with champagne and felt a momentary pang of sadness in the midst of all the celebrating. Martha would have been so happy to be here today, and Hud too.

And Elodie . . . ?

Savvy couldn't think about Elodie. Not now. She felt too guilty that her confession had brought about her reconciliation with Luc in Monte Carlo. And these heady, whirlwind days since.

Being with Luc, being *engaged* to Luc, made it almost

impossible to think about the past. She looked down at the enormous square-cut diamond on her ring finger, feeling the back of it with her thumb. It was every bit as big and glamorous as she'd always dreamed her engagement ring would be. But it felt strange on her finger. Overwhelming. A constant reminder that *everything* had changed overnight.

It was just after Luc had kissed her in the moonlight in Monte Carlo that he'd popped the question. It had been so natural. So emotional. And when she'd whispered yes, they'd kissed again, until Savvy had felt blissfully and completely lost.

But as Luc was sweeping her up into his arms and carrying her towards the bed, he'd told her that he wanted to wait until their wedding night to make love. To make it proper. To be old-fashioned. To make even more sure they'd remember it for the rest of their lives. They'd both been so emotional that it had seemed the right thing to do at the time and, overwhelmed by his gentlemanly and romantic gesture, Savvy had fallen into a deep sleep in his arms.

But now she wished that they had at least cemented their feelings physically too. She knew she should feel confident and strong, but she needed his touch now more than ever. She needed confirmation that what was happening – what she'd always secretly dreamed of happening – was real.

And now, as Paige grinned at her, Savvy felt even more insecure. How could she explain to Paige that her over-the-top enthusiasm was very endearing, but it wasn't what Savvy needed. She needed time and privacy with Luc. All this . . . this sudden exposure was too much.

Savvy glanced at the clock on the wall. She'd been watching it all evening. Counting the minutes until she had to say goodbye to Luc. In less than two hours he'd be gone. And she'd be alone.

'Quite a party,' Savvy told Paige.

'It was only an impromptu thing, but we couldn't go back to Shangri-La without celebrating.'

Luc suddenly appeared and slipped his arms around Savvy from behind and nuzzled into her neck.

'You two lovebirds,' Paige said, laughing. 'We've got a flight to catch soon,' she reminded him.

Luc needed to be back in Shangri-La and he'd asked Paige to go with him to help. It made sense, he'd told Savvy. Paige knew the project backwards and Savvy needed to be in Vegas to represent the Hudson Corp at the industry awards. They couldn't all go and even though Savvy had wanted to desperately, she'd had to play it cool. She was, after all, the boss. She had to be in charge.

'I can't wait to tell everyone over there,' Paige said. 'There'll be a few broken hearts when people find out Luc's no longer a free man.'

'Paige,' Luc scolded.

'It's true. You're the Shangri-La pin-up. You must know that.'

'Well, not any more,' Savvy said firmly.

She didn't like Paige teasing her and Luc about their relationship, or thinking it was public property. It was too new. 'Listen, Paige, please don't make a big fuss. I don't see why everyone has to know every detail.'

'Are you kidding me?' Paige said. 'The phones have been ringing off the hook. "The romance of the century," they're calling it. You're marrying Elodie's fiancé, but Luc was the love of your life all along. It's . . . *hot*.'

'How did they know that?' Savvy asked.

Paige glanced at Luc. 'He filled me in.'

'No secrets,' Luc said, smiling down at Savvy. 'Not any more.'

Savvy smiled back nervously. She wasn't sure she wanted such personal details exposed so soon. But she was in no position to complain now. She was a Hudson – the head of the Hudson Corporation. What she did *was* a public affair, whether she liked it or not.

'In fact, we've had an amazing idea,' Paige said.

Savvy laughed in spite of herself. She'd never seen Paige this animated, or happy. 'Another one? Go on then . . . tell me.'

'I know you said you wanted to get married here in Vegas . . .'

Savvy frowned. She saw Paige glance at Luc, then grin back at her.

'But I . . . we . . . had a brainwave.'

'Enlighten me.'

'We're going to get married in El Palazzo. On launch night,' Luc said.

Paige was jumping up and down. 'Isn't that just the best idea? I've thought it all through. We'll turn the meeting room into the chapel. You know it's got

458

screens down the whole of one end wall? Well, we can project a backdrop of an English country garden or a beach and—'

'Hang on. Married? In Shangri-La?' Savvy interrupted.

'Oh, please say yes, Savvy,' Paige said. 'It makes perfect sense. Everyone will be there. And if you're getting married, then the world's press will be there too. We'll spin out the story. "El Palazzo is the hottest venue in Asia to get married." Think of the business! And you said yourself that you wanted to upstage the Good Fortune on the night of their baccarat championship. Well, this is the perfect way to do it.'

'But it's less than six weeks away.'

And besides, Savvy wanted to shout, this is about me and Luc. Not the business. Not the press. And what about their special wedding night? It couldn't be special if they were hosting launch night at El Palazzo at the same time. Why did the two biggest nights of her life suddenly have to be combined?

'I'd marry you right now if I could,' Luc said, grinning at her. He put his arm around her waist and leaned down to kiss her. 'But Paige is right. Launch night would be perfect. The beginning of a new adventure. The start of the rest of our lives.'

Paige clasped her hands together and cooed. 'I'm just so happy, I don't know what to do with myself,' she said.

Savvy looked between them. Her eyes settled on Luc. The confidence . . . the sheer joy on his face . . . It swept her doubts aside.

Why not? she thought. Why not make it happen as quickly as possible? He was right. Why put their lives on hold when they could be moving forward right now?

'OK, OK,' she said, laughing. 'But how are we going to get organized? I mean, I haven't even got a dress.'

Paige grinned triumphantly. She picked up a clipboard and handed it to Savvy. 'Your schedule, ma'am,' she said with a flourish. 'It's all planned out. Tomorrow morning, starting at nine, I've got all the best designers coming to present their dresses and bring samples.'

Luc leaned down and kissed Savvy again. 'After we're married, I promise, after we're open and launched, I'm going to take you on the most amazing, romantic honeymoon you could ever imagine. The best hotels, the finest wine . . .'

Yes, Savvy thought, holding his hand tightly now. And no business. Just the two of us. Somewhere as beautiful as Peace River Lodge. Somewhere we can be ourselves . . .

She couldn't wait.

It wasn't until the party was over and Luc and Paige had left for the airfield that Marcus arrived. Savvy had been about to go to bed when he screeched up in his Ferrari to the White House doors. He'd come straight from work and looked healthier than Savvy had seen him look for months.

'I heard what happened at the Good Fortune,' he said. 'Babe, are you OK?'

Savvy smiled, touched that Marcus still presumed to call her 'babe'. She liked the fact that, even though she was his boss, in private conversations he still treated her like he always had.

'I guess that's another of my nine lives I've used up.'

There was an awkward pause.

'Is it true?' he asked. 'You and Luc . . . ?'

Savvy waggled the sparkly engagement ring towards him. But Marcus didn't smile.

'You just missed the party,' she said.

Marcus stared at her. His face was serious, his green eyes searching out hers.

'This is your cue to congratulate me,' Savvy continued, unnerved by his silence. 'Especially seeing as you didn't make my party.'

'Jesus, Savvy.' Marcus walked away from her and ran his hand over his dark hair.

The smile dropped from her face. She'd never seen Marcus look so upset.

'What's the matter?'

He turned to face her, his hands on the waist of his midnight-blue shirt. 'Have you forgotten what he did? Last time I noticed, he'd broken your heart and sent you into a downward spiral that – believe you me – was bloody difficult to rescue you from. Where was Luc Devereaux then? But all of a sudden, now you're successful and rich, he's back on the scene—'

'Stop it,' Savvy gasped, feeling a deep flush inside her. 'Take that back. You have no idea what it's like.'

'Then enlighten me. Because all I can see is you making another huge mistake.'

'I love him,' she said.

Marcus threw his hands up in despair and groaned, as if she were being delusional.

'Not that I'd expect you to understand,' Savvy snapped. 'What do you know about love?'

'Plenty.' Marcus glared at her. His eyes bored into hers. It was the first time he'd shouted at her and she stepped away, fighting back tears.

She should never have presumed to be friends with Marcus. She should have left him in her past, where he belonged. It was impossible to truly be friends with someone with whom she'd had such murky history.

And now she had nowhere to go. They couldn't be friends any more, but he still worked for her. She couldn't exactly fire him, just because he had doubts about her marriage to Luc.

'I'm sorry you feel that way,' she said. She fought to keep her voice level. 'But since you do, I suggest that we don't discuss it again. I think we should try and keep things professional between us.'

'Fine,' he said, in a tone that made her think there was a whole tonne of stuff he hadn't said. She felt a pang of sadness that it had come to this. He wouldn't be coming to the wedding now, that was for sure.

Marcus squeezed his lips together. He seemed to be composing himself. He coughed. She guessed their row had hurt his feelings too.

'As it happens, it's a professional matter I wanted to see you about,' he said.

'Which is?' Savvy tensed.

This was it then, he was going to quit.

Marcus sighed. 'I've got some information. About your father,' he said.

Savvy felt tension spreading like a spider's web across her back.

'Go on,' she said, steeling herself for what she might be about to hear, thinking of all the lies written about Hud already.

'I found the madam who used to supply girls for Hud. Like you asked me to. And let me tell you, it wasn't easy. She's called Peaches Gold, but she's retired now. It took me ages to get her to talk.'

Savvy felt a stab of fear.

'And?'

'And the latest kiss-and-tell is from a girl who Hud last saw years ago. And I mean years. It's not a recent story. But what she's saying *is* true. He made them all wear blonde wigs and he filmed them. That's why Peaches stopped supplying him.' Peaches reckoned Hud had given up the whole call girl thing entirely anyway just after that. Over five years ago now. After he'd first got ill. She'd been as surprised as anyone by the manner of his death.

Savvy knew she'd asked for it. This was the information she'd wanted Marcus to track down and now she had to deal with it, but it was still hard. Every time she thought about Hud's last night – about what he'd done, right here in this house – she felt totally conflicted.

If what Marcus had found out was true, it was only a matter of time before some greedy journalist with a grudge to bear tracked down one of those tapes. And what then? That kind of sleazy press could ruin all her carefully laid plans and scupper the launch of El Palazzo *and* her wedding.

Was this how Hud had felt about her? Savvy wondered now. When her name had been dragged through the press? When her antics, or her loud mouth, had brought shame on the Hudson name? Well, maybe he was getting his own back from beyond the grave, she thought grimly.

'Thank you, Marcus,' she said.

He nodded. 'OK. I'm going to go now.'

He wouldn't look her in the eye. 'Marcus,' she said. He turned in the doorway. 'I still need you to find that girl. If you can . . .'

'I'll try,' he said. But as the door closed, she had no way of knowing whether he would or not.

She was still standing there, fiddling with her engagement ring, as she heard Marcus's Ferrari spin up the gravel outside the front door and speed away into the night.

CHAPTER FIFTY-THREE

Lois stood next to Aidan on the steps of Banyan's Boatyard, as the water taxi containing Mike and Jeanie Hannan and three DEA operatives sped away.

Then they turned back towards the French doors. A lawn stretched out before them, broken only by the hoops and stumps of a croquet set. Pink bougainvillea trailed over the doorway and a hedge of rhododendrons buzzed with bees. In the afternoon heat, the quiet calm of the colonial surroundings somehow made what had happened here seem even more monumental and permanent.

'You think he'll play ball?' Lois asked Aidan.

'He's got no choice.'

'You're going to have a tough time explaining this one to Fernandez,' she told Aidan, as they reached the worn stone steps. 'He'll want his head.'

Aidan shook his head and whistled. 'Don't I know it.'

But that was nothing compared to how Roberto Enzo was going to react when he found out that Jai Shijai's drugs money had been behind the consortium which had funded the Good Fortune.

One of Aidan's team, a Chinese guy called Jet, approached, removing an earpiece from his ear.

'Well?' Aidan asked.

Jet was the liaison with the Chinese government. 'We're good to go,' he said. 'Once we've got the conclusive evidence on Jai Shijai locked down, then they'll have to go public.' He glanced at Lois. 'Very public. They'll want a big arrest. Show that they're not going to tolerate corruption. They're gonna hang Jai Shijai out to dry.'

Aidan glanced at Lois. 'Then it'll have to be at the baccarat championship. That's the next time that we know for sure we've got him cornered. And it's the most public place he's likely to be. You're going to have to do that sweet-talking we discussed and get him back.'

Lois felt shaky. Terrified of what the operation involved, she thought how tactfully and skilfully she'd have to play it to get back in Jai Shijai's favour.

They walked through to the lounge area.

'So what will happen now?' she asked Aidan.

'I'm afraid you'll have to go back to Shangri-La and act like nothing has changed. And I'll have to quietly gather all the evidence I can from Mike, and then it'll all be over.'

Lois laughed, without pleasure. 'You make it sound so easy. But it's going to be hell.'

Six weeks of keeping her mouth shut. Of deceiving everyone in the Good Fortune. Six weeks when she knew that she couldn't be in contact with Aidan. That she'd have no way of knowing if he had everything he needed. Six weeks . . .

Aidan squeezed her arm. 'You know, you did good today. Real good. You impressed the hell out of my team.'

'Did I?' Lois turned on him. His compliment couldn't make up for the turmoil she was feeling.

'I know what you've done. What you've sacrificed, Lois.'

'Do you? If Jai Shijai goes down, then the Good Fortune will go down with him. I can't bear for that to happen. All my team . . . all they've sacrificed. All their hard work. And Roberto . . . he's part of the syndicate that built it too. I know he raised finance on the Enzo Vegas, so that'll be on the line. Not to mention his reputation.'

She hadn't yet had to look Roberto in the face, but already she felt like a traitor. Aidan had sworn her to secrecy. She couldn't tell anyone what was happening, not even the man to whom she owed her whole career.

Because if word leaked out about what was going down, then the chances were it would result in Mike and Jeanie Hannan's death. And Jai Shijai would get away.

'I'll do what I can,' Aidan said, but they both knew

that he couldn't make any promises. 'I'll talk to Fernandez.' He put his hand on Lois's arm and turned her to face him. 'Listen to me,' he went on. 'One of the first things you ever told me was that you wanted to make the world a better place for the little guy. To make it safe. Well, this is your chance.'

'But—'

'Doing the right thing is never the easiest option,' Aidan said.

She nodded. 'But how do I know I've done the right thing?'

'Because you have. Morally, you've made the right call. You'll have to trust me on that one.' He raised her face so that she could meet his eyes. His lovely, honest, kind eyes. The eyes that melted her, every time she looked into them. 'You're going to have to trust a man one day, Lois. And I really want that man to be me.'

CHAPTER FIFTY-FOUR

Savvy couldn't sleep. In Hud's old bedroom at the White House, she sat on the window seat and looked out at the view of the lake and the lawns stretching in all directions to the high walls. She'd always hated the White House in the past, but recently she'd grown fond of the place. For all the bright lights of Vegas beyond the walls, Hud had created this oasis of peace. But she wondered now, as she listened to the silence of the house, whether he'd ever got lonely here by himself.

Luc and Paige had left hours ago to go back to Shangri-La and now that Savvy was all alone, she felt unaccountably emotional. Perhaps it was the argument with Marcus that was bugging her.

She felt angry that he had been so dismissive of her and Luc. And now she pined for Luc, for him to make Marcus's cruel words go away.

She should be feeling happy, she knew. She had everything she wanted. Her business empire was about to flourish in Shangri-La, she was rich and she was engaged. To Luc. The man she'd loved from the first moment she'd laid eyes on him. The happy-ever-after she'd always wanted was just around the corner. She just had to get the wedding over with. Then she had a real chance of making a new future – a new family even – with Luc. A chance to build a wall of privacy around them, away from the prying eyes of the world.

But somehow . . . somehow, she felt a sense of melancholy that she couldn't shake. With Paige so excited about the wedding, Savvy had no one to talk to about her doubts. About how she'd been left reeling by the sheer speed of everything. About how she no longer felt truly in control of her own destiny.

She looked down and realized that she'd been unconsciously fiddling with the friendship bracelet on her wrist. Now she stared at it in the moonlight. It would have to come off, she realized. She couldn't try on couture wedding gowns in the morning while wearing something so tatty and old.

And yet the thought of it made her feel even sadder. As if cutting it off would be casting a part of herself adrift too.

She sighed, thinking of Red on his island in Scotland.

Was he happy? Was he in love too? Was he engaged? The thought made her heart beat faster. Was he staring at someone else with those wolf-like eyes? Those eyes that had once made her feel so safe. So grounded. So true to the person she'd nearly become.

But she pushed the thought away. Red was in the past. Whatever he did with his life was none of her business. Why should it bother her, if he'd found love? He deserved it, didn't he? Just like she did.

She should get out of here, she thought, getting off the window seat. Being in Hud's room was just making her feel maudlin.

But as she walked towards the door, she stopped.

He liked to film the girls . . .

Suddenly, the conversation she'd had earlier with Marcus echoed through Savvy's mind. It was like her subconscious had been quietly working away on a problem and had at last come up with a solution.

And now she realized why she couldn't sleep and why she was here.

At the foot of Hud's bed was a large walnut-veneered cabinet. Savvy strode towards it and opened the doors. Inside was a giant television. She opened the drawer underneath and the front flicked down, revealing an old video player.

She knelt down and searched in and around the TV cabinet.

Think, she told herself. If she were Hud, where would she hide the tapes?

She thought for a moment, then walked over and opened the closet. Her father's clothes had been taken away. Only a few empty shoe boxes remained and a load of wooden hangers, which rattled as she moved them aside.

She stood inside the closet, feeling the side wall of it, knocking and tapping at the panels.

She jumped as one of them sprang open.

The hidden compartment housed around twenty digital tapes on a shelf, each of them labelled with a date and a different girl's name.

Savvy's hand was trembling as she put the most recent digital tape in the player. She sat on the edge of her father's bed with the remote in her hand and pressed play. The TV flickered into life.

An empty room. *This* room. Savvy stared down at the case. The date was from five years ago.

Five years . . .

All that time ago, and yet Savvy and Elodie had been around then. Grown-ups. And they'd had no idea of Hud's secret life.

She jumped as her father walked into shot. He was naked.

She froze the picture. Cut the sound.

'Oh Hud,' she breathed.

She squeezed her eyes shut. This was all a big mistake. She shouldn't be here. Doing this. It was wrong. All wrong.

But at the same time, she knew that if she was ever going to get any closer to understanding what had happened to Hud, she had to finish what she'd started.

Steeling herself, she pressed play again. Hud continued to walk. He turned and smiled at a woman who now came into shot.

She started to strip at the head of the bed Savvy was sitting on now.

Savvy went cold.

Then she turned and looked at the screen and then back at the bed. The angle meant that the camera must have been positioned in the top corner of the room.

She played more of the tape and paused it again, seeing the woman on the screen in colour this time. She had dark skin and large nipples which made the blonde wig on her head even more ridiculous. She was half lying on the bed, her knees spread open to reveal herself.

Savvy looked at the picture, then looked around the room.

So where was the camera?

She sat in the same position as the woman. Then she stood up and dragged the bedside table over to the bookcase on the opposite wall.

She climbed up. She could only just reach the top shelf. A book fell off, just missing her head and landing with a thump on the thick carpet.

Her fingertips patted along the dusty shelf. And then they hit something. A book that felt too wide.

She'd never have seen it from the bed, she thought, but as she lifted off the book casing, she saw what she'd suspected. A hidden camera. It was hooked up to a power cable. She stretched, pulling the cable free and grabbing the camera.

She yelped as she fell away from the bookcase, breaking her fall on the bedside table. She landed in a crumpled heap on the carpet and swore.

She limped over to her father's bed and turned the small video camera over in her hands.

Inside there was still a tape.

Savvy was shaking as she set up the digital tape to play through the TV. Hud had been as meticulous as with the other tapes. He'd labelled it before he'd set it to record. The date on it was the night he'd died. All that was missing was the woman's name.

A woman came into shot with her back to the camera. She had a shoulder-length blonde bob. Was it a wig? It was impossible to tell.

Savvy watched as the woman took a small package from her pocket. She unfolded the paper and poured the powder – a lot of it – from the slim package into the glass of wine by the bed. Then she wiped her finger over the paper and rubbed it around her gums.

Cocaine. It had to be. Several grams. Enough to explain the amount found in Hud's blood. More than enough to trigger a heart attack in a man in his condition.

Murder. The word lodged itself in Savvy's mind.

She held her breath, leaning right forward now, staring at the television, as she let the tape run on. The woman undressed, her robe slipping to the floor. She was wearing a black bra, a thong and suspenders with black stockings.

And now Hud came into shot.

He was dressed in one of his business suits, as if this were the end of the day. The woman still had her back to the camera, watching as Hud undressed. He seemed to be chatting to her.

The woman strutted towards him. She was holding the wine glass which she now passed to Hud, encouraging him to drink. He downed it nearly in one.

But he'd been teetotal. The doctors had banned him from drinking . . .

Before he'd even finished undressing, the woman pushed him back on the bed, straddling him. Savvy could see that Hud was half expecting this and he laughed. But when he tried to move to finish taking off his shoes and socks, the woman forced him back down.

The woman pulled two silk ties from under the pillow. Hud shuffled up the bed and submitted to being tied up. This had clearly happened before. He still seemed to be talking to the woman, who quieted him, kissing him lingeringly.

Savvy closed her eyes briefly as the woman ripped away Hudson's pants and took him in her mouth. Savvy concentrated on watching Hud's face. His brow creased as the woman's head bobbed up and down.

The woman then stood on the bed, peeling off her thong. She squatted down on Hud, impaling herself on him.

Savvy felt bile rise in her throat as the woman started to ride him. There was something so confident about the way she moved, so assured, but alarming too.

Her movements became more aggressive. Angry. Clinical. It was like she was thrusting. Stabbing.

That was when Hud started to struggle. His expression twisted, became contorted. He was trying to get out from under her, but his hands were still tied.

He looked like he was shouting, but the woman struck him hard across the face. Hud strained against the ties, but the woman stuffed her thong in his mouth.

Now Hud's legs began spasmodically twitching beneath the woman, who was leaning down now, talking into his ear. She unhooked her leg, easing herself off him, to sit on the edge of the bed. Her back was to the camera.

Hud jerked and spasmed on the bed, thrashing against the ties. He was clearly gasping for breath.

But the woman ignored him. She stood up and pulled on a pair of jeans that had been lying on the floor. She didn't turn round.

Hud's face was contorted with pain. Veins popped like ropes on his neck. He curled up his legs, his whole body bucking.

Now the woman reached up and untied his wrists, pulling at the silk ties, slowly, tortuously, as if she were enjoying his agony. The second the ties were undone, Hud clasped his chest, rolling on to his side, clawing one hand out towards the woman. But all she did was take the thong from his mouth.

Tears streamed down Savvy's face. Her father was trying to stand up, but he couldn't. He was dying. She could see it in his eyes. She knelt in front of the television as her father stared up at the camera, a look of horror and desperation in his eyes.

'No,' she sobbed. 'No.'

She watched as the woman stood to leave, pulling the blonde wig from her head so that her auburn hair tumbled down her back.

Savvy watched her father die. Right there. She saw him, on the tape, take his last breath, his eyes looking directly into the camera.

Behind him, the woman walked out.

And that was when Savvy finally caught a glimpse of the woman's face. Through her tears, the anguish ripping her apart, this new sight made something inside her freeze.

Because even before she'd paused the tape to check, she'd recognized the familiar sly smile.

It was Paige.

CHAPTER FIFTY-FIVE

'And the winner is . . .'

In the circus ring the industry awards ceremony had reached its conclusion. Again, the lights criss-crossed the auditorium, but all eyes were turned towards Savannah Hudson and Lois Chan on their tables.

As the drum rolled, nobody felt the weight of expectation in the air more acutely than Lois. Beneath the table, her knees were shaking. She hated this attention. She hated this air of expectation. She hated that the focus was on her. She didn't want to win . . . and yet, she didn't want *not* to win. She just wanted the whole thing to be over.

On the stage, Dusty Redfern, the Vegas legend, opened the embossed envelope.

'The Good Fortune, Shangri-La,' he announced. 'What do you know!'

Tristan stood up and punched the air.

Lois put her hand over her mouth as the realization hit her. It was unbelievable that they'd won such a prestigious accolade after the fire had wrecked their opening night. But the industry had nevertheless honoured her . . . them . . . the Good Fortune.

Had Roberto rigged this? she wondered. She glanced across at him. He nodded, grinning.

'Off you go,' he told Lois. 'It's your casino, not mine.'

The whole of the Enzo Vegas team and the guys she'd brought over from Shangri-La were on their feet as Lois took to the stage, picking up the skirt of her dress.

She felt her heart fluttering with panic. She hadn't expected to win and she hadn't prepared an acceptance speech. Perhaps the best thing to do would be to deflect the attention away from herself, before anyone discovered what a huge fraud she was.

'Thank you,' she said, leaning forward to talk into the microphone, after kissing Dusty Redfern on his parchment-like cheek. 'This means a lot.' She looked at the heavy gold trophy in her hand. 'The Good Fortune is truly an amazing place. One I am so very proud to have been involved with. But I'd like to accept this on behalf of the whole team at the Good Fortune. They've worked as tirelessly in the face of adversity as they have done in the face of success. I guess we all take our work ethic from the man who made it all possible. So I'd like to dedicate this award to my mentor. My hero . . . Roberto Enzo.'

She couldn't see Roberto's reaction as she held the

trophy aloft. The lights were too blinding. She felt surprisingly emotional as she left the stage to a standing ovation. Flustered, she went back to the table, accepting kisses all round.

Then she leaned forward to talk to the usher, who wanted to direct her through the crowd to the photographers' area at the back of the tent.

But as she walked between the tables, receiving congratulations from all sides, Savvy Hudson stepped into her path.

These last few months, Lois had got so used to seeing Savannah Hudson on TV, coquettishly flirting with the press, strutting around in her power suits. But standing in front of her now, she looked less like a mogul and more like a kid.

There was a moment of embarrassed, expectant silence. Lois had never realized how piercing her eyes were before.

'Don't tell me you're going to congratulate me?' Lois said, her voice loaded with sarcasm.

'Actually, for what it's worth, you deserved to win that award,' Savannah said. 'I wanted to win, but I was thinking back there . . . it was the right decision. The Good Fortune was . . . *is* . . . an outstanding achievement.'

Lois stared at her. She couldn't believe she'd just heard right. This girl had tried to sabotage the Good Fortune's launch. Completely. How *dare* she pretend to be so gracious in public? When she knew so many people were watching them, wondering where this face-off would lead.

'My father was very wrong about you, Lois,' she continued. 'He should have employed you. Not tried to destroy you.'

What was *that*? An apology? A job offer? Lois was too flabbergasted to answer.

Then suddenly, to her utter surprise, Savvy stepped forward, as if to kiss her. But instead she leaned in close to Lois's ear.

'I need to talk to you,' she whispered. 'Please don't say anything. Just meet me outside in ten minutes. Alone.' Then she squeezed Lois's arm tight, just once. 'Please,' she urged and Lois suddenly heard the desperation in her voice.

But then she pulled away, smiling, as if nothing had happened.

Outside, Lois sighed in the cool night air and took off her shoes, letting her bare feet sink into the sand. Her head was pounding.

This was ridiculous, she told herself. Why was she out here? What could Savannah Hudson possibly want from her? Why did they need to meet alone?

And yet she hadn't been able to refuse the request. And now she shivered, looking back at the tents.

The canvas encampment behind her was fake. It had been purpose-built ten kilometres out in the Nevada Desert for tonight's awards ceremony. The sponsors of the *Arabian Nights*-themed bash would no doubt hail tonight a glorious success, but Lois couldn't wait for it to be over.

Hummers and jeeps stretched off as far as the eye

481

could see, along with catering trucks. The massive central marquee poked towards the sky like a wizard's hat, the lasers from the stage show beaming through. She could hear applause and cheers as the acrobatic show wowed the audience, but Lois was in no mood to enjoy the spectacle.

She took a few steps away from the white flare of the lights, relishing the quiet moment of solitude.

Out here the stars were breathtaking. Millions of them stretched out before her, sinking down to the horizon. It was a beautiful, humbling sight.

She remembered being at Jai Shijai's island and how Aidan had told her that the stars always gave him a healthy sense of perspective. She'd never believed in fate, but now she marvelled at how a chance meeting like that with Aidan had led all the way to this.

She sighed again, wishing she believed in the power of the stars now. That they could give her the sense of perspective she needed. That she could believe that this whole mess she was embroiled in didn't matter in the greater scheme of things.

But she couldn't. And it did.

Lois looked back over her shoulder, knowing that Roberto and the team from the Enzo Vegas would be wondering where she was. In a moment's time, she'd have to step right back into the lion's jaws, with a bright, proud Vegas smile so that no one could tell she was dying inside.

The pressure was almost too much to bear. She couldn't stand lying to Roberto like this, even publicly lauding him, knowing that by helping Aidan she was actively bringing about his ruination. The future of Shangri-La that Roberto was in there right now claiming was so certain, was anything but.

Again, she felt doubt overwhelming her. Was she doing the right thing? Could she really trust Aidan? Would he do his best to ensure that Roberto wasn't buried alive in the demolition of Jai Shijai's house of cards? Because this was her industry, her world, her people. She should be closing rank, not conspiring with an outsider.

And Aidan *had* lied to her once. And yet . . .

And yet . . .

Again, she remembered his face. And his words echoed in her ears. This *was* about her trusting him. He'd been right about that.

And she did want to trust him. She wanted to with her whole heart. And she knew that there was a place, right at her core, that knew she already had, despite her doubts, despite her fear. It just seemed that her brain was taking time to catch up.

Aidan was a good guy. And he saw the good in her. What could be so wrong about that? He was a risk she'd have to take. She had no choice.

She knew that she had to look at the bigger picture. If someone didn't take a stand against criminals like Jai Shijai, if she just turned a blind eye and let him win, then it would be the same as letting Chief Blakeney get away with ruining her career, all over again.

And when it was over? Well, who knew what everything would be like? Perhaps she'd have nothing. But she hoped she'd have one person who'd stick by her after all this heartache. One person who mattered to her more than she dared to admit.

She heard soft footsteps. Turning, she saw the dark silhouette of a woman walking towards her.

So this was it. Savvy Hudson was here.

She was wearing a long white Grecian-style evening dress. It fluttered in the breeze, making her seem skittish, as if any second now she might bolt.

Even so, Lois's first instinct on seeing her out here alone was wariness. She knew damn well how sneaky and duplicitous this woman could be.

But as Savannah Hudson now stopped in front of her and looked directly into her eyes, Lois felt something else too. Guilt. Guilt over the fact that she'd never returned Savannah's phone to her. Guilt over the fact that Mario – and now the DEA grunts, God knew how many of them – had sweated for hours over the private recordings her phone had contained.

But Savvy was the one who should feel guilty, Lois corrected herself. Was she out here to confess to arson? She looked as if she had something important to say.

Gone was the camera-bright smile. She seemed exhausted . . . fragile even. Gone too was the magnanimous superiority she'd displayed.

Now Savvy stepped forward so that she stood side by side with Lois. She reached into her small clutch bag and took out a pack of Lucky Strike cigarettes and a plastic lighter.

She put a cigarette between her lips and lit it. Her face was illuminated in the glare of the flame.

Lois couldn't stand it any more. She needed to find

out what was going on and get back to her team inside.

'They said it was an electrical fault that caused the fire at the Good Fortune, but I don't believe it,' she said. 'There's no one else here. Just the two of us. So you can tell me. Did you do it? Did you start the fire? Did you deliberately ruin my launch night?'

Lois had been around enough poker players to know the tells that gave them away. So now she stared hard at Savannah Hudson as she exhaled a stream of smoke over Lois's shoulder. But something in the way Savvy Hudson shook her head made Lois realize all at once that she was innocent.

'You really think I'd do that? That I'd set fire to myself just to rain on your parade? Are you crazy?'

'But . . . but you were in the spa area, right there when the fire began.'

'We might be rivals, Lois, but believe me, even I wouldn't go that far.'

Savannah Hudson sucked on her cigarette and Lois stared at her.

She felt tripped up, caught out. She realized now what a big mistake she'd made. She'd assumed Savannah Hudson was guilty. She'd taken one piece of evidence and jumped to the wrong conclusion. Her personal feelings had so clearly overridden her judgement.

How many times had she railed at the injustice of people assuming her guilt over Billy-Ray's death? And now she'd proved that she was just as susceptible.

'So what do you want then?' Lois asked, trying to recover her composure.

Savvy smoked for a moment longer, then stubbed the cigarette out beneath her toe. Her voice was soft . . . nervous. 'I need your help.'

'*My* help? Why?'

'Have you ever had the feeling that you're going mad, because what you're seeing right in front of your eyes is all lies?'

A sudden memory of Billy-Ray's funeral flashed into Lois's head, because the feeling of horror, of betrayal, was something she saw in Savannah Hudson's eyes now. And that world-weary stoop of her shoulders, as if everything was too much to bear, was something Lois had experienced all evening.

'The thing is . . . I suspect that my life is in danger,' Savvy said, and her voice cracked. 'I need someone I can trust, Lois. Someone that no one in my organization would ever suspect I'd go to. Someone who will do the right thing, no matter what. And I've got a feeling you're that person. I'm *counting* on you to be that person.'

Lois nodded, too shocked to speak.

'Can we walk for a while?' Savannah said, glancing over her shoulder back towards the party. 'I don't want anyone to hear this.'

And as they stepped together towards the shadows, Lois knew that the future had just become a whole lot more complicated.

'Go on,' Lois said, cautiously.

Those two little words were all it took. Savannah Hudson started to talk. And the more she told her, the more Lois Chan knew she couldn't turn down her plea for help, in spite of the risks. As Aidan had told her only a week ago, doing the right thing was never the easiest option.

And somehow being trusted, as Savannah Hudson was trusting her now, helped Lois believe in herself again.

She was still here to make the world a better place.

CHAPTER FIFTY-SIX

In the two weeks since the relaunch of the Good
Fortune, people had started flocking to Shangri-La.
And tonight they had more reason than ever.

Outside the Good Fortune, the crowd swelled in the
courtyard, hoping to get a glimpse of the celebrity players in tonight's inaugural Shangri-La Open Baccarat
Championship.

Over the road, the spectacle was even greater as
TV crews jammed the sidewalks to film the coloured
fountains outside El Palazzo, which was finally on show
to the world for the very first time. Helicopters flew
overhead, filming from above, the world's attention
focused on these few square miles of Shangri-La, as
the lasers and pomp of El Palazzo's opening ceremony
lit up the sky.

Oblivious to the excitement outside, Lois stared at
the meeting-room door in the Good Fortune's hub,

knowing that her future was being decided behind it. The mood outside was jubilant – triumphant even – but Lois's heart felt like lead.

'Jai Shijai has just left his hotel room. He's on his way into the casino,' Mario told Lois, glancing at the screens.

But Lois didn't have time to look, her attention now snared by the meeting-room door opening. Aidan stepped out on to the walkway. He looked tense, but then he caught Lois's eye and his face softened. He gave her a solitary nod. His signal.

This was it, then. *Tonight it was really going to happen.*

The Chinese authorities and the DEA were going to attempt to take Jai Shijai down.

Now Joshua Fernandez stepped through the door too and straightened the jacket of his smart suit. He was just as handsome as Lois remembered him. But he looked older and more serious than before. Lois wondered whether the last six weeks had been as nerve-racking for him as they had been for her.

She'd heard from Aidan that Fernandez had been horrified that Mike Hannan, his personal friend and long-standing bodyguard, had betrayed him, and even more upset that he'd had no choice but to go along with the deal Aidan had struck.

But it had worked. Tonight Aidan's team had enough conclusive proof from Mike Hannan to arrest Jai Shijai.

Several more Chinese officials followed Fernandez out of the office. Roberto Enzo was between them. He looked ashen. As if he were being led away to the gallows.

'Lois ... the eyes in the sky. Looks like we meet again,' Fernandez said, walking towards Lois and shaking her hand. He smiled, his eyes so warm that Lois couldn't help but smile back, despite the seriousness of the situation.

She saw him glance at her neck and the St Christopher that he'd given her.

'I see you still wear it,' he said.

She touched the silver pendant. 'It's kept me safe,' she told him. Then she glanced across at Roberto. 'How did Roberto take it? And how are you going to treat him now? Because you need to know this: I will stand by him. Fall by him, too. Because I trust him. He's the victim here. He's done nothing wrong.'

Lois knew she'd just revealed how scared and tense she was, but there was no point in denying it.

'He understands what has to happen here tonight, Lois,' Fernandez said, his tone soothing. 'It helped having the government officials there. This coup is good for them. They're spinning it well. It'll herald the start of more open and honest international relations between East and West. We'll make sure the world knows that Roberto Enzo brought it about. He'll be standing tall when Jai Shijai falls.'

'And the Good Fortune? Enzo Vegas?' Lois had to ask. As insignificant and as selfish as she felt ... it was still her and Cara's future on the line tonight.

'Enzo Vegas will be fine. This place too. You see, the Chinese government realize that shoring up the finances behind the Good Fortune is the least they can do. Either that or watch the whole of Shangri-La flounder and possibly fail. Roberto will get out what he put in and a future percentage share of the profits. Your boss won't be out of pocket. And in time, I guess, neither will you. The rest of the deal will be refinanced. From legitimate sources this time.'

But the game was over for Roberto in Shangri-La. That much was clear.

And if it was over for Roberto, then Lois knew it was definitely over for her too.

'Lois, it's time,' Mario said.

She nodded, walking with Fernandez towards Aidan and the Chinese officials.

'I'll be there, to greet Jai,' Roberto said to Fernandez. 'And to put him at his ease. Apart from anything else, I want to look that bastard in the eye.'

Fernandez nodded. 'The team's in place, Roberto. There's nowhere he can run to. He thinks he's safe here.'

Roberto glanced once at Lois. 'We always meant people to feel safe in our casinos. That was the whole point.'

Lois felt her heart aching. She could tell how furious he was with her. How betrayed he felt. But tonight couldn't have happened if she'd played it any other way. Surely he had to understand that?

'You coming, Lois?' Aidan asked.

She shook her head. She sensed that Roberto needed to do this alone.

As the others walked away, Lois found herself beside Senator Fernandez once more.

'You know, Lois, you may be able to give me some

help,' he said. 'I'm commissioning a new task force back in San Francisco. There's someone in line for the job to head it up. An ex-police chief. But I've done some digging and I'm not sure that he's the right man for the job. In fact, you might know him? A commissioner. Blakeney's his name.'

Lois stared at him, hardly able to take in what he was saying.

'It's a highly paid and prestigious role. At the very forefront of anti-corruption. And I'm thinking that maybe someone with your experience . . . ?'

He smiled at her and there it was again, after all this time – the feeling she had when she'd first met him on Fight Night – that airborne feeling, the feeling that she was in the presence of someone great. Who could make real things happen. Who really could make the world a better place.

'You'd better get down there,' she said, nodding to the screens and the pictures of the police cars arriving outside the Good Fortune's entrance.

'You're really not coming?' he asked. 'Don't you want to see?'

She shook her head. The scene downstairs was going to be public enough. Lois didn't need to be there to witness it.

Besides, the Good Fortune wasn't the only casino in Shangri-La with a police presence tonight.

And right now, there was somewhere else she needed to be.

CHAPTER FIFTY-SEVEN

Across the strip in El Palazzo, Lois and Mario met Savannah Hudson at the door nearest to the security hub, as they'd planned. She was wearing the most exquisite long black dress Lois had ever seen. It was appropriate that tonight her outfit was black and not white. But as Savvy had told Lois earlier, she'd got to wear a white wedding dress once. On the night of the awards ceremony.

One glance across at Mario confirmed how sensational Savvy looked. In the last few weeks, Mario had become quite a fan of Savvy Hudson. But he wasn't the only one. Lois knew that what they planned to do tonight was the most daring thing she'd ever witness.

'You ready?' Lois asked her. 'They've redirected the guests?'

Savvy nodded. 'Let's do it,' she said. Her voice was grim.

A mutual respect had blossomed between Lois and Savannah since their talk in the barren Nevada Desert. Their two business empires might still be at war, but from now on Lois knew that the battles they fought would be along much cleaner lines.

Savannah Hudson might be her father's daughter, but plenty of things round here were about to change.

A view of the Chapel of Love – Hawaiian, Elvis-themed – filled the bank of monitors on the hub's wall. But the chapel was nearly empty.

Chester Malone, El Palazzo's head of security, turned to Savvy, a panic-stricken look on his fat face. 'But they're . . .' he began, looking at Lois and Mario. He knew exactly where they were from.

'I'm expecting you to cooperate with our special guests, Chester,' Savvy said, a steely edge in her voice. 'Please let Mario use your workstation.'

'But—'

'Now!'

She nodded to Mario, who waited for Chester to get out of the way and then quickly sat down at Chester's station and started rattling his fingers across the keyboard.

Lois went to stand next to Savvy. She knew that the guests had already been diverted to the main hall, where the reception would take place, as they'd discussed.

Savvy had wanted to make a public spectacle, but Lois had convinced her that this was a private affair.

One that should not damage the opening of El Palazzo. And standing next to Savvy now, feeling her nervous energy, Lois knew she'd made the right call. One that Savvy would thank her for later.

Because now there were only two people in the chapel. Luc Devereaux was standing at the front. Ahead of him, the wall was filled with a view of the beach, as if he were standing on the sand, waiting for his bride. He turned round and looked towards the doors at the back.

Paige Logan was in her pink, short bridesmaid dress. She walked up to Luc and shrugged, clearly confused too. Lois could see that they knew something was very badly wrong. The guests should be arriving now. But the chapel was eerily quiet.

Suddenly the chapel doors at the back slammed shut and both Luc and Paige jumped. Lois could see from the computer screen Mario was operating that four burly members of El Palazzo's security team were guarding it from the other side, out of Luc and Paige's view.

Savvy nodded to Mario. 'Play it,' she told him.

CHAPTER FIFTY-EIGHT

Savvy felt her heart thumping wildly as she watched Luc's expression when the lights dimmed and the view of the beach scene changed to the view of the top suite in El Palazzo, taken from a camera on the outside scaffolding.

The sound was dubbed perfectly, recorded by the hidden microphones in the ceiling lights. Lois and Mario had done an amazing job of secretly infiltrating El Palazzo and bugging the whole place. Lois had called in some favours from her contacts back in the SFPD to help. They couldn't have done a more conclusive job.

The bed in the background was messed up. Luc was pulling on his shirt.

'Don't crack up on me now, baby,' Paige said. 'Not after everything we've been through. We're so, so close.'

'I know. But . . . but it's all just too complicated.'

'If you'd done the job properly, she'd already be dead,' Paige said. 'I did my part.'

Luc rubbed his eyes. 'Jesus Christ, I tried, OK? It wasn't like I didn't take the first chance I got. I told you. I busted all that sealant at the Good Fortune. Savvy was right there in the spa. The fire should have killed her. I only just made it out of there myself.'

'Well, unfortunately, our little problem is still very much alive,' Paige said.

'Savvy's not a little problem. She's starting to sound convincing. More and more like her father. Like she doesn't need us at all.'

'Convincing? You really think that some dumb-ass ex-junkie who flunked school can run a successful business?' Paige said, pacing in front of Luc. 'She's nothing without us. Nothing. And anyway, who gives a shit if she's like that bastard Hudson or not. Once the wedding is over and she has her little accident on your honeymoon, then legally it'll all be yours . . . ours. Just like we planned all those years ago.'

Paige's voice dropped. 'I've been waiting so long for this, Luc. We can't blow it now. This is the perfect plan. Because nobody would ever suspect us. And people like her . . . they don't deserve the money or the success. Those Hudsons . . . they've trampled on everything, taken, claimed, when they've had no right. She's been doing it ever since she stole my first boyfriend, and Hud for even longer. Since he bankrupted your papa and ruined his dreams. Don't you remember when you said we'd devour Hud's business, from the inside out? We're so close, Luc. So very close . . .'

497

*　　*　　*

Even though Savvy had watched the recording a hundred times already, every time she noticed something different. Today she saw the manic expression in Paige's eyes, as she stroked Luc's face. The same slyness she'd seen in her expression on the night she'd killed Hud.

Savvy had been through every emotion since Mario and Lois had shown her the tapes last week. There'd been disbelief, anger, humiliation, betrayal, grief, loss, but finally, now, she felt relieved.

The view on the screens cut back to the chapel.

Luc – her Luc – the man who'd told her that he loved her and always had – was staring up at the camera through which Savvy was watching him.

He knew she was here. That she'd done this.

But she was untouchable now. Just like he and Paige must now know they were trapped and their sick plan was over.

This was the moment Savvy had been waiting for. This exact instant of her revenge. The split second she'd made the Chinese cops promise her she could have, before she'd given them a copy of the evidence that would put Luc and Paige away for a very long time.

In her mind, it was like the final turn of a roulette wheel, as the silver ball stopped rattling and dropped into its slot.

The gamble was over. The chips were down. And the wheel had spun exactly as she'd hoped.

She'd won. She'd beaten them. She'd destroyed

those who'd set out to destroy her and her family. This dumb-ass ex-junkie who'd flunked out of school had just turned up trumps and she'd done it for keeps.

Paige tried running, but it was useless. There was nowhere to go. The chapel doors had burst open. Police rushed in and grabbed her. She was shouting out to Luc, but it was too late. In a matter of seconds they were both cuffed and taken away, like the common card sharps they were.

Savvy felt a hand on hers. It was Lois Chan. 'Are you OK?'

Savvy nodded. She'd never forget Lois's kindness or how much she'd helped her. She cleared her throat and turned away from the screens. It was over now. History.

'So it's really over at the Good Fortune?' she asked.

Lois nodded. 'For Jai Shijai, yes. All hell will be breaking loose over there right about now.'

Savvy smiled. 'At least that'll give my guests down there something to talk about other than the fact I didn't get married to that snake. On this particular occasion, I don't mind the Good Fortune upstaging me.'

Lois laughed. 'Savvy, believe me, nobody is ever going to upstage you.'

She paused, wondering how she could possibly tell Lois how grateful she felt. 'So if we can't be rivals, you think we'll make it as friends?' she asked.

Lois smiled. 'It's worth a punt,' she said.

Savvy smiled at her, then hugged her.

Lois pulled back. 'You'd better go,' she said. 'Get down there where you belong. You have a kick-ass casino to launch.'

'Thank you. From the bottom of my heart, thank you.'

CHAPTER FIFTY-NINE

It was nearly a year since Lois had left Shangri-La. On a crisp September morning, out in San Francisco Bay, a white yacht sliced through the choppy water. On board, Lois stood behind Cara, covering her eyes with her hands.

'Ready?' she asked. She grinned up at Aidan, who was standing at the wheel. And then she winked at Zak, who was sitting hugging his knees.

She flicked her head, letting the breeze blow the hair from her face.

'Mom!' Cara exclaimed.

Lois lifted away her hands. Then she leaned down and pointed towards the shore, so that Cara could see their new harbourside house.

'That one,' Lois said. 'The blue one.'

'You're serious? *That*'s where you're going to live? And I can come and stay? Whenever I want?'

Lois nodded. 'You like it?'

'Like it? Oh Mom, I love it!'

Lois laughed, thrilled at her reaction. She couldn't wait to call Roberto and tell him the good news. After Shijai's arrest, Roberto had been astounded by what Lois had done to make it happen. Emotionally, he'd declared her to be his white knight and pledged his undying respect and friendship. He'd retired happily, his final bow-out a global recognition of his outstanding contribution to the gaming industry. Finally, with a ringing endorsement from Savannah Hudson, Roberto had achieved the adulation he deserved.

Enzo Vegas, from what Lois had heard, was going to be at full capacity for the next year at least. With Mario in charge, the place was thriving.

Roberto had insisted on buying Lois the house as a thank-you present, when she told him she was bowing out of Shangri-La and taking Fernandez's offer to head up his anti-corruption task force in San Francisco. Roberto had been quick to give the move his blessing. Lois already knew that she and her fiery Italian-American mentor would remain close for life.

Fernandez was thrilled that she was joining him and had finally come good on the favour he owed Lois, putting her in touch with a family lawyer, who'd successfully started negotiations with Chris to give Lois wider access to Cara. So far it was going well, especially since Fernandez had reopened the Lawnton case, in order to clear Lois's name and prove once and for all that she hadn't been responsible for Billy-Ray's death. That, and the fact that Lois was back in the States for good, had resulted in Chris being fairer about her spending time with Cara in the vacations.

And that was what this was. A well-earned vacation.

It had started well. Lois had spent last week organizing a secret retirement party at the Cultural Center for her mother. Lois had taken great pleasure in announcing in a speech that, thanks to a little help from Joshua Fernandez, a special funding programme for refugees from China had been set up in Beverley Chan's name. A lasting way to ensure that her tireless contribution continued to be recognized.

Her mother had been overwhelmed by the honour, but she'd only started laughing and crying at the same time when Lois told her mother's friends and fellow workers that she was moving back to San Francisco to take care of her.

And now Lois could truly relax. Aidan put his arm around her shoulder as Zak chased after Cara, who ducked down the stairs into the galley, laughing.

'You see. I told you they'd get on,' Aidan said.

'She's having the time of her life. I don't think she's ever had this much attention.'

Lois put her arm around Aidan, squeezing him tight, as they looked out towards the Bay Bridge. Their future was as wide as the horizon, she knew. She couldn't wait to see what fate had in store for her next.

CHAPTER SIXTY

'That must be it,' Savvy shouted through the head-phones.

James, the pilot, nodded and tipped the nose of the helicopter down towards the remote Scottish island.

Savvy stared out of the window. All she could see was a small cottage and lots of gorse-covered hills, with sheep. Lots of sheep. The waves crashed against the high craggy rocks, sending plumes of white foam into the air. But there was a rawness to the place, a ruggedness that she could see must appeal. This was just about as far away from her world as it was possible to get.

And boy it was good to get away.

The last few months had been a whirlwind. There would be more probing to come into the true extent of Luc and Paige's deceit, she was sure. And in three months' time she'd be in the witness box in the most sensational trial of the decade.

But Savvy knew that the trial was a date in her diary, not the rest of her life. The storm would blow over and it would be business as usual.

And business was booming. Her latest project was to coordinate the members of her select consortium who were making a bid for the Good Fortune. Shangri-La had taken off big time. El Palazzo was going from strength to strength. Things in Vegas were looking good too. Marcus had helped formulate Savvy's plans to turn the White House into a small luxury casino and club that he'd eventually manage.

As for Paige Logan and Luc Devereaux? The last Savvy heard, they were in separate detention centres awaiting the trial. No bail had been granted.

A few minutes later the helicopter landed and Savvy thanked James, knowing he'd be leaving straight away and waiting on standby back on the mainland.

But now, as she opened the passenger door and stepped out into the cold whirlwind of the rotor blades, she felt sick with nerves.

Squinting through the wind, she saw a man running from the cottage towards the helicopter. Struggling against the vortex, Savvy moved towards him.

She ducked as the helicopter took off.

And then she was alone, face to face with Red.

He'd stopped and was staring at her, open-mouthed, waiting until the noise of the helicopter subsided and they could speak.

'Savvy . . . what the hell?'

He'd changed since she'd last seen him. His hair was

505

longer and he looked bigger, somehow, but that could be the thick Aran sweater he wore with his jeans.

'I hope you don't mind. I thought I'd drop in.' She bit her lip and smiled.

He didn't say anything and she laughed, thrilled that she'd rendered him speechless.

She stamped her feet up and down. The breeze from the sea certainly was bracing.

'Is this remote enough, or what?'

'How did you find me?' he asked.

'I ran into your brother a while ago. He inadvertently tipped me off on a very unusual investment opportunity.'

Red stared at her. 'It was you? The rescue package was you?'

She shrugged and smiled. A month after having Red's finances privately investigated, she'd anonymously arranged through a local lawyer to invest in his business venture here.

'Savvy. Oh Savvy.' He laughed. Suddenly, he scooped her up in a hug, twirling her round and putting her back down. 'I don't know what to say. Come,' he said, grabbing her bag, then gesturing for her to follow. 'Come in. Into the warm.'

They reached the croft door and Red pushed it open. 'It's not quite what you're used to,' he said.

He wasn't kidding. As far as des-res status went, this place, half buried as it was in the granite landscape, was strictly niche market. But then *Red* was niche market. He was the man she'd just travelled halfway around the world to see.

It was only now, as he opened the door, that she wondered what she might find behind it. A girlfriend? A wife? Or even a child? She had absolutely no idea of Red's circumstances, only that she was compelled to make the surprise visit and her schedule had presented the gap she'd been hoping for, for months.

The croft was untidy, but homely. A tiny shot glass stood with a sprig of heather in it on a small wooden table. A ratty-looking mongrel dog was asleep in the basket by the wood-burning stove and a delicious smell rose from a hearty casserole cooking on the hob.

All in all, though, it didn't look like a woman had been anywhere near this place. If ever. There were only shirts on the wooden washing rack hanging from the ceiling and muddy boots stood on the draining board of the butler's sink and only male coats were slung over the back of the wooden chairs. All of which contributed to the sensation Savvy now experienced of feeling very, very much at home.

It felt safe. As if the whole world, the press, her responsibilities, were a million miles away. Red had put her bag on the floor and was staring at her.

'I still can't believe you're here,' he said.

'I came because . . .' she started, but she stopped.

She knew why she was here. Because she still wanted to believe that anything was possible. After the emotional hell she'd been through, she still wanted to believe that there could be happily-ever-afters.

She didn't finish her sentence. Couldn't. Because Red was staring at her.

'It's really *so* good to see you again,' she said.

'And you.'

His eyes locked with hers. His lovely, honest eyes. She couldn't help but blurt out the question that had been on her mind so much.

'Red, why didn't you ever call me?'

His eyebrows furrowed together. 'But I did. I even came to see you in Vegas. When I heard your father had died. I saw your friend Paige. Didn't she ever tell you?'

Savvy felt her heart thump hard. Yet another act of betrayal. Yet another way Paige had tried to destroy her. But she hadn't succeeded, Savvy reminded herself.

'She told me that you'd moved on and not to contact you.'

'Oh,' Savvy said. She didn't know where to start. Should she tell him how Paige had betrayed her? Or that he'd been right about Luc all along? That her obsession with him had nearly cost her everything?

In time, yes. But right now it didn't matter. All that mattered was that he'd been to see her. That he'd tried. Which could mean only one thing.

'So you *did* regret walking away from me that day?' she said.

'Almost straight away. I just hoped you'd follow. When the time was right.'

'Well, here I am,' she said.

'Here you are,' he said, grinning. 'But I'm wondering what the hell a sophisticated Vegas girl like you is planning to do with a grizzly sheep farmer like me?'

She shrugged and then laughed. 'I have absolutely no idea.'

And she didn't. Would it work? Between her and Red? With him wanting to be here and her needing to be running her business empire around the world? She had no idea, but it was worth giving it her best shot. She'd take it as it came. Day by day.

People changed. Red had taught her that. And plans changed too. She'd learned that for herself.

But for now, all that mattered was this moment. This wonderful feeling of life in freefall, of waiting for fate to take its course.

And then it hit her. *This* was the feeling she'd been chasing all her life.

And it had nothing to do with gambling at all.

Acknowledgements

Firstly, I'd like to thank Linda Evans and all the fabulous team at Transworld. Also, thanks to my wonderful agent Vivienne Schuster and to everyone at Curtis Brown, especially Felicity Blunt, Carol Jackson and Elizabeth Iveson. A big thank you to my early readers Toni Savage, Dawn Howarth and Sara Sims who gave me so much support and invaluable feedback. Also to Laurel Lefkow and Rebecca Choi for their advice and expertise in American and Chinese matters. Thanks to my family – especially my three girls – and to the friends who helped in various ways along the way, Katy Whelan, Jacob Potts and Lisa Campbell-Bannerman. And lastly, my never-ending heartfelt thanks to my amazing in-house editor, tea-maker, pep-talker and the person without whom this book would never have been written, Emlyn Rees.

PLATINUM
by Jo Rees

'Heaven sent for sunbathing'
Heat

Hell hath no fury like three women scorned . . .

Peaches Gold – a tough-talking, knockout brunette. She's LA's most infamous madam, with a flourishing business and ambition to match.

Emma Harvey – a happily-married, multi-talented redhead. She's English society's darling, but her latest investment has just put her whole future at risk.

Frankie Willis – a super-smart, adventurous blonde. She's the new stewardess on board a luxury mega-yacht and is about to find love where she least expected.

Three different women. One common enemy . . .

Yuri Khordinsky – the ruthless, all-powerful billionaire. Whatever he wants, he gets.

But this time he's crossed the wrong women.

And now it's revenge time . . . female style.

'Sizzling, juicy summer read'
Eve magazine

'The summer's sexiest book'
Company

'Steamy sex, glamorous women and a plot that races along at top speed'
Daily Express

9780552156073